The Protectors:
Book 1 in the Protectors Saga
By P. M. Dooling

Copyright 2011 Paige Dooling

Table of Contents

Chapter 1
Chapter 2
Chapter 3
Chapter 4
Chapter 5
Chapter 6
Chapter 7
Chapter 8
Chapter 9
Chapter 10

Chapter 1

The long cold steps seemed endless as she rushed towards the screams of her friends. Why had she just left them? Were they alright? These were the thoughts that raged through her mind as she finally reached the enormous stone doors. She flung the doors open with as much force as she could muster and then entered into the impeding darkness with both fear and anger weighing on her heart.

Once she was inside the chamber the doors slammed shut behind her. She couldn't see or hear anything, but she felt him. Everything inside of her knew that he was close. Then, out of the darkness, his voice bellowed. Chills ran throughout her body as he spoke, "How does it feel to be so powerful and yet not able to save the people you really care about?"

Her confusion was laced with despair, and her voice trembled as she spoke, "What are you talking about? Why did I hear the screams of my friends?"

His laugh was cold and hard as he answered, "The screams of the dying are often heard for miles, and I don't think your friends hold any exception to that."

She felt the bile of panic rising up in her throat, "You're lying," she shouted, "my friends are at home, and alive, and out of your reach!"

"Poor child," he scoffed, "you are so naïve; so young, and you have no idea as to how far my reach can extend. All together the Protectors became, and now all together you shall die."

"You speak to anger me and it's working…now…where…are my friends?" The silence that followed was broken as she screamed, "*Show me!*"

A second later a mist began to rise from the floor and in the middle of the room a luminescent glow began growing. Then, the glow started to turn into ghostly images. She saw the figures of her friends, her family; the people she knew and loved. She watched in horror as hordes of the darkest kinds of Demons raided her village, her home; the place where she had crept away from in the middle of the night, telling no one where she was going. She had done it for them, to protect and save them, and now all she could do was watch as they died without her. She kept silent as the destruction played out in front of her, until the image of her best friend, her most loyal fighter; laying dead on the ground in a pool of her own blood forced a scream of pure pain to echo throughout the empty chamber. Her legs gave out and she fell to the floor, unable to stop the tears.

"Now, now," said a cold voice from behind her, "as much as your crying may delight me, it certainly won't bring back your little companions." He paused a moment, savoring her anguish, "As much as I'll miss you and your friends getting in the way of my plans, everything must come to an end."

"But…the prophecy," she whimpered, still kneeling on the ground, "the prophecy said that if I came alone, it would only be me…it would be over. No one would get hurt…only me." She could barely get out the last words.

He laughed, "Prophecies are just mist and dust. No one believes in them, except for fools." He delighted in the fact that his words made her tears fall harder as he continued, "You really only have one course of action left, my dear."

Desperation crept over her as she stared at the cold stone floor, praying for the answer to what she should do. She knew what it was that the Emperor wanted. He wanted to fight her; if he were able to defeat the leader of the Protectors his reputation alone would be enough to secure his place as a God amongst the darkness.

I can't do it, she thought to herself, he's too strong and I'm so weak. I've never been anything but weak…I'll lose. Then the knowledge that she had already lost consumed her. What was the point in fighting if she had already lost everything?

"Get off of your knees." He was getting impatient, "Fight me…*now*!"

She wiped away the warm tears off of her cheek. It took only seconds for her to make a decision, but to her it seemed like an eternity.

With sleek eyes she looked up at him and spoke with a soft defiance, a defiance that came from the knowledge that she wasn't about to give him the pleasure of killing her, "You are right about one thing Emperor; I do only have one course of action left."

She swallowed hard and drew in what she knew would be her last breath. Her movements were quick and precise as she drew the long steel dagger out from sheath strapped onto her waist. She thought how strange it was that holding the dagger would give her comfort. Even though she knew what she was about to do with it, to her, it was like an old friend. She raised her head towards the heavens, but all she could see was the dingy stone ceiling.

She spoke quietly, only audible enough for her own ears and couldn't stop the tears from re-forming in her eyes, "Forgive me."

In one swift movement she plunged the dagger deep into her chest and through her heart. There was no pain, only a dull sense of discomfort and a tightening that grew with every beat that her heart could not make. But even without pain she knew that she was dying; she was a skilled warrior and her aim was accurately deadly. The life was draining out of her and she could feel it, feel her body growing limp, and the air around her becoming colder. As she fell back onto the floor, in her last moments, she searched for the guilt she knew she should feel. The leader of the Protectors ending her own life before attempting to fight for this universe was an unheard of thing. A thing of guilt and shame, but she felt none of it, only a silver thread of relief. Relief that maybe it was finally over; all the worry, pain, and responsibility; everything that her life had been made up of. Although, there was something deep down inside of her that told her it wasn't over, that this wasn't it; a chapter had ended, but the story was far from being finished.

"Noooooooo!" The Emperor screamed with such fury it seemed to shake the chamber walls.

It had all happened so fast, too fast for the Emperor to stop her, and now he was deprived the acclaim of killing her. An act he knew he would have accomplished. In her condition, beaten down by grief and without the aid of her fellow Protectors, she would have been no match for him at all.

The Emperor walked over to her lifeless body and knelt down beside it, wanting nothing more than to bring it back to life so that he could strangle the life out of her with his own two hands. After a while he became amused at the irony of the situation. From the second of her birth he had hated her and wanted her dead more than anything else in the world, but now that she was actually dead, he realized he hated her more than ever. He began to gently stroke the torn flesh around the area where the dagger had pierced through her skin.

His thin lips traced the outline of her ear as he spoke to her body, "Avery," he breathed her name, "I may not have the honor of your death on my hands, but now there is almost no one left standing in my way. Soon, even your little warriors won't be a threat. In the end, I suppose you made it easier for me. In the end...you lost."

The large chamber doors flung open once more, but this time instead of a single Protector walking through them, it was an assembly of some of the vilest beings alive, dark Demons from the underworld, brutish trolls, foul ogres, and monstrous beasts; all of the things that nightmares are made of, and all of the creatures that the Protector's spent their lives eliminating.

"My friends," The Emperor gushed, standing up from the body, opening his arms out to his visitors, "I'm so pleased you could all come."

A large Demon, humanoid in appearance, except for the fact he was covered in red scales, was the first to notice Avery's body lying on the ground, "Is that her?" He asked, a hint of shock in his voice, "Is that the Protector's leader, dead on your floor?"

The Emperor smiled slowly and motioned towards the body, "Yes, I suppose she was."

"You actually succeeded." Another Demon spoke, this one was grayish and covered in rancid ooze that smelled like stagnant water, "Although, I do not sense your power on her...you did not kill her with your own hand."

"That is irrelevant!" The Emperor shouted, he was not about to let any of these putrid insects begin to challenge him, "I provided the false prophecy which led her here! I created the illusion of her village's destruction, and if she had not been too weak to fight me I would have torn out her heart with my own two hands!"

A hush fell throughout the room. Not one of the creatures wished to anger the Emperor, fearing his power and wrath.

"The body of a Protector is still a grand trophy!" A massive green troll, standing against one of the far walls said, "You should display it outside for all to see!"

"Leave the body where it lies." The Emperor bellowed, "Trust me, it'll be much more effective this way."

"What do we do now, my Lord?" The red scaly Demon asked.

The Emperor could barely conceal the anticipation in his voice, "We wait until they come, and when they do…we show them the same kindness that our previous guest received."

Chapter 2

"I can't believe we let her go alone!" A girl in blue riding a buckskin horse yelled over her shoulder.

Another young girl, wearing gray, and mounted atop a smaller white horse, shouted back, "Nobody let her go alone, Jade! Nobody even knew she was going!"

"Bunny did!" Jade shouted, pulling her horse up and cutting off the other girls riding behind her, so that they had to stop as well.

"Jade, what are you doing?!" The girl in gray asked, surprised, having to hold onto her reins tight as her horse bucked up slightly from the sudden stop.

"I'm getting some answers, Skylar." Jade spat out, "Like, why, in God's name, would Bunny show Avery some obscure little prophecy, in some archaic little book, found in the very back of our dusty little library, that basically tells Avery to go off and die!"

"I had to show her." A girl in green, on a dark brown horse, spoke nervously, the beginning of tears wetting her eyes, "Avery's our leader; we have to go to her first about anything. She had me looking through the books for anything that involved the Emperor, and then I found the prophecy, and I showed it to her, and she begged, she ordered me not to tell the rest of you. Especially, you, Jade." Bunny began to cry uncontrollably, "I already told you all of this. She gave me an order, and she made me promise not to tell, and I broke both!"

Jade stared at Bunny in disbelief, shaking her head. She couldn't believe that Bunny had been so weak and so stupid and now, because of that, Avery was in trouble.

"You told us thirty minutes too late, Bunny!" Jade shouted.

Bunny wiped at her nose with her hand, trying to get a hold of herself, "Besides," she hiccupped, "the prophecy didn't say anything about dying; it just said that two leaders, one of light and one of dark, shall meet alone and from their sacrifice of blood, peace could be had by both sides."

Jade's mouth dropped open, "How is that good?!" She screamed, "Sacrifice of blood, Bunny! Sacrifice of blood!"

"That's enough!" A fourth and final girl in red, saddled upon a dusky gray horse, yelled angrily, "Bunny feels bad enough as it is, don't make it worse. Avery knew what she was getting into when she went off by herself. That's what our *leader* is best at…doing things by herself and telling us about it later."

"Sasha, don't you even start with me." Jade gave Sasha a stare that would have sent most other people running away crying, "If anything happens to her…" Jade's voice trailed off. She couldn't even force herself to finish the thought, "Let's just ride."

They kicked their horses into a run and continued down the dark forest path which led to the Emperor's fortress. None of them were focusing on anything but the road in front of them.

Once the Protectors exited out of the thick woods, the fortress immediately came into view. Until now, they had only seen it from a distance. It was a dark crumbling fortress, permanently surrounded by darkness and mist. Up close, it seemed even more foreboding than it did in the nightmares they had about it in their sleep.

The Protectors rode up to the massive wall that surrounded the fortress. The huge front gates lay open a crack, beckoning them inward. They dismounted their horses and sent them on their way, not wanting them to get hurt.

The gates were old and decaying and made horrible screeching noises as the Protectors heaved them open. Heavy stone gargoyles guarding the entrance to the fortress cried out warning alarms, as the Protectors entered into the desolate courtyard.

The troop of mountain trolls that began to charge them, may have, on another day, been able to hold them back for a while, but not today. Today things were different. Today they weren't fighting out of duty or power; they were fighting for one of their own.

They drove the trolls all the way back inside the fortress and towards the circular stone steps which led up to the top chamber. They battled them up the staircase and through the enormous doors, into the same darkness that their leader had entered into not long ago.

As soon as they all set foot into the black room, the remaining trolls retreated, closing and locking the heavy doors behind them, effectively trapping the Protectors inside.

The Protectors stood deadly still for a moment, panting and bleeding, listening to the sounds of bulky footsteps and the clink of weapons building up on the outside of the doors.

"What's that?" Bunny asked, pointing, breaking the tense quiet.

All their eyes followed to where Bunny was pointing at. In the very center of the chamber a dim light was gleaming down from the ceiling, but it was what the light was shining on that captured the Protector's attention. There, in the middle of the light lay a body, a body with a dagger plunged deep into its chest.

The Protectors stood paralyzed, making the room seem all the more lifeless. In a matter of seconds, everything that had just previously happened seemed like a million years ago to them. The silence in the room was deafening, a pin dropping would have sounded like thunder.

Skylar was the first one to step forward, followed wordlessly by the other Protectors. It wasn't until they moved closer that they were able to see the full effect of the scene. Avery's once white corset was now stained a bright shade of red. The red continued to form a wide circle around the body, although, it was hard to make out against the dark stone floor. Avery had always been porcelain pale, but now her skin was a ghostly white, almost translucent, void of any color or life. Her lips were parted slightly and had taken on the color of lavender. The Protector's had seen enough death to know what it looked like. They knew she was dead; they just couldn't bring themselves to rationalize it.

When they reached the body, Bunny collapsed down by Avery's side. Picking up Avery's ice cold hand, she held it in her own and began to cry.

Jade had gone numb the moment they spotted the body. She felt like nothing in her physically or mentally was capable of functioning, but now watching Bunny crying, feeling was beginning to come back into her body. It felt like the shockwave right before the explosion hits.

"She's not dead…she can't be dead." Jade's voice was louder than was necessary and quivering with fear, "Pull the knife out of her…*hurry*!"

Jade looked around to the others, but no one moved.

When Jade realized that nobody was going to do anything, she ran up to Avery's body, pushed Bunny out of the way, and gripped the ivory hilt of the steel dagger still embedded in Avery's heart. She pulled with all of her strength. There was the slight scraping of blade against bone as the dagger was dislodged with enough force to send Jade stumbling backwards. The wound had stopped bleeding awhile ago, but the removal of the weapon had caused the body to jerk and fresh blood to spill out of the opening in her chest.

Bunny, who was closest to the body, released a whimper from deep in her throat. She strode towards the back wall and placed her head against the bricks, trying to wipe out the image of Avery's wound.

Jade caught her balance and stood stone still for a moment, waiting for something to happen, but when nothing did, she staggered back over to the body. Jade fell to her knees beside Avery's corpse, looking it up and down. The blood was cool against the side of Jade's face as she lay her head upon Avery's chest, listening for a heartbeat, waiting for Avery's body to rise as her lungs filled with air, but there was nothing.

"Breathe...come on, breathe!" Her voice was starting to crack and tears were beginning to sting her eyes, "Don't you dare leave me!"

Jade lifted her head up and began pushing on her chest, giving her mouth to mouth, but nothing worked. After a few minutes of trying that, she began shaking the body and pounding on it harder and harder with her fists, shouting, "Fight! Damn you...fight!" She picked Avery up into her lap and rocked her for a few moments, whispering into her ear, "Please...please don't go. We can't do this without you...please, please."

Jade lay Avery's body back down and began beating on it again, but she wasn't allowed to do this for very long. Sasha and Skylar grabbed Jade by both arms and ripped her away from the body.

"Let me go! I have to help her!" Jade screamed and kicked as she struggled to free herself, "Let me go!"

"You can't help her," Skylar shouted at her, as she began to cry herself, "you can't! She's gone, Jade...she's gone."

A savage scream escaped Jade's lips and echoed throughout the chamber. She raised her hand to her hair and pulled, still screaming. When her voice had finally worn out, she collapsed into Skylar's arms, and they fell to the floor together, holding each other and crying.

"How can this be happening?" Bunny uttered, still facing the wall where she was leaning her head, "What are we suppose to do?" Her voice began to get more hysterical, "This can't be happening!"

"Bunny, calm down!" Sasha spoke for the first time since they entered the chamber. "We'll figure out what to do." She walked up to Bunny, grabbing her by the shoulders and turning her around, trying to steady her.

"Avery's dead, Sasha." Skylar looked up at her from the ground, still holding Jade, "What exactly is it that you think we should do?"

"First things first, we take Avery's body back home. We get Gumptin, he might know of something we can do." Sasha was taking over the role of leader, "Right now, though, we have to get out of here, or we're going to end up getting killed ourselves."

"That's just what I had in mind," said a voice from the darkness.

They all turned towards the direction the voice had come from just in time to see the Emperor emerge from the blackness.

Their swords were all drawn instantaneously, and Jade was halfway across the chamber towards the Emperor before Sasha stopped her.

"Jade...no!" Sasha bellowed, "We can't do this right now! We have to get Avery back to Gumptin! You know we do!"

Jade just stood there staring at the Emperor for a minute, and Sasha thought she might not have heard her, but then a shiver seemed to run through the length of Jade's body and the grip on her sword loosened. Jade and the Emperor exchanged one last cold hard look before she backed down.

Sasha stepped forward, so that she was just a few inches behind Jade, "Today is not our day to fight Emperor. The only thing we wish to do is return Avery's body back home."

The Emperor's laugh rolled over the Protectors like an earthquake, "Do you think me a fool?" He asked, "The last thing I would let you do is drag off your leader to your little magician.

Besides, I already have a perfect place on the battlements picked out for her corpse."

At these words Jade and the other Protectors moved into fighting position.

The Emperor continued to speak without emotion, "The only thing that would make this day more perfect is to have four more bodies to go along with hers. So, you see, you were right about one thing; it's not our day to fight, it's your day to die." He snapped his fingers once and a second later the locked doors burst open and an army of trolls, Demons, and beasts flooded into the chamber.

The fiends moved in quickly. Now that they knew the Protectors were leaderless, they found a new confidence. They were like sharks in the water that had smelled blood and were going in for the kill.

The battle was intense and the Protectors fought hard, but without Avery their power wasn't strong enough to keep the enemy back for long. They were weakening and the sense that they weren't going to win this battle began to envelope them.

Bunny was the first one to fall. A Bacci Demon, muscular and wolf-like, trapped her into a small corner of the chamber. She thought she had seen an opening in the Bacci's defenses, so she raised her sword high above her head, intending to bring it down on the Bacci's upper arm, but he anticipated this and took advantage. Right before Bunny was about to strike, the Bacci made a lightning quick turn and drove his own sword deep into Bunny's abdomen. As the Bacci pulled his sword out, he howled with excitement and blood lust, he knew he had just killed himself a Protector.

Bunny fell to the ground, holding her stomach. Blood was pouring from her wound and she knew she was dying. She tried to call out for help, but the words stuck in the blood pooling in her throat and all that came out was a gurgle. She died with the taste of blood overwhelming her senses.

Skylar switched her sword from her right had to her left because the deeply embedded arrow sticking out of her right shoulder made any movement impossible. The next arrow flew towards her from somewhere in the crowd of Demons. It struck her in the upper thigh and forced her to the ground.

"Ugh!" She grimaced in pain.

She used her sword as a brace and struggled up off of the ground. Skylar had just barely righted herself when an enormous ogre, ax held high in his hand, rushed her. She lifted the sword she was using to balance on and plunged it into the ogre's neck. The ogre fell down dead, and Skylar, now without her support fell back down as well. She was laboring so hard to get back up that she never even saw the thick silver arrow split through the air towards her. The arrow hit her with such force, that she was flown backwards five feet until she hit the stone wall behind her, with a crushing force.

Skylar lay on the floor for a few moments, trying to register what had happened before she attempted to get up. When she finally did try to push herself up off the ground, she realized that she couldn't move. She couldn't feel any part of her body below her neck. She was paralyzed. Skylar didn't know if it was from the force of hitting the wall or the three foot arrow protruding out of her midsection, but she did know that this was the end of her fight. She began to cry warm tears that she could no longer feel once they slid down her neck.

Skylar looked over at Avery's body, so still amongst the chaos going on around it. She couldn't believe it had come to this, and then she died.

Sasha had seen Skylar hit the wall and immediately tried to make her way over to her. She took out the troll she was fighting easily. With a quick kick she took him to the ground, and then cut off his head with her sharp sword. When Sasha got to Skylar, she bent down and checked for a pulse, even though, she knew there wouldn't be one.

She bent down and kissed her fallen friend on the forehead. It was the only way she knew of to say goodbye. Standing up to face the battle she knew would claim her life, Sasha let out a long sad sigh.

There was a large group of swamp trolls rushing towards her. Sasha knew that there were too many of them for her to win, but she quickened her pace to meet them none the less. If Sasha was going to die, she was going to go out fighting.

Her fierceness took the trolls off guard, and she quickly took down the first two. Sasha flipped over the shortest one, severing his head off with her sword on the way down. The second one received her dagger in the back of his skull.

Sasha was so into the battle that she never saw the colossal troll moving up behind her. The troll lifted its massive stone club high into the air and brought it down directly on the back of Sasha's skull. There was a terrible crunching sound, and Sasha fell to the floor. She lost all sense of everything in an instant. The only thing her brain could focus on was trying to get herself up off the ground. She was scrambling around on the floor, attempting to get control of her limbs, when the troll swung his club down onto her head once again, this time on her left temple. Thick blood poured from her head in a small stream. Her body jerked twice before all movement stopped completely, and she was dead.

Jade glanced around the room and saw that she was the only Protector left. Instead of breaking her, it only made her fight on harder. She knew when they started their journey to the fortress, that if they hadn't found Avery alive, this was going to become a suicide mission. Jade found herself oddly fine with that, but she was going to take down as many villains as she could before she died, and hopefully, most importantly, the Emperor.

Jade slowly made her way over to where the Emperor was standing against the wall, buried in the darkness. She punched and ogre square in the face, knocking him out cold. Using her Protector strength, she picked up a smaller Demon, throwing him backwards.

The swamp troll that had killed Sasha ran at Jade, his killing club held high. Jade spun out of his way, slicing across his belly with her sword in the process. She was able to kill the troll, but by doing so she had left her right side exposed to a Succubus Demon, holding a small blade. The Demon drove the blade into Jade's left side. Jade howled in pain and removed the blade from her body, stabbing the Demon in the eye with his own weapon. She ignored the sharp pain in her side and continued on towards the Emperor, sword held tight in her hand.

Jade heard someone approaching from behind her, so she kicked back hard sending a troll flying. This kept her occupied for only a split second, but that was long enough for another troll to stab a discarded arrow deep into her right shoulder. Without missing a beat, Jade switched her sword to her other arm and swung it around wildly at the troll, severing his head and spilling putrid green blood out all over her.

Jade could feel the blood pumping out from the wound in her side, weakening her, but adrenaline and the idea of revenge kept her going. She was only yards away from the Emperor when two long arrows shot out from the crowd of monsters and struck her in the right hip, tossing her to the floor and making her legs virtually useless.

Once she was on the ground, Jade had her sword knocked away from her and received a swift kick to the face. She grabbed on to the offending foot with her only good arm and wrenched it upwards, effectively discarding her attacker.

Jade turned herself over onto her belly and began to crawl towards the Emperor, dragging her wounded legs and arm with her. She reached down and untied a small crossbow that had been securely fastened to her belt. She lifted the crossbow up and took aim at the Emperor, but before she could get a shot off, a Bacci Demon took hold of Jade's leg and began dragging her backwards. Jade flipped over and shot the Demon through the heart with one of her crossbow arrows. Right after she took the shot, another large swamp troll descended upon her, knocking the crossbow out of her hand. She grabbed a dagger she had hidden in her boot and brought it up, straight through the troll's chin and up into his brain.

As Jade rolled the troll off of her, she was able to see at least ten more deadly trolls only seconds away from reaching her. Jade dismissed any instinct she had to want to fight them off and instead rolled back over onto her belly and continued on her path to the Emperor. Knowing she wouldn't be able to reach him, she stared him dead in his vacant black slits for eyes, and let her hatred show all over her face as she spoke to him.

"I promise you Emperor, one way or another, I *will* see you again." Jade growled.

A second Succubus Demon made his way through the crowd of trolls. He reached Jade and stood over her, one leg on either side of her body. The Demon glanced up at the Emperor, and the Emperor, in return, gave him a quick nod of approval. With that, the Demon raised the massive broadsword he was holding high in front of him, and a split second later, brought it down straight through Jade.

Jade made one last reach towards the Emperor, before she let out a final breath and lay on the floor dead.

Outside of the fortress the Emperor could hear the sky going wild. Thunder roared and lightning beat down upon the ground. The scent of damp rain mixed with the coppery scent of blood and made for a heady concoction that seemed, to the Emperor, a perfect perfume for the occasion. The Emperor laughed to himself, wondering if the storm raging outside was the planet's way of weeping for its lost Protectors. He hoped so; he loved the idea of causing so much pain.

The Emperor's fiendish army stood covered in blood, some of it their own, some belonging to the Protectors. They stood and waited for the Emperor's orders, ready to do his bidding.

The Emperor took a deep breath, still savoring his morbid perfume, "Take this garbage," he waved a dismissive hand towards the bodies of the Protectors, "and place it on stakes along the front gate. Let our enemies see what becomes of those who try to fight us."

A large number of swamp trolls moved in to carry the bodies away, but before they could even reach the first body, something began to happen. The Protector's bodies began to emit a warm soft glow, like there was a fire burning on the inside of them. The glow became brighter and brighter until the Emperor and his armies could no longer see the bodies, just five bright orbs of light. Then, in a giant explosion of white light the Protectors were gone.

The Emperor screamed, in a rage, "That pathetic little magician!" He spat out, and then turned to speak to his army, "Go to the Protector's village and bring their bodies back to me!"

A small Demon with snake-like features stepped forward, "But, my Lord, the Protector's village is located near King Draven's territory."

"So?" The Emperor asked.

"Well, Draven has a large army," the Demon continued, "and he protects his lands and the forests surrounding them well. He will know if an army of our size is in the area, and he won't take it well. It would be foolish to risk it just to retrieve a few corpses. I think it would be wiser to…"

His words were cut short as the Emperor plunged a steel sword deep into his stomach, and he fell on the floor dead.

"Does anyone else have anything to say?" The Emperor asked with a threatening edge to his voice, still holding the bloody sword. "Now, go...I want those bodies!"

Chapter 3

The small Wizard fell backwards, exhausted. The items he had been holding in his hands fell the to ground, a silver necklace belonging to Avery, a small knife belonging to Jade, Sasha's hair comb, a bracelet of Bunny's, and Skylar's compact mirror, all personal items belonging to the Protectors.

Gumptin had used them for the summoning spell he performed. When the Protectors had been killed Gumptin had sensed it. Being a Wizard since birth, he had a stronger connection to the elements around him, and he had felt it in the air, whispering to him…the Protectors were dead.

The villagers had gathered around Gumptin, standing in the center of their village. They had been worried ever since the Protectors took off in the middle of the night.

In another flash of blinding white light, the Protectors bodies re-appeared on the grassy ground where Gumptin and the rest of the villagers stood.

Skylar's mother screamed at the sight of her bloodied and torn daughter lying dead on the ground. She brought her hands up to her eyes to block the image and turned into her husband's arms, weeping.

Avery's mother had fallen to her daughter's side and was now cradling her in her arms, letting her tears dampen her dead daughter's long hair.

"Gumptin, you have to do something!" She choked, staring up at the Wizard, pleading with tearful eyes.

The short old Wizard hobbled up to Avery's mother and placed his hand on her shoulder, "I…I do not know if there is anything I can do."

"What do you mean you don't know if there's anything you can do?!" Jade's father shouted angrily, "You're their mentor! You're supposed to look out for them…now you do something!"

Gumptin ran his hands through his long gray beard. There was only one spell he knew of that could bring the Protectors back from the dead and it was far beyond his power to perform. In fact, he knew of only one group powerful enough to perform the spell that would even grant him an audience.

"I will go and see the Elementals." Gumptin told the villagers, making up his mind.

The villagers looked at Gumptin with apprehension. Everyone knew that the Elementals preferred to watch rather than intervene in the lives of humans.

"Are you sure they'll help?" Jade's mother asked from the ground, where she was seated next to her daughter's body.

"No," Gumptin answered honestly, "but there is nothing else we can do."

Gumptin turned away from the tragic scene in front of him and walked into the thick forest surrounding the village. He walked along the main road as fast as his little body allowed him to go. After a half a mile he turned onto a smaller path that diverged from the road, the path was unmarked and overgrown, but Gumptin knew it was the one which would take him to where he needed to go.

As he walked, Gumptin tried to think of what he was going to say to the Elementals. After all, the last time he had spoken to them was over sixteen years ago and that time the Elementals had come to him, not the other way around. They had come to him and told him that they were going to create five warriors. The Elementals were a group associated with the order of the Ancients. The Ancients are the most powerful of beings, capable of almost any kind of magic. There are good Ancients and there are bad Ancients, but mainly they just believe in keeping a balance in the world, the fragile balance between good and evil, and no group believe in that more than The Elementals. That was why sixteen years ago they came to Gumptin and told him that they sensed evil was becoming stronger than good. So, in order to keep the balance they were going to give five unborn human souls each a different power. One was to have the power of water, one with air, another with fire, one with wind, and the fifth one would be given the power of energy and would be fated to be the leader. The Elementals would make them stronger, faster, and hardier, with more adept senses and reflexes than the average human. They had told Gumptin that the five warriors would be called the Protectors and would be destined to protect the planet and fight against evil.

Then, they commanded Gumptin to be their teacher and guardian. They instructed him to go to the village of Havyn. He was given the names of the Protectors would be parents and told to wait for the five of them to be born. That was over sixteen years ago, and Gumptin had done what The Elementals had told him to do without question. He had trained and guarded the Protectors. Now, he hoped, that The Elementals would do what he was about to ask.

Gumptin continued down the overgrown path for over a mile before he finally reached his destination. It was a large pool of crystal clear water, surrounded by a wall of opalescent rock. It was beautiful, but there was nothing particularly magic about it, that is, until Gumptin reached into one of the pouches tied around his belt and pulled out a handful of white powder. The powder was made of ground up crystals, snake scales, sand, and five tears from a broken heart; it was a common summoning powder.

He threw the powder into the pool and recited the words, "Deax ploria avu Domuvita Elementia!"

A few seconds later, the water in the pool shot straight up into the air in one long stream, and came crashing back down, but instead of landing back into the empty pool, it stayed hovered a few feet above it. Gumptin watched as the water began to move and churn, until it took on the shape of six figures, three female and three male, all made out of water, except for their eyes which glowed a pale shade of blue.

"Gumptin the Wizard," spoke one of the female figures in a watery almost songlike voice, "why have you summoned us here?"

Gumptin gave a small bow of respect to the Elementals before he began, "The Protectors have been killed."

"We are already aware of this information." Said one of the males in the same sing-song voice, "Tell us what it is you summoned us for."

Gumptin swallowed hard, "I am asking for you to bring them back using the Spell of Rebirth. They have been dead for less than twenty-four hours, which is the only requirement, and I know you have the power to do it."

There was silence and for a horrifying moment Gumptin thought that they might simply decide to leave without dealing with him anymore.

Finally, the first female spoke, "Gumptin, that is a spell that hasn't been done in thousands of years," she blinked her pale eyes and tilted her head towards Gumptin, "and for good reason."

"But this planet needs the Protectors!" Gumptin pleaded, "The Emperor grows stronger every day, and without them there is almost no chance of stopping him. They are too important to let die!"

This time, another male spoke, "We created the Protectors, Gumptin, we know of their importance. However, they were mortals and mortals die. It is fate that decides when."

"Then change their fate!" Gumptin shouted. These girls weren't just his students; they had become his family, and he wasn't going to leave without getting them back, "If anyone deserves a second chance it is them. They have done nothing but fight for the greater good all of their lives. They devoted their lives to the burden that you placed upon them, and *yes*," Gumptin spoke quickly before the Elementals could protest, "it was a burden...you know it was. They deserve a second chance."

The male was about to speak again, but the first female held up her hand to silence him and spoke instead, "What you are asking is not lightly done. You are asking us to affect life and death, the natural order of things."

Gumptin started to speak, but this time the female held up her hand to silence him.

She continued, "The Inamri Ancients cast a spell not very long ago, a dark and extremely powerful spell, a spell that will have dangerous repercussions, a spell that could very well tip the balance in evil's favor forever. We were going to take the Inamri to the Council of Ancients and have their spell revoked. However, if we do this, if we bring the Protectors back, we lose all authority to challenge the Inamri. Whatever they did will remain done."

Gumptin knew the Inamri were the darkest of the Ancients. Above all the others they desired power, not balance, and unfortunately, power could usually be obtained through evil.

"What spell did the Inamri cast?" Gumptin asked.

All six Elementals shook their heads, "We have told you all we can. Now, you must choose."

Gumptin knew it should have taken him longer to decide, being a Wizard dedicated to fighting for good, but weighing one dangerous spell against the Protector's lives was no choice for him, "I want you to bring them back."

All six water figures merged together as one, forming one large ball of water that glimmered the same pale blue color as their eyes. They stayed in that glowing ball of water for almost a minute. Then, when they emerged back into their human water forms, five of them, all except for the female who seemed to be in charge, were holding radiantly glowing orbs the size of a peach in their hand.

"We have collected the Protector's souls." The female told Gumptin.

Gumptin gasped and fell backwards a step, focusing on the fact that he was actually staring at the Protectors.

"Souls remain in the atmosphere for twenty-four hours before they move on." The main female Elemental informed Gumptin, "That is why the spell must be performed within a day of the individual's death."

"So, you shall do the spell?" Gumptin asked, barely able to breathe from excitement.

"Yes," she answered, "the souls will be placed back into the mothers of the Protectors to be reborn. They will then be sent through the Ora Gateway."

"What?" Gumptin exhaled weakly.

Being a Wizard, Gumptin of course knew about the Gateways. There were thousands of them spread across the universe, and they always came in pairs, one on one planet and its twin on a separate planet. They were, just as their name suggested, gateways, or doors, from one planet to another. They allowed an individual to step through a door on one planet, travel through space in a matter of seconds, and exit through the other door on whatever planet it's located. There were five different gateways scattered across their planet of Orcatia, but no one outside of the magic folk knew where they were located, or to which planets the Gateway's connected. Gumptin, as part of the magic community, knew that the Ora Gateway was located only a few miles from the Protector's village and that it connected to a planet called Earth.

"Why would you send them through a Gateway?" Gumptin asked, not liking the idea of the Protector's on another planet.

"There are many reasons, Gumptin." The Elemental answered, "Foremost, this planet cannot wait years for the Protectors to be born and grow up. It would be pointless to bring them back if that were the case. We can manipulate the Gateways. As we send them through space, we can also send them through time. We will send them back in time sixteen years to the planet Earth. There, they will grow up, and when they reach the age they were when they died, you will go and collect them. We will come to you when it is time. Only a few days shall go by here on Orcatia. Because they will be born on Earth, they will age at the normal rate. However, their parents, being born Orcatian, will not be able to age on Earth. Make sure you tell them this."

Gumptin thought about that for a moment. He had been so wrapped up in bringing the Protectors back to life he hadn't really stopped to think about them being re-born or growing up. His head began to ache. He tried to think of a way around the Gateway and sending them to the past, but he came up with nothing. In the end, Gumptin realized that he had no choice but to do it the Elementals way.

"There is one more thing you should know." The Elemental bowed her head in a way that left Gumptin nervous to hear the rest of what she was about to tell him. "There are certain consequences that come with doing a spell this powerful."

"What kind of consequences?" Gumptin asked feeling disheartened.

The Elemental lifted her head, "With the Spell of Rebirth, those being reborn are born without their memories."

Gumptin felt the blood drain from his face. Apart from being told that the Protectors would have to stay dead, he couldn't imagine hearing worse words coming out of the Elementals mouths.

"For how long?" he asked, "Will they regain any of their memories?"

"Over time they might reclaim a very small amount of their memories," The Elemental answered honestly, "but they will never remember everything."

Gumptin nodded his head; there was nothing else he could do. If this was the price for getting the Protectors back alive, he couldn't argue against it.

The five Elementals that held the Protectors souls began to mold back together into the giant water ball.

"Go," the last Elemental told Gumptin, "prepare the parents; we will meet you at the Ora Gateway in three hours."

When she finished speaking the female Elemental merged into the water with the others. They remained swirling around for a few seconds before vanishing in a bright explosion. The remaining water fell back into the pool and Gumptin watched the water still, as if nothing had happened.

Gumptin walked back to the village at a much slower pace than he had used to reach the Elementals. He was lost in thought, mulling over everything that had just been discussed. On one hand, he was relieved; the Protectors were being given a second chance. They would be brought to life and Gumptin couldn't be anything but overjoyed by that, but there were aspects of them being re-born that left him uneasy. They were going to be growing up on a distant planet, with no memory of ever being a Protector. He could only hope that when the time came for them to return to Orcatia they would be able to step back into the role of a warrior.

When Gumptin returned to the village he found the villagers, who were in a panic.

Apparently, when the Elementals had taken the Protector's souls, their bodies had turned to dust, leaving the parents in a state of hysteria.

Gumptin quieted them down and explained to the villagers everything that the Elementals had told him. Slowly, the parents began to calm down and take in everything he was saying.

"So," Sasha's mother choked, "you're telling us they're going to be alright?"

Gumptin nodded and the whole village seemed to breathe a sigh of relief.

The parents were more than willing to do what the Elementals had asked of them, travel to Earth and raise their children all over again for sixteen years; that was nothing to them.

The parents and Gumptin left the village immediately to go meet the Elementals at the Gateway. It wasn't a very long walk, less than an hour, even following Gumptin who wasn't the fastest of walkers.

Their destination was at the end of a small dirt path, which lay a mile down the main road; it opened up into a small clearing about ten feet around, surrounded by dense overgrown trees. At the far end of the clearing were two exceptionally large oak trees, only a few feet apart and out of place from the other trees.

Gumptin picked up a small rock and threw it between the trees. The parents heard it land somewhere in the thicket of the forest.

Gumptin picked up a second small rock, but this time before throwing it between the trees he spoke the words, "Ora Gateway."

There was a small charge that went off between the trees, like a miniature lightning strike. When Gumptin threw the stone, the space between the trees rippled as if someone had thrown a pebble into a pool of water. This time the stone didn't land on the other side; it disappeared completely.

Gumptin turned to the parents, "That stone is lying somewhere on Earth now. That is how the Gateway works; you have to name it. Once you say its name, it stays open for approximately ten minutes."

"You, however, will not need to use the Gateway once you travel to Earth." The ethereal voice came from behind Gumptin and the parents.

They all turned to see six figures, human in appearance, but made up of what looked like smoke and dust, although, they still had their gleaming pale blue eyes. Five of the Elementals were still holding the glowing souls.

The Elementals addressed the parents, the main female speaking for the group, "We will send you all to the planet Earth, with your children's souls. Once there, we will provide you with a place to live and a means to support yourselves. You will have normal lives and raise your children as normal girls." The Elemental gave the parents a penetrating gaze, "Never speak of this planet or who they really are. You will not use the Ora Gateway to travel back to Orcatia until Gumptin comes to retrieve you; do you understand?" She waited for each of the parents to tell her they understood, before asking, "Are there any questions?"

The parents only wanted their children back alive and were willing to do whatever the Elementals demanded of them. The parents shook their heads and the five Elementals holding the souls walked forward towards the mothers.

Avery's mother was the first to be given her daughter's soul.

The Elemental walked up to her, cupped the soul in both palms, leaned down to her stomach and whispered words, "Sula Dunna Nacht."

The words were too old for even Gumptin to understand, and that was saying a lot, considering he was a Wizard with extensive knowledge of the old languages.

There was a bright flash of bluish light, and then the soul was no longer in the Elemental's hands.

"Take care of her." The Elemental told Avery's mother, and she nodded in agreement, holding her stomach, tears begin to form in her eyes.

The other Elementals followed suit. First, Jade was given to her mother, then Sasha, then Skylar, and finally Bunny.

Bunny's mother seemed hesitant and the Elemental backed away, "Are you sure you want this?" he asked her, "It must be all of them that go back, or none at all."

All of the parents looked at Bunny's mother, pleading and warning with their eyes.

"Of course, I want this!" She cried, "I just can't believe everything that's happened today." Her voice cracked as she steadied her stance, readying herself to accept Bunny's soul.

The Elemental nodded once, then continued to place the soul into her body.

Once the Elementals had done their job of placing all the souls, they ordered the parents into the Gateway.

The five Elementals who had carried the Protectors souls went through the Gateway first, followed by the parents. The main female stayed behind for a moment.

"Thank you for doing this." Gumptin told her, overcome with gratitude after seeing the souls safely put where they belong, knowing his Protectors would soon be returning to him.

"Just remember, Gumptin," The Elemental answered, her sing-song voice taking on a melancholy tone, "you were the one to ask for this. Whatever happens, good or bad, do not come to us for any more favors."

And with those words, she turned and walked into the Gateway, leaving Gumptin standing alone, pondering what she had said.

Chapter 4

Eeeeeeeeeerrrrrrr!

Avery Kimball's head shot up from her desk so fast that she nearly managed to knock herself out of her seat. She had almost fallen asleep when the ear piercing bell, signifying the end to her final class, slammed her back into reality. She checked her desk and the side of her face for drool. There was hardly anything as embarrassing as falling asleep in class and drooling all over the place, and this she knew from experience.

Avery slumped her backpack onto her shoulder and started to file in line with the rest of the students pilling out of the compact classroom and into the crowded corridors.

"TGIF, right?" a slight Asian girl, with dyed purple hair, standing beside Avery asked.

"Tell me about it." Avery responded, keeping her eyes fixed on the two double plexi-glass doors which led out to the parking lot and to freedom, "I thought this week would never end."

"So, are you going to Mitchell's party tonight?" The girl asked.

Avery let out a sigh, but before she could continue and officially say no, the girl cut her off, "Avery, you have to go! It won't be the same without you there. Plus, now that Mitchell and Jenny are a thing of the past, he totally has eyes for you!"

Avery thought about that for a moment. She had always held a small torch for Mitchell Becker and his big brown puppy dog eyes, ever since the third grade when he had shared his bag of gummy snacks with her. She let herself fantasize about his eyes for a few more seconds before deciding against making a play for his affection.

"Sorry, Ming, I can't." Avery said, hoping she wouldn't later come to regret her decision, "I've got an English literature paper that desperately needs my attention."

Ming shook her head, "You've gotta knock it off with all this studying, girl. We're only juniors; we have another whole year before we have to start worrying about grades and college."

Avery gave Ming a light motherly pinch on the cheek, "It's never too early to start worrying…or so my parents tell me"

Finally, they exited the doors and were out of the student packed corridors.

Ming waved goodbye, smiling broadly, "Well, we'll miss you tonight, but I'll give Mitchell a big kiss for you."

Avery smiled back, telling herself that Ming's comment was just a good humored joke and not an actual declaration of something she was intending to do. Otherwise, smiling would be the last thing Avery would do.

"I'll see you Monday, Ming." Avery shouted her goodbye.

Phoenix Mountain High School was located right next to a large park, filled with dozens of bulky trees and green bushes overflowing with petite white flowers that extracted a spicy sent into the air.

It was by the curb at the far side of the park that Avery always parked her car. In the far distance, she could see the sun glinting off the hood of her beloved Dodge Challenger. She didn't care that it was over thirty years old, with a peeling dark blue paint job, missing windshield wipers, a sticky gear shift, and sun visors that randomly decided to fall off. Avery didn't even care that she had ended up putting more money into it than what she had initially paid for it. That car was her baby. It was the first thing she had bought with her money earned from working at her Mom's flower shop, and more importantly, at this moment, it was her ride to home. Of course, she had to make it to the car first.

Avery would have inhaled to take in a deep breath of that delicious scent of the tiny white flowers, but first she had to cross the car packed student parking lot blocking her way to the park. There was nothing that she hated more about school than the student parking lot, with its smoldering black top, insane teenage drivers, and asphyxiating exhaust clouds. Avery glanced over longingly at the green oasis that was Cactus Wren Park.

That was something that always astounded Avery about Redemption, how green they were able to keep their parks in the middle of the desert.

Avery had been born and raised in the town of Redemption, Arizona. It was a town of about five thousand people, located in the middle of the Sonoran Desert, the kind of town with one local theater and a good thirty minute drive to the nearest mall. It was home to farmers, cowboys, and your average citizen looking to get away from the large over-populated cities. Avery always figured her parents fell into the latter category. Although, they never talked much about their past, she knew her parents hadn't been born there. She figured they had moved from some big city to Redemption, so that her Mom could open up a small flower shop, while her Dad worked at the local bank. It didn't matter to Avery why exactly they had moved to Redemption; she was just grateful they had. She loved everything about living in the town, the desert lightning storms, the friends she had made, the dry weather, working part time at her mom's flower shop, even going to her out of date and poorly funded high school.

 Car horns began honking as cars raced to get out of the parking lot. Avery stepped down off of the curb and onto the blacktop. She had made it half way to sanctuary when she heard someone from behind her shout, "Avy!"

 There was only one person who called her by that, and Avery really did not want to have to deal with her right now. Avery steeled herself, fighting every instinct that told her to ignore the voice, knowing that if she just kept walking she would be given an earful about it tomorrow morning. So, she put on her politest smile and turned around to see Sasha Seraphina and one of her many male admirers strolling up to her.

 Sasha was the kind of girl that every boy wanted and every girl wanted to be. She was tall, a good six inches taller than Avery, and pretty much all legs. Her olive skin was kept baby soft with expensive moisturizers whose names Avery couldn't even pronounce. Sasha's dyed copper hair was always professionally clipped and styled into a perfect pixie cut. She had chestnut eyes and brows that were sculpted into perfect arches. To complete her look, she always wore the most fashionable name-brand outfits that detailed every curve of her long body.

 "Hey." Avery replied, as Sasha and her male friend, who Avery now recognized to be Toby Burke, a Varsity wrestler, reached her.

 "Hey." Sasha said, stepping up to Avery closer than she needed to, invading Avery's personal space so that she was now looming over her.

Avery just sighed and glanced up at Sasha with her eyes, refusing to raise her head. She knew what Sasha was doing. Avery knew she could be a pretty enough girl. She had thick, long, auburn hair that fell in unruly waves down to the small of her back and could either make Avery look like a princess when behaving itself, or a hot mess when it wasn't. Her ivory skin gave her an ethereal glow, even though it meant she could never leave her house without applying sun-block, unless she wanted the Arizona sun to turn her redder than a cooked lobster. She had curves enough of her own, but her favorite form of attire, a pair of warn jeans and a flannel shirt didn't exactly emphasize anything but her laid back attitude. Her deep emerald eyes were framed by dark lashes that sparkled particularly bright when she flashed her wide smile, which was often.

Sasha also knew that Avery could be a pretty enough girl, a fact that Sasha didn't like. That was why every time they spoke Sasha always did her best to make sure the only real things Avery felt self-conscious about was in the spotlight…her height. Avery had been petite her whole life, always shorter than most of her friends, but she had continued to hold out hope for a much wanted growing spurt. However, at sixteen years of age, Avery was faced with the hard truth that she was most likely going to be stuck with her current five-foot-one height for the rest of her life. Often times, Avery wondered if she would actually be alright with her shortness, if not for friends like Sasha.

Avery pushed that thought aside and addressed the insecurity pusher, herself, "What's up, Sash?"

Sasha stared down at her, "What are you in such a rush for?"

Had she not heard the final bell ring, Avery thought sarcastically, before saying, "I'm just in a rush to get home. You know, to food, nap, homework, and then more napping…probably in that order." All things which you are keeping me from, Avery had to bite her tongue to stop herself from saying.

Sasha smirked, "What an exciting life you lead, Avery."

Sasha meant it as a joke, but only partly. It had the appropriate amount of Sasha sting connected to it that Avery knew, loathed, and tolerated.

Avery raised her eyebrows and smiled back, wondering how she and Sasha had ever become friends. In fact, she knew exactly how, and it was more by force than choice. Since before Avery could walk, Avery's parents along with Sasha, Jade Kai, Bunny Claiborne, and Skylar Bavol's parents had gotten together and organized a play group for their children. Even now, they still did family activities, like picnics and softball matches together. They had all been forced to grow up together, and despite their strong personality differences, a strong bond had been formed between the five of them.

Sasha was really the only one Avery ever had any problems with. Since she could remember, Sasha had always loved to give her a hard time, always questioning her, poking fun, and generally agitating her. Of course, Sasha did that to almost everyone, so Avery couldn't really complain much. Avery loved Sasha, but most of the time she just wanted to punch her in the face.

Avery decided to give it one more go before turning around to leave, "What did you want, Sasha?"

Sasha shrugged, getting to her reason for stopping Avery in a slow pristine fashion, "I just wanted to know if you and the girls were going to the party tonight?"

Avery stared; she had been allowing the heat off of the blacktop to slowly cook her alive just to be asked about the stupid party again, "Well, I'm not going, and I'm pretty sure there's no way in hell Jade's going, but you'll just have to ask the others yourself, because I have no idea."

Sasha looked at Avery the way Avery looked at one of her dogs when it deliberately disobeyed a command.

"Fine," Sasha sighed, "go live your exciting life at home. I'll see you later."

With a dismissive hand wave goodbye, Sasha turned to go. Toby gave Avery a toothy smiled and winked at her before following Sasha.

Avery shook her head. That had just sealed it. This had been the absolute worst few minutes of her day. It could only go up from here.

Avery watched as Sasha and Toby piled into Sasha's blue two-door convertible that her dad had bought her for her birthday. Those were the kind of presents you got when your dad was one of only two lawyers in the town, especially, the only one of the two who was actually any good.

Avery waved good-bye as Sasha attempted to speed out of the parking lot. Now that that interaction was thankfully over with, Avery turned around and continued to make her way out of the parking lot.

As she stepped onto the grass of the park, she was finally able to take a breath of that longed for spicy flower scent. Avery had made it, she was free, it was Friday, and she had effectively avoided Sasha peer-pressuring her into attending a party she hadn't wanted to. Avery slipped her backpack off of her shoulder and grasped it in her right hand as she started spinning in several whirling twirls of joy, not even caring who might see her.

Teetering and almost losing her balance, Avery decided it might be a good idea to stop spinning. She had resumed walking in a straight line towards her car when something out of the corner of her eye caught her attention.

Someone was staring at her from behind one of the parks big Mahogany trees. At first, she mistook it for a child because of its size, but as she looked at it more closely, she realized it wasn't a child at all. In fact, Avery wasn't even sure if it was completely human. It looked almost like some sort of elf out of a children's book.

In an attempt to hold onto reality, Avery blinked her eyes hard and shook her head. When she opened her eyes a second later, the little creature had disappeared.

She was about to walk over to the tree and look to see if she had really seen what she thought she saw, when she re-thought the idea.

"Avery," she told herself, aloud, "you just thought you saw some freaky little fantasy creature spying on you from behind a tree…and now you want to go and look for it?! No, no, no, no, no, no way…just go home and get some much needed sleep."

Changing directions slightly, Avery tried to put as much distance between her and the large Mahogany tree as she possibly could. She had barely taken five steps, when the small being she had seen leapt directly out at her from behind another bulky tree.

Avery screamed at the top of her lungs and swung her backpack around in front of her to act as a barrier between her and the creature.

From close up, Avery was able to see that the little being actually resembled a man, about half her height. He had long pointy ears that somehow fit his more rounded features and a long white beard that moved up and down with every twitch of his button nose. His deep set eyes shone like two shiny sapphires behind bushy gray eyebrows and seemed to contain oceans of knowledge. His graying hair stuck out in tufts from underneath his triangular shaped gray pointy hat. He wore an oversized brown robe that fell just below his feet and would have been too long to allow him to walk if it hadn't been held up by a weathered leather belt fastened around his waist. There were at least a dozen small pouches attached to the leather belt, along with a very small dagger looped through it, which is what Avery was keeping her eyes on at the moment.

"Oh, for Great Wizarding sake!" the little man spit out in a gravelly voice that Avery found impressively deep for such a little body, "There is no need to cause a scene with your screaming. I've been waiting for you for over an hour."

Avery stared hard at the little man for a long while, still holding up her backpack between them as a shield. She was trying to regain some focus through her confusion and make sense of what he had just said.

"Are...um...are you talking to me?" She asked in a shaky little voice. It was the only question her mind would form at the moment.

A look Avery could only make out as disgust flashed across Gumptin's face, "Of course I am talking to you," he answered brusquely, "do you see anyone else around?"

Even through the insanity of the situation, Avery couldn't help but think the little man rude, which was actually a good thing since it helped to chase away some of her fear and replace it with annoyance.

Swallowing hard, Avery placed her backpack back over her shoulder, "Well, no, but I...I don't usually have elves jump out at me from behind trees and start talking to me."

The man frowned as if Avery had said something offensive, "I am not an elf; I am a gnome. There is a *big* difference."

Avery's mouth fell open in shock. Out of all the necessary information she needed from him to make sense out of what was going on, that seemed the most trivial.

"Oh, I'm sorry, Mr. Gnome," Avery said sarcastically, still desperately trying to understand what was going on, "my mistake. Now, why don't you tell me who exactly you are, what you're doing here, and why you're talking to *me*?"

The small man cleared his throat, "My name is Gumptin; I am a Wizard, a forest gnome, and a trainer of extraordinary beings. You and I already know each other." Gumptin looked at Avery, a lilt of melancholy in his eyes, "Unfortunately, you will not remember knowing me, or even who you are for that matter."

"Ok." Avery's mind seemed to have gone blank. She was seriously starting to believe that she may have inhaled too much car exhaust from the student parking lot and was now hallucinating, "So, you're saying we already know each other; I just don't ever remember meeting you or know myself?"

"Exactly!" Gumptin grinned and clapped his hands, happy Avery was following him, "But, there is so much more that needs to be explained; this just is not the place to do it. Come with me and I will show you everything you need to know."

"Right," Avery said, nodding her head up and down vigorously, "that sounds like a great idea, Gumptin the gnome, but I think I'm gonna pass on that for now. Nice meeting you, though."

Avery wanted to run away as fast as her legs could take her, but she fought the urge and calmly turned around, securing her backpack on both shoulders, making it easier to run that way if needed. She started to slowly walk away from the Gumptin, heading back towards the school.

"Wait!" Gumptin shouted anxiously, "Wait, you cannot leave!"

Avery started to slowly pick up her pace as she heard Gumptin attempt to follow her.

"The insane little man is chasing me! The insane little man is chasing me!" Avery chanted to herself, trying to remain calm, "Just keep on running; it'll be alright; he's got little legs; you can outrun him!"

She was right. Gumptin's little legs could not move very fast and he quickly gave up the chase.

"You cannot run from who you are, Avery!" Gumptin shouted after her, in a last attempt before she got away, "It is your destiny! You are a Protector!"

With those words Avery stopped dead in her tracks. Besides the fact that she had never told Gumptin her name, there was something in the way that he said it that made her turn back around and face him. There was something so familiar about it, as if she had heard him say it before. Of course, she knew that wasn't possible. Avery was sure she wouldn't have forgotten meeting a two and a half foot gnome, but then there was that word…Protector. It had stirred something deep inside of Avery; something scratching on the very edges of her mind, begging to be remembered and released.

Gumptin was still breathing heavy from his very short run as he approached her, "I am glad you came to your senses." He puffed, "Now, are you ready to go?"

"Gumptin," Avery gaped at him, "I stopped running, that doesn't mean I'm going to go anywhere with you." Avery was still very cautious. Just because a certain word, and Gumptin saying her name sounded familiar, didn't mean she was ready to listen to anything he said, "You could be a psycho!"

Gumptin either didn't hear Avery or ignored her, because he began to walk towards a grove of trees near the center of the park.

"This way." He motioned for Avery to follow him.

Reluctantly and against her better judgment she followed Gumptin. After all, they were still in the open space of a large park, and she was twice the size of Gumptin; what could possibly happen?

"Fine," Avery shouted towards him, "but I'm not getting into any cars or confined spaces with you!"

Gumptin stopped in between two massive Beech trees and swung his head around to make sure they were alone. Avery stopped behind him, wondering what the difference was from this spot compared to where they had just been standing. Avery sighed and shifted her weight from one foot to another, thinking maybe Gumptin was just crazy after all, and she was even crazier for following him.

Just as Avery was about to speak up and say something, Gumptin waved his right hand in the air and said the words, "Ora Gateway."

Now, Avery was sure he was crazy, but before she could tell him this she was distracted by a movement from between the trees. It started out as a slight swirling, which for a moment Avery thought could be the wind, but then the swirling came in bigger and faster circles, widening in circumference. Within seconds, the churning stopped and Avery was staring at what looked like a circular pool of water standing up-right in mid-air.

Avery didn't realize she had stopped breathing, until her body forced her to take a large gulp of air just to stop her from fainting.

"What…what did you just do?" She stammered, pointing at the liquid-like circle.

"This," Gumptin said, pointing towards the floating pool, "is the Ora Gateway, and I just opened it. It is the gateway to Orcatia, the planet you come from. Well, the first planet you come from, anyway." Gumptin shrugged his shoulders, "After all, you were born on Earth as well."

The World started spinning inside Avery's head; she stood frozen, just staring at Gumptin. There was no way she should believe what he was saying, but at the same time there was a magic gateway floating a foot in front of her.

"Alright," Gumptin told Avery matter-of-factly, "walk into it."

It was those words that knocked Avery out of her frozen trance. She began laughing, a small giggle that got bigger the more she thought about what Gumptin had just told her to do.

"If you think for one second that I'm going to walk through that enchanted puddle, then you really are nuts." Avery told him, her laughter dying down.

Gumptin sighed and Avery could tell he was losing his patience, "I need to explain something to you, Avery. This is going to be hard for you to hear, but I need you to understand that you are a Protector. It is not a choice, it is your destiny." Gumptin said seriously, "Protectors were created to fight the evil that not only threatens to take over Orcatia, but the whole Universe. You were born on the planet of Orcatia and you lived there and served as a Protector for sixteen years…until you were killed."

Avery opened her mouth to tell Gumptin again how insane he was, but Gumptin held up his hand to silence her. She obeyed, more because she was entranced by his story than out of obedience to him.

"You were killed," Gumptin continued, "and then magic was used to send you to Earth, so that you could be re-born. Then, when you reached the age you were when you died, I would come to bring you back."

Avery placed her hands over her eyes and shook her head, trying to wipe away what Gumptin was saying. Avery wasn't sure if it was coming from her head, heart, or soul, but a very small part of her was confirming Gumptin's words as truth. His words were sparking something inside of Avery's brain, like a memory she knew she should have, but didn't. It felt like Gumptin was picking at a giant scab covering her mind. Avery didn't care that a part of her felt the truth in Gumptin's words; right now, she was just telling that part to shut up and keep quiet.

While Avery had her eyes closed, Gumptin moved around behind her and began pushing her from behind, towards the Gateway.

Avery moved forward one step, then another; then she opened her eyes and realized what Gumptin was doing.

"What the Hell!" Avery yelled, smacking Gumptin's hands away from her backside, where he had been pushing her.

"You have to go through the Gateway." He told her firmly, moving his hands up to start pushing her again.

She dodged out of his way, putting some distance between herself and the gateway. Avery had had enough, she didn't care that some small part of her knew Gumptin was telling the truth; she was done with all this insanity; it was time to return to reality.

"Listen," she shouted at Gumptin, to make perfectly clear he understood what she was saying, "there's no way I'm going down some freaky white rabbit's hole just because some gnome tells me it's my destiny!"

Avery turned around and began to walk away from Gumptin and the madness.

She had gone a few steps; then yelled over her shoulder towards him, "Go and scare somebody else!"

"What about your family and friends?" Gumptin yelled back to her.

When Avery spun around, she saw Gumptin hadn't made any attempt to follow her. He was still standing by the gateway where she had left him. She strode up to him. Bringing her loved ones into this was stepping over a line. Every ounce of confusion, fear, and disbelief Avery had been feeling before was replaced with a hot anger.

"Are you threatening the people I care about little man?!" Avery demanded, shoving her finger hard into Gumptin's chest.

"Of course not," Gumptin said softly, soft enough to calm Avery down slightly, "but the Emperor will."

There it was again, a tinge of recognition that played in Avery's brain. The Emperor, she could sense she knew that name. She could also sense the chill that name sent throughout her body.

"He is the one responsible for your deaths." There was a sadness to Gumptin's voice as he spoke, and it caused Avery to take back her finger with a trace of guilt for having shoved him so roughly with it. "If the Emperor discovers you and the others are still alive, he will move the planets to see you destroyed. He will kill you and everyone close to you. If you come with me, I can prepare you, give you another fighting chance."

Avery noticed that Gumptin had said 'another'. That's because he supposedly killed you the first time, she told herself sardonically.

"If you do not come with me," Gumptin continued, "if you walk away from who you are, you are not just condemning yourself and the lives of those you love, but also planets full of people…to a terrible death."

Avery thought that a bit overdramatic, but his point had hit home. She still wasn't sure she believed absolutely everything Gumptin was saying, but there was no way she could walk away if it meant there was even the slightest chance she could put her family and friends in danger. Gumptin had used the one card that would make Avery go with him. There was a moment when Avery thought she might either cry or vomit, but she was able to control both reactions.

She couldn't believe she was actually about to do this, "Fine," she told Gumptin, "let's go."

Avery took tentative steps towards the gateway, until she was just inches away from it. She could feel energy reflecting off of it, like static electricity. Avery lightly grazed her fingers over the watery substance. Tiny ripples formed where her fingers made contact and branched outward. It felt cool to the touch, but to Avery's surprise, not wet.

Goosebumps broke out all over her body; it was telling her how insane she was for doing this. Avery closed her eyes, took a deep steadying breath, and then walked into the liquid.

For a moment, Avery felt nothing, as if she had simply taken another step in the park, but a second later head-to-toe tingles, similar to tiny little pin pricks, burst across her flesh. Avery's eyes shot open as she experienced the strongest pulling sensation she had ever felt, like someone had tied a rope around her waist and attached it to a herd of stampeding elephants.

Whatever was happening was happening too fast for Avery to focus and see anything. It was mostly blackness, and small smatterings of light that passed by so quickly, if Avery were to blink she would miss them.

It felt to Avery like she didn't even have a body anymore, just a brain to absorb what was going on. It was like the craziest roller coaster she had ever been on times a thousand.

In a blink it was over, as quickly as it had began. The entire trip had only taken seconds, but Avery's head and stomach were doing a good job at convincing her it had taken an eternity.

Avery had been catapulted out of the gateway with too much force for her to effectively catch her balance and she ended up falling flat on her face in the grass and dirt.

Avery heard Gumptin come through the gateway behind her, and from the sound of it, he had no problems staying on his feet.

"You could've given me a little warning about how much that was gonna suck!" Avery groaned as she lifted herself onto her hands and knees, wiping at the dirt she was sure was smudging her face.

"You will get used to it." Gumptin said dismissively, walking past Avery.

That gave way to Avery having a horrifying thought; she was going to have to go through the Gateway again. Now, she was surer than ever that following Gumptin was a bad idea.

When Avery picked herself up off of the ground, she looked around and saw that she was in the middle of a tiny clearing in the woods somewhere. The trees surrounding the clearing were massive; Avery had to lift her head almost all the way back to see the tops of them. The thick green carpeting of foliage blocked out most of the sky, but let in enough rays of sunlight to give the entire forest a warm glow. Mossy emerald carpeting covered the forest floor, except for small patches where multi-colored flowers and odd shaped mushrooms sprouted out from.

Avery saw Gumptin disappear into a small patch of the forest, and she trotted to keep up with him. As uneasy as Gumptin made her feel, Avery would still prefer to be with him then on her own in an otherworldly forest.

As Avery approached the spot Gumptin had vanished into, she saw that he had actually gone down a small overgrown dirt path. She spotted movement in the thick undergrowth a few feet ahead. Determined not to lose Gumptin, Avery walked onto the path, grumbling as she pushed wispy hanging branches and low-lying vegetation out of her way. The unruly waves of her hair kept getting caught on protruding tree stems and, she cursed the fact she didn't have anything to tie her hair up with. Of course, she had no idea when she woke up that morning that she was going to be following a gnome while he traipsed around Sherwood Forest on another planet.

Thinking about the forest, Avery was just about to shout out to Gumptin, asking how much longer she was suppose to endure the onslaught of nature, when the small path they were on exited out onto a much larger road. This looked, to Avery, like a main road of some kind, although she had no idea from where to where. The road was about ten feet wide and was either maintained or used frequently enough to keep the underbrush off of it.

Gumptin was waiting for Avery in the center of the road.

"Where are we going?" Avery asked him, pulling a leaf out of her hair.

"You will see." Gumptin told her; then turned to the left and started walking down the road.

Avery grumbled under her breath and followed him, knowing that there was most likely nothing she could say to make him tell her.

Avery stayed a few feet behind Gumptin. She kept noticing him glance around the forest, more alert than he had been back on Earth. Whatever he was keeping an eye out for, Avery didn't want to know. Just being here was scary enough for her; she didn't want to have something else to worry about. So, Avery decided, that for just this one time, she'd let Gumptin have a secret.

As they walked, Avery could feel the forest pulsing with life around her. The call of multiple birds floated in on a soft breeze that lightly swayed her hair around her face. She heard the tiny rustling of small creatures scurrying around inside the thick forest, and she thanked her lucky stars that she could tell they were small. The leaves of the trees danced in the wind, giving off a low whistle which sounded almost like a lullaby. Everything around Avery smelled fresh and clean, like nothing she had ever experienced back on Earth, and as they continued walking she found herself being lulled into, what she knew, was a false sense of peace.

After walking for about twenty minutes, Avery began to hear something besides the wind, birds, and animals of the forest. At first, Avery couldn't make it out, but as they got closer and she strained to listen, she realized she was hearing the voices of people. She could hear men and women talking, the laughter of a child, the high whinny of a horse, some clanging and thumps, and the sound of people working.

"Gumptin!" Avery screeched in an elevated whisper.

"What?" Gumptin asked, turning around, not bothering to whisper.

"I hear people." Avery said, walking over to him and leaning down to be close to his ear so that she could keep her voice low, "Where are we going?"

"We are going to Havyn." Gumptin told her.

Havyn...that word hit Avery hard in the chest, like a brick falling on it. It was another word she knew she was familiar with, a word that brought her comfort. Avery felt a flood of memories wanting to pound into her brain, but stopping short before she could actually remember anything.

Avery straightened up and looked into the distance. She could almost see what lay at the end of the road, a small village filled with people.

"Havyn's where we lived." Avery told Gumptin.

"Do you remember?" Gumptin asked her, and Avery could see a small glimmer of hope flicker across his face.

Avery laughed dismissively, "No…no way," she told him, "I just had a feeling."

"That is good!" Gumptin shook his head up and down, "Feelings are good, sometimes even better than memories."

Avery wasn't sure if Gumptin was just trying to cheer her up or not. What she decided not to tell Gumptin, was that if he was right and she had actually been killed by some evil Emperor, then she was more than happy not to have any memories of this place.

After Avery nudged Gumptin onward with her knee, he flashed her a look of contempt that brought Avery a surge of mischievous joy. He might not have liked being pushed around, but he did as Avery's knee instructed and walked forward.

Just a few steps later, Avery could begin to see small glimpses of the village through the trees. She could see a woman in a green tattered cotton dress throwing something on the ground for the chickens surrounding her to munch on, a wheelbarrow leaning up against an old stump, and the tops of a few other people's heads. She knew the villagers weren't yet able to spot her and Gumptin, not behind the large trees and thick shrubs of the forest.

Where the road ended and the village began, there were two wide bushes with tiny purple flowers decorating them located on opposite sides of the road.

Avery ambled up and stood behind one of the overgrown bushes. Out of sight, she was able to view the village in full for the first time.

As she took in the village, she saw that there were no conventional homes, the kind made out of mortar or brick, or wood. Instead, all of the homes were actually built into enormous trees; the size of ten large Sequoias fused together. Avery lifted her head up to try and see the tops of the trees, but they seemed to go on forever and all she could manage to see was the greenish hue color of the distant leaves and some rays of light. It was easy to tell these trees were being used as homes, since every one of them had a doorway and multiple windows built into the trunks. Avery couldn't tell how far down the tree homes went, but she guessed there were at least fifty or sixty of them rooted in a crescent moon shape, outlining the center of the town. Some of the trees had signs attached near and above their doors. Avery could make out one sign that said, 'Blacksmith & Ferrier' and another one that read, 'Bott's Apothecary & Sweets'. Avery thought that an odd combination, but considering she was on another planet didn't figure she had much to compare it with.

Beyond the trees, scattered in the background amongst wide farming fields, Avery could see a few normal homes that appeared to be made out of wood and clay.

The center of town didn't have much. There were no roads running through it, just a generous sized area of cleared land covered with grass and dried leaves. In the middle, there was a large water well made out of dark colored stones and covered with a wooden roof supported by four stone posts. Towards the outlying right end of the village, Avery could barely make out what looked like three large tables and six benches. They looked as if they could easily fit at least fifty people each.

Avery was still absorbing some of the sights of the village, like the extensive vegetable gardens that lay beyond the tree houses, a few farm animals in small pastures, and the swords lying against the trunk of the Blacksmith's tree house, when she realized something was tugging at the pocket of her jeans. She glanced down and saw Gumptin trying to pull her towards the entrance.

"Lay off!" Avery hissed at him, smacking his hand away.

That was the second time in an hour Avery had to smack Gumptin away from pushing her around, Avery hoped this was a habit they weren't going to keep.

"We do not have time for you to stand here and try to build up some nerve." Gumptin scolded her, "Going back to your village is the easy part, Avery."

He pushed her hard in the small of her back, towards the village, causing Avery to jerk forward, run into something, and tumble over it. As she spun around and was falling backwards, Avery was able to see what Gumptin had pushed her into. It was a wooden post, a foot taller than Avery, with a sign on the top of it that read. 'Welcome to Havyn, Pop. 236'.

Avery tried to make a grab for the sign, but only managed to graze it with her finger tips, which spun her body back around so that she landed on the ground flat on her face instead of on her butt.

"Son of a bitch!" Avery yelled at the top of her lungs, picking herself off the ground and rubbing her throbbing elbow that had landed on a small rock. She spun around to face Gumptin, her mind set on killing the little man, "What the Hell did you do that for?!" Avery shouted at him.

She felt sure she just might throttle him. Avery noticed that as she was yelling at Gumptin, he was looking past her. That only pissed Avery off more. He could at least have the decency to look at her after what he had just done; so she could properly scold him.

"Avery?" The voice came from behind Avery, and she froze as it began to dawn on her what Gumptin was most likely staring at.

Avery turned around slowly, still holding her wounded elbow. She saw that the voice had come from a boy, not much older than her. He had shaggy brown hair, and tanned skin smudged with dirt. The clothes he wore, brown cotton pants and a blue tunic with a belt cinched around it looked well worn. Just by looking at him Avery could tell he definitely worked hard for a living.

The boy wasn't the only one staring at her; he was surrounded by five other villagers, and Avery noticed a multitude of other people stopping what they were doing, coming out of their houses, and making their way over to where she stood.

Oh, my God, she thought, the whole freaking village is on their way to come see me.

Gumptin had come up to stand beside Avery, "I told you I would bring her home." He addressed the villagers, "She is just as she was."

Gumptin looked Avery up and down, scrutinizing, and Avery had a strong suspicion he didn't believe what he had just said.

The boy who had said her name ran up and gave her a tight hug, "Thank God, you're back." He said into her ear.

Avery gasped, not knowing how to deal with this reaction. She lightly hugged him back.

When she pulled back from the boy the rest of the villagers were waiting to follow suit, some hugged her, some patted her on the back, and a few even shook her hand. There were a small amount of them crying, but the rest looked as happy as if they were receiving presents on their birthday.

Avery heard people say things to her like, 'We were so scared the Protectors wouldn't return to us' and 'I knew you were too strong a warrior to stay dead' or 'Without you, the Emperor would surely take over Orcatia'. Then, there was Avery's favorite, 'How could you be so stupid to go and get yourself killed'.

Avery looked pleadingly at Gumptin. She had no idea what to say to these people. They were all acting like they knew her, like they needed her, and she had no idea who any of them were.

"That is enough! That is enough!" Gumptin said, pushing the villagers away from Avery. He had seen her distress and decided it would be best not to freak her out any more than she already was, "You must keep in mind, as I told you," Gumptin told the villagers, "Avery has no memory of who she was, of this place, or of you."

Avery saw the recollection dawn on all of their faces and most of them looked as if they had just been hit by a falling tree.

"I am sorry." One of the village men said to Avery, "It was awfully terrifying not having you here to protect the village anymore. We saw you again, and I guess we just…forgot."

Avery smirked slightly; she found it humorous that the man was apologizing for them forgetting that she had forgot everything.

"It's really not a problem." Avery told them.

Gumptin, who was still trying to push some of the villagers away, spoke up, "I need to speak with Avery alone now. You all go back to what you were doing." At the villagers' reluctance to leave, Gumptin told them, "I need to speak with her before we can go back and get the others. Do not worry; she is here to stay."

Avery startled at Gumptin's words. Everything had happened so fast. Her mind was still struggling to keep up, but even with everything she had already discovered, this was the first time she realized Gumptin had meant for her to stay here on this other world permanently. Avery threw that thought quickly out of her brain before it caused her panic. She had enough to deal with in the now to think about the future.

As much as Gumptin's words had disturbed Avery, they had calmed the villagers, and they had begun to disperse back to their houses and work.

When they were alone, Gumptin led Avery over to a small clearing on the outskirts of the village near the border of the forest.

There were two small wooden benches in the clearing and Gumptin motioned for Avery to have a seat on one.

Avery sat and Gumptin began to talk, "I brought you back here first, on your own, for a reason, Avery. I am going to need your help in bringing the other Protectors back here."

Avery snorted, "What are you going to need my help with?" She couldn't begin to imagine how she would be able to convince someone to take a wild ride through a magical portal to another world, "Can't you just jump out from behind some tree and scare them senseless until they agree to come with you?"

Gumptin continued, unfazed by her sarcasm, "You are their leader Avery. You are *the* leader; the leader of the Protectors. You have to re-establish your leadership, gather your warriors, and get them back here to fight."

This was becoming too much for Avery. She didn't know if she could handle the responsibility of being told that she was not only some magical warrior, but also the leader of these magical warriors.

Avery stood up off of her bench, "Look, Gumptin, this is all just getting a little too crazy house for me."

"Avery!" Gumptin yelled loudly, stopping Avery in her tracks and capturing her full attention, "Look around you, young lady. You can no longer deny that this is real. It is not your imagination. It is not a dream, and you are not going insane. I know you know everything I told you is true. I know that you feel it as truth inside your very bones."

Avery looked around her at the houses built into giant trees, the villagers who were staring over at her as they pretended to work, and the thick green forest surrounding everything. Gumptin was right. Even though she'd never admit it to him; a part of her belonged to this place and she knew it. It played on her memories like a barely remembered dream.

Avery was still lost in wistful thought, gazing at her surroundings, when Gumptin said, "Plus, there is also this you cannot ignore."

Then, Gumptin pulled the small dagger out from his belt and lunged at Avery. Avery reacted instantaneously, she spun to the right and grabbed Gumptin's wrist with her left hand, while at the same time clasping his arm to her body with her right hand. Avery brought her knee up and slammed Gumptin's wrist against it, forcing him to drop the dagger. He let out a small grunt of pain and she flipped him onto his back on the ground, all the while still holding on to his wrist, so that she was able to pin it. A second later, Avery had his other wrist pinned to the ground with her knee. She picked up his dagger with her free hand and placed the blade across his throat.

"Are you insane?!" Avery shouted into Gumptin's face. She was breathing heavy, more from the shock of being attacked with a knife than from exertion. "I knew I shouldn't have trusted some creepy fantasy creature! You tried to kill me!"

Gumptin lay on the ground calmly, not trying to struggle away from Avery or the knife she was holding at his throat.

"I was not trying to kill you." He told her, "I simply wanted to show you what you are capable of."

Avery looked down at Gumptin, puzzled, minutely easing the knife away from his throat.

"I wanted to show you that you are truly a Protector." Gumptin continued, "All of the powers and abilities that the Protectors possess are inside of you, a little dormant perhaps, but they are there. I knew that in a fight or flight situation you will always choose fight, it is who you are, and instinctually you would use your skills."

What Gumptin was saying wasn't making Avery feel much better, "So, you're saying you were testing me...with a *knife*!"

"Oh, for Wizarding sake, girl," now Gumptin did struggle a little to free himself, but Avery kept him firmly cemented to the ground, "I was not testing you, I was showing you! Look at what you did! In just a few seconds you were able to disarm me, throw me to the ground, and take advantage of the situation. Now, get off of me!"

It was then that everything that had just transpired hit Avery like a lightning bolt. She had no idea how she had done what she did. She didn't even really remember seeing Gumptin come at her with the knife; her body had just reacted. Avery had to admit to herself that being able to whip Gumptin's little ass was pretty cool.

"Get off!" Gumptin huffed for the second time, below her.

Avery obeyed and released him, but as he stuck his hand out for her to give him his knife back, Avery threw it to the ground.

Gumptin may have just been trying to show Avery she had warrior instincts, but he had still lunged at her with a knife, and that wasn't something she was entirely grateful for.

Avery sat back down on the bench; thinking about her newly discovered fighting skills. Gumptin picked up his knife from the ground, placed it back into his belt, and walked over to her.

He placed his little hand on her shoulder, "You are the leader of the Protectors Avery. The Protectors are five beings created by the Elementals, a powerful group of sorcerers. You were created to keep the balance between good and evil. Before you and the others were born, darkness was taking over, becoming too strong for most of us to fight back. Demons, trolls, harpies, were beasts, and other horrendous creatures began to roam this world unchallenged, but then the Protectors were born and things changed."

Avery placed her head in her hands. Gumptin talking about Demons and trolls made her want to go back home to Earth and sleep away this whole experience.

Gumptin sat down beside her, his hand still resting on her shoulder, trying to comfort her, "The Protectors have the power of the elements. You have the power of energy, another has water, another earth, one fire, and one wind. You can harness the power of your energy and use it as a weapon."

Avery looked up at Gumptin, "You mean I actually have *power*, power, not just strength and all that fighting stuff."

Gumptin shook his head, "Well, that fighting *stuff* is important," he scowled, "but yes, you do actually have powers. Of course, none of you ever really learned to use them very well, just tiny things. I am afraid they will likely remain dormant until the day you die." Gumptin caught himself, "Well, you know, die…again."

Avery thought that was one of the dumbest things she'd ever heard, "What's the point in having powers if you can't even use them!" She asked.

"Avery, you are just a human, remember." Gumptin told her, "None but the Elementals fully comprehend the complexities of your powers, but from what I understand; it takes complete mastery of one's own body, mind, and emotions to even begin to know how to use a power like yours." He paused for a moment, as if thinking about something, and then said, "If it makes you feel any better, I once saw you zap a troll with a small bolt of electricity, and it left a very nasty burn mark on his face."

Avery stared at Gumptin like he had just eaten a fly. She couldn't believe he was so remarkably bad at making a person feel better.

"Anyway," Gumptin went on, not seeming to notice Avery's dissatisfaction, "this world needs the Protectors. The Elementals know that; that is why they brought you back after the Emperor killed you all."

Avery wished Gumptin would stop bringing up the being killed thing; especially if he was trying to set her at ease, because that wasn't going to work.

Taking another tactic, Gumptin said to Avery, "The Elementals sent your parents to Earth with your souls so that you could be re-born. They were given jobs and a place to live, unable to age until they could come home to Orcatia. They were forced to live sixteen years on a planet that was not their home, keeping their secret, especially from you, just so that you could be kept safe and alive."

Up until this point, Avery had never even thought about her parents; which, looking back, she actually found rather dumb. She couldn't wrap her head around the fact that her parents had known about the whole Protector, being from another planet, thing for her entire life and said absolutely nothing. Her parents had never really talked about their past, but Avery had just always figured it was because it wasn't very interesting, how wrong she was. She had never even questioned the fact that they looked the same now as they did in old baby pictures with her. All of a sudden, Avery felt very blind and stupid.

"Gumptin, if my parent's didn't age on Earth and I did, does that mean that I won't age on Orcatia?" Avery had this image of her looking like she was sixteen forever, and she wasn't quite sure if that was a good thing or a bad thing.

"No, you were born on Earth, so you are part Earthling now. Earthlings age and die no matter what planet they are on. You shall age at a normal rate on both Orcatia and Earth." Gumptin told her.

Typical Gumptin answer, Avery thought, full of certain death. Then, another thought popped into her mind, "Gumptin, what about my sister?"

Gumptin looked surprised, "You have a sister?" He asked.

Avery nodded her head, "Yeah, and she's younger than me, which means she was never even born on Orcatia...*ever*. What does that mean for her?"

"Nothing," Gumptin said, still looking surprised by the knowledge that Avery had a younger sister, "like I said Earthlings age wherever they are. She will have the same manner of life here as she does there."

Avery snorted; she knew that wasn't even remotely possible.

"I can't believe my parents never said anything to me." Avery grumbled as she ran her fingers through her long hair, attempting to collect herself and her thoughts.

"You know they could not." Gumptin told her softly, "They could not risk anyone or anything finding out. Plus," he added, almost absentmindedly, "you truly needed to be given a normal life."

That was one of the problems Avery was struggling with; all she knew was a normal life, and it wasn't a bad life. Now, here was Gumptin, the Wizard gnome, telling her that she'd have to leave everything she knew, to become the warrior she didn't remember being, to fight the thing that had apparently already killed her once before. She wished her parents could have at least prepared her to accept the fact that her cozy little life was just temporary.

Avery wiped at her eyes, making sure to stop the tears before they had a chance to spring out. She didn't know Gumptin well enough yet to allow herself to cry in front of him,

"Gumptin," Avery said, her voice slightly strained, "I don't remember *anything*."

"I really do not believe you shall ever get your memory back." Gumptin shook his head, "It was one of the prices for bringing you back to life."

Even though, Avery was acutely aware Gumptin said *one* of the prices, she decided it was best not to bring that up at the moment. She decided to ask him about it later when her head stopped spinning.

"But, now," Gumptin said, standing up, "we must go back to Earth and fetch the other Protectors."

Gumptin walked through the village entrance and back onto the main road, headed back towards the Gateway.

"Wait a second!" Avery shouted, running to catch up with him, "You still haven't told me who the other Protectors are."

Gumptin stopped mid-stride, "Have I not?" He asked Avery, and she shook her head, no.

"Well, that is because I figured you would have already guessed it." He told her, "They are Jade Kai, Skylar Bavol, Sasha Seraphina, and Bunny Claiborne."

Of course, Avery thought as realization hit her like a lightning bolt. That was why their parents were always forcing them together, always making sure they did things as a group. From before they could speak, their parents had been preparing them to be a unit.

The thought of Sasha flashed into Avery's mind, and the idea of being the leader didn't seem so daunting anymore; because, if there was one thing Avery had longed to do all her life, it was to boss around Sasha Seraphina.

Avery's mind then began to drift towards another girl, "Hey, Gumptin," She told him, "when we get back to Earth I know who we're going to go tell first."

"No!" Was all Gumptin said, and he picked up his pace.

"What?!" Avery asked, wondering why she had been so easily shot down, "Why?"

"Because I know who you are referring to," Gumptin told Avery, "and I am not going to deal with her until the very last moment that I have to."

Avery raised her arms in frustration, "How could you possibly know who I'm referring to?! I'm just telling you that I know which Protector I want to tell first."

"And I am telling you no, no, no, no!" Gumptin picked up his pace even more so that he was almost at a run.

Avery watched him scurrying away down the road and let a huge smile break out on her face. She would let Gumptin protest as much as he wanted and act as childish as he wanted. All the while, she would revel in the knowledge that she and her car were going to be Gumptin's only mode of transportation back on Earth.

3.

Jade Kai lived in the Rebel Moon Trailer Park, located on the far outskirts of town. It was a short fifteen minute drive through desert landscape down a two lane highway before Avery and Gumptin would reach the turn-off for the trailer park, marked by its old beat up blue and yellow sign, which hadn't been updated since the sixties, standing large and tall, guiding people to the entrance.

Avery rolled down the window of her old Challenger to let the desert wind blow warm on her face. Going through the Ora Gateway was bad enough once, but going through twice had left Avery's stomach flip-flopping and her head thumping painfully.

It hadn't taken Avery too much convincing to get Gumptin to agree to go see Jade first. He had caught on quickly to what Avery had already known; that if Gumptin was going to go anywhere it was going to be in Avery's car with her driving.

Gumptin sat in the passenger seat, staring out the window the whole way to Jade's place. Avery could tell he was fascinated with the scenery, the flat desert, the cacti, the craggy looming mountains in the background.

"The deserts on Orcatia are not like the deserts here. They are really quite lovely." Gumptin told Avery, still looking out his window, and a pang of remorse sliced through Avery's heart. She didn't want to have to think about leaving Redemption.

"We're here." Avery said, turning into the dusty entrance of the trailer park, thankful to be able to put her mind on something else.

Jade's dad worked as a mechanic at the only auto repair shop in town and her mom as a clerk at the twenty-four hour grocery store. They both worked long hours, which meant Jade was alone most of the time. That time she spent either restoring motorcycles, listening to classic rock, or hanging out with Avery and her family. In fact, Jade spent more time over at Avery's house than she did at her own. It had been that way ever since they were first forced together as children. They had become inseparable, seeing each other almost every day for the past sixteen years. They considered each other, not only as best friends, but also sisters.

Avery knew the one person that she could count on was Jade. Jade had looked out for Avery her whole life. When they were little, she had beat down any bully who had ever tried to start anything with Avery. In second grade, Jade had given Alex Marquez a bloody nose for stealing Avery's lunch box. Then, in the sixth grade she ended up giving Megan Dominguez a black eye for creaming Avery in the face with a dodge ball during gym class. This was a habit that had continued throughout their entire school years. The latest victim was Camilla Roberts who Jade had caught kissing Avery's ex-boyfriend before he was officially ex. As for the ex-boyfriend, Alex Marquez, he ended up with another, much worse, bloody nose.

They were protective of each other, but Jade had a tendency to get over-protective. This was the reason, as Avery stopped her car in front of Jade's rusty blue trailer that her nerves began to dance inside her stomach. Avery knew she had to tell Jade everything, but she wasn't quite sure how Jade was going to react when she found out Avery had followed a magical gnome to another planet without even talking it over with her first.

Avery told Gumptin to stay in the car, then got out and slammed the door shut. She spotted Jade lying on her back in her front yard, working on an old motorcycle that had definitely seen better days.

Jade's prize 2001 Suzuki Hayabusa motorcycle that she used to ride around town terrorizing the residents with speed and noise, was perched in its usual spot, under a large canvas shade covering next to her family's trailer. Jade had purchased the bike relatively cheap two years ago, it was run down and broken, but she had spent two straight months fixing it up and airbrushing it a slick black. It was now her pride and joy.

"Jade?!" Avery called out as she approached her. She grimaced a little as her nerves made her voice crack, something she was not expecting.

Jade lifted her greased stained face towards Avery. Even smudged in grease and oil, Jade was still beautiful. It was a different kind of beauty than Sasha's, whose looks were more sophisticated, or Avery, who always had a sort of ethereal beauty. Jade had none of that, her beauty was strictly dangerous. She stood a good few inches taller than Avery and had flawless pale skin covering her slender, but muscled body. She had straight midnight black hair that fell down to her mid-back and pouty vixen lips. Her cat-like eyes were a dark chocolate brown, but turned a dangerous black when she got angry.

Jade knew her looks were intimidating, and she played it up, always wearing black and motorcycle boots, driving around town, breaking the speed limit on her bike, skipping school, and acting tough.

The people of Redemption saw her as a troubled girl with absentee parents, too much anger, and no future. Jade knew what they thought of her, so she played the part, but Avery knew the truth. Avery knew that Jade was like a double sided coin. One part of her was the tough, motorcycle riding; devil-may-care girl from the trailer park, but the other side of her was sensitive, vulnerable, insecure, and even goofy. It was the people that were close to her who got to see that part, and that was the part of her that Avery loved.

Jade stood up from the ground, wiping a dirty wrench off on her black jeans, "Avery?" She asked, looking a little puzzled, "What are you doing here?"

Jade knew that the trailer park had always made Avery uncomfortable. Although most of the residents of Rebel Moon Trailer Park were perfectly lovely, there were a few who were not the most respectable in Redemption. One in particular was Curt Weiner who lived next door to Jade. Avery hated how he couldn't put one sentence together without having at least four explicative's thrown in, or how he never wore a t-shirt over his wolfman chest, all the while telling Avery what a pretty girl she was growing up to be. Plus, Avery knew for certain that it wasn't an herb garden he had begun planting on the side of his house. Then there was the Draper family who lived three trailers down and collected guns the way some people collect Pez dispensers. Their favorite form of entertainment was getting black-out drunk and shooting their guns into the sky.

Thinking about the usual uneasiness she felt in the trailer park, Avery realized her nerves were blotting out her discomfort. For the first time in her whole life, Avery actually began to appreciate the value of being nervous.

Avery was about to explain to Jade why she had come, but as she stared into Jade's dark eyes, she found herself lost for words, "I...um," she struggled for something, anything to say, "you weren't at school today." Avery knew that was lame, but it was the first thing that popped into her head.

Jade laughed, "Avery, the real news flash would be if I actually went to school. I'm never there...you know that better than anyone." She picked up a towel lying across the seat of the motorcycle and began to clean the grease off of her face, "Don't tell me you drove all the way out here to give me my homework." That made Jade laugh even harder, the thought of her actually doing homework, mixed with the thought of Avery actually driving to the trailer park to give it to her.

Jade's laughter help erase some of Avery's nerves, "You know, it wouldn't kill you to do homework once in awhile, Jade. It is something you have to do to actually pass high school. Well, that and showing up." Avery scolded Jade. Avery hated the laissez-faire attitude Jade took towards school and she could never understand why Jade didn't care more.

"Oh, Avery, I love you to death," Jade said, sauntering up to Avery and placing her hand on Avery's shoulder, "but," she shrugged, "let's face it; you're the geek in this pair. You always have been and you always will be." Jade flashed a sharp side smile, "I'm just the incredible looking brawn."

Avery rolled her eyes, thinking how unbelievable Jade could be sometimes.

A car door slammed behind Avery, causing her to freeze. She saw Jade's eyes grow wide, and she knew exactly what Jade was looking at.

"Who the hell is that?" Jade asked, pointing the wrench she was still holding in her hand towards the direction of Avery's car. All the humor and laughter was gone from her voice.

Avery turned around, already knowing what she was going to see.

Gumptin had gotten out of the car and was now standing in front of it, in full view of Jade.

Avery scolded herself for actually trusting him to do what she said and stay in the car. Up to this point, he hadn't made anything easy for her; why should he start now?

There was nothing else that Avery could do, but simply tell Jade the truth.

"That's Gumptin." Avery said, her brain unable to form any other thought at that moment.

Jade looked at Avery like she had gone insane, "Oh, that's Gumptin, is it." She said sarcastically, "Well, that explains everything, doesn't it?"

This wasn't getting off to the start that Avery had hoped for. She opened her mouth to try and say something else, to explain who Gumptin was, but her mind and mouth seemed to be having a communication problem.

"Um…" Avery began. However, it didn't really matter what she was going to say next, as Jade barged in with her next question, not bothering to wait for Avery's fumbling explanation.

"Did he just get out of your car?!" The abrasive tone in Jade's voice and the way she was staring at Avery, like a parent getting ready to take away every toy from a disobedient child, made Avery desperately wish she could lie to Jade. Unfortunately, she needed to tell Jade everything and that included Gumptin. So, Avery steadied herself for the admonishment she knew was about to come her way and answered Jade's question, "Yes." She said.

Jade grabbed hold of Avery by her shoulder and moved the two of them farther away from Gumptin, "How can you be so naive?" Jade hissed.

That struck a nerve in Avery. If she had been anything today, it wasn't naïve. It wasn't like she had decided to follow some little man down a rabbit hole because he offered her candy. She hadn't even agreed to go with Gumptin until he brought up the safety of her friends and family.

"Jade, I'm not a child." Avery said, defending herself, "I can make my own choices."

Jade shook her head in disbelief, "I can't leave you alone for a *second*." She told Avery, tightening the grip on her shoulder, "You just don't go around picking up circus freak strangers."

From behind her Avery heard Gumptin cough, "If you two are done with the domestics," he said, as Avery turned towards him, "it would be nice to get to the point of why we are here. We really do not have time for the two of you to stand around tongue-wagging."

Jade's eyes became dark daggers as she stared Gumptin down. Then, those daggers switched over to Avery.

"So, not only did you pick up a stranger," Jade told her, "but you picked up an ass."

Gumptin snorted in the background.

Avery backed away from Jade, freeing her shoulder, "Look," she said, "he's not technically a stranger...to me, or to you."

Jade gave Avery a 'what the hell are you talking about' look.

Just say it, Avery urged herself...just say it, "Alright, Jade," she began, "I'm about to lay some pretty heavy stuff on you, and I just need you to keep your mouth shut until I finish, alright?"

Jade looked like she was about to argue, so Avery made her eyes look as puppy dog as she could and added, "Please."

This maneuver had always worked with Jade in the past and Avery was more than sure it would work now. No matter how upset Jade got she couldn't argue with Avery's well practiced sensitive eyes.

Not looking too pleased about it, Jade took a deep breath in and nodded in agreement.

Now that she had as much cooperation as she was going to get from Jade, Avery decided to just start at the beginning, "Alright, like I said," Avery started, "this is Gumptin." Avery pointed behind her to where she knew Gumptin still stood, "I met him at the park by the school and he's...um," Avery began to falter. Suddenly the idea of just blurting out the truth didn't seem like such a good idea, but she was too into it now to stop, "well, he's, um...he's a gnome."

Even though Avery had told Jade to keep her mouth shut, the look Jade was directing towards Avery, like Avery had just told her she had ridden there on a unicorn, compelled Avery to ask, "So, what are you thinking right now?"

Jade stood silent for a moment just shaking her head, which wasn't like Jade, she usually had something to say about any and everything.

"Honestly, Avery," Jade said after a few seconds, "I don't even know what to say to that. I mean, obviously gnomes don't *exist*, but up until this minute I thought you knew that."

Avery rolled her eyes and thought that if Jade ended up calling her naïve again she was going to have to slap her, "I know they're not *suppose* to exist," she barked, getting agitated, "but, I mean, just look at him!"

Jade glanced over Avery's shoulder towards Gumptin, a deep scowl forming between her brows as she looked him up and down.

Gumptin stared unflinchingly back at Jade, giving her a small little wave.

Avery continued on, stopping Jade from further protesting the believability of Gumptin's existence, "Jade, you're gonna have to wrap your head around the whole magical creature thing, because that's just the start. He came from another world, which, I guess, as it turns out, happens to be our world as well. Well, one of our worlds." Avery felt herself getting off track and quickly tried to remedy that, "Anyway, he came from this other world to get us…you, me, Bunny, Sasha, and Skylar, and take us back. You see, apparently we were some hard core warriors and we were killed by this evil Emperor. Although, I don't actually know how hard core we were if we ended up dying, but, whatever," Avery shook her head, realizing she was straying from the point, "it doesn't matter, because this planet really needs us back to stop the guy that killed us."

From the start of Avery's explanation Jade hadn't moved a muscle. She just stood with her arms folded, keeping her mouth shut like she had agreed to, until now, "Did he drug you?" She asked seriously, "Because if he drugged you I'll kill him."

Avery's mouth opened, but she had no idea how to respond to Jade's question. So, instead, Gumptin spoke up.

"That was one of the most pathetic explanations of anything I have ever heard in my life, and I am over a thousand years old." He said.

"Hey," Jade shouted gruffly, arms still folded, "you don't get to speak until I find out exactly who you are."

Gumptin rubbed at his forehead with his little fingers, "This is why I wanted to avoid dealing with you until the last possible moment." He said more to himself than to Jade or Avery, "Fine," Gumptin sighed, "I am Gumptin, I am a gnome, and Wizard and I was your mentor back on Orcatia, the planet you were originally born on. You…are Jade Kai, a Protector with the ability to control the power of water and one of the most aggravating individuals I have ever known. You were killed on Orcatia by the Emperor, a powerful dark Warlock who controls an army of over twenty thousand vile creatures. You were sent to this planet to be re-born.

Your memories will not be returning to you, and, now you must come back with me to Orcatia to save the planet from certain destruction."

Avery was in awe. The only thing she couldn't figure out, is if it was because Gumptin had summed up in a few sentences what would have most likely taken herself an hour to explain, or because for the first time in Avery's life, she was witnessing Jade completely dumbstruck. Jade had no retort, no sarcastic comeback; she could only look at Gumptin like he had just appeared out of thin air.

"Well?" Avery asked, nudging Jade out of her trance.

At Avery's question Jade shook herself out of her mesmerized state and slapped her eyes back onto Avery.

"What do you want me to say?" Jade shrugged, "Obviously, I don't believe a word of it."

Avery didn't believe her, "Oh, come on," Avery urged, "you have to admit a lot of what Gumptin said somehow sounds familiar to you."

Jade scoffed.

"I saw your face when he said Protector." Avery continued, "When he said Orcatia. Those words mean something to you, even if you don't know what it is. The same thing happened to me."

Jade waved her hands in the air, as if she was trying to swat away everything Avery was saying to her, "That's enough, Avery...enough!" She shouted, "Even if some of the things he said sound vaguely familiar in a very tiny part of myself, that doesn't mean that I'm about to throw reality aside."

A small cloud of dust rose up as Avery stomped her foot into the ground. She grunted in frustration. It upset her that she was having to argue so hard to get Jade to come back with her when Avery was pretty certain she didn't even want to go back herself.

If telling Jade the cold hard facts weren't going to work, Avery decided to try a new tactic...pleading, "Look, I know how insane I sound. Believe me, I know. When I first met Gumptin and he tried to explain everything to me that he just told you, I wanted to call the crazy police and have him locked up, but instead I went with him." Jade opened her mouth to say something, but Avery held up her hand and stopped her, "I went with him and saw that everything he said was the truth." Avery decided to leave out the part about how she had really only gone with Gumptin because he said the people she cared about could be in danger if she didn't go. Avery felt that might not go over too well with Jade right now,

"Jade you know me." Avery continued, "You know me better than anyone else in the whole wide world." Avery saw Jade's face soften, her disapproving scowl disappearing, "I would never lie to you. As crazy as it sounds, I'm telling you that Gumptin's telling the truth. Please, Jade, please just come with us, so we can prove it to you."

Jade raised her hand to her face and began slowly massaging the brow between her eyes with her middle finger. She always did this when she was struggling with a decision. This gave Avery hope, because if Jade was struggling to decide, then she wasn't completely shutting out the idea of going with them.

Unfortunately, all of Avery's hopes were dashed with Jade's next sentence.

"Avery," She said, face softening even more as she looked Avery in the eyes, "you know I trust you. I'd trust you with my life, but this is just too unbelievable."

Avery could practically feel her whole body deflate.

"There's just no way I'm going anywhere with that creepy psycho," Jade nodded towards Gumptin, "and, you know what, neither are you."

Jade grabbed hold of Avery's wrist, hard and pulled her towards the trailer. Avery tried to pull her wrist free, but Jade, whose lean muscles had always made her strong, had a vice-like grip on her.

"You're going inside this trailer," Jade told Avery, once they had reached the trailer door, "and you're staying there till I get rid of this guy."

Being man-handled by Jade was the final straw for Avery. She had gone through enough today already, but she absolutely refused to be thrown into a trailer by her best friend. Avery did the only thing she could think of. She grabbed Jade's thumb and wrenched it back as far as it could go.

"Owwww!" Jade hollered in pain, releasing Avery's wrist.

Avery took a few steps back from Jade, so that she wouldn't be able to grab hold of her again.

Shaking her head, Avery felt crazy for thinking that Jade was going to believe her. After all, it had taken Gumptin actually bringing Avery to a whole other planet, through a magical gateway, to make her believe. That was when Avery decided the only way to get Jade to believe was for her to see it with her own two eyes, just like Avery had.

After all of Jade's protests, Avery knew of only one way to get Jade to come back with her and Gumptin, and she knew Jade would agree to come, even if every fiber of her being was screaming at her not to go.

Avery thought back to all the times Jade had refused to let her walk home by herself. She thought back to Alex Marquez and his poor beaten-up nose. She remembered, how for Christmas, Jade had given her a Swiss Army knife and portable pepper spray.

She thought back to all of these things, and then told Jade, "Fine, you don't have to believe us. You can stay here, but I'm going back with Gumptin...alone."

Avery turned around and started walking towards her car where Gumptin was still standing. She began counting down in her head, "...5, 4, 3, 2..."

"Wait!" Jade called from behind Avery, right on cue.

Avery stopped in her tracks and tried to stifle the huge smile that was forming across her face as she turned around to face Jade.

"You know I think this is certifiable," Jade said, walking up to Avery, "and I'm gonna have to beat some serious sense into you later, but there's no way in hell I'm letting you drive off alone with him." Jade motioned towards Gumptin with disgust.

Gumptin, who had moved into the passenger seat and was now sitting, shouted from the car, "Jade Kai, shut your mouth and get in this car." He lifted his little head out the passenger seat window, "We all know you are going to end up coming with us, anyway. So stop wasting our time!"

Before Jade could shout something back at him, Avery slapped her on the back, "All good then, let's get going."

Avery slipped into the driver's seat and waited for the other two to get situated.

Jade opened the passenger door, reached in, and grabbed hold of Gumptin by one of his oversized sleeves, yanking him out of the car.

"You're in the back Gump." Jade told Gumptin, pulling the passenger side seat forward and motioning for him to get in.

"The name is Gumptin!" He barked, tugging his sleeve free from Jade's fist.

Gumptin straightened his tunic out, all the while glowering at Jade. He turned his nose up at her, signifying his disapproval.

"You," he sniffed, "have not changed one bit."

Jade shrugged and shoved him into the car, "I'm taking that as a huge compliment." She told him, a sly smile playing at her lips.

Gumptin positioned himself in the back seat behind Avery, as far away from Jade as he could get, "Trust me," he grumbled, "that was anything but a compliment."

Once Jade sat down and slammed the door shut, Avery started the car. She thanked her lucky stars that they were finally on their way. The frustration of trying to convince Jade to believe her, mixed with having to listen to Gumptin and Jade bicker like two old ladies had taken a toll on her already frazzled nerves.

Avery gripped the steering wheel tight as she turned back out onto the highway, grateful that both Jade and Gumptin seemed content to keep their mouths shut.

"And I shall tell you another thing, young lady," Gumptin said from behind Avery, "once we get back to Orcatia, you shall see that that repellent mouth of yours will not do you an ounce of good."

Avery felt her eye begin to twitch as Jade shouted back, "Stow it, short stack!"

In her rearview mirror, Avery saw Gumptin open his mouth to say something back to Jade.

"That's enough!" Avery yelled, before Gumptin got the chance to continue the argument, "I don't want to hear another word out of either of you until we reach the park!"

"He started it!" Jade exclaimed at the exact same moment Gumptin hollered, "She started it!"

"Not another word!" Avery shouted, taking her right hand off of the steering wheel and pointing her finger at both of them.

Both Gumptin and Jade stared out of their respective windows, looking at the landscape fly by, seeming, for the moment, to take Avery's scolding to heart.

Avery clicked on the radio and turned it to a classic rock station that she knew Jade would like. Knowing that the steady guitar riffs pounding out of the car's speakers would calm Jade's inner beast.

Avery hazarded to look into her rearview mirror again and saw Gumptin staring at the radio like it was an attacking beast that needed to be shot. Anticipating that Gumptin might have something to say against the rock that was vibrating throughout the car, Avery turned up the radio to drown out any protests he might have.

Three long rock songs later, Avery was pulling up to the curb of the park. Jade had her eyes closed and was silently air-guitaring along to Jimi Hendrix's 'Purple Haze', when Avery shut off the car.

Broken out of her musical trance, Jade slinked out of the car and glanced around the empty park.

"Yeah," she said to Gumptin, as he tumbled out from the back seat, "it looks like something really supernatural happened here."

Completely ignoring Jade, Gumptin made his way over to the two Beech trees bookshleving the gateway.

"Well, we're here," Jade told Avery as she walked up to stand next to her on the sidewalk, "now what?"

Avery nodded towards Gumptin, "Now, we follow him."

Jade rolled her eyes and followed Avery over to where Gumptin was standing between the large trees. They stopped behind Gumptin and waited as he glanced around the park to make sure they couldn't be seen. Avery heard Jade sighing next to her and couldn't help but suspect that Gumptin was taking an especially long time in order just to annoy Jade.

Finally, after what Avery was sure was more than enough time to visually canvas the entire park, Gumptin cleared his throat and spoke the words, "Ora Gateway."

It happened just as Avery had remembered it the first time, the air between the trees beginning to swirl and come alive, whirling into a liquid that became the circular pool which was the gateway.

From next to her, Avery could feel Jade stiffen. When she turned her head to look at Jade, Avery saw that she was shaking her head slightly, her jaw clenched tight, and a look of complete shock in her eyes.

Jade began slowly backing away from the spinning gateway. "Are you alright?" Avery asked.

She could see in Jade's eyes that the truth was slamming down on her. The truth that everything Avery had told her had been true. Avery could also see Jade's mind struggling to accept what she was now seeing as the truth.

Jade shook her head in response to Avery's question. She stumbled backwards over her own feet. Avery made a move to catch her, but Jade held up her hand, righting herself before she landed on the ground and letting Avery know she needed a second to herself.

On wobbly legs, Jade staggered over to a wooden picnic bench sheltered next to the trunk of another shady Beech tree, about a hundred feet away from the gateway. Once there, she plopped herself down on the bench and placed her forehead in her hands.

Avery stood back, watching Jade for a few minutes, letting her absorb everything. Then, she walked over and joined Jade at the picnic table, taking a seat across from her. Jade looked up, made eye contact with Avery, and then placed her head back into her hands again. Avery just sat across from her, silent. She was more than content to give Jade as much time as she needed, especially considering she knew exactly what Jade was feeling, how confused she was, how scared, and intrigued, and probably just a little bit nauseous.

After a minute, Jade ran her fingers through her long black hair, and said to Avery, "I know what I saw. I just don't know exactly what it was that I saw."

Without nerves or emotion to distract her into rambling again, Avery calmly told Jade everything. She started with Gumptin surprising her by jumping out from behind a tree after school let out. She described seeing the Ora Gateway for the first time and how her reaction wasn't much different than Jade's, except she tried to run away. Avery told Jade the reason she had decided to follow Gumptin into the Gateway, how he had explained the possible dangerous repercussions of her deciding not to. She told her about Orcatia and their village and how weird it was to have everyone know her when she hadn't known anyone. She explained to Jade everything Gumptin had told her about the Emperor and dying and being reborn on Earth into the past, about being a

Protector and all the powers and responsibilities that went along with it.

To Avery's surprise and relief, Jade listened without any interruptions, something that was rare for her. In fact, even her facial expression had been pretty stone faced, just one small smile when Avery had explained their fighting abilities and powers, and a slight crease in her brow when Avery had talked about them dying.

"So," Avery asked when she had finished explaining everything, "what are you thinking?"

Jade opened her mouth to speak, but then closed it again when nothing came out.

After a moment, she shook her head, "There's so many different thoughts going through my head right now, I wouldn't even know how to begin to explain any of them."

Avery nodded her head in understanding, not wanting to push Jade.

"How did we die?" Jade asked Avery, the confusion in her eyes disappearing for the moment as she focused intently on her question.

"I told you," Avery answered, "Gumptin said that evil douche Emperor killed us."

This answer hadn't satisfied Jade, "But how did he kill us?"

"What do you mean?" Avery asked, confused by where Jade was taking this conversation.

"I mean," Jade said, firmly gripping the table in front of her, "we're supposed to be these five super horse-power fighting machines, right? So, how did he manage to kill all five of us at once? These are things we need to know, to avoid it happening again in the future."

Avery gave Jade a blank stare. She hadn't even thought about that till Jade brought it up, "I don't know. I don't think Gumptin knows."

Jade scrunched up her face in a particularly disgusted look, "You didn't ask?"

Avery blinked, she knew Jade was going to make a thing out of this, but she didn't know how to avoid it, "No." She answered

Jade laughed exasperatedly, "You see, that's just another reason why you don't run off to strange places without me...not ever."

Before Jade had the chance to mention the words innocent or naive, Avery spoke up, and loudly, "Look, a magical gnome had just put a bender on my whole reality! I was in more of an absorb than question mode, alright?!"

Jade couldn't stop herself from laughing at Avery's frustration. She knew Avery hated it when she got over protective, but she couldn't help it. Ever since they were kids, she just felt it was her role to protect Avery, and as Avery was the person she cared about most in the world, sometimes she took her job a little too seriously.

"Alright," Jade said, still trying to suppress her laughter, "I'm sorry. I'll just ask Gumptin later."

The mood had lightened, and Avery was thankful for this. What she had to say to Jade next, she knew Jade wasn't going to like, but she wouldn't be a true friend if she didn't say it to her.

"Listen," she told Jade, "I know that Gumptin said we had to return to Orcatia, but if you really don't want to, if this is just too much for you, I want you to know that you don't have to come with us. I'll talk to Gumptin. I won't be mad or upset if you decide to stay."

Jade leaned forward and smacked Avery hard on the side of the head.

"Ow!" Avery shouted, rubbing her stinging head.

"Don't be such an asswipe, Avery." Jade said, standing up. "Of course, I'm coming with you. I'm coming for the same reason I came to this stupid park in the first place."

Avery stood up, still across from Jade, "I'm just saying that if you did decide to stay in Redemption I wouldn't be mad at you."

A flicker of hurt crossed over Jade's eyes, "Don't you want me to come?"

Avery had to back pedal, for as tough as Jade was, when it came to certain things she was as soft as a cotton ball, and one of those things was definitely Avery.

"Of course I want you to come with me! I can't even imagine us being apart." Avery told Jade, placing her hand over her heart,

"I just don't want you to do something you feel forced into doing, and I definitely don't want you to get hurt."

The pain was gone from Jade's eyes and a small smile tugged at the side of her lips, "Avery, I live in a trailer park with parents who I barely see. I spend more time at your house than I do my own. I'm flunking out of school, and the whole town thinks I'm either gonna die or kill someone by the time I'm eighteen…maybe both. It's not like I have a lot to stay for."

Avery laughed, it was sad, but everything Jade had said was unfortunately true.

Jade walked over to Avery and took her hand into her own, squeezing it slightly, "You're my family. You and me, that's what I've got in this whole world. If you're going through that gateway, then I'm going with you."

Avery squeezed Jade's hand back, a silent thank you for confirming to her just why Jade was her best friend.

"Then, let's get going before Gumptin throws us both into the gateway with his bare hands." Avery laughed, pulling Jade by her hand towards Gumptin.

Jade groaned and allowed herself to be pulled, "Ugh, for one beautiful moment I forgot about him."

Avery smiled, wondering how any could possibly forget about a supposedly non-existent magical being.

By the time they had finished talking and had made their way back to Gumptin the gateway had once again closed. So, Gumptin said the words once more and opened the watery gateway in front of them.

"That is just trippy." Jade said.

"Alright, in you girls go before I grow roots and end up being trapped on this planet." Gumptin told the girls as he pushed them towards the gate.

"Wait a second," Jade interrupted, slapping Gumptin's hand away from her, "you're not going in first?"

Gumptin shook his head, "No, I am going to stay here until I see you go through the Ora Gateway with my own two eyes."

Jade nodded, pursing her lips, "Just can't get enough of my ass, huh."

For the first time since Avery had met Gumptin, he looked genuinely shocked.

"Sorry, Gump," Jade continued, "I know its awe inspiring, but you're far too old, too non-human, and definitely too irritating for me."

"Insufferable." Gumptin mumbled and ushered them forward, although this time he made sure not to put his hands on Jade at all, especially anywhere near her backside.

Just before Avery was about to jump into the gateway she turned around and faced Jade, standing just inches from her.

"You know, you were wrong." She told Jade.

Jade gave Avery a quizzical look.

"I'm not the only thing you have in Redemption." Avery said, "You've also got your bike."

A huge smile formed on Jade's face, "That's true, I do have my baby."

Avery nodded in agreement, "Of course, it sucks," she said, "'cause you know you can't bring her with you to Orcatia."

As Avery leapt into the gateway she heard Jade shout from behind her, "Son of a bitch!"

Chapter 5

Avery landed hard on Orcatia once again. She staggered forward and would have been able to remain on her feet if it weren't for a pesky tree root sticking up out of the earth. As her foot hit the root she knew she was headed straight for the ground. At least she had time to prepare her body this time, placing her hands out in front of her.

Once she was on the ground, Avery rolled over and sprang up quickly, making sure she was out of the way when Jade came pummeling through.

Jade came flying out of the gateway even faster and harder than Avery had. She landed face first on the ground without even a chance to stumble around and try to get her footing.

"Son...of...a...bitch!" Jade shouted, lifting herself up on her arms.

Avery thought it appropriate that Jade's last words on Earth would also be her first words on Orcatia, however inappropriate those words might be.

Before Jade had the chance to fully lift herself up onto her hands and knees, Gumptin came crashing out of the gateway, landing directly on Jade.

"Get the hell off of me!" Jade yelled at Gumptin.

In an effort to prevent Jade from physically picking Gumptin up and tossing him off of her, Avery ran over and helped Gumptin roll off of Jade. Once Avery had managed to help Gumptin stand up, Jade was on her feet in one cat-like move. For a moment, Avery thought Jade may try and smack Gumptin, but instead she just brushed the dirt off of her black tank and jeans, grumbling to herself as she did so.

"Thank you, Jade," Gumptin said as he took off down the overgrown path which led to the main road, "that was a much softer landing than I had been expecting. I suppose you are good for something after all."

This time Jade did make a leap for Gumptin, but Avery grabbed on to Jade's shoulder tightly, holding her back.

"Just let it go." Avery told her, "You obviously made it sixteen years on this planet without killing him, so just do me a favor and try to get through today."

Jade very reluctantly agreed, and they followed Gumptin out on to the main road.

Once they reached the road, Avery noticed a dozen or so fresh horse shoe impressions in the mud that hadn't been there before they had left.

"Hey, Gumptin, look." Avery said, pointing out the impressions in the road.

"Yes," said Gumptin, barely taking any notice of it, "by the types of shoe imprints and number of horses, those were left by members of the King's army, nothing to worry about."

The fact that there was a King didn't surprise Avery in the slightest. From everything she had heard and seen of Orcatia, it was exactly the type of place to have some sort of royalty ruling.

Gumptin continued, "We tried to keep word of your deaths a secret, but with the Emperor and his followers boasting about the death of the Protectors all over Orcatia, whispers began forming everywhere. When King Draven heard the news, he sent some of his men to watch over the village in case the Emperor decided to attack. After a few days the soldiers left, but they return once a day to make sure everything is alright. Now that you are back, there will be no need for the King's men to check on the village anymore."

The name Draven sounded familiar to Avery, but just like with everything else, she had no idea why.

"Wait a second," Jade spoke up after listening to everything Gumptin had to say, "we don't follow this King do we?"

Avery knew exactly why Jade had asked. Jade had never been one for following orders, either from parents, teachers, police, especially not from Gumptin, and Avery knew not from any King either. Avery wondered how she had ever been able to get Jade to do anything she had ordered her to do when she was leader, or even how she'd get Jade to follow her this time around.

"Havyn technically falls into the Nightfell Kingdom," Gumptin explained, "which belongs to King Draven, but the Protectors are a law unto themselves. Every King in every province recognizes your authority." He caught himself, then said,

"Although, not all of them agree with it. You will most likely have issues with a few of them in the future…if you live long enough."

Avery giggled, "That's not a problem for Jade. She's use to people in charge having issues with her."

Jade reached over and smacked Avery across the arm which only made Avery giggle harder.

"What's King Draven like?" Avery asked through her giggling.

"He is a good king." Gumptin answered.

Avery waited for him to elaborate, but that was all he offered her, "Well, have we ever met him?" Avery questioned, not content to let the subject drop yet.

"No, you have never met." Gumptin's short answers were beginning to get on Avery's nerves. It was the first time since she had met him that she actually wanted him to talk more.

Avery persisted, "Don't you think it's weird that the Protectors have never met the King of the kingdom that they live in?"

"Yes." Was all Gumptin said.

Avery grunted in frustration and looked over at Jade who just shrugged her shoulders as if to say, "Don't look at me to try and deal with him."

They were content to walk the rest of the way to the village in silence. Avery let her mind wander, mainly to King Draven and why Gumptin was being so tight-lipped about him. She wanted to push Gumptin further on the issue, but knew if she did he would only clam up again. Plus, she didn't know enough about Gumptin to know if he was even hiding anything important or just being evasive for annoyance sake. Instead of dwelling on it any further, Avery looked down at her muddied and scuffed burgundy Doc Martens and wished she had chosen to wear her cheap no name sneakers that morning instead.

The familiar sounds of the bustling village, distant voices, the whinny of horses, a hammer banging against something metal, took Avery's mind off of her messed up shoes and on to the fact that they had almost reached Havyn.

They passed the entrance sign that Avery had tripped over her first time entering the village and walked out into the main center of Havyn.

Just as before, the villagers came rushing up to them in packs, stopping what they were in the middle of doing and exiting out of their houses to come and see Gumptin and the next Protector he had brought back to Orcatia.

As a large number of villagers began to approach Avery glanced over at Jade. She wondered how Jade was going to react to them, knowing full well Jade barely tolerated people, especially not strangers, and definitely not strangers who were all crowding around to see and talk to her.

"Well I'll be damned," a burly villager wearing a dirt stained smock and carrying a rake, spoke to Jade, "if it isn't Jade Kai come back to haunt us." He smiled broadly and clamped Jade on the shoulder.

Jade grimaced, but made no move to shove the villager away from her.

A pudgy older woman, with a thick mop of gray hair piled atop her head, wearing a pink and white striped dress with a red apron, and smelling sweetly of cinnamon and flour, pushed her way to the front of the crowd and laid a giant bear hug on Jade. Jade's eyes got as wide as a startled horse's.

"Oh, come here, you little rascal." The woman said, still holding on to Jade tightly. Avery recognized her as the woman who had come running out of Bott's Apothecary & Sweets.

Jade didn't hug the woman back, but again she didn't make an attempt to get away from her either. Avery smiled to herself as she realized Jade was trying to be polite. This was a rarity for Jade, so it showed Avery just how much Jade was willing to do to follow Avery with the whole Protector thing.

"Didn't they feed you on Earth?" The woman said, releasing Jade and running her hands over Jade's shoulders and arms, pinching at her flesh, "Why, you're nothing more than a splinter."

That was it for Jade; the small amount of tolerance she was attempting to display had begun to fade. She stepped away from the woman and out of the reach of her flesh pinching fingers.

"I eat just fine, thanks." Jade told the woman, smiling tightly and trying not to make her voice sound too clipped.

Avery was perfectly happy standing back and watching Jade's uncomfortable interaction with the villagers when a familiar face in the crowd caught her eye. It was the boy who had hugged her when she had first came back. The very first person she had seen on this planet. Avery motioned for him to make his way up to them. She was grateful for the familiar face even if she didn't know anything about him. Something about his laid-back countenance and gentle smile made Avery feel at ease around him.

The boy smiled and made his way up to stand off to the side of Gumptin. Avery noticed it was the furthest spot he could stand away from Jade without looking too obvious that he was trying to avoid her.

"Jade," Avery said, getting Jade's attention away from the other villagers, which Avery could tell by Jade's look she was grateful for, "I want you to meet…" Avery stopped as she realized she had no idea what the boy's name was.

"The name's Pip." The boy told Avery, seeing her confusion, "I work over at the stables with Thomas, my boss. I've been taking care of village's, including the Protectors, horses for over half my life." He smiled brightly while speaking of the last part and Avery could see the pride behind his eyes.

"Hey." Jade said, sticking out her hand for Pip to shake it.

Instead of taking Jade's hand, Pip shook his head and laughed, "Never thought I'd see the day when ya'd offer to shake my hand. Truth is you ain't too fond of me, never have been." Pip laughed harder at Jade's disconcerted face, "In fact, last time I ever saw ya, ya threw a stable brush at my head for putting your saddle back on the wrong rack."

Jade shrugged one of her slender shoulders and threw Pip a baiting smile, "Sounds like a perfectly reasonable thing for me to do. Get it right from here on out and I won't throw things at you."

Pip laughed even harder, "Good to see your attitude wasn't lost along with your memory." He reached out and took Jade's hand, which was now resting on her hip, "Good to have ya back."

"Hmmm," Jade said, leaning in to whisper in Avery's ear, "I can see why I wasn't too fond of him before."

After shaking Jade's hand he placed his hand on Avery's shoulder and gave it a light squeeze, "If ya need anythin' I'll be over in the stables." As he took off, he turned back around and shouted, "I'll see ya later, Avery!"

It startled Avery to hear Pip say her name with such familiarity. Part of her wished she could remember Pip, Gumptin, the sweet smelling lady who liked to hug Jade, and all the other villagers, but another big part of her didn't want the memories, knowing that on top of everything else they might just cause her to curl up in a little ball and refuse to move.

Jade grabbed Avery by the shoulder, shaking her out of her deep thoughts. She turned Avery towards her and gave her the, 'Get me the hell out of here' look.

Avery decided that before Jade got past just conveying meaningful looks to her and went straight to yelling at people; she would take Jade someplace private away from swarming villagers.

Avery told the villagers she was taking Jade away to get some air and then took her over to the two small wooden benches on the outskirts of the village where Gumptin had attacked her with the knife. When they reached the benches Avery took a seat, taking in the quiet of the forest behind her, happy to be away from their overzealous greeters. Jade paced back and forth in front of Avery, refusing to sit down.

"So, how you doing?" Avery asked, already knowing the answer.

Jade stopped pacing and sat down next to Avery, "Well, everyone seems to know me and that's weird. Plus, there was way too much hugging and touching for my liking, but," she took a deep breath in, "at least it's not a trailer park."

Avery nodded, thinking back on all her horrible memories of Rebel Moon Trailer Park.

"So," Jade said, looking around the village, "which one of these freaky tree-house things are mine."

"Ummmm…" Again Avery had no clue.

Even when she had first seen the giant trees with their windows and doors, the idea that she had actually lived in one of them had completely escaped her. Before Avery had a chance to let down Jade again with her lack of knowledge involving their life on Orcatia, Gumptin came up and interrupted them.

"You two done holding hands, yet?" He asked them brusquely, "We have got to go back and get the others."

"This should be fun." Jade scoffed, standing up, "They're not gonna believe this in a hundred years. Especially Sasha, that girl's more stubborn than I am, and that's saying something."

Avery thought about it for a second, "You know," she said, "I think we should try a different tactic than I did with you. I say we just get them to the park somehow, we'll lie to them, and then once they're there, we'll show them Gumptin and the Ora Gateway." Avery could foresee hours of mindless explaining if they talked to each girl individually, "Then, even if they try to argue we'll have Gumptin there to point out the gateway and explain the truth."

Jade nodded her head in agreement to the plan, "Plus, that way, if they try to make a run for it, we can just push them through the gateway."

"Brilliant!" Avery beamed, wondering if they'd actually have to pull off that last part of the plan.

The landing back on Earth wasn't any smoother than the landing on Orcatia had been. The only difference was this time Jade made sure to pick herself up off of the ground fast enough to avoid Gumptin falling on top of her.

"So, where to first?" Jade asked, once they were all up and situated.

"Well," Avery said, hesitantly, "I was thinking we'd stop by your place first."

Jade looked at Avery suspiciously, "Why?" She asked.

"That way we can split up and get things done faster." Avery tried to sound convincing, but Jade wasn't having any of it.

"You just want to split up so you won't have to go get Sasha!" Jade accused Avery, nailing her motivations on the nose.

"No!" Avery shouted, trying to look offended and make her lie seem believable.

"Don't even try to play me; I know you too well." Jade told her, "Besides, you're the fearless leader, don't you think it should be your duty to retrieve your followers."

"Hey!" Avery huffed, annoyed that Jade was already bringing the leader detail into her arguments, "I'm not leader on Earth; I'm just Avery. Look, you know Sasha won't put up as big of argument with you. She's too scared you'll punch her! Plus, Bunny annoys you anyway. I'll go pick up Bunny and Skylar and you get Sasha." Avery knew she had Jade right where she wanted her at the mention on Bunny's name.

Jade sighed, "Ugh, that girl does get on my nerves for some reason."

"Also," Avery said in a sing-song voice, "you'll get to ride your big noisy bike around Sasha's snooty rich neighborhood."

"Dammit!" Jade yelled, genuinely upset that the idea of riding her bike for maybe one of the last times ever, mixed with pissing Sasha and her uppity neighbors off, made it impossible for her to say no.

Avery smiled and turned to walk towards her parked car, but stopped abruptly when she realized Gumptin was following her.

"Where do you think you're going?" She asked him, placing her hands on her hips in an authoritative stance.

"With you, of course." he responded, looking at her like this was well known information.

Avery laughed mockingly, "Oh, no, you're not, not this time. You saw how well that worked with Jade. No, this time you're going to wait right here until we get back."

"Wha…what am I suppose to do while you are gone?" He stuttered, acting very put-out.

Avery shrugged, "Why don't you hide behind a tree…you're good at that."

Avery could hear Gumptin quietly fuming to himself from behind a large tree as she and Jade got into her car.

After Avery dropped Jade off at her trailer, she drove down the highway until she reached Main Street. Once there, she took a right and drove down the town's central fairway. She passed all the small shops, the bakery, the hardware store, the town's one doctor's office, and her mom's flower shop. Avery noticed that her mom's car wasn't parked out front, which was unusual for the time of day, but she didn't have time to dwell on where her mother might be.

After driving a few more blocks, Main Street turned into a small suburb area. It was there that Avery made a left, passed five houses, and then stopped at 113 Tumbleweed Dr, also known as Bunny Claiborne's house.

Bunny's house was a red brick two-window building, with yellow shutters and door. It was smaller than most of the other houses on the block with only two bedrooms and one bath, but what it lacked in size it made up for in character. The entire front yard of the house was basically one giant garden. There were carrots, lettuce, tomatoes, and strawberries secluded in a soil bed on the right side of the front yard. Pruned citrus trees offered blankets of shade over the entire front yard. There was a cobblestone pathway leading from the street to the yellow front door, entirely lined with rose bushes of every color blooming big and bright. The left side of the yard held a small white bird bath in the shape of a crescent moon and was surrounded by a carpet of perennial flowers. Bunny had always had the most extraordinary green thumb. She tended to and kept every single plant alive year-round, no small feat in the blistering Arizona summers.

    It was only Bunny and her mother that lived in the house. Although, no one really knew Ms. Claiborne that well, not even Avery and she was over at Bunny's house all the time. Ms. Claiborne mainly stayed in her room when she wasn't working as a file clerk at the city courthouse. She hardly ever spoke, even at work. In fact, the most she usually said to Avery was, "What would you like for dinner?" or "See you later, dear." Admittedly, Bunny's mother was a bit of an enigma, but then again, so was Bunny.

    Avery got out of her car and walked up the cobblestone path to the front door, breathing in the scent of the flora as she did. She rang the doorbell, which chimed a whimsical little tune and stood there waiting. A little tabby, one of Bunny's many cats, purred and rubbed itself along Avery's legs, and Avery knelt down to stroke it. As she was petting the purring cat she heard the door open. When Avery looked up she saw Bunny's smiling face staring down at her.

    Bunny was tall and thin with straight chestnut brown hair that fell to her shoulders, which she always wore in a braid with shaggy bangs covering her wide forehead. She had sun-kissed skin, crystal blue eyes, and a bright easy smile that always made Avery happy just to see it. Bunny was all limbs, long legs and arms, but despite that she still managed to move with a slow grace. Avery assumed it was because of Bunny's artistic soul. Bunny loved anything to do with the arts; she drew, knitted, gardened, painted, and played the flute. She was the studious one of the group. The one the other girls came to when they either needed help studying, or more likely, their homework done for them.

Avery had always considered Bunny to be one of her closest friends, even before she knew about their shared destiny. It was during one of their group playgroups, when they were about five years old, and Avery had stolen Bunny's Rainbow Brite lunchbox, and Bunny had swiftly whacked Avery over the head with a plastic sandbox shovel, that a connection had been formed between them. From that day on they never went more than two or three days without seeing each other, even during the summer.

Avery thought of Bunny as a sweetheart, quieter and meeker than the rest of the girls; the one she needed to protect, but there was also a darker side to Bunny that not many people besides Avery got to see. For instance, once in junior high when Avery was walking with Bunny to her house after school, Alex Marquez had ridden up next to them on his bike and began poking fun at Bunny's new haircut. Bunny acted as if it didn't faze her, but after Alex had finished with his teasing and sped up to ride away, Bunny picked up a rock the size of a lemon and pitched it at the boy. It hit his wheel, denting it, and sending him flying over the top of his bicycle, splitting his head open on the cement, and requiring fifteen stitches to close him up. The whole thing had freaked Avery out, but Bunny didn't seem bothered in the slightest by it. To this very day it was a secret that Avery and Bunny shared. Everyone else, including Alex Marquez, just assumed he hadn't seen a large rock in the road, hit it, and flipped his bike.

"Avery," Bunny said, fixing her bright smile on Avery, "were we suppose to do something today?"

It wasn't at all unusual for Bunny to forget whether she did or didn't have plans. It was another characteristic that Avery attributed to her artistic soul, her flightiness.

"No." Avery answered her, standing up and shooing the small tabby cat into the house.

"Alright," Bunny said, not sounding the least bit fazed by Avery's answer, "do you want to come in?"

"No," Avery shook her head, "I really don't have time." Avery thought it was best to just tell Bunny outright what she wanted her to do. After all, she might get lucky and Bunny would say yes without any question. That way, she wouldn't have to muddle through some terrible lie that she was sure Bunny would see right through anyway, "Bunny, could you do me a favor and come with me somewhere?"

"Come with you where?" Bunny asked, curiosity spreading over her face.

So much for getting lucky. Avery still didn't want to take a lying approach, so she decided to beat around the bush, "There's something I want to show you in the park by the school, I just can't tell you what it is right now." Avery saw curiosity turn to suspicion in Bunny's eyes, so she quickly added, "It's a surprise!"

Bunny stared at Avery silently for a moment, and then she shrugged, "Whatever," she said, "it beats staying here."

Avery sighed, that was so much easier than it had been with Jade. Of course, Bunny still didn't know the real reason Avery was abducting her, but that was a technicality. Avery should have known that Bunny would be an easy sell. It was in her easygoing nature.

After Bunny had gotten her purse and locked up the house, Avery told her, "Oh, by the way, we have to stop and pick up Skylar."

Bunny shrugged again, "Whatever."

Avery only hoped that Skylar would be as easy as Bunny.

Skylar Bavol resided in one of only two apartment complexes in the entire town, Cowboy Palace Luxury Apartments, the nicer of the two. It only took them three minutes to reach their destination. When they got there, Avery parked the car under the pink plastic parking-lot awnings. Bunny opted to stay in the car and read.

As Avery swung open the white metal gate that led into the inner apartment complex, the smell of chlorine from the gated swimming pool smacked her right in the face. She walked over to the rusty green iron staircase and climbed it up to the second floor. Avery knocked on door number 12B and a moment later Skylar's mom answered.

Skylar's mother was a tall woman with shoulder length blond hair that stuck out in every which direction. Ms. Bavol made a living by reading people's palms, tea leaves, and tarot cards. In the sixth grade, she had read Avery's palm and predicted that she would be a strong leader for good one day. At the time, Avery had thought it had been a cool prediction, but knowing what she did now, she realized it had been less of a prediction than actual knowledge...sneaky woman. Most of the town thought Ms. Bavol a bit of a nutter, considering she went around town passing out chakra beads, hugging trees, and organizing solstice parties. Despite all this, Avery found her completely likeable. Granted, Avery thought she might have been certifiably crazy, but she was a genuinely good person with something nice to say about everyone, and Avery admired that, just so long as she stayed away from her palms.

"Avery, my dear girl," Ms. Bavol exclaimed, wrapping her wispy arms tightly around Avery, "I just knew you'd be here soon. You have seen your true path laid out beneath your feet and now you walk it. Destiny waits for no one."

Avery pulled back and stared up at Ms. Bavol. For a moment Avery thought she was just spouting out some of her new-age self help jive, but then Avery realized she was actually talking about being a Protector. She knew their parents had all their memories from living on Orcatia, but she wondered why Ms. Bavol would bring it up now.

"How did you know that I know?' Avery asked.

"Oh, silly little lark," Ms. Bavol said, bopping Avery on the nose with her finger, "the Ora Gateway has been used. Your parents and I, true Orcatians, felt it inside." She pounded her fist to her chest, "Like a string pulling us to home.

"Alright," Avery smiled politely, not really sure what Ms. Bavol was telling her and not really wanting to hear any more of it, "is Skylar here?"

Ms. Bavol swooshed her arms back and forth inside the door jam, imitating a breezy dance, "My daughter of the wind is partaking in her other calling at dance practice."

Avery scolded herself for not trying to reach Skylar at dance practice first. Skylar was at dance practice more often than she was at her own home; if Avery would have thought of that she could have avoided Ms. Bavol's awkward insights into her life.

Avery thanked Ms. Bavol and made her way back to her car. When she reached her car she found Bunny beginning to doze off in the passenger seat, her open book lying on her lap.

When Avery sat down she closed her car door hard enough to wake Bunny up.

"Where's Skylar?" Bunny asked, rubbing the fresh sleep out of her eyes.

"Where do you think?" Avery answered, starting the car.

"Her precious practice." Bunny mumbled, "Next time," she yawned, "don't wake me up unless you need me."

Avery pulled up in front of Saguaro Dance Hall, a large red brick building with two purple and green awnings over the arched entrance way and a bright pink neon sign flashing the studio's name. The building not only served as a dance studio for many of the girls, and two or three boys from the town, but it also served as a bingo hall every Thursday night, and a senior citizens line-dancing club every Friday.

Leaving Bunny in the car, Avery opened up the building's front doors and walked through the over-plush sitting area, filled with crimson colored cushioned chairs and couches, and deep purple wallpaper with tacky velvet paisley lining.

She walked into the main wood-floored dance hall, and the first thing Avery noticed was an image of herself on the mirror-lined wall opposite her.

"Oh, my, God!" Avery said aloud, momentarily forgetting everything except the image in front of her "I look vomit worthy!"

Her hair was completely untamed, even more so than usual, with auburn curls sticking out in every direction. To make matters even worse, as she turned her head a bit, she saw she had a small twig caught up in one of her misbehaving curls. Avery cursed everyone she had seen that day who had failed to mention the offending twig. Her jeans were covered in grass stains from falling out of the gateway onto the ground and her purple plaid shirt had a tear in the pocket revealing a peek at her pink bra underneath.

"Now I actually do look like I've come back from the dead." She said mournfully as she reached up and pulled the twig out of her hair.

Avery yelled at herself to try and snap out of it. She told herself there were more important things to do like find Skylar and save the Universe, that what she looked like didn't matter, but deep down she was contemplating whether or not she had time to go home and get changed. In mid-contemplation she spotted Skylar pirouetting across the long wooden dance floor.

Skylar was the most talented dancer in all of Redemption. In fact, some town members speculated in all of Arizona. She had been dancing since she was old enough to walk, and her one dream was to travel to New York after high school and pursue a career as a professional dancer. Everyone expected her to accomplish it; she was that good. Skylar had the skill, and she had the looks. She was beautiful, incredibly tall and slender, with long, wavy, electric blond hair and wide violet eyes highlighted by dark lashes.

Despite Skylar's angelic appearance and ballerina poise, she was definitely the wildest and craziest person Avery had ever known in her entire life. In the eighth grade, she had flashed a bus full of choir boys in town to give a Christmas performance at the local Catholic Church. At the end of semester dance her freshman year, Skylar had somehow managed to take three different boys as her dates, and even more amazing was the fact that she was able to keep it a secret from all three of them. That is, until the next Monday at school, when Bunny spread the truth all over campus, and the boys got suspended for trying to kill each other in the middle of the cafeteria.

One of the things that Avery loved about Skylar was that she brought out Avery's wild side. Whether it was ditching school to drive down to Phoenix and hit the dance clubs early, dying their hair the most ridiculous shade of pink or just skinny dipping in Sandy Gulch Creek, Skylar was always behind it.

Even Jade was a fan of Skylar's, although she always got anxious about Skylar and Avery spending time alone together. Especially, since two years ago Skylar had suggested horseback riding through Rattlesnake canyon and Avery's horse had spooked, tossed Avery, and broke her wrist. Jade had been furious, but Avery didn't mind and two weekends later she was back hanging out with Skylar, Dune Buggying through the desert.

"Skylar!" Avery shouted, wincing as her voice echoed throughout the dance hall.

Skylar stopped mid-pirouette and turned to face the disheveled looking Avery.

"Avery?" Skylar said, looking surprised at first, but then abruptly busting out into a roar of a laugh, "Why do you look like you just went through a garbage disposal?"

Avery reached up and tried to straighten out her hair, to no great success. Again, she had to tell herself to ignore Skylar's comment and ignore her appearance.

Skylar walked over to Avery, away from the rest of her dance class, "What's going on?" She asked.

"Hey, Sky," Avery said awkwardly, "I was wondering if you could come with me right now to the park by the school?"

Skylar squealed, startling Avery, "Are the Sunshine County Fire Fighters doing their work-out routines there again?" Skylar lightly jumped up and down in her excitement.

"Ummm…that would be a no." For a second Avery thought she should have said yes. In fact, she thought that might excite Skylar more than a gateway to another world, "Look, I promise that what I have to show you will be just as equally interesting."

"Alright," Skylar agreed, always up for a surprise and a good time, "just let me go grab my stuff."

Avery waited for Skylar in the parking lot. Once Skylar was changed and ready she met Avery out by her car. Avery suggested that Skylar just drive her own car and follow Avery out to the park. Avery was always in the mindset that the more people with their own transportation the better. So, Skylar piled herself and her stuff into her yellow Volkswagen Beetle and followed Avery to the park.

When they reached the park, Avery could see Jade's bike parked up alongside the curb; she pulled up behind it and Skylar behind her. She got out of the car and saw Jade leaning up against a tree, her hands stuffed into the pockets of her fitted leather jacket, and Sasha sitting on a picnic table nearby, chatting away into her phone.

"Was' up Kai!" Skylar shouted, walking up to Jade and giving her a side hug.

Jade smiled despite herself, the way she always did around Skylar, "Sky." She said and then nodded towards Bunny in a much less friendly manner, "Bunny."

Bunny nodded back along with a small hand wave.

"So, when's the big reveal?" Skylar asked, "What are we all doing here," she rubbed her hands together, "the anticipation is killing me?"

Avery looked around for Gumptin. She wondered if he was waiting for her to announce his presence. He had a large dose of arrogance to him, so that's what Avery assumed he was doing.

Before Avery did officially announce Gumptin's presence, she noticed that Sasha was still talking on her phone, "Hey, Sasha, could you get off the phone?"

Sasha either didn't hear her or completely ignored her, so Avery got right in front of Sasha's face, "Sasha," she said, hand gesturing for her to hang up the phone, "get off the phone."

Sasha held up her finger, giving Avery the 'one minute' sign. Before Avery had a chance to ask Sasha to hang up again, Jade came over, grabbed the phone away from Sasha, and shut it closed.

"Rude, Jade!" Sasha shouted, grabbing her phone back, "I'm only here because you threatened to mess up my face for tonight's party. I have a lot of stuff I still have to do before tonight!"

Well, Avery could think of no better time to let Gumptin handle things than right now.

"Girls!" Avery shouted loudly, getting everyone's attention, "Jade and I brought you here to meet somebody who's pretty much going to explain things to you that'll turn your world upside down." Avery looked to the tree she saw Gumptin sneak behind before they had left to get the others, "Gumptin, come on out!" Avery yelled loudly and waited for him to pop out from behind the tree, just like he had done to her, but after a few beats nothing had happened.

"Gumptin sounds like a fungus." Sasha told her sarcastically.

"If he's a guy, I hope he's hot!" Skylar gushed, taking a seat on the bench next to Sasha.

"Gumptin get out here now!" Avery continued to yell, but nothing happened. She looked to Jade and Jade rolled her eyes, letting Avery know she wasn't surprised by him not showing.

Avery walked over to the tree she had seen Gumptin scurry behind before she left, looked around it, and saw him curled in a small ball next to a large root, sleeping. She reached over and picked him up by the collar of his tunic, shaking him out of his sleep.

"How could you have fallen asleep?" Avery huffed, continuing to shake him, "You're making me look like an idiot, Get up!"

Gumptin smacked his lips together and rubbed his eyes, "I have not had a decent sleep since the five of you were killed. It is exhausting being your guardian."

Avery didn't want to hear it; she waved her hands in the air, "They're all over there waiting, go do to them what you did to me."

Gumptin straightened his wardrobe and ran his fingers through his beard, attempting to brush out all the dirt and debris he had collected while napping under the tree; it was only about half successful. As he walked off to go confront the girls, Avery stayed behind the tree, leaning her back and head against the strong wood. She took a deep breath and decided to stay where she was until after Gumptin had made his introductions, not wanting any more questions thrown her way.

Avery heard a collective gasp from the girls and a small squeal from Bunny, so she assumed they had now all seen Gumptin.

She heard Sasha screech, "Oh, my, God! What are you?" And she heard Skylar mumble, "Well, he's definitely not hot."

Gumptin was in the middle of listing off the girls names and how he knew them when Jade appeared in front of Avery's face, "Wanna take a walk?" She asked, and Avery agreed, grateful to take a breather away from all the craziness.

Jade and Avery walked over to the picnic bench they had sat on together after Jade had been shown the Ora Gateway. It was out of earshot of Gumptin and the girls, so they could just sit there in silence listening to the distant cars pass by, the birds in the trees calling out to each other, and neighborhood dogs barking. It was a peace they both appreciated, knowing that they wouldn't have too many peaceful moments in the near future.

Avery wasn't able to hear what Gumptin and the girls were saying, but she could still see them. She saw emotional Bunny with her hands over her eyes just rocking back and forth. True to fashion, Sasha was up in Gumptin's face arguing, and Skylar just sat on the bench smiling, not giving any emotion away by just looking at her. The conversation only continued for a little bit longer before Gumptin motioned for them to follow him.

"Ooh," Avery said excitedly, "he's taking them over to the gateway!"

Jade, who had been leaning back looking at the sky, turned herself around, "Well, this I've got to see."

They watched as Gumptin said the words, and then watched each of the girls' reaction as the Ora Gateway appeared before them. Bunny began to get teary eyed, which Avery could have predicted. Sasha shut up for the first time since Gumptin had emerged in front of her, and Skylar began laughing so hard that she doubled herself over.

Jade turned back around to face Avery, "For the first time since I've met Gumptin, I actually feel sorry for the little jerk." Then, she laid her head in her folded arms to rest her eyes.

Gumptin continued talking to the girls for another twenty minutes before leaving them by the gateway and walking over to Avery and Jade.

"I am taking them back to Orcatia now." He told them when he reached them, "You two best go back to your houses, gather your things, and get your family."

The thought of dealing with her family made Avery queasy. She still wasn't sure if she was mad at them or not for keeping everything a secret from her. Plus, involving her family made everything completely real, there was no turning back after that.

"You don't want us to come with you guys?" Avery asked, hoping to stall for a little more time before she had to face her family.

"No," Gumptin told her, dashing her hopes, "when the girls return and are ready to leave they will contact you on your voice communicators." Avery figured Gumptin was talking about a phone, but she knew it pointless to tell him what they were really called since he'd most likely just forget it anyway, "Also," Gumptin said, turning away to leave, "you are human, so the fewer times you travel through the gateway the better…what, with breaking down of your molecules and everything."

Avery and Jade exchanged looks of horror. Avery instinctively hugged herself, willing her molecules to stay in place, "Thanks for telling me after my fourth trip, you evil gnome!"

After watching each of the girls go through the gateway, some more reluctantly than others, Avery and Jade walked over to their vehicles. Avery felt lucky that she had asked Skylar to take her own car, that way she didn't have to worry about how the other girls were going to get home when they got back to Earth.

    Avery got in her car and pulled away from the curb. She turned her car back out onto Main Street and drove home the same way she had every single school day for the past year. She continued driving left on Main Street until it was no longer called Main Street anymore, just a small pot-hole filled two lane road called Roadrunner Boulevard. Avery traveled slowly down the Boulevard, making sure the old broken road was delicate on her tires. After traveling a mile down the Boulevard, passing subdivisions of houses built in the seventies, a public swimming pool, and a strip mall filled with a sizeable and flamboyant pink and orange building whose purple neon sign flashed "Coyote Dave's Bowling Alley, Roller Rink, and Diner! Open till the rooster crows!!" Avery reached the turn she wanted. She turned right on Dust Devil Avenue and her stomach clenched, it would only be a few more minutes before she reached her home. She stared out her window at the open desert and mountains stretching in front of her and tried to clear her mind. To the left of Avery was a large park with basketball courts and a large baseball field where the little league teams played. It had a picnic area where every spring multiple families would have barbeques, and a small playground with a rickety swing-set and plastic green slide.

    Across from the park, on the right side of the road, was the neighborhood that Avery lived in. Tall Jacaranda trees and brown lampposts lined the sidewalks. Avery turned her car in to the third street down and stopped in front of the first house on the left, 5821 West Sunset Drive, Avery's house.

    She got out of the car and began to walk up to her house, but stopped shortly afterwards. Instead, she leaned against one of the tall jacarandas planted in her own front yard and just stared at her house for a little while. It was just a little after four and the sun was beginning its slow descent in the sky, throwing its bright rays on to her peach adobe house, making it almost look like it was glowing. She looked over the three large oval windows with the brown shingles and stopped at the third window, knowing her bedroom lay just behind the glass. Avery got choked up as she took in the entire front exterior of her house, the green front yard with multi-colored flowers scattered throughout, the different shrubs, the pecan tree, and the dark green vines with heart shaped leaves covering most of the adobe on her house. Just looking at her house she thought of how comfortable and safe it made her feel, and now those things weren't hers to keep anymore.

Knowing she couldn't stand out there wallowing all day, especially with the sun beginning to set, she made her way up the yard, under the vined archway and up to the light blue front door. Instinctively, Avery turned the doorknob, not really expecting it to be unlocked, but to her surprise the door swung wide open.

Avery's two giant German Shepherd's Justice and King bounded up to her, knocking her back against the entry wall and showering her face with slobbery kisses. Bailey, the family's old Great Dane waited patiently behind the two younger dogs for his chance to give his master some love.

"I missed you guys, too." Avery laughed as she pushed them off of her and scratched all their heads lovingly.

Avery walked past her three dogs, out of the walkway, and turned the corner into her living room. She stopped dead in her tracks when she saw her parents sitting on opposite sides of their over-stuffed floral couch, and her sister Cinder sitting in between them. They were all just staring at Avery, as if they were expecting her.

Immediately, Avery's eyes went to her younger sister, Cinder. Cinder was only seven years old with blond curls that fell to her shoulders, big baby blue eyes, and peachy tan skin. Cinder was the little golden child with a lovely exterior, infectious laugh to go along with her dimpled smile, and a sweetly independent spirit. Avery's parents spoiled Cinder, showering her with attention and praise, buying her cute outfits and stuffed animals to go with her baby doll looks. Still, Avery couldn't resent Cinder the attention or the gifts, for she absolutely adored her sister. Cinder was always the one cheering Avery up at home when she felt depressed or stressed. Cinder would come into her room and show Avery the new tap dance she learned that day or tell Avery a story about how a kid at her school was so dumb he had to wear a helmet just so his brains wouldn't leak out of his ears. All of her life Avery had looked out for Cinder, making sure she was never picked on and that she always had her homework done, so that she never fell behind in class. Cinder gave Avery two very important things in life, joy and responsibility. If Avery could have, she would have told her parents to give Cinder all the attention.

Of course, thinking about it now, Avery realized they might have given Cinder so much consideration because they knew one day they would have to take her to a world that wasn't her own and away from everything she knew. Because, even though both Cinder and Avery had no prior knowledge of Orcatia, Avery figured at least her parents knew that, at one time, Avery had had a life on Orcatia, even if she couldn't remember it, whereas poor Cinder only ever had this life on Earth. Plus, Avery figured the whole being a Protector thing probably caused her parents to worry about her more in some way, like dying, and less in other ways, like how it might emotionally scar her to leave the place she thought of as home.

Whatever, Avery thought; she didn't have time to worry about herself. Now, like her parents obviously were, she was worried about Cinder.

Avery walked up to her little sister and knelt down in front of her. She saw that Cinder's eyes were slightly red from crying.

"Are you alright?" Avery asked her sister gently.

Cinder nodded, sticking her lower lip out in a slight pout, "Mommy and Daddy said we have to leave and I'm not gonna see my friends anymore."

Avery sat up a little and gave her sister a hug, "Well," Avery told her, "I'll be there and we're not just sisters, but we're friends too, right?"

Cinder smiled and wiped at her already dried tears, "Yeah, plus we get to bring Bailey, Justice, and King, and they're my *best* friends!"

Avery nodded in agreement, somehow alright with being placed fourth behind three dogs.

"And," Cinder continued, excitement in her voice, "Mommy says that there are a lot more animals where we're going, and really big trees, and waterfalls, and magical stuff, and a lot more kids for me to play with!"

Cinder's trademark dimples appeared, as the more she talked, the more and more excited she got.

"Sweetheart," Avery's Mom stopped Cinder before she could go on with the hundred other things she was looking forward to, "I already packed your clothes. So, why don't you go get your pink duffle bag, go to your room, and fill it with the things you want to take with you."

"Alright!" Cinder said joyously, bounding up from the couch and away from Avery.

"Remember," Avery's mom shouted after her youngest daughter, "just the items that you really want!"

Avery could already foresee Cinder crying her eyes out an hour from now when she'd want to take more than her parents would allow. Avery bemused at how quickly a child's emotions could change and wished she could be able to express her feeling with as much abandon as Cinder did.

Once Cinder was gone and out of earshot, Avery stood up and faced her parents. Jaw clenched and arms folded, she stared them down. Avery knew why they had kept everything a secret, she could even understand it, but that still didn't stop her from being angry with them about it. She had given her parents that hard, I'm pissed face enough times for them to know exactly what Avery was thinking. Instead of trying to defend themselves or explain they both stood up from the couch and walked over and hugged their daughter. The daughter they had traveled to another planet for, just to bring her back to life.

It didn't take Avery long to cave and hug them back, "You could have said something." Avery said, her face buried in her mother's shoulder.

"I'm sorry, baby," Her mother told her, stroking Avery's long auburn hair, "but we just couldn't risk it."

Avery pulled away and looked up at her mother; a pretty middle-aged woman with short dark brown hair and gray eyes, "Mom," Avery said loudly, "my whole world just got turned upside down in one single day!"

"We were strictly told not to tell you anything, Avery," Her father, a tall, sturdy man with sandy brown hair and a beard, said to her, "and we weren't going to go against anything the Elementals told us to do."

Avery shook her head and turned away, biting her lip to keep from crying. With everything that had happened she hadn't cried once today and she planned on keeping it that way.

"Honestly, Avery," Her mother told her, coming up and placing her arm around her, "it was sort of a relief for us to have you grow up as just a normal girl. We didn't have to worry about you the way we did on Orcatia and *you* didn't have to worry about things like you did on Orcatia."

Avery wished her mother would stop talking. It was bad enough that she couldn't be angry with her parents like she wanted to, but she didn't want to have to be grateful at this very moment, as well.

"I know you can't remember anything, sweetheart, but if you could I know you'd be happy you had this time on Earth to just be a girl." Her mother said.

Avery pulled away from her mother; she didn't want to hear anymore, "Why do you think I'm upset?" She told her parents, "I'm upset because I love my life! I really love everything about it! It's not about me not being ready for it to change; it's about me not knowing if I want it to change!" Saying it out loud almost forced the tears out of Avery's eyes.

Avery's mom looked like she was about to cry herself.

"Believe us, Avery," Her dad said, "if it was our choice, we'd stay in Redemption."

Avery wondered if that was really true. Gumptin had made it sound like her parents had given up a full and whole life to come to Earth, which made Avery wonder about what her life was like back in Havyn. Whatever it was like, she wasn't going to imagine it now. Right now, she wanted to distract herself.

"I'm gonna go to my room and pack my stuff." She told her parents, and when she saw their still upset faces, she added, "I'm really alright. I just needed to vent a little, but the more time I have to let it sink in the more fine I am with it." She lied.

The walk down the hallway seemed excruciating long to Avery. She passed Cinder's room and looked in and saw her little sister scrambling to fit every stuffed toy she owned into her child's sized pink duffel bag.

Avery reached the door with a poster of the Orion Nebula taped onto it and opened the door to her room. The smell of the vanilla candles she burned every night hit her nostrils, and Avery walked into the room she had thought of as her sanctuary. Its violet walls, wallpapered with posters of her favorite bands, far off galaxies, a ridiculously large horse calendar, and multiple clippings of actors and actresses taken from magazines.

It felt good to Avery to be able to heave the backpack she had been lugging around with her all day onto her bed, which was covered with a dark purple bedspread and far too many sparkly pillows. She dumped her school books out on the bed and began filling the backpack back up with her most desired possessions. First, went in her poetry books, Avery figured a little Edgar Allen Poe after a hard day of fighting couldn't hurt. Next, went in her photo album and all the photo's she had in frames around her room. Then, her journal, her favorite nail polish, a few pieces of jewelry, a stuffed coyote she had since she was six, and a few other necessities. Avery looked longingly over at her shelf of trophies, some for the Chess Club, a few for the Astronomy Club, some for Junior Rodeo, and one very proud looking National Watermelon Seed Spitting Championship trophy. She wanted to grab them all and take them with her, but knew that trying to travel with them would be ridiculous.

After she was done packing her backpack, Avery joyfully took off her disheveled clothes and threw them in the hamper of dirty clothes that would never be washed. She threw on a pair of black skinny jeans, lacing her boots up over her jeans, and a black plaid flannel shirt. Avery reached into her closet and pulled out her black duffel bag and began filling it with jean, shirts, undergarments, socks, and jackets. She figured she probably had clothes back on Orcatia, but if her style had been anything like what she saw the other villagers wearing, she was definitely bringing her own Earth clothes with her.

Before Avery tried to pack everything she owned into her bags she decided it was time to leave. She threw her backpack on, grabbed her duffel and hurried out of her room. Avery was out the door with the lights turned off in a matter of seconds, making sure she didn't turn around and take a final look. She wasn't sure she would be able to leave it if she did. Luckily, her phone going off in her right back pocket gave her a reason not to think about it.

"Hello?" Avery answered her phone.

"Hey, it's Skylar." The voice on the other end said.

"You're back!" Avery said excitedly, curious as to how Skylar and the others had taken the trip to Orcatia, "How are you? How did everything go?"

Skylar took a long sigh, "Well, when you told us you had a surprise for us, you really weren't kidding."

Avery couldn't think of anything to say to that, so when she didn't, Skylar continued, "Basically, Sasha argued and bitched until Gumptin told her if she didn't come back and help he'd have the Elementals undo the whole life spell on her."

Avery wasn't really sure if Gumptin would or even could do that, but she thought it a brilliant strategy for handling Sasha.

"Of course," Skylar said, "Sasha started to feel a little bit better about the whole thing when I told her she'd definitely be the hottest chick on Orcatia…total lie by the way. Plus," a lightness entered Skylar's voice, "being a Protector is kind of like winning a huge popularity contest. Bunny was basically quiet the whole time. You know her, introverted."

Listening to Skylar, Avery thanked her lucky stars that she didn't have to be there to deal with all of that.

"Skylar," Avery said, "you're awesome."

Skylar laughed, "I know, but you're not so bad yourself. Anyway, I just called to tell you we're all back and should, I repeat *should*, be ready to leave in an hour. Gumptin told us to go on through and he'll be waiting for us on the other side."

That surprised Avery, "Wow, he's actually throwing a little trust our way."

Skylar grunted, "I think it more had to do with him being sick of dealing with Sasha than actually trusting us."

That caused Avery to laugh, thinking it was most likely true, "I'll see you in an hour." Avery told Skylar.

"I'll be ready for one wild ride." Skylar said, "See ya then."

Avery hung up and pocketed her phone, knowing that she wouldn't be able to use it where she was going, but wanting to keep it anyway as a sort of security blanket.

When Avery walked outside she saw that her parents had already loaded up most of their stuff into the family's red van. Just as Avery had suspected, Cinder was going on about how it was impossible for her to be expected to load her life's collectibles into one small bag.

Walking to the back of the van to pack her luggage, Avery saw Justice, King, and Bailey already loaded into the back seat next to Cinder's crated white Persian cat Romeo. Avery loaded her bags around the menagerie of pets and hoped that nothing would get crushed or destroyed by furry butts and paws.

The drive to the park was a silent one, with each member of the Kimball family lost in their own thoughts. All except for dogs and cat whose barks, whines, and meows provided Avery with a much wanted distraction.

As Avery's dad parked their van up against the curb at the park, Avery saw that Jade and her family had already arrived. They were standing in silence over by the Ora Gateway. It wasn't uncommon for the Kai's to not talk to each other. Their trailer had seen a lot of silent nights. Of course, there were just as many nights yelling at each other. The fact was that Jade's parents just didn't know how to deal with their daughter's wild ways. Now that the truth was known about who they really were, Avery figured Jade's parents probably saw their daughter heading down the same dangerous and reckless path that led to her death, even if she was on a different planet.

Avery unpacked her stuff and walked over to Jade. She nodded to Jade's parents who nodded politely back. Avery had always felt a slight resentment coming from Jade's parents. She thought it had been because they resented Jade spending so much time with Avery and her family when she barely saw them. Now, however, Avery thought it might have something to do with her leading their daughter down that path to death on Orcatia. Maybe it was a combination of the two. Either way, Avery just smiled politely and then pulled their daughter away so that they could talk out of earshot.

"So, how'd it go?" Avery asked Jade.

Jade shrugged, seeming agitated, "When I got home they had already packed my stuff."

Avery shook her head; she couldn't see what the big deal was.

Jade continued, exasperated that she had to explain it any further, "Avery, my mother and I barely exchange glances, let alone a fashion sense. I had to unpack everything, re-pack, and all the while listen to my parents go on about how I better be more careful this time because their hearts couldn't take losing their only daughter again."

Avery let Jade act like it had irritated her, but she knew that deep down Jade had really been touched by her parents concern. Jade may act like she didn't care, but Avery had been on to her act since they were five. Secretly, all Jade wanted was acceptance and love, and she desperately craved it from her parents. Avery suspected that was why Jade always acted out so much.

A car door slammed catching Avery's attention and signifying Skylar's arrival. Skylar, Skylar's mother, and their small black Cocker Spaniel, Shalom, all piled out of Skylar's tiny Beetle.

Next, Sasha and her parents arrived, along with Sasha's younger brother Shawn. Shawn was only ten years old and in the same position as Cinder. He had never had a life on Orcatia and was now being forced to go there, and as far as Avery could see he didn't look happy about that fact at all. Oh, well, Avery had her own sister to worry about; she would let Sasha and her parents deal with Shawn.

Twenty minutes had passed since Sasha and her family had arrived, and there was still no sign of Bunny and her mom.

The girls and their families had all piled around the gateway, some sitting, some standing. Avery sat on the ground with Jade and Skylar, listening silently to their parents talking a few feet away. They talked mainly of superficial things, what kind of food they had missed living on Earth, and what kind of foods they were going to miss now that they were going back, how they would assimilate back into their old jobs, about certain villagers they were looking forward to seeing again, Avery recognized the name Mrs. Bott and Thomas, but that was it. Every now and then the parents would quiet their voices to barely a whisper and Avery would have to strain to hear them. She missed most of it, but she picked up the word Emperor and Elementals, and she was pretty certain she heard Sasha's mother say something about praying things go differently this time.

"Do you think she skipped town?" Jade asked Avery, pulling her away from eavesdropping any further.

Avery knew Jade was talking about Bunny, she just didn't know if Jade was joking or being serious.

"She'll be here." Avery told Jade. Jade's opinion of Bunny wasn't always the best and Avery didn't want to say or do anything to stoke that fire.

Bunny's mother's blue four door sedan rounded the curve of the park and Avery breathed a sigh of relief. For a moment she had wondered if Bunny really had become overwhelmed and decided to runaway.

A few of the parents walked over to help them with their baggage. Avery noticed that although Ms. Claiborne didn't seem particularly overjoyed, there was a certain excited glow in her eyes, which for her, was more emotion than Avery had ever remembered seeing.

Ms. Claiborne volunteered Avery and Jade to assist in carrying Bunny's large flower printed suitcases over to the gateway, leaving Bunny lagging behind them having to carry only her small purse. By the time they had lugged the heavy suitcases the few hundred feet over to the gateway, Avery was sure Jade was going to use one of the flowered bags to beat Bunny and her mother to death with, but she behaved herself as well as she could, instead throwing their luggage hard onto the ground. Avery could tell she was disappointed when it didn't burst open scattering Bunny's possessions all over the dirt.

"Well, now that we're all here," Jade said, throwing a sideways glance towards Bunny, "maybe we should get this parade started."

They all agreed, although reluctantly. It seemed as if no one was especially ecstatic about going back. The Protectors were enlisting into a life of duty they had no memory of, and their parents were going back to a planet where their children risked their lives every single day. Still, they all knew it had to be done.

Avery nervously stepped up to the gateway. She had only ever seen Gumptin open the gateway before and had never actually tried it herself. Avery had to admit, she was excited. It wasn't every day a person got to open up an intergalactic gateway.

"Ora Gateway!" Avery shouted louder than she probably needed to, just to be sure. It earned her a snigger from Sasha that she quickly ignored.

Just as it had for Gumptin, the Ora Gateway swirled and opened for Avery. Avery knew it wouldn't have mattered who said it, but she felt a great sense of accomplishment, none the less.

Family by family, they took their turns going through the gateway. The animals posed a small problem, but after some coaxing and a lot of pushing the dogs went through. Cinder insisted jumping in carrying her crated cat Romeo, and Avery just hoped the gateway was smart enough to make sure her sister landed on Orcatia intact, without any new cat parts.

Finally, it was just Avery, her father, and Jade left standing on Earth. Jade had stayed back when her parents went through, wanting to wait for Avery.

"You go ahead dad. We'll be right behind you." Avery told her father, knowing he had intended to be the last person through, just to make sure everyone went in safely, but Avery wanted a moment alone to say goodbye to Redemption, "It'll be fine."

"Alright, but you two hurry up." He told Avery and Jade before jumping into the gateway himself.

Avery grabbed a hold of Jade's hand and smiled up at her. She was so glad it was the two of them standing alone together on Earth for the last time, in Avery had no idea how long. There were so many things she wanted to say to Jade. She wanted to thank her for always being there for her and looking out for her. She wanted to tell her that knowing Jade was going to Orcatia with her made everything less painful, but all she could manage to say, was, "You go on now, too. I'll be right behind you."

"Fine," Jade sighed, sensing Avery wanted to be alone before she hopped in, "but don't bum around, because I'm not going to wait for you."

Avery laughed at the ridiculousness of Jade saying something like that to her, "Yes, you will." She said.

Jade sighed harder, "You're right, so don't dawdle. You know how much I hate waiting."

Just before Jade stepped her foot into the liquid, she stopped and turned around, "Avery," she said, becoming serious all of a sudden, "for what it's worth…this world was only ever temporary. Maybe if you think of it like that, it won't hurt so much."

Avery pursed her lips and looked away, again fighting back the tears that had been so dangerously close to escaping. She put on her best fake smile and motioned for Jade to hurry up and get going. Avery watched Jade go into the watery gateway. She knew she couldn't take too long, everyone was waiting for her back on Orcatia.

To the west the sun was setting, causing the sky to dance in flames of oranges and cool purples, casting a husky glow on everything around her. Avery tried to take a mental picture of the place she considered home. She gazed across the park to Main Street, to the subdivision of houses beyond that, and then to her beloved desert which seemed to stretch out forever beyond the borders of the town. Her eyes took in everything, the fiery sky, the vast mountains, and the lush park. Avery shut her eyes and reveled in the fact that she could still see the images burned inside her mind.

As Avery said her silent goodbye's to Earth, all the emotions that had been racing around inside of her throughout the day, everything that she had kept pushing down, and the feelings she had pushed away, came rushing to the surface. For the first time that day, after everything she had been through, she began to cry. Avery wiped at the salty tears streaming down her cheeks; she would be damned if she landed on Orcatia with a blotchy face and bloodshot eyes and everyone staring at her. Once she was sure her face was sufficiently dry and semi blotch free, Avery turned to step into the gateway.

When she approached closer to the gateway, Avery saw something that seemed to be floating inside the liquid, but she couldn't quite make out what it was. All she could see was a small red glow. Avery moved closer to the gateway until her nose was almost touching the swirling substance. She stared intently as the red glow started to take shape, becoming clearer and darker, until the red had turned into an almost black color. Finally, she saw what it was, clear and unmistakable, two black snake-like eyes looking directly at her.

Avery gasped and leapt backwards as the two penetrating eyes glared at her from inside the gateway. Avery stood rigid, breathing heavily, staring back at those eyes that held her. They were the coldest eyes Avery had ever seen, reptilian with no emotion or humanity to be found inside of them, completely black except for a small sliver of red running down the center. Avery wanted to look away, but she couldn't; she was paralyzed with horror, and her whole body went cold.

"Aghhh!" Avery cried in pain and fell to the ground clutching her chest.

A searing pain like nothing she had ever experienced before raged inside her chest. Avery tore her gaze away from those horrid eyes, and within seconds the pain began to alleviate. She calmed her breathing down and wiped at the sweat that had begun to form on her brow. After a moment, she risked glancing back up at the gateway, but the eyes were gone. Avery stood up shakily, still holding her hand to her chest, she began to massage it slowly, the memory of the pain still fresh in her mind and her nerves.

Chapter 6

"I'm going back." Jade told the others, getting ready to jump back into the gateway and journey back to Earth.

"Would you stop acting like her mother!" Sasha snapped at Jade, "She'll get here when she gets here. Cut the cord already!"

Jade put her hands in her pockets to stop herself from smacking Sasha, "You know, Sasha, that mouth of yours…" Jade was stopped from finishing her threat as Avery came tumbling out of the gateway.

Her encounter with the eyes back on Earth had made Avery shaky. Her legs were virtually useless when she landed on the ground, but instead of wobbly stumbling forward flat on her face Jade was able to catch her under her arms in time and keep her upright.

"What the hell took you so long?" Jade asked at the same time Avery heard her mother ask, "Are you alright?"

Avery had no intention of telling anyone what had happened to her back on Earth, no matter how much it had shaken her. She knew they would only worry and fuss over her and that Jade would go on about it for weeks wanting to know every little detail. Avery decided to mention it to Gumptin sometime later, but for right now, she was keeping her mouth shut.

"I'm gone for like three minutes and you guys freak out." Avery said, trying to add a hint of levity to her voice, "Geez, I'm not a baby, you know. I'm fine."

Jade looked Avery over suspiciously, but allowed her to pull away and didn't ask any more questions about it.

With everyone lugging their bags and possessions with them, the walk back to Havyn took a lot longer than it had the first two times Avery had come back. This wasn't good for Avery, considering she spent the whole walk back thinking about the eyes she had seen in the gateway. They had been so menacing and terrible, but they looked at her as if they knew her. Avery wondered whose eyes they were and why she even saw them in the first place. Not to mention, what that pain she had felt in her chest was. It had hurt so badly that she thought her heart had exploded.

Eventually, they all reached the village and Avery gratefully was able to switch her focus over to the village and villagers.

Their parents, who actually remembered everyone, heartily hugged their friends they hadn't seen in sixteen years. They shared smiles and short stories on how Earth had treated them and what they had been doing all this time. The Protectors patiently let their parents reunite. They could see how much their parents had missed everyone and how happy they were to return to the place they considered home. Avery and the rest of the Protectors hung-back.

While letting their parents catch up, they glanced around Havyn, their new home. They wondered which enormous tree house were theirs, or if they lived in one of the smaller normal houses farther in the background. Avery didn't care where she ended up living; she just wanted a bed and a bath before she lay right down on the ground in front of everyone and fell asleep.

Just as she was contemplating physically pulling her parents away, her father said, "Let's go, Avery, time to be getting on home."

"About time." Avery mumbled, shifting her heavy duffel bag farther up her shoulder. She said goodbye to the girls and followed her parents to her unknown house.

While the Protectors were still in earshot, Gumptin shouted to them, "I shall see the five of you tomorrow at dawn to start your training. We will meet by the well in the center of the village. Do not be late!"

He then turned around and walked into the lush forest before any on them had a chance to protest, which was a wise thing for him to do since Avery was getting ready to pitch a fit. Avery looked mournfully over at Jade who looked angrily back at Avery. The last thing they had been planning for tomorrow was to be up before dawn. Avery shook her head and continued to follow her parents. She would worry about it tomorrow. Right now, all she wanted was sleep.

Her parents walked diagonally across the center of the village towards the enormous tree at the furthest left side of the semi-circle of tree houses. The sun had almost completely set, so Avery had to get pretty close to the tree she was about to consider home to make out the details of it. The tree itself was a dark deep mahogany color, with leafy heart shaped vines and rich green moss crawling all over it. Avery could see four large circular windows on the front of the tree, all with wooden flower beds underneath them filled with petite yellow flowers. There were two balconies protruding from the tree's trunk, one on the right side and one on the left. Both balconies had dark wooden railings surrounded in purple flower-covered vines. There were different sized pipes sticking out of the tree in various areas. Avery assumed these were for stoves and ventilation. Two round stone steps led up to the blue circular front door. On either side of the front door was a small wooden bench. There were dozens of pots and beds filled with Sunflowers, Carnations, Lilac, and Roses. Avery could see that her mother's love for flowers came about long before she left to Earth.

To the left of the Kimball's home were the stables. The long building was built right on the very edge of the forest and formed an almost barrier between the side of the forest and the village. There were a row of hitching posts on the outside of the stable and a wide door-less entryway which led into the interior where the horses were kept. The outside of the building was a red stained wood. There were four small square windows on each side of the entryway. Avery craned her neck a little to see if she could see any of the horses that were whinnying and snorting on the inside, but all she could see was a back wall filled with hanging tack and a warm orange flame from the lights. Avery sniffed the air slightly to see if living next to a stable would prove unpleasant for her nostrils. Luckily, as she took in a deep breath of the air around her, all she could smell was a slight musky scent of hay and leather, and a delicate saccharine perfume from a patch of delicate blue flowers growing wildly around the circumference of their giant tree house.

Avery's father turned the oversized brass doorknob on their blue front door and opened up the house. Avery stepped over the threshold onto a crocheted welcome mat. The dogs had been let off their leashes and were now bounding around the dark house with eyes able to see in the darkness what humans could not. As the dogs ran around their new surroundings, Avery and the rest of her family waited on the welcome mat for her father to turn on the lights. Eventually, one light went on, and then another, and another, until the whole house was bathed in warm glow.

Cinder threw her pink duffel bag down on the floor, let Romeo out of his cat cage, and began to run and romp around the house with the three dogs. Avery took things more slowly. She walked farther into the living room, letting her eyes absorb everything there was to see. The walls were painted a dusty rose and lined with multiple paintings of flowers, landscapes, castles, and people who Avery didn't recognize. The wooden floors were covered with dozens of plush rugs, everyone a different color. There were so many that Avery could barely see the actual wood floor beneath them. A huge overstuffed blue velvet couch sat in the middle of the room, with two comfy looking blue velvet chairs to match on either side of it. A heavy dark oak coffee table lay in front of the couch, covered with books and a glass chess set. There was a large stone fireplace on the far right side of the room with a good sized mantle hanging over it. Above the mantle was a sizeable painting that immediately caught Avery's eye. She walked up to the fireplace and gazed up at the painting. It was a portrait of Avery and her family. Avery knew the painting couldn't have been done too long ago since, in it, she looked relatively the same age as she did now. In the painting Avery was wearing a white empire waist dress with her hair pulled back. She couldn't stop staring at the picture of herself. Appearance wise everything about herself and the girl in the painting were identical, but there was something behind those green eyes that seemed foreign to Avery. There seemed to be a sadness inside of them and a stoniness Avery didn't recognize. They were eyes Avery had never remembered seeing looking back at her in the mirror every day for the past sixteen years of her life.

Avery forced herself to stop analyzing herself. There was a door off to the right of the fireplace, so she opened it and looked inside. It was a study with dark green walls and leather furniture. Avery knew it had to be her dad's and that there was nothing in there that would interest her, so she shut the door.

Avery could see her mother walking around the kitchen with its red brick stove through a doorway behind the living room.

There was a small hallway off to the right of the kitchen, with a wooden staircase leading up to a second floor at the beginning of it. Avery secured her bags on her back, grabbed hold of the banister, and made her way up the stairs. The stairs led up to a second floor landing which entered into a narrow dimly lit hallway. The walls were wallpapered with a dark green floral pattern and covered with small circular paintings of different farm animals, a rooster perched atop a fence, a horse standing in a field, cows grazing on yellow grass. To Avery's left, at the end of the hallway, was an extremely slim stairway leading up to a third floor. There were three doors down the cozy hallway. One was located at the very end of the hallway to the right, facing outwards. For some reason Avery couldn't quite explain, she knew that was her room. She walked towards the round door and turned the tarnished sliver doorknob.

    The room would have been completely dark if it weren't for the two arched glass doors, leading out to a small balcony, letting the moon glow flood into the room. The bright glow allowed Avery to see the lamps attached to the bedroom walls. The orange hues replaced the cool blue ones as she turned on the lamps and looked about her new bedroom, which was, in actuality, her old one.

    The floors were covered with thick shaggy rugs in shades of deep blue and purple. They looked soft and Avery couldn't wait to take her shoes off and run her bare feet over them. The walls were painted a periwinkle blue and completely bare, except for about a dozen maps nailed up around the room. Avery walked up to one of the maps and glanced over it. It was a map of Havyn and the surrounding forests and villages. There was writing scribbled all over parts of it, and as Avery took a closer look she recognized the writing as her own. She had drawn an arrow pointing towards a dense looking spot in the woods with the words, 'Demon attack – February 11th – Bacci Demon – defeated with right sword strike to head' written above it. Another arrow pointed at a spot on a small road, which diverged off of the main road, with 'Ambush site – twice in one month – 4 trolls' written next to it. There was one scribbling that pointed towards a village named Fallin, located about ten miles away from Havyn and half its size, that said, 'Battle – January 3rd – Emperor's army – 50+ strong – Sasha (broken arm) – Jade (2 broken ribs) – Myself (stabbed through left shoulder)'.

    Avery pulled her shirt down and looked at her shoulder. There was nothing there except smooth pale skin, no mark at all.

Whatever her body had been through on Orcatia, she had been spared the physical ramifications of it after being reborn on Earth. In fact, the only scar Avery had on her entire body was a small crescent shaped one under her right top rib, where she had tripped over her dog while playing chase with her sister and fallen onto her opened dresser drawer. Looking at the map with all its markings about battles, ambushes, dangers, and scrimmages, Avery realized her one small little scar would probably soon have company. Avery decided to stop looking at the maps for now, so as not to have nightmares of terrible beasts, and broken bones, and stab wounds.

There was a large king sized bed in the middle of the room, covered with a heavy dark purple bedspread and multiple fluffy dark purple pillows. There were two blue end tables on both sides of the bed. One had nothing on it and the other had a lamp and book. Avery picked up the book and read the title, 'Demon Species of the Western Wintara Mountain Range'. Riveting, Avery thought sarcastically, tossing the book back down on the table.

Avery walked over to the large silver painted wood wardrobe against the far wall. She swung open its two light weight doors to reveal the clothes inside. Tunics, bodices, vests, and tight shirts with lace up closures hung from the wooden hangers next to multiple pairs of pants. Avery touched the pants; they were mostly leather and other tough materials. Avery couldn't help but be disappointed in her previous taste. There wasn't one stitch of color to be seen, everything was either brown, black, or white. Wide belts hung from hooks on the inside of the door, and on the inside of the other door hung a full-length mirror. Avery didn't much see the point of that, considering with so little variety of outfits she probably looked the same every day. At the very end of the wardrobe were two long dresses, one in light blue and another in burgundy. Avery moved them to the middle, so she'd at least have a little color to look at. The bottom of the wardrobe was lined with a variety of boots, all different lengths. Scanning over the inside of the wardrobe, Avery was sure she hadn't brought enough of her clothes from Earth. Disheartingly, she shut the doors.

There was a massive chest of drawers against the wall opposite her bed. It was painted the same silver color as the wardrobe, and there was a ridiculously large silver framed mirror resting on it. Even though the chest of drawers took up most of the wall space, there was hardly anything on it. There was a thick bristled hairbrush, two glistening sliver daggers with gold hilts, that looked like they had more been haphazardly discarded than strategically placed, and a small silver jewelry box with an etching of a horse on the top of it. Avery opened the jewelry box and a sad haunting tune filled her room. There was nothing much in the jewelry box, itself, except a silver bracelet and a few strips of ribbon. Avery left the box open so that the melody could continue to play.

As Avery stared down at the sparse items on the dresser top, she couldn't help but think back to her dresser on Earth. It had been so covered with jewelry, and books, makeup, pictures, stationary, and a dozen other knick-knacks that she had never ever really been able to see the actual top of the dresser. If the top of her dresser on Earth had been bad, her actual drawers had been atrocious. This made Avery curious, so one by one she opened up the drawers of the silver dresser.

The first drawer she opened contained rolls of white bandages, a pair of scissors, different sizes of needles, thread, and a small sharp looking knife. Avery cringed and shut the drawer quickly. She didn't even want to think about how many times she had to use the contents of that drawer. The next drawer clanked and tinged as she opened it. She looked inside and saw over a dozen glass vials filled with different colored liquids. Avery picked up a thin-necked glass vial with a round bottom and a pink liquid sloshing around inside. For a brief moment she thought it might have been perfume, but as she pulled the cork out of the top of it, a distinct medicinal scent hit her nose. The second vial she took out was squat and round with a lid that screwed on. Inside it was a green hued gel. Avery unscrewed the lid and again a medicinal menthol scent was released. Avery tried two more glass bottles, but both contained medicative liquids.

So far, Avery was not liking what she was seeing, bandages, healing tonics, needles, boring monochromatic clothes, and maps that read like a horror novel. Avery wondered what kind of person she had been to think these things normal.

Avery turned around in a circle, taking in her whole room. There was nothing personalized anywhere, no pictures, stuffed animals, books that didn't have to do with killing monsters, no diary...nothing. It was as if she had had no personality at all, and that definitely wasn't Avery. She decided to try one more drawer before she wrote herself off as having had been the most boring person in the world. The drawer was filled with undergarments, all neatly folded in rows and all white. That was it, she was thoroughly depressed by the person she use to be. Avery reached in and scooped up all the perfectly white undergarments into her arms. She disposed of them in a corner of her room. Avery unzipped one of her small carry bags that contained all of her undergarments from Earth. She dumped the contents of the bag into the drawer without bothering to fold anything. Avery smiled at the purple boy shorts covered in tiny pink skulls wishing her a happy Monday.

"That's much more like it." She told herself aloud, feeling a sense of relief in making the room slightly more to her taste.

Avery spent the rest of the evening unpacking her bags and attempting to turn her room into something she could be proud to call her own. She placed a few photos of her family and friends that she had brought with her on her nightstands and nailed a few to her wall. She had wanted to take down the maps, but decided against it, knowing they contained valuable information, horrific, but valuable. Avery made quick work of covering the dresser with items, jewelry, makeup, and books. She then made room in the wardrobe for all of her clothes and shoes.

If Avery had been exhausted before she started unpacking and redecorating, afterwards she was about ready to collapse. Before she let herself lay down on the inviting bed Avery walked over to the two glass doors that led out to the balcony. She opened the doors up and a cool breeze rushed into the room, blowing back Avery's long hair form her face. Avery stepped out onto her small wooden balcony. The railing was covered in leafy vines with purple flowers that extended onto the floor of the balcony, up the tree, and surrounded the glass doorway. Avery let the cool air and the sweet scent of the flowers wash over her. She looked up at the sky and saw the moon. It looked almost exactly like Earth's moon, except much closer, like a wolf's moon. The moon was surrounded in a blanket of a thousand stars, and Avery felt comforted that at least the night sky remained the same to her eyes. Before she turned to go inside, Avery leaned over the balcony rail and gazed across at the rest of the village. There weren't many villagers left in the center of town, only a few holding brief conversations in passing on their way home. It was strange for Avery to see the lights of the tree houses shining through the trees. It looked almost as if the inside of the trees were on fire. She could see images of people walking around inside the houses and could even make out a figure or two standing out on their balconies. Avery wondered if any of those people might have been Jade, or any of the other girls, for that matter.

Avery slammed down on her bed without even bothering to undress. She turned over on her side and groaned as she stared out her balcony doors. She had turned the lights off, but hadn't bothered to close the curtains, and now she imagined how the soothing moon shine flooding into her room would eventually turn into harsh sun rays. Avery contemplated getting up and pulling the thick purple velvet curtains closed, but when she couldn't will her body to move, decided it really didn't matter that much. The last thing Avery remembered seeing before drifting off to sleep was a small firefly buzzing around busily on her balcony.

Chapter 7

"Avery! Avery, it's time to get up!" Avery's father's voice drifted into her subconscious. It sounded like a hundred drums being pounded on inside her head.

"Avery!" The voice called again, "You're supposed to meet Gumptin and the others in five minutes, get up!"

Avery grunted and turned over in her bed to look out the balcony doors. She pulled the covers down over her head and saw that it was still dark outside.

"Guess I really didn't have to worry about those curtains after all." Avery spoke into her pillow and snuggled back under the cover.

"Avery!" The voice shouted.

"I know!" Avery shouted back, "I'm up!" Avery groaned grumpily as she realized she was going to have to actually get up.

She slowly sat up in bed and glanced around the room with puffy eyes. She thought, disgustedly, how unnatural it was to get up before the sun had even begun to rise. Avery's movements were slow and laborious as she got out of bed and changed her clothes. She decided to go with a pair of jeans and long sleeve thermal shirt she brought from Earth.

Avery was still groggy as she descended the stairs, and she found herself exceedingly grateful for the handrail, as she almost tripped a few times.

When she did finally manage to make it down the stairs without tripping and breaking her neck, she saw her father sitting on the living room couch reading a long piece of parchment. As Avery approached closer she was able to see the words 'Havyn Ledger' scrolled across the top of it in bold letters, with the headline, 'Protectors Return' written just below it. Avery wasn't sure how she felt about being part of a headline.

After grabbing an apple from a bowl on the kitchen table, Avery proceeded to the front door.

"Bye, honey." Her dad called to her from his seat on the couch.

Avery waved her apple filled fist goodbye to him and walked out the door. The sun was just beginning to peak over the horizon, lighting up the tall mountain tops to the west. Even though it still seemed ridiculously early to Avery, a good portion of the villagers were already up and outside working on their gardens and crops, or opening up their shops and beginning their tasks.

As Avery approached the spot where they were all told to meet she saw Bunny sitting on the side of the well and talking to Skylar who was balletically dancing around in front of her. From the looks of it, both of them seemed to have enough energy to spare, which was a good thing since Avery was having trouble even mustering enough energy to walk over to meet them.

She spotted Jade walking towards the well from the other side of the village. Jade was wearing all black, as usual, with her hair pulled back and her signature stony expression planted on her face. She had just finished munching on an apple and threw the core over her back shoulder. When she spotted Avery making her way over she let a smile escape and picked up her pace to meet her.

"Good night's sleep?" Jade asked Avery when they reached the well and Skylar and Bunny.

Avery shook her head, releasing a giant yawn, "Good, but not nearly long enough."

"I hear that." Jade agreed with her, "Gumptin's out of his tiny mind if he thinks we're going to keep meeting him at freaking dawn."

Bunny turned her head and looked over at Jade from her perch on the well, "It's really not that bad." She told Jade, "If you think about it, we're supposed to be soldiers, and soldiers are supposed to get up and train early every day. Maybe you should thank Gumptin for wanting to give us the proper training time to keep us alive, instead of complaining about him."

Avery couldn't stop herself from letting a guffaw escape her mouth. She didn't know if it was seeing Jade first thing in the morning or just being on another planet, but it was one of the first times she had ever seen Bunny chastise Jade, and she couldn't help but love it.

"Listen, band geek," Jade told Bunny, getting almost directly in her face, "we're not all used to getting up at the ass crack of dawn. So don't give me any of your five cent comments, alright?"

Bunny shrugged her shoulders dismissively and turned her head away from Jade. Jade walked over and stood next to Avery, letting her body language tell Avery exactly what she thought about having to spend multiple hours every day training around Bunny.

Sasha sauntered over to them a few moments later. She wasn't exactly on time, and as Avery looked over her perfectly done hair, lightly painted face, and matching sneakers and work out outfit, Avery knew why. Perfection took time, and Sasha looked nothing less than perfect even when she was about to get all sweaty. Avery wondered how many days of training sessions it would take for Sasha to stop caring about how good she looked. She assumed the lack of male admirers would drastically cut the time in half.

Thinking about Sasha's tardiness made Avery question aloud, "Where the hell is Gumptin?"

All the girls began to look around, and then, as if on cue, Gumptin appeared from behind a large shrub at the edge of the forest, "I am right here." He shouted loudly, startling Skylar enough that she jumped back and almost knocked Bunny down the well she was sitting on.

"Don't ever do that again!" Avery yelled at Gumptin, grabbing her heart from the fright of having him pop out of nowhere.

Jade, who would never admit she had been startled, but who was, none the less, grabbing tightly a hold of Avery's arm, snapped at him, "Stupid elf...where have you been?! If we can be here on time, you damn well better be!"

Gumptin walked up to them, dragging behind him a brown leather sack about twice the size of him, "First of all, and for the very last time," he addressed Jade, "I am a gnome, not an *elf*! Second, only two of you lay-a-bout's were here on time, Bunny and Skylar. You and Avery were approximately five minutes past due, and Sasha was a weighty ten minutes late."

"Whatever," Jade replied, too tired to argue, "can we just get on with it?"

Gumptin motioned for them to follow him, but before they left he pointed to the brown sack he had been dragging, "You carry that." He told Jade.

"What?!" Jade asked, taken aback, "Why me?!"

"Consider it as part of your training, which officially starts now." Gumptin turned around and started to walk towards the forest, intent on ignoring any retort Jade was going to give, "You are a Protector; you have the strength of ten men Jade. It is hardly a major inconvenience. Just pick it up and follow me."

Jade looked towards Avery, and Avery nodded her head to tell Jade to just do as she was told. Jade picked up the sack and slung it over her shoulder with hardly any effort. Of course, that didn't stop her from grumbling heatedly to herself as she followed Gumptin and the others towards the forest's border.

Gumptin led them down a small nameless dirt path deep into the woods. For a little nothing path it seemed fairly used. There was no undergrowth or overhanging tree limbs and bushes. They walked for a quarter of a mile until they reached the end of the path. It had led them to a large clearing the size of a baseball field. Short yellow-green grass covered the clearing and towering thick trunked trees surrounded it. To Avery, the trees seemed to form a barrier between the clearing and the rest of the outside world. The ground was soft beneath Avery's feet. The loose dark soil was soft and pillowy, not anything like the hard compact dirt road that had led them there. The air inside the clearing seemed somehow crisper than the air outside of it. It felt as if the whole place crackled with electricity.

In the dead center of the clearing was a black stone altar. It was about waist high with a thick width. The stones looked old and worn, and there was a delicate green moss crawling around it. On the top of the altar, attached to it, was a large rusted metal bowl.

"This place is called Elysianth." Gumptin told them, "It was created thousands of years ago by the Ancients. Back before there was such a thing as good and evil. Before the Ancients split into different factions, this was one of the places they would meet to perform powerful magic. This place is alive with magic; you can feel it."

Gumptin looked around the clearing with reverence as he spoke. It was obvious to the girls that this place held a special meaning in Gumptin's soul and most likely a lot of other magic folk's souls as well.

Gumptin continued, "Over the centuries, many battles have been fought for this little piece of land. Eventually, it fell into the possession of the Elementals. This is the place, over there at that altar, where they created your powers. In a way, this is where you were created. That is why they gave this place to you. It is yours to protect and to train in, a place where you can truly learn to eventually control your powers."

"So, to be clear," Jade spoke up once Gumptin had finished speaking, tossing the sack he had given her to carry on the ground, "The Elementals created us so we'd have to fight the most horrible evil scum you could imagine, which would most likely, as past events have proven, lead to our premature deaths, and all we got out of the deal is a patch of land."

At first, Avery had thought the idea of claiming ownership to a patch of magical land kind of cool, but Jade always had a way of forcing Avery to see things from a different perspective. She wasn't sold on it being cool anymore.

Although Avery thought Jade had a good point, Gumptin certainly didn't, "It is a great honor to be given Elysianth, young lady. You and this land are a part of each other." He flared his tiny nostrils, "You have fought to defend this land against countless enemies who wished to use it for their own purposes."

This time it was Avery who spoke, "Wait a second, you mean we've had to fight things over this land? We could have been killed defending a piece of land that no innocent people actually live on?" Avery could understand risking her life fighting to protect people's lives, but the idea of doing it for a patch of grass was a little more than she bargained for.

Gumptin looked back and forth between Avery and Jade, a look of displeasure on his face, "You two do understand that you do not need to make everything an argument, right?"

"Yes." Avery said hesitantly, nodding her head.

"No." Jade said without hesitation, shaking her head.

Gumptin frowned at them, and then asked Bunny, Sasha, and Skylar, "Do you three have anything to say on the matter?"

Each one of them shook their heads, no.

"Fine," Gumptin said, "let's begin training before any of you have a chance to open your mouths anymore."

Gumptin led them through what he considered basic training routines, but what the girls considered torture. After they finished stretching, they started off with push-ups. Gumptin made sure they each did three hundred before moving on.

"Come on, keep the pace up!" Gumptin shouted at them as they pushed their bodies up and down off of the ground, "Keep going! Your abilities have been dormant for over sixteen years, all your strength, speed, reflexes, senses, powers; your bodies have to remember them all over again."

It was only the very beginning of what Gumptin was going to have them do, and already Avery knew she was going to be in trouble. Her arms felt like they were on fire. When she looked over at the other girls, Avery could see they shared her pain, especially Bunny who lay face first on the ground, not moving.

Once push-ups were finished, it was time for sit-ups.

Sasha was on sit-up two hundred and sixty five when she collapsed on the ground, "I think I'm dying." She moaned, her pretty face in the dirt.

"You are not dead yet, Sasha," Gumptin told her, pacing back and forth in front of the girls, "and until you are, keep going!"

Sasha reluctantly picked herself up and kept going.

After sit-ups it was pull-ups on some low-lying tree limbs, two hundred of them, and then knee lifts, two hundred of them as well. They were followed by squats and jumping jacks that seemed, to the girls, like they were never going to end.

"Alright, enough." Gumptin told them.

The girls fell to the ground. Avery lay on her back, breathing heavily, looking up at the baby blue sky dappled with big white fluffy clouds.

Gumptin looked down at the girls trying to catch their breath, "That was quite pathetic." He said.

"Are you nuts?!" Avery retorted, lifting her head up to look at Gumptin, "I've never worked so hard in my life!"

Gumptin snorted, "Maybe not in this life, but in your pre-Earth life, that was about half of what you usually do."

There was a collective groan from the girls at the thought of doing any more.

Gumptin ignored their displeasure, "Alright, time to run, get up."

The girls didn't move, except for Jade, who lifted her arm up and flipped Gumptin off.

"Get up!" Gumptin continued, "Get off of the ground! Move it, move it!" He kicked at each one of the girls until they were all on their feet and jogging in laps around the perimeter of the clearing.

Avery tried to clear her mind as she ran, focusing on the cool air and soft grass, the forest around her teeming with life, anything to keep her mind off of the stitch forming in her side and the feeling of her lungs about to explode. She had no idea how long Gumptin had had them running for, but the sun had now become fully visible in the sky. Jade and Avery had been running side by side and ahead of the others, when suddenly Jade stopped. Avery followed suit and looked back at her.

Jade had her hands on her knees, and she was shaking her head, "Nope, no more, I'm done."

"Oh, thank God!" Skylar exclaimed stopping as well, along with Bunny and Sasha, "I don't know how long you planned to have us running, but that's it."

Gumptin shrugged his shoulders, "I did not have anything planned. I was just waiting for you to go as long as you could before you had to stop."

Before any of the girls had a chance to yell at Gumptin for neglecting to mention that before they had started running, and especially before they had reached the point where they felt like vomiting, Gumptin walked over to the oversized leather sack he had Jade carry. The girls watched as he untied the sack and took out its contents. The first thing Gumptin unpacked was a handful of cotton cloth strips.

"Tie these around your hands." He told them, "It is time for your real training to begin."

The girls did as they were told, just relieved that they were done with the exercise routines. They tied the strips of cloth around their hands, forming make-shift gloves.

Gumptin led them to the very far edge of the clearing, where nailed to five separate trees, were leather sacks a foot taller than Avery. Avery pushed against one of the sacks and it gave way a little. It felt, to her, as if it was filled with sand, making it a semblant punching bag.

"These are your sparring partners." Gumptin said, pointing towards the sacks.

Gumptin directed each one of them to a different bag and then made sure they were all in the appropriate fighting stance. Feet shoulder width apart and firmly under you, knees slightly bent, weight evenly distributed between the balls of your feet, hips at a ninety degree angle to your opponent, shoulders square over the hips, and the back straight, head turned to face your opponents with your right fist up just below eye level, left arm brought up in front of the body with the fist just underneath the chin, elbows kept close to the body at all times. It sounded complicated as Gumptin was explaining it to them, but after a short demonstration the only one of the girls who required extra attention to get her stance correct was Bunny.

Once they were all in their starting stances, Gumptin led them through a rigorous training routine. He had them doing multiple kinds of jabs, standard jabs, twisting jabs, and collapsing jabs, until sweat was dripping down their faces. He had them doing cross punches, hook punches, and uppercut punches. After they finished their punches, Gumptin had them move on to kicks. He had them doing side kicks, back kicks, sweeping, thrust, and rising kicks, snap kicks, and roundhouse kicks. Gumptin then had them do multiple maneuvers in mixed order.

Gumptin called out, "Hook, twisting jab, side kick, back kick, uppercut!"

He barely left a breath between his words and the girls were expected to follow him without mistake. In fact, they weren't allowed to stop with the exercise until they had performed five consecutive routines to perfection. To Avery's surprise the skills and routines came relatively easy to her. Her muscles were killing her, and she was sure she'd never breathe right again, but she found that all the punches, jabs, and kicks, and doing them in different patterns came habitual to her. They were as easy as riding a bike back on Earth. She didn't even have to really think about what she was doing; it was as if the nerve endings in her body remembered these activities.

Bunny, however, was having slight problems and was responsible for that particular training session lasting an extra twenty minutes. When she finally managed to get it down without fault, Gumptin gave them ten minutes of rest.

Avery hugged the tree she had just released a considerable beating on, letting it support all of her weight. She cringed as her sweat drenched face stuck to the leather punching bag, but it beat collapsing onto the dirty ground along with Skylar and Sasha.

After what seemed to Avery like thirty seconds, Gumptin announced, "Your ten minutes are expired. Let's move on to ground work."

Avery stayed glued to the tree, hoping that someone, especially Jade, would protest, but after a few moments of silence, she turned her head around and saw Jade literally crawling on her hands and knees over to the near center of the clearing where Gumptin was directing them to go. It was then that Avery pushed herself up off of the tree, thinking that whatever Gumptin was about to do to them, it couldn't get much worse.

It wasn't long before Avery realized how wrong she was. Gumptin first had them work on basic ground roll techniques. They were made to do forward, side, backward, and diving rolls. They weren't difficult compared to everything else they had been doing, and they didn't require much energy, which meant the girls took as long as they possibly could drawing out their different rolls. Gumptin, however, was not fooled and had them quickly moving on to cartwheels. First, just free form and then cartwheeling while picking up an object up off of the ground. He used a long stick as their prop.

Next, Gumptin moved on to handsprings and flips, and this is when the girls became hesitant. As Gumptin explained the technique that went into the acrobatic maneuvers he wanted them to do, the girls looked back and forth at each other, more than sure that one of them was going to break something; they just hoped it wasn't their neck. Avery could have bet money that Bunny was definitely going to fracture something.

When he finished explaining, Gumptin pointed to Avery, "I want you to do a handspring into a front flip, run five paces, do a cartwheel into a back handspring, followed by a double front flip."

Avery's mouth genuinely fell open. She was pretty sure she wouldn't even be able to verbally repeat what Gumptin had said, let alone do it.

Next to her, Avery could hear Sasha snickering under her breath, "Yeah, Avery," Sasha squeaked out through her giggles, "show us what you got, big bad leader."

"Stow it, Sasha!" Jade barked, glaring at Sasha from the other side of Avery. She turned to Gumptin, "This is going beyond sadistic drill instructor, alright. She could seriously hurt herself."

Gumptin shook his head, "No, no, no, she will be fine. Your bodies remember everything. It is just like a cat landing on their feet, completely instinctual."

As Avery moaned at the unsatisfying analogy of being compared to a cat, Jade scoffed at Gumptin, "It's also instinctual for me to want to duct tape your mouth shut, but you don't see that working out too well, do you?"

Avery knew Gumptin and Jade were just going to keep talking in circles without agreeing. So, she decided she would rather injure herself doing something productive, than get a migraine listening to them bicker.

"I'll do it!" Avery shouted, above Gumptin and Jade's heated voices.

Before Avery walked out to prepare for her aerial gymnastics, Jade grabbed on to her elbow, "Whoa, whoa, whoa." Jade told her.

"Relax," Avery said, tugging her elbow free, "I'm cat-like, remember." She said it as much to assure herself as she did to assure Jade.

Avery walked up to Gumptin, telling herself to keep calm despite her sweaty palms and racing heart.

"Just remember," Gumptin told her, "get a running start, breathe, and let your mind go free. Your body will do all the rest. Just do not over think it."

It wasn't the most calming thing Gumptin could have said to her, but Avery took his advice. She took a couple deep long breaths to calm herself and tried to clear her mind. It was difficult at first with the thought of pummeling to the ground in mid jump darting through her head. A petite white flower sprouting up from the ground a few feet in front of Avery caught her attention, and she focused all of her attention on it. Soon, Avery's mind was free of any thoughts except that tiny flower and the jumps she was about to do. Taking a final deep breath, Avery took off into a run.

One step, two steps, three steps. On the fourth step, Avery leapt up off of the ground. She bounced into a handspring, then from there into a front flip. She hit the ground a little off balance, but quickly recovered, took five paces, then sprung into a cartwheel, a back handspring, and finally a double front flip. Her landing was a little rocky and she ended up stumbling forward a few feet, landing on her hands and knees, but she had made it without damaging herself, and that was all Avery could have hoped for.

It took Avery a few seconds of kneeling on the ground before she was fully aware of what she had just done. Avery heard cheers from the other girls standing behind her.

"Oh, my God," Skylar hollered, running up to Avery, "I cannot believe you just did that!"

Jade ran over to Avery as well, grabbing under her arms and helping to pick her up off of the ground, "Are you alright?"

Avery allowed herself to be picked up and placed on her shaky feet.

"I can't believe I just did that either." Avery uttered, walking around to regain her balance.

One by one, Gumptin had the girls each do an individualized routine. Just like Avery, they got through them, shocked that their bodies could perform such tumbling maneuvers. Of course, not one of them got the landing perfect; Skylar landed on her butt; Sasha fell on her face; Jade landed so hard on her right ankle that it caused her to curse and fall to the ground, and poor Bunny overestimated her speed, came out of the routine too fast, and slammed into one of the large trees surrounding the clearing.

Gumptin had the girls flipping, tumbling, cartwheeling, and handspringing until they were all proficient in everything, including the landings. They weren't allowed to stop until they were almost too dizzy to walk, let alone, whirl through the air.

"Aren't we done yet?" Avery whined, sticking her head between her knees to stop the queasiness in her stomach caused by all the spinning.

"We are done with the tumbling." Gumptin told her matter-of-factly, "Now, we move on to weapons training."

Avery could swear she heard Skylar begin to cry behind her at Gumptin's words.

Gumptin let the girls collect themselves for a whole minute, and then moved them back over to the edge of the forest where their punching bag trees were. Between two of the trees was a broad rectangular hole dug into the ground. A brown canvas blanket rest on top of the hole and was covered with fallen leaves and other debris. Gumptin had Avery lift the canvas cover off of the hole. Inside were four round tire-sized bull's-eye targets, eight wooden swords, and a dozen sticks about six feet in length, a pile of arrows, three bows, two crossbows, and about a dozen sacks of different sizes. Last, but not least, resting on top of everything were three straw stuffed dummies, the size and shape of actual men, attached to a metal pole with a metal bottom base.

Gumptin had the girls drag the life-sized dummies to the edge of the clearing. He carried with him one of the sacks that had been in the hole. Gumptin dumped out the contents of the sack, which consisted of twelve thick curved metal spikes and two bulky hammers. The metal base of the dummies each had four round holes in it. Gumptin had the girls stand the dummies up straight and hammer a spike into each hole. This anchored the dummies to the ground making them unyielding.

Once they had finished staking the dummies to the ground, Gumptin gave them each a wooden sword. He stood them all in row and slowly explained the footwork, the different cuts to make with the sword that are the most effective, cuts to the leg, body, and head, assorted thrusts, and blocks. All the girls listened and followed Gumptin as best they could, but were honestly getting lost once he started to add more than five or six cuts, thrusts and blocks together.

"You are Protectors," Gumptin shouted at them after their tenth failed attempt at a series of techniques he had told them to do, "you should know this! You are not trying hard enough! You must focus, because we are not stopping until you get this right!"

Jade quit what she was doing in mid sword thrust and turned towards Gumptin, "What is this 'we' crap!" She hollered, "I don't see 'we' doing anything. I see the five of us working our asses off while you stand their shouting at us!"

Gumptin kept pacing in front of the girls, barely acknowledging Jade's outburst, "Trust me Jade, it is far more painful watching the five of you pathetically labor through your elementary training routines, than it is for you to do them."

"You're like a little satanic monster, you know that." Jade told Gumptin, throwing down her wooden sword, refusing to continue.

Gumptin still didn't turn to acknowledge Jade, which Avery was sure he only did to frustrate Jade more, "For every minute that goes by in which you refuse to train, I will add an extra twenty push-ups onto tomorrow's warm-ups for everyone."

Jade stood with her hands on hips, not moving, but Avery could tell she was torn. It was only her pride that was keeping her from picking up the sword.

"That is twenty extra push-ups." Gumptin said, "Shall we try for forty?"

"Jade, you pick up that sword, or I'll strangle you while you sleep!" Sasha shouted at Jade.

Avery wasn't about to let Jade's pride cost her forty extra push-ups, "Jade, pick…it…up!" Avery made sure to say it in a tone that let Jade know if she didn't pick it up, there were going to be serious consequences for

Jade.

Jade snarled and stomped her foot before bending down to pick up her sword and continue with the exercise.

Disheartened by the idea of extra work the next day and the fact that they had been out there for over six hours, they all concentrated exceptionally hard and got through Gumptin's maneuvers in just a few short tries. Once they had completed that task, Gumptin moved them towards the stuffed dummies and had them practice their sword work on them. Three at a time he called them up and shouted commands out to them.

"Right knee cut, turn, left head cut, body thrust, turn, right body cut!" Gumptin called out.

They all muddled through the orders imperfect in some way, but not enough for Gumptin to make them keep doing the same ones over and over again.

After the sword work was over, Gumptin had Bunny bring over six of the long sticks Avery had seen in the hole. Gumptin explained that they were called quarterstaffs and were a very useful and effective weapon.

Jade complained that it was pointless to have to learn how to use a weapon that didn't even have a pointy end. The only thing that shut her up was Gumptin's threat to add more sit-ups to tomorrow's exercise.

Avery was just done all together. She was sore; she was tired, and she really didn't want to have to learn how to fight with a giant stick. These were the thoughts running through Avery's mind as Gumptin handed Avery a staff and described the proper way to hold it, with both hands.

Having been through the sword practice before made it easier to grasp using the staff. They learned glides, and strikes, sweeps, and jabs. Once again, Gumptin had them practice on the dummies before letting them move on to the next weapon.

When they had finished training with the staff's, Gumptin had them move on to the bow and arrows. The girls pulled out the round targets with the bull's-eye on them and placed them each at a different distance from where Gumptin was having them stand to shoot. He led the girls in a straight path back into the woods, where there was still clear sight and shot to the targets, but so they would have a longer distance to shoot from. The first target was placed a hundred feet away, the second at two hundred and fifty, the third at four hundred, and the fourth and last target at a whopping five hundred feet away from them. Looking at the targets from where she stood, Avery thought it laughable that Gumptin expected them to hit the targets at all, let alone any of the bull's-eyes. The furthest target, even though it was the size of a truck's tire, looked to Avery like the size of a Frisbee.

Gumptin explained that right-eye dominant archers hold their bow with their left hand, have their left side facing the target, use their right hand to handle the string and arrow, and take sight of the target with their right eye. Avery closed one eye, then the other, and back again, trying to figure out her dominant eye. When her blinking technique failed to give her an answer, she just figured, since she was right handed, her dominant eye was most likely her right one.

Sasha was called to go first. She picked up one of the sturdy wooden bows and a stiff arrow with a long thin metal tip on one end and three bright red feathers on the other end.

Gumptin instructed Sasha to move her body perpendicular to the target, with feet shoulder length apart. He had her point her bow downward and get her arrow ready. Then, he showed her how to bring the bow up, and pull the arrow back in one quick fluid motion. He had Sasha take a few deep breaths, aim, and release.

Sasha's arrow flew towards the target one hundred feet away and landed just a few inches away from dead center. Since Sasha was the first one to go, and the rest of them had nothing to compare her shot with, they couldn't help but be impressed and gave her a round of applause.

Her second shot went about as well as the first one, but her third shot from four hundred feet away didn't land exactly near the center. In fact, the only part of the target it hit was one of the wooden legs holding it up. Sasha's last shot was just as bad, except this time it landed in the ground a few feet in front of the target.

"This is ridiculous." Sasha complained, handing the bow back to Gumptin, "I'm not some Neanderthal who needs to go out and bow hunt for my supper."

"Practice, Sasha," Gumptin told her, "more practice. By next week, I want you to at least hit the last target. The object is to hit your enemy with the arrow, not to have it land next to him so that he may see how dangerous it looks."

Next to go was Bunny, who did about as well as Sasha did, although, her last shot landed somewhere in the forest behind the target instead of in front of it. This pleasantly surprised Avery; Bunny seemed to have a lot more strength than Avery would have given her credit for.

Skylar went after Bunny. She hit the target near dead center with her first two shots, but her third was more than a few inches off. However, her fourth shot actually landed on the target, the very outside edge of the target, but so far it was the best shot of the day.

Next was Jade. She didn't take as long to aim as the other's had, but even so, her aim was scarily accurate. Her first two arrows landed right next to Skylar's near dead center. Her third shot was only a few centimeters from center, and her fourth and most difficult shot, flew through the air, slamming into the target a whole three inches closer to the bull's-eye than Skylar's.

Finally, it was Avery's turn to go. Jade handed off the bow to her and Avery ran her hands over it. The sensation of the wooden bow in her palms seemed familiar to her body, even though she had never handled one in her life. She picked up one of the arrows off of the ground and got into position. She tried to remember Gumptin's words about not over thinking, about letting her body remember the skills it had and letting it do all the work. Avery was skeptical her body would do what she wanted it to do, but she decided to try and give it an attempt. If she failed, she would just blame Gumptin and his stupid reasoning. Avery closed her eyes and let her left hand feel the strong center of the bow, her right hand the delicate tip of the arrow and tight tension of the string. Her body was telling her she knew these feelings, and she forced her mind clear before she could argue away what she was feeling. She took one long deep breath, raised her bow and pulled back on her bow string in one swift movement. It took Avery only a split second to decide and aim at the fourth and furthest target first. It seemed like the world around her went black and the only thing she could see was the bright red center of the circular target. What had seemed so tiny to her just ten minutes ago was now the clearest thing she had ever seen. Her hand released the arrow and it sailed through the air, whistling its way towards the target before hitting dead center in the middle of it.

After she watched her arrow hit its mark, the world came back into focus for Avery, color returned and the target went back to looking like an unreachable speck.

"Well, screw me!" Jade whooped, standing behind Avery, staring open mouthed at the shot she had just made.

"Thanks for making me look pathetic, Avery." Skylar pat Avery on the back.

Avery looked over at Gumptin and noticed a small smile on his face.

"What are you smirking at, weirdo?' Avery asked, a little embarrassed at all the attention her perfect shot was getting.

Gumptin's smile broadened, "I knew you would do well if you let yourself. You were always excellent at the bow and arrow. After practice or patrolling, you would come out at night when the moon was bright enough and practice it for hours."

It seemed like Gumptin was fond of the memory, so Avery smiled back at him and nodded, deciding not to tell him that there was no way in hell that was ever going to happen this time around. Avery didn't think anything could possibly suck more than added voluntary training after what she had already been through today.

After the bow and arrow, Gumptin moved them on to the crossbow. Unfortunately, it didn't go quite as well as the bow and arrow training had.

Sasha had difficulties drawing the bow string back by hand, and before she was able to get it set, it snapped back on her fingers, leaving her with a horizontal red mark across her left hand.

Skylar hadn't been paying attention when Gumptin talked about being prepared for the recoil after a shot was taken, and as a result, she was not prepared and ended up with a good sized bruise on her shoulder.

Avery, whose aim was still impeccable, hadn't expected the trigger on the crossbow to be as delicate as it was, causing her to accidentally fire before she had lifted the crossbow up to her shoulder. As a result, it fired while she was holding it at chest level, giving herself a bruise to match Skylar's right above her right breast.

Avery was still rubbing at her bruise when she witnessed Bunny make the worst mistake of the day. Bunny had just been handed the crossbow, and while she was jokingly asking Avery for any tips on how to avoid personal injury, she unintentionally fired the crossbow; sending one of the sharp crossbow bolts sailing into a tree trunk centimeters from Gumptin's head. Even though Bunny apologized profusely, she wasn't allowed to use the crossbow any more that day, and Avery guessed probably ever again.

Jade, however, did more than exceptionally well, liking the fact that unlike the bow and arrow, she didn't have to use both hands if she didn't want too.

After finishing up their mostly disastrous crossbow training, the girls were hoping that they were done for the day. They couldn't imagine what else Gumptin could possibly have them do.

"Can we please go home now?" Avery whined, longing to leave the clearing and all of its tortures behind.

Gumptin sighed, "You five never complained this much before, not even you, Jade."

Jade was sitting on a large rock, looking far too exhausted to give Gumptin any sort of sarcastic reply.

"You may leave after the final training exercise." Gumptin told them, "It is time to take what you have learned and put it into practice. You will spar one on one with each other."

"Spar?" Jade asked, "You mean you want us to fight each other?"

Gumptin nodded, "That is correct. I will give you each a wooden sword and pair you up against one another. The first person to make what would be considered a killing blow shall win."

"Hell, I'm down with that." Jade said, jumping off of her rock with new found enthusiasm.

There was no way Avery could think of that this was going to go well. They were tired, sore, and grumpy, and now they were suppose to beat each other up.

Gumptin was wearing his usual oversized belt with at least seven different small pouches tied and attached to it. He undid a purple velvet pouch with a gold string and untied it. Inside the pouch was a bright red powder that he used to create a giant circle outline, ten feet in diameter.

"You must stay inside the red circle." He told them, "You win the match if you inflict your opponent with what would be a killing blow, or you get them outside of the circle."

Gumptin handed each of them a wooden sword, "Jade and Skylar, you two go first."

Jade stepped into the circle, twirling her sword around in her hand. Avery could tell she was excited. This was Jade's element; she loved competition, and she loved fighting. Avery was sure Jade would have chosen to go against Bunny or Sasha, preferring to kick their ass, but she would make do with Skylar.

Skylar stepped into the circle, across from Jade. She didn't seem as enthusiastic about it as Jade was, but didn't complain about it either. Skylar dealt with it the same way she handled most everything, with a light and flighty approach. She danced around in a small circle, stretching her long legs out one at time. She stretched her neck and moved her shoulders around, like a dancer warming up for a performance.

"You're going down, trailer trash!" Skylar threw out a little pre-fight trash talk. Skylar was one of the only people Jade let call her trailer trash. Mainly, because Jade liked Skylar, and she knew Skylar meant it lovingly. She just had a crazy way of showing her affection.

Jade just smiled and set her body into its fighting stance. She let Skylar have her trash talk, confident enough to know that the outcome of the fight would speak for itself.

Jade went on the attack right from the start. She lunged at Skylar, striking at her left side with her sword. Skylar twirled to the right, avoiding Jade's initial strike. She raised her sword up quickly to protect her body as Jade swung around, swiping at Skylar's mid-section. Skylar brought her left knee up and kneed Jade hard in the back, right where her ribs were located. Jade grimaced, arching her back slightly. That was all it took to piss Jade off past the point of trying to make it a prolonged fight. Jade bent her knees and then back flipped through the air, landing directly behind Skylar. Before Skylar had time to appropriately react, Jade reached around Skylar's chest with her right arm. Then, with all her strength, Jade swung her body hard into Skylar's. Placing her left hand on Skylar's back, Jade, literally, flipped Skylar's body up over her head. A second before Skylar's body hit the ground; Jade whipped her body around and, fast as a flash of light, gave Skylar a quick kick to the stomach.

Avery grimaced and looked away, shutting her eyes. Gumptin had said the Protectors possessed a high tolerance to injury and an ability to heal quickly. After watching poor Skylar tossed like a rag doll and kicked in the gut, Avery sure hoped he was right.

The kick sent Skylar rolling backwards and out of the parameter of the red circle. Skylar stopped rolling and sat up, groaning. She winced as she attempted to stand up, obviously in some kind of pain.

Jade walked over and helped Skylar delicately stand up, "Are you alright?" She asked, in a tone that intentionally kept concern out of her voice. It showed that she wanted to make sure that Skylar was alright, but that she wasn't sorry for winning the fight.

"I'll be fine." Skylar groaned, stretching out a little as she stood, "I just have to re-learn how to breathe."

Gumptin shook his head in approval, which was as close as he got to clapping, "Good job, very good job. You must go into every fight with everything you have. Your enemy will never go easy on you."

Jade had definitely set the tone. There would be no going easy on each other just because they were friends.

"Very well done, Jade." Gumptin told her, "In this instance, your natural aggression actually comes in handy."

Avery noticed Jade smile slightly, then quickly turn away so that no one, especially Gumptin, would notice he had said something that pleased her.

"Skylar," Gumptin continued, "you need to react faster. Your movements are graceful and fluid, but you must find a way to add speed, especially to defend yourself."

Skylar, who was now sitting down outside the circle, resting her wounded self, gave Gumptin an encouraging thumbs up.

Avery thought Skylar's black and blue body tomorrow would be more motivation for Skylar to work on her speed, than anything Gumptin could say to her.

"Next, Avery and Sasha shall fight." Gumptin said, pointing towards the circle.

Avery did as she was instructed and followed Gumptin's finger into the circle. Watching Jade and Skylar's fight had made one thing blaringly clear to her, she wanted to avoid getting hit or kicked at all costs.

Looking ahead of her, Avery saw Sasha getting into position. Sasha didn't seem nervous or scared at all. In fact, she seemed cocky, giving Avery a little smile and tilt of the head. Sasha seemed completely sure she was going to win this fight. Suddenly, everything became very clear cut to Avery. She was being given the chance to do something she had wanted to do for over ten years, to kick Sasha Seraphina's ass. Avery didn't care what it took; there was no way she was going to lose this fight.

The moment Avery got herself into a fighting stance, Sasha came charging at her. Sasha swung her sword at Avery's head, but Avery managed to duck in time. Before Avery righted herself again, Sasha tried to side kick Avery with her right leg. Avery took her sword hand and slammed it into Sasha's leg, forcing her leg down. Sasha gasped in pain and Avery stood up, cutting her left hand across her body and punching Sasha square in the jaw.

Avery heard Jade whoop from outside the circle, but she didn't let it distract her.

Sasha swung at Avery hard with her right fist, obviously upset that Avery had been able to hurt her. Avery spun to the right, avoiding Sasha's fist. As she spun, Avery switched her sword from her right hand to her left, this allowed her to reach up with her right hand and grab a hold of Sasha's wrist as her arm was still extended. Once she had Sasha's wrist firmly in her grasp, she pulled Sasha forward and towards her, at the same time she brought her left leg up, kicking Sasha across the chest. Sasha staggered backwards and fell to the ground. Avery walked over to her, about to thrust her sword into Sasha's exposed chest. Sasha, never one to go down without a fight, came off of the ground in a backwards hand spring, shoving the heel of her boot into Avery's chest on her way up. The pain hit Avery like a bolt of lightning. It was all Avery could do to flip out of Sasha's way as she came at her with her sword raised high. As Avery flipped over Sasha, before she hit the ground, she pushed both of her legs hard backwards, slamming Sasha in the middle of the back. Sasha was sent falling forward landing on her face. Avery landed delicately on her hands and knees, rolling over and springing onto her feet in less than a second. While still lying on her stomach Sasha attempted a backwards kick, once again aimed at Avery's chest as Avery walked towards her, but this time Avery was prepared for it. Avery grabbed Sasha's ankle and flipped Sasha from her stomach over to her back. The moment Sasha was on her back, Avery had her wooden sword pointed right in the center of Sasha's chest.

The girls clapped from the sidelines, happy to see Avery defeat Sasha.

"That's my girl!" Jade shouted, clapping louder than the others.

Sasha ripped her ankle out of Avery's grip, stood up, and pushed Avery away from her, hard. It didn't faze Avery at all as she stumbled backwards from Sasha's shove. She had defeated Sasha, and that was something that would keep her happy for weeks to come.

Angry about being beaten, Sasha walked over to the sidelines and complained to Gumptin, "I'm so done with this crap! Yesterday I was the girl every boy wanted to date and every girl wanted to be! I was hot, popular, smart, and wealthy!"

Avery and the other girls exchanged looks, shaking their heads and rolling their eyes. For as long as they had known Sasha, no one had ever thought Sasha Seraphina was as perfect as Sasha herself did.

"Now," Sasha kept going, "today, I'm getting beaten up by Avery Kimball! My life has gone to shit!"

"For crying out loud," Skylar exclaimed, as sick of Sasha's tantrum as the rest of them, which was rare for Skylar since she got along better with Sasha than any of the other did, "stop being such a sore loser."

"I don't think Sasha knows how to be anything else." Jade added. You could always count on Jade to make a tense situation even tenser.

Sasha turned on Jade, "Jade, sometimes you really need to know when to keep that trashy mouth of yours shut!"

"Oh, is that so?" Jade asked, walking towards Sasha, still clutching her wooden sword.

Gumptin held his hands up, silencing everyone, "Enough!" He bellowed, "Sasha, you lost, collect yourself and move past it. Your life may not be what you want it to be. I am sure you are not the only one of the Protectors to feel that way, especially after today."

Gumptin looked around at all the girls. He knew very well that none of them, except maybe Jade, would have ever voluntarily chosen to give up their lives on Earth and travel to another planet to battle monsters. Gumptin felt for them, but he also had to make sure that they realized they really didn't have any choice in the matter; it was their destiny.

"I know it is hard for all of you," Gumptin said to them, "but this is a birthright that you cannot escape. You are only alive now because the Elementals gave you a second chance at life. They gave you a second chance so that you could come back and fulfill your destinies as Protectors. If you forsake it, if you forsake them, they could take your life away from you as easily as blowing out a candle."

Silence crept over the girls as they let Gumptin's words sink in. They had to except the duties of a Protector so that the Elementals would let them keep living, and they had to keep training so that they had the skills not to be killed by a hideous enemy. All of a sudden, the girls got the feeling of being very small and very not in control of their own lives. Avery wasn't convinced the Elementals would actually kill them if they chose not to fight as a Protector, but it wasn't a theory she would ever be willing to test. Of course, whether it was true or not didn't matter, since it managed to shut Sasha up real quick. Sasha valued her life far too much to ever put it in even more unnecessary danger.

"Now, if all the complaining is over, then let us continue." Gumptin pointed to Jade, "You and Bunny get in the circle."

Bunny stood across from Jade looking ready, if not just a little bit frightened. Avery didn't blame Bunny for being scared about being paired off against Jade. It hardly seemed like a fair fight. Jade could have wiped the floor with Bunny back on Earth, and that was before they had all their super human Protector powers reawakened.

Jade and Bunny ran towards each other. Before they met in the middle, Bunny vaulted over Jade. This surprised Jade as much as it did the other girls. None of them figured Bunny would have the foresight to do a move like that. Jade was shocked, and the half a second it took her to recover from her shocked state cost her. Bunny landed facing Jade and managed to backhand her along the side of her skull before Jade could defend herself. Jade tripped sideways shaking her head. Bunny advanced on Jade. She lifted her sword to swipe at Jade's side, but this time Jade was ready for Bunny's attack. Jade lifted her elbow up to deflect the blow; then gave Bunny a hard side kick to her midsection. The kick caused Bunny to flail backwards, giving Jade a chance to go on the attack. As Bunny righted herself, Jade whacked the sword away from Bunny's hand with her own sword. Once Bunny's sword was on the ground, Jade laid a hard roundhouse kick on Bunny, causing her to fall face first onto the ground. Jade reached down and grabbed Bunny by the back of her shirt, preparing to flip her over, but before Jade could do anything, Bunny spun herself over and hit Jade hard on the side of her head with her fist. Jade backed away clutching her head, a trail of blood was beginning to run down her face.

The girls gasped at the sight of the blood. It hadn't seemed like Bunny's punch could have caused such a bloody wound, but when Avery looked over to Bunny, she saw Bunny clutching a good sized rock in the fist she had struck Jade with. A flash of the Alex Marquez incident from their youth popped into Avery's mind.

As Jade was still clutching at her head, Bunny rolled forward on the ground; knocking Jade over. Bunny picked up her sword from where Jade had knocked it away from her, walked over to Jade, stood over her, and placed the tip of her wooden sword on Jade's neck.

"Too bad for you, but you're dead." Bunny said, smirking, looking down at Jade.

The girls stood silent, holding their breath, shocked at what they had just seen. Little Bunny had actually defeated Jade in a one on one fight. Of course, she had pummeled Jade in the head with a rock to win. Avery wasn't sure if she was more shocked because Bunny had actually won, or because Bunny had done something bordering on dangerously vicious to win.

Jade snatched the sword away from Bunny and stood up in one fluid movement.

"Bunny!" Jade growled savagely, advancing on Bunny, clutching the sword like she was about to strike her with it, "What the hell was that?!"

"I'm sorry." Bunny said meekly, backing away from Jade. She had transformed back to her usual submissive self. All signs of the formidable warrior Jade had faced were gone, "I really didn't mean to hit you with the rock. When I landed on the ground I just…"

"You just what?" Jade angrily interrupted her, "You just unwittingly grabbed onto a rock and accidentally knocked me on the side of the head with it?!"

Jade lifted up the wooden sword a little more, and Avery was sure she was going to hit Bunny with it.

"Alright, alright," Gumptin said, stepping in between them as tears began to form in Bunny's eyes, "Jade, just calm down. I never said you could not use foreign objects to fight with. In a real battle, if you are weaponless, a rock is a perfectly acceptable means to defend yourself. However," he looked towards Bunny, "I would discourage from using such tactics against your fellow Protectors." He gave Bunny an anxiously unsure look.

Bunny nodded in agreeance and assured Gumptin and Jade it would never happen again.

Jade threw the sword down, "Unbelievable." She said in disgust, walking back over to Avery.

"I guess Bunny was out for blood...literally." Skylar told Jade, staring at the red stain on her face.

Avery took out a crumpled unused tissue she had stuck in her pocket before she left her house and handed it to Jade to help clean herself up. There was a lot of blooding running down her face, but the wound itself didn't look too bad.

"Well, since Bunny won," Gumptin scrunched up his face, "however controversial, that means Avery and Bunny will fight each other."

Avery stepped into the circle and glanced around the ground, searching for any visible rocks. The last thing she was going to do was let Bunny near any of them. Across from her, Bunny seemed to have gotten over inadvertently slicing Jade's head open. She looked ready and determined.

Avery and Bunny circled each other for a minute, getting closer and closer. When they were only inches apart, Bunny thrust her sword towards Avery's stomach. Avery deflected it with a swipe of her own sword. Then, Bunny went on the attack. She struck left with her sword, swiped right, thrust, and swiped left. Avery deflected the blows, but Bunny's aggression was throwing her off. After watching Bunny defeat Jade, she had known going into the fight that Bunny was a much better fighter than she would have ever given her credit for, but her tenacity was something Avery hadn't been prepared for.

Bunny brought her sword up and attempted to bring it down on Avery's shoulder. She struck left, right, left again, and finally straight down on Avery's head. Avery managed to stop each blow. Getting tired of being on the defensive, she took a step backwards and threw her sword from her right hand to her left. Avery watched as Bunny's eyes followed her sword from her right to left hand, and in that fraction of a second that Bunny took her eyes off of Avery's right hand, Avery closed it into a fist and clocked Bunny hard on the left side of her face. The few seconds it took Bunny to collect herself allowed Avery to handspring away from her and into an offensive position. Bunny shook her head, as if she was trying to wipe Avery's punch away. Bunny charged towards Avery, and Avery let her get within just a few feet before her body made the unconscious decision to fling her sword at Bunny. The sword sailed through the air before striking Bunny directly in her chest, knocking her to the ground.

"Oh, yes!" Jade cheered from the sidelines, "Too bad for you, Bunny, but I think you're dead!"

Avery walked over to where Bunny was laying on the ground, on her back, and offered Bunny her hand, "You ok?" She asked, hoping her blow hadn't hurt Bunny.

Bunny smiled and grabbed onto Avery's hand, pulling herself up, "I'll live." She told Avery, "I lost to you, which is a hundred times better than losing to Jade."

"Very well done, both of you." Gumptin said, smiling broader than he had all day, "Now, you may put everything away."

The girls weren't thrilled about having to put away all the weapons and other equipment, but they knew that once they did, they would be that much closer to being able to go home, and that made them ecstatic.

The girls placed all of the weapons away back into the large storage pit, then began trying to un-stake the target dummies from the ground. As Avery was helping Jade loosen one of the heavy metal stakes, her eyes glanced over to the black stone altar in the center of the clearing. She had been practicing around it all day, but now as she stared at it, she began to wonder why it was even there and what purpose it served. With all the misery Gumptin had put them through throughout the day; she hadn't had a moment of calm to think about it.

When they had un-staked the targets, Avery let the other girls carry them back to the pit. She walked over to the altar in order get a better look at it. The black stones that the altar was made from were smooth, like river rocks. The altar, itself, stood as tall as Avery's waist, and the broad metal bowl attached to the altar reached her chest.

Gumptin meandered over to Avery, watching Avery examine the altar.

"What exactly is this, Gumptin?" Avery asked, walking around the altar, letting her fingers delicately brush the green moss growing on it.

"That is the Elysianth altar." Gumptin answered her, "I told you this clearing was powerful, well this is the epicenter of the power. It is where someone with the skill and knowledge of the old magic would perform a spell or ritual to harness or tap into the power of Elysianth."

Avery tilted her head and looked into the oversized metal bowl connected to the top of it. She didn't really expect to find anything in it, except maybe a few leaves and some dust. That's why when she saw the ashy remnants of something having been burnt she was surprised.

"Do people use this to light fires in?" Avery asked Gumptin, wondering if maybe that's what the Protector's used the altar for if they were ever out there at night.

"What?!" Gumptin said, a bit more loud and abrupt than Avery thought necessary, "This altar has not been used for at least a century."

Avery snorted, "Well," she said, running her index finger through the burnt debris, "somebody used it as a fire pit not too long ago."

Gumptin rushed over and stood directly next to Avery. Avery took a small step to her left, so that he wouldn't be plastered against her leg."

"What is in there?" Gumptin sounded anxious, "What do you see?" He stood on his tip-toes trying to see into the bowl, but barely made it eye level to the top of the altar, let alone, the bowl.

Avery glanced at Gumptin, curious as to why he was acting so paranoid, "Nothing, really," Avery told him, "just burnt stuff. I have no idea what it was, maybe paper or leaves."

Avery continued to swish her fingers through the ash in the bowl. All of a sudden, her finger hit something solid.

"Hold on a second," Avery said, reaching both her thumb and index finger in and pulling out the object, "I think I found something."

Next to her, Gumptin moved around nervously, impatiently waiting to see what she had found.

Avery pulled it out and dusted it off, still not quite sure of what it was. She continued brushing the gray ash off and turning the thin finger-length object around in her hand. Then, in a flash, she realized what it was. It was a blackened and burned, thin, finger-length bone.

"Ewwww!" Avery exclaimed, dropping the bone on the ground and quickly wiping her hand off on her pants.

Gumptin immediately bent down and snatched up the bone off of the ground. He looked the bone up and down carefully. When he brought it up to his nose and sniffed it, Avery thought she might throw up. Gumptin tucked the bone away securely in one of the tiny fabric pouches he had hanging on his belt.

"Was there anything else in there?" He asked, "Any bits of flesh?"

"Flesh?!" Avery hollered, "Gross….I don't know, everything's burnt away except that icky little bone."

"This is very unusual." Gumptin said, more to himself than to Avery, "A spell cast here involving a bird bone cannot be a good thing."

Avery continued wiping the ash off on her pants, "Spells, and bird bones," Avery griped, "you magical people are just freaky. What do you think happened here?"

Gumptin shook his head, "I am not sure. I will have to consult the Elementals; only they would know."

Avery didn't have near enough energy to listen to Gumptin talk about Elementals and spells performed in sacred places. She could tell that Gumptin was concerned about whatever had happened here, but she also knew that Gumptin was one of the most diligent and dogged beings she had ever met. Whatever had happened, she knew Gumptin would figure it out.

"Fine, you'll talk to the Elementals. Can we please, please just leave now?" Avery walked over to join the other girls finishing up putting everything away.

Avery threw one last wooden sword into the pit, then covered the hole up with the large canvas and helped spread debris on top of it, making sure it was camouflaged, something Gumptin said was very important. By the time they had finished with everything, the sun was beginning to set in the sky, giving a deep purple glow to the now empty clearing.

"Very good," Gumptin told them when they had finished, "now, follow me."

It was only because Gumptin started walking in the direction of the village that the girls did as he asked.

The walk back to the village seemed to go on forever. Avery's body fought her the whole way. After twelve hours of the most grueling work Avery had ever done, her body demanded she lay down and stop using it. She tried to keep her mind on her soft comfy bed and a warm shower, just to give her enough motivation to follow Gumptin back to the village.

When they did finally make it back to the village, the girls began to disperse in their separate ways, not one of them saying or waving goodbye.

Gumptin was still walking ahead of them, and without even turning around to see that they were each on their own paths to go home, he said, "Before you return to your homes, I need the five of you to follow me." Before any of the girls had a chance to protest, Gumptin added, "You can come with me tonight, or you can come with me tomorrow after you have trained for an extra hour added on for not coming with me tonight."

Avery groaned. From where she stood she was able to see her house. There was smoke coming out of the side metal chimney and warm yellow lights shining out from the bottom floor windows. She could even see her balcony, protruding out from the large tree trunk in the growing darkness. Avery knew just beyond that balcony was her room, and in that room was a bed that she longed for more than she had ever remembered longing for anything in her life. It was hard for Avery to turn away from the inviting sight in front of her, but there was no way in the world she was going to train for an extra hour tomorrow.

The rest of the girls shared Avery's mind set, even Jade. Avery could see Jade's jaw clenched tight, a clear sign she was biting her tongue, fighting the urge to actually say what she was thinking.

They each fell in line silently behind Gumptin, following him to wherever he desired. Where he desired, as it turned out, was a large tree house. Avery wasn't going to count the trees on either side of it, but she was pretty sure the house was in the center of the village. The bark of the tree was dark and there were only two very small square windows in it, both in the front of the tree. The door leading into it was round and the same color as the bark of the tree. If it weren't for the ornate brass lock and round doorknob, it would look as if there was no door at all. There was a glass lamp on the right side of the door.

Gumptin waved one of his small hands towards the lamp and said the words, "Siata Doso Illumia."

Inside the lamp there was a small red flicker, and then it burst into an orange glow.

The girls stood, shocked. They had known Gumptin was a Wizard, but besides seeing him open the gateway, which they were told anyone could do, hadn't actually seen him do anything magical.

"Dude, that was awesome!" Skylar shouted, clapping Gumptin on the back, "If this was Earth, you could totally own Vegas!"

Once the lamp was lit, the girls could see that above the door, a small wooden sign hung from a metal post stuck into the tree. Written in dark green calligraphic letters, the sign said, 'The Library'.

"After everything you've put us through today, now you made us follow you to a library?" Jade blurted out, finished with biting her tongue, "Unless we need to learn how to fight a librarian, I'm going home."

"This is not like the libraries you are use to Jade." Gumptin told her.

Avery laughed out loud at that idea and couldn't stop herself from saying what came out of her mouth, "I don't think Jade's ever been in a library in her life, so she has no basis for comparison, Gumptin." Avery laughed even harder the more she thought about the idea of Jade in a library. Jade rarely went to school voluntarily, let alone a library.

Jade reached over and punched Avery on her upper arm, "Don't mock me in front of the elf, stupid!" She yelled at Avery.

Ignoring the fact that Jade had once again inaccurately called him an elf, Gumptin continued explaining, "This is not an actual library, per se. This is the Protectors home base. It is in here that you have your meetings, discuss your course of actions, and where Avery gives her orders."

Avery saw Sasha roll her eyes on that last part, and she wondered if the joy she felt from knowing how much it tormented Sasha to think of taking orders from her made her a bad person. It only took a brief second for Avery to come to the conclusion that she didn't care, and that she would continue to relish Sasha's aggravation.

"Inside are stockpiles of different weapons." Gumptin went on, "There are maps of every region and village on Orcatia. Notes and journals on your battles and exploits are kept in the library, some written by you, some written by me, and even others by a third party. Any letters you receive asking for help or thanking you are also kept in there. Plus, although, it is not an actual library, in the literal sense, the second floor is entirely used as a library for the Protectors." Gumptin's voice began to carry a hint of excitement as he talked about this, "There are hundreds and hundreds of books containing information on different monsters and spells, Wizards, Demons, and prophecies. There are history books detailing any and every event that has ever occurred on Orcatia." As he spoke, it was obvious how much Gumptin cared for the books, much more so than any weapon he had showed the girls how to use that day.

When he finished explaining to the girls exactly what the library was, he reached into another cloth satchel hanging from his belt and pulled out six large silver keys. He gave one to each of the girls, and held on to the sixth one for himself.

"Keep these on you at all times, and whatever you do, do not lose them." Gumptin said this, staring directly and intently at Bunny.

The key was as large as Avery's hand, and she had no idea where she was suppose to keep it. It certainly wasn't going to fit on any key chain she had ever seen. The key, itself, was tarnished silver with a fancy letter 'L' engraved into it just below the top ring loop.

Gumptin stuck his oversized key into the oversized lock and turned it, opening the door.

The girls walked into a dark and narrow entryway. From just a few feet ahead of them, they heard Gumptin shout, "Siata Doso Illumia Allea"

A few seconds after he uttered those words, every lamp inside the tree house burst into light.

Now, with everything lit up, the girls shuffled farther into the headquarters. The entryway stretched on for a few feet and was only wide enough for two girls to walk side by side comfortably.

Avery and Jade were the first two in behind Gumptin, and they squeezed their way through the entryway, their arms pressed up against each other.

It was easy enough for them to see over Gumptin, to the main room of the library. It was a large room, with the walls painted a dark green, and shaggy brown rugs scattered across the wooden floor. In the center of the room was a broad, circular, dark wooden table. There were seven chairs, all different sizes, with different colored cushions, spread around the table. On top of the table were several maps, a book entitled, 'Forces of Great Power During the Xenic Age', and multiple scraps of paper with writing on them.

As Avery moved closer to the items on the table, she was able to get a better view of the maps. Unlike the maps stuck to the wall of her room, with past events written upon them, these maps seemed to have plans for future actions drawn on them. There were red arrows drawn onto the map, pointing towards a forest region called Darksin Forest, located around the Emperor's fortress. Above the red arrows were written the words, 'Weak point, 500+ strong needed, Elves from the right, Horses to fortress gate'. Avery had no idea what it could possibly mean, but she noticed it was written in her hand writing. Another thing she noticed that was written in her hand writing were some of the notes on the strewn pieces of paper. She picked up one of the notes and read it, 'October 11th- Emperor's army at Blackmore's border. Reports of 800+. King Jeremus's army holding off invasion on western front. 200 dead. October 15th- Blackmore still holding. King Jeremus asking for help (unable to lend aid). King Draven sending part of his army to help. October 25th - Led Protectors into Hunthill. Small group of Emperor's army trying to advance on the Eastern front (were able to hold them off). Battle lasted four days. 250+ dead. Sasha received head wound (not too bad, but keep eye on her). October 27th - Stormfell Mountain dwarves joined Emperor. Heading to Stormfell to stop invasion of mountain villages. October 31st - Back from Stormfell. Village of Gunning lost.

Dwarves and Emperor's army held back (for now). Injured right shoulder. Body is sore. November 3rd - Emperor's army regrouping. Pushing harder on Blackmore. King Draven sent rest of army south to Kellington where Emperor is trying to invade from southern border. November 5th - Fight in village of Klover. Enemy led by two Were Demons. One Demon forced to talk - said Emperor will attempt to take over villages on the coast (better access to ocean ports). Leaving to port town of Secregorn tomorrow. (Body still sore - rewrap wounds before journey). November 10th - Back from Secregorn. Few small battles. Emperor's army still mainly congregating near Darksin. 4 more villages have fallen in our absence. Emperor advancing more heavily on Blackmore. King Jeremus close to falling. Port villages defended, but weak. More and more going over to Emperor. Gumptin searching for solution in his old books. Sasha and Skylar injured. Jade hurting (though she won't admit it). Bunny struggling. My body is so sore. November 13th - More fighting. Trying to advance, but not making any headway. Need the use of the King's army and the elves, any others willing to help. Over 1500+ Orcatians confirmed dead. Protectors are failing'. The last entry was dated November 17th, the day before they had died. It said, 'Nothing but more fighting. Can't hold Emperor back. More people die. Protectors grow more tired and hurt. Bunny was right, something has to change'. Below the last line were written words that had been crossed out. Avery brought the paper up to her face, to try and make out what was scratched out. The words said, 'I'm so tired. So tired. Too tired'.

 Avery read the notes she had written in her previous life on Orcatia and couldn't stop the cold knot forming in the pit of her stomach. Everything was written as simply as if it were a grocery list. Avery was surprised at the ease and detachment her previous self could have written about death and fighting. Just reading the notes made Avery feel like curling up in a little ball and crying. She wanted to curl the paper up into a little ball and throw it in the trash, but resisted since she was sure it contained information they might need sometime in the future. So instead, she let the laundry list of despair fall back onto the table. There was a momentary thought she had to try and study the notes more to get a better idea of what she should expect as a Protector, but Avery knew full well that her mind wasn't yet ready to accept the fact, that at some point in the near future, she too would have to live through the events she had written about.

Next to the notes with her writing on it, Avery spotted a piece of paper with what she recognized as Jade's hand writing. It read, "November 11th - Patrol with Skylar on the Selvin Road, encountered small group of trolls, one ugly bastard escaped (Skylar wouldn't let me follow it into Darksin - Per Avery's orders to keep out of that area), witnessed Emperor's army advancing on Blackmore - (Note: inform Avery)'. Avery smiled, it comforted her that Jade seemed at least slightly similar to her previous self. For her own part, the more and more she found out about her Orcatian life, the more tightly she wanted to hold on to the life she had on Earth.

The other girls walked up to the table to look at the maps and read the notes.

"Wow," Skylar said, after picking up Avery's notes and reading over them, "this is crazy heavy stuff. I can't believe you wrote this, Av."

Jade grabbed the paper out of Skylar's hand and glanced over it. Once she had gotten the general idea of what Avery had written, she looked up at Avery, concern written all over her face. It was obvious she hadn't liked what she read.

"Skylar's right, this is pretty heavy stuff." She told Avery, setting the piece of paper back on the table and staring back up at her, "You ok with this?"

Avery shrugged, not quite sure if she was or not, but not wanting to concern the others with any anxiety the notes had given her, "Don't worry about me." She told Jade and the rest of the girls, "I remember as much as you guys do, which is nothing. I don't remember living through those things, let alone writing about them."

"Sure," Jade said, not wanting to push her any further, "if you're fine, than I'm fine. You just don't really sound like the Avery I know in these notes."

Tell me about it, thought Avery. She turned her attention to the rest of the room to take her mind off of her past Protector activities. The dark green walls were covered with maps, just like her room. They were maps of different kingdoms, the mountainous kingdom of Blackmore, and the kingdom of Espria, which seemed to consist of mainly grasslands. There was the kingdom of Greycian, surrounded on three sides by large bodies of water. The kingdom of Eternel had dark forests and rocky mountains. Then there was a map of their own kingdom of Nightfell, with their village, Havyn, located on the map, surrounded by the Wildwood forest. King Draven's castle rested in the center of the kingdom, acting as the focal point of the map. There were a dozen other maps mounted on the walls, all of different kingdoms, with different mountain ranges, forests, villages, and oceans. Avery sincerely hoped Gumptin wasn't expecting them to learn all of the different locations and landmarks.

There was an open doorway off to the left side of the room. It led into a narrow hallway that led off to two separate smaller rooms. The first of the two rooms was a cramped weapons storage room. The walls were lined with different weapons, there were rows of crossbows, swords, axes, knives, whips, bows, and staffs. The second room was just as cramped, except this room was filled with three flimsy looking straw beds, each with one pillow and one blanket. Avery assumed they must have slept over here when they were busy and needed a quick nap. Although she couldn't imagine getting any sort of restful sleep in those awkward beds. There was one small wooden nightstand in between the first two beds with a dim lit lamp and a short stack of books. Avery didn't bother to look at what the books might be, figuring they were most likely in the same vein as the book on her bedroom night stand, involving spells, and creatures, and how to defeat them.

After a quick examination of both rooms, Avery walked back out to the main room. There was a large spiral staircase off to the right side that led up to the second floor. Avery grabbed onto the thick wooden banister and proceeded up to the next floor. The staircase was wide enough for Avery to lie down straight across the stairs head to toe, and dark burgundy carpeting covered each wooden step. It spiraled around twice before leading Avery out onto the second story landing.

The first thing that Avery noticed was the smell. The scent of dust and old books, mixed in with an almost musky cinnamon smell, floated up her nose. The floor creaked beneath Avery's feet as she walked farther into the room. There were rows and rows of bookshelves, most of them stretching over ten feet high, hitting the top of the ceiling. On the outside of the bookshelves were handwritten signs, labeling the different categories of books. Avery walked down between the two shelves labeled, 'Ancient Demons, 2000 yrs. +, M-Z', and 'Poisons, A-S'. The shelves were packed so tightly with books of every different size that some books sat on top of each other at odd angles, just daring a reader to try and grab one without causing the entire stack to topple over. Some of the books appeared fairly new, but others looked so old and tattered, Avery was sure if she tried to take them off of their shelf, they would fall apart in her hands. Avery blew on one of the rows of books on poisons beginning with the letter E and small cloud of dust blew up in her face. She coughed and cleared the air in front of her face with her hand. Rubbing at her nose, which the dust was beginning to make tickle, Avery turned her attention to the row of bookshelves. The books on Demons weren't as dusty and in much more disarray, an indication they received a lot more use than the books on poison. A black leather-bound book on the bottom row caught her attention. It was sticking out about an inch over the bottom shelf, like someone had been recently reading it and put it away hastily. Avery reached down and picked up the book. In faded red letters and a stylized cursive that Avery could barely make out, the title read, 'The Nexus Demon by Leoflin the Wizard', Avery heard someone else coming up the stairs and bent down to quickly put the book away. She didn't bother to kneel down or squat, which meant the book, looked just as it had before, sticking over the edge.

    The end of the two stacks led out to a narrow middle walkway lined with overstuffed and battered old plushy looking chairs. Brass pillar candleholders with sturdy white candles sat next to the chairs and helped to light up the room. As Avery got closer to the candles, she realized they were releasing the soft cinnamon scent gently filling the air. Avery stepped into the hallway and looked it up and down and back and forth. There were more rows of bookshelves lining the other side of the hallway. At least twenty rows of shelves, from what Avery could tell, and that was just on this side of the room. The lack of windows, burgundy walls, dark wood, candlelight, and cramped quarters lulled Avery into a relaxed state, reminding her just how tired she really was. She glanced over at a lumpy blue velvet chair and wondered if she curled up in it and fell asleep it would bother the others.

Avery was about to sit down in the chair, just to rest her aching body for a second, when Gumptin called from downstairs, "Ladies, can I see you all down here for a moment?"

Avery stopped herself half-sit, and ignoring her screaming thighs, made her way down the stairs. She was followed down the stairs by Bunny, who had a book in her hand. Avery had figured that if one of them was going to walk out of there with a book in hand, it would be Bunny.

When Avery arrived downstairs she saw Jade, Skylar, and Sasha entering from the weapons storage room and that Gumptin had laid out a few weapons on the large round table. Among other things, there were five broadswords tied together with a leather buckle strap.

"These are yours." Gumptin said, handing out the swords to each of the girls.

Each sword was different, and the one Avery was handed had a thick steel cross-guard with an intricate scroll work etched into it. The grip was white pearlescent and the pommel at the top of the hilt was a silver crescent moon with a crystal jewel inlay. The sword was safely tucked away in a black leather scabbard that silver horses emblazoned on it.

Avery unsheathed the sword and held tightly onto the smooth handle. She swung it back and forth a little, making sure she didn't hit any of her fellow Protectors in the process. The sword was heavy, but not so much that it gave Avery trouble to wield it with just one hand. Avery couldn't understand or describe how holding the sword was making her feel. She had practiced with a wooden sword in the clearing earlier today, but something about holding this particular sword, at this moment, was causing some sort of feeling to stir up inside of her. Avery would have thought it was a feeling of comfort, if she hadn't believed it utterly ridiculous to be comforted by a metal object used for killing things.

"These are all of your everyday weapons. They were summoned back to the village with you after you died." Gumptin told the girls, as he handed out the rest of the weapons he had placed on the table.

"I just love how you talk about us dying, with about as much emotion as you would have ordering a drink." Jade said sarcastically, grabbing onto a ragged silver handled knife Gumptin was handing over to her.

Gumptin scrunched up his nose, "I never drink," he said, shaking his head emphatically, "it has devastatingly awful affects on my Wizarding abilities."

Avery smiled, imaging the incident that led Gumptin to that realization.

Gumptin handed Avery three different daggers, a medium sized one with a white handle and jewel on top, that Gumptin told her went into her belt, another medium sized dagger with a thin brass handle that went into her boot, and a third long steel dagger in a black leather sheath with two straps that went around her wrist and arm. The second Avery took the dagger out of the sheath, a flash of an image went off inside of her head, she saw herself unsheathe the dagger, and then saw a flood of red cover her hands. The image lasted less than a second, and then it was gone. Avery grabbed on to the table to stop herself from teetering over.

"Are you alright?" Jade asked, concerned, about ready to put down the dangerous looking curved dagger she was stroking admiringly and rush to Avery's side.

"I'm fine," Avery said, stopping Jade by holding up her hand, "it's just hitting me how tired I am."

"You and me both." Skylar quipped, "Not even dance practice prepared me for this."

Avery smiled at Skylar and avoided eye contact with Jade. She figured it was probably just some weird déjà vu she was having from her life before Earth. Nothing to worry herself over, she told herself, and certainly nothing to worry Jade over.

Gumptin handed Avery a wide black leather belt with a silver buckle and what looked like another smaller black leather belt with straps attached to it. Avery just stared at it, not taking it from Gumptin's hand. The belt, itself, she understood, but she had no idea how she was suppose to wear the smaller belt with the straps.

"Get down here." Gumptin grumbled, frustrated he was having to actually show her how to put it on.

Avery kneeled down. Gumptin strapped the belt around Avery's ribcage, just below her chest. Gumptin pulled it tight and attempted to fasten the buckle into the well-worn second belt hole.

"Ouch!" Avery cried out as Gumptin braced his shoulder against Avery's body and pulled with all his strength on the belt, finally fastening it.

"There, how is that?" He said, panting, looking proudly at the fastened belt.

"Tight," Avery grimaced, trying to move her ribcage around under the constrictive belt, "it hurts."

Gumptin stared at Avery and the belt scrutinizingly, "Hmmm, I think you have gained a few pounds since you have last worn that."

Avery stopped squirming under the belt and glared at Gumptin with a look that could kill. Standing above Avery, Sasha guffawed, and even Jade couldn't stop herself from snickering a little.

"Now, that's a real ouch." Skylar joked, laughing.

Completely oblivious to the laughs of the other girls, Gumptin suggested, "Perhaps we should try to loosen it one belt loop."

Sasha burst into laughter.

"It'll be fine!" Avery snapped, abruptly ending the weight part of the conversation, "Just show me what to do with the other straps.

Gumptin took the straps, which were attached to the back of the belt, and crisscrossed them over Avery's shoulders and across her chest, where they attached into two little holes on the front of the belt. Now that Avery was all strapped in properly to the contraption, she still had no idea what purpose it served.

Gumptin reached up to the table and picked up what looked like an oversized sword sheath with two small circular straps on the underside. It was made out of black leather, just like Avery's belt and had the same silver horse design emblazoned on it as her sword sheath did. There were fifteen long arrows with white feather tips sticking out from inside of it.

"This is a quiver," Gumptin said, "it is used to hold your arrows in."

He strapped the quiver onto one of the straps crisscrossing Avery's back. Then, took the sheath for Avery's sword, and with two small leather straps, tied the sheath on to the second strap crisscrossing Avery's back.

Avery picked up the sword Gumptin had given her and slid it into the sheath. Once the sword was in its sheath, Avery reached back with her right hand and pulled the sword out. She felt the blade of the sword graze her hair, centimeters away from her ear. Avery made a mental note to practice that move some more before trying it again and at a much slower speed.

Next, Gumptin grabbed one of five bows that had been leaning against the table. The one he handed Avery was made out of a dark wood, so dark it almost looked black, with a silver vine design encircling it. If Avery had been standing it would have reached up to her waist. The ends were curved slightly and had silver metal tips. Gumptin hooked the bow around the quiver on Avery's back.

"Stand up," he told her, "stand up and turn around. How does it feel?"

Avery did as Gumptin instructed. She stood up and moved around, turning and bending.

Gumptin smiled, "Feels good, does it not?" He said, "You use to wear that all the time before you went to Earth. It was like a second skin to you."

Honestly, to Avery, it didn't feel good at all. It felt constrictive and cumbersome, and Avery couldn't wait till she was able to take it off.

"Whatever," Avery sighed under her breath, and then, not wanting to upset Gumptin's smiling and proud face too much, she said loudly, "It feels great."

"I knew it would." Gumptin beamed and continued to pass out the rest of the weapons to the girls.

By the time Gumptin had finished distributing all the weapons, Avery not only had her sword, bow, arrows, and daggers, but also a crossbow and whip that Gumptin told her attached to the saddle she would be using on her horse.

"Are we done, already?" Sasha asked, trying to hold on to all of the weapons Gumptin had just given her, but doing a poor job as a tiny dagger the size of a toothpick slipped out of her hands and onto the floor, "Can we go home and try to get some sleep," She said angrily, picking up her dagger off the ground, "or is there some new torment you'd like to put us through?"

Gumptin shrugged nonchalantly and shook his head, "No," he answered, "you may leave now."

The girls let out sighs of relief and began to try and amble out of the library.

"Just remember," Gumptin called out, before any of them had a chance to make it through the door and out to freedom, "dawn tomorrow, same place, and this time make sure you are all on time! I would hate to have to make you work any harder than you already fail at doing!"

All of the girls ignored him, except for Jade, who for the second time that day, presented Gumptin with her middle finger raised high up in the air.

Avery and Jade were the last two girls left in the library, when Avery turned to Jade and said, "You go ahead. I'm going to have a little talk with Gumptin about tomorrow's training session."

"I'll stay with you for that." Jade told Avery, "I'd like to have a little *talk* with Gumptin about our training sessions, too."

Avery chuckled, "No, that's exactly why you should go. If you end up *talking* to Gumptin, we'll all end up spending an extra two hours in training."

Jade hesitated for a moment; then gave in, "Fine," she said, "just don't waste too much time with him. I can tell that little bastard isn't gonna go easy on us, and you need to make sure you get some rest."

"I will." Avery told her, "See you tomorrow."

The real reason Avery had wanted to talk to Gumptin alone had nothing to do with training. She wanted to speak with him about the incident involving the eyes in the gateway at the park. Avery had wanted to talk with Gumptin alone so as not to worry the other girls, and with this new life of hers being so hectic, now seemed like the only time she would be able to do it. Avery walked over to where Gumptin was sitting at the table, writing something down on a large yellow parchment of paper.

"Something is troubling you." Gumptin said, continuing to write, "You may have changed a great deal Avery, even more than I would like to admit, but you would never come speak to me alone unless something were bothering you," Gumptin looked up at her, "and that has not changed."

Avery sat down in the seat next to Gumptin and proceeded to tell him about the terrible black eyes she had seen floating in the Ora Gateway before she had jumped in and how they had produced the sharp pain she had felt in her chest.

Gumptin listened intently, taking in every detail of Avery's description. When she had finished, Gumptin sighed and hung his head, a weary look clouding over his face. Avery could tell Gumptin knew exactly what it was she had seen and that it might be worse than she had thought.

"That, Avery," Gumptin said, a tired strain in his voice, "was the Emperor. Those were his eyes. He is powerful enough to use the gateway as a mirror to see into different worlds. If you saw his eyes, it means that he saw you, and that he now knows the Protectors are alive and back on Orcatia. It means that he will most likely try and attack soon, sooner than I had hoped. It means you will not have time for much training before returning to fighting." Gumptin sighed even deeper, "This is very troubling Avery. Someone must have told him of your return; it is the only way he could have known what gateway to look through and when." He rubbed at his temples, "I really must speak to the Elementals, and soon."

The sight of Gumptin looking so weary troubled Avery more than what Gumptin had to say. Yes, Avery could admit that the eyes she had seen had been terrifying, but besides what she had been told, a pair of glowering eyes, and some random scribbling on a few pieces of paper, Avery had no real experience with the Emperor. To Avery, Gumptin might as well have been talking about some villain out a scary story. She tried to convince her mind and body to be scared or apprehensive, but as of this moment, it just wasn't working.

The one thing that did concern her slightly, she decided to ask about, "Gumptin, what was that pain I felt in my chest when saw those eyes?"

Gumptin shrugged, not seeming near as bothered by it as Avery was, "It was most likely just the Emperor's power causing your body to remember something it connects with Emperor. More like an echo of pain than actual pain."

This took Avery back, "Echo my ass, it actually hurt!" She protested.

"Yes, I suppose it would," Gumptin told her, "but it won't actually physically harm you in any way."

That was all Avery could take hearing for the night. The Emperor knew they were back, Gumptin was going to talk to the Elementals, and her heart was intact and damage free. Anything else Gumptin had to say, Avery was way beyond too tired to listen to. Avery stood up and gathered all of her weapons into and under her arms.

"Well, I hate to leave when you look so depressed," She said to Gumptin, "but you kicked my butt too hard today for me not to go home and try to get some rest."

When Gumptin didn't answer her after a few seconds, lost in thought, staring down at the paper he had written on not long ago, Avery took it as her queue to leave. She gave Gumptin one last concerned look, then walked out of the library and into the dark Orcatian night.

Avery could see the large trees of the forest silhouetted through the moonlight in front of her. The black still forest was in sharp contrast to the busy village going on around her. Bright lights shone out from the giant tree houses to her right and left, and out of those same houses poured the delightful smells of evening dinners. Avery took a deep breath in, the smells of meats, breads, and spices made her stomach growl, letting Avery know just how much it was craving food. Gripping tighter on to the weapons she was holding, so as not to drop any, she turned to her right and began to make her way home.

Three tree houses down she stopped in front of Bott's Apothecary & Sweets. She hadn't meant to stop, but the delicious scents of cinnamon, vanilla, yeast, and chocolate, literally stopped her in her tracks, and once again caused her stomach to scream out its hunger.

Mrs. Bott was standing in the open doorway sweeping off a yellow welcome matt with her broom. Her hair was up in a bun piled on top of her head, just as Avery had always seen it, and stuffed under a purple bonnet with a pink bow on top. She wore a purple dress with a pink and red striped apron tied around her plump waist, although, Avery didn't see the point of her wearing an apron at all, since she seemed to have more flour stained across her actual dress than on the apron.

When Mrs. Bott glanced up and saw Avery gazing into her shop, a huge smile swept over her face and she exclaimed, "Avery, what a lovely surprise!"

She threw her broom down behind her, not caring where it landed and quickly shuffled over to sweep Avery up in an encompassing hug. Avery grunted as the impact of the hug caused the crossbow she was carrying under her arm to slam into her side.

Mrs. Bott, still smiling broadly, released Avery, and then with just one breath, rushed to tell her, "Oh, it's so nice to see you! What are you doing here?" She looked down at all the weapons Avery had in her hands, "What on Orcatia is all that stuff you're lugging around? Oh, you must be here to see Wilbur! Are you sure you can carry all of that by yourself; you're such a tiny little thing. Wilbur," she called out, "Avery's here! Of course, I suppose you can carry heavy stuff better than any man here. Wilbur, get out here!"

Avery gazed at Mrs. Bott, shocked at how the woman could say so much in just one breath. Avery didn't know how to respond to her, or if she was even suppose to for that matter.

"Wilbur!" Mrs. Bott yelled, again, "Would you please get your string bean butt out here?!"

A split second later, a skinny bald man with a gray beard and bushy eyebrows, standing over six feet tall, came rushing out of the shop. He was hurrying so fast, he didn't see the broom Mrs. Bott had discarded on the ground. His large right foot caught under the broom handle, tripping him, causing him to pummel forward, right into Mrs. Bott's back. Luckily, she was sturdy enough for the impact only to move her a step forward. She turned and looked at the poor man as if he had just spanked a chicken.

"Sorry, Beatrice," He told her timidly, "I think somebody left something in the doorway that I tripped over."

Mrs. Bott scoffed, hitting Wilbur lightly in the stomach, "Don't be ridiculous, no one would do such a thing."

Wilbur nodded and coughed slightly, "Yes, dear, whatever you say."

"Anyway," Mrs. Bott said lightly, changing the subject, "Avery is here to see you."

Avery, who hadn't said a word since Mrs. Bott had seen her, suddenly realized she was going to have to speak. Watching Mrs.

Bott and Wilbur had been like watching a film. So much so, that she had actually forgotten she was supposed to be a part of the interaction.

Avery shook her head, focusing her thoughts, "No…no," she stammered, "I'm not here to see him." She nodded her head towards Wilbur, unable to point with her hands so full, "I was just walking home from training and stopped to smell your food. It smelled soooo good, I couldn't help it."

"Oh." Mrs. Bott said, sounding slightly surprised, and then bursting into laughter, "Oh, dear me." Mrs. Bott laughed so hard she had to wipe her eyes, "To think of it," she giggled, "Avery Kimball here for my treats."

Mrs. Bott was laughing so heartily, Avery almost felt like she should laugh along with her, but the fact she had no idea what the woman was laughing at stopped her.

"Beatrice," Wilbur said, placing his hands on Mrs. Bott's shoulders, trying to stop her from laughing, "the girl doesn't remember anything from this life."

Mrs. Bott's laughter died down till she was almost frowning, "Oh, dear, I keep forgetting. You poor little thing. Let me explain, you see Wilbur, here," she pointed to where he was standing behind her, "he's actually my husband, Mr. Bott. Now, I know it's hard to believe that someone as appealing as myself, would marry such a gigantic splinter of a man, but sometimes you just can't fight the obstacle hurdling power of love."

Avery stifled any laughter rising in her throat, pretending she had a cough, just in case Mrs. Bott wasn't joking.

"Anyway," Mrs. Bott continued, "he's the apothecary in Bott's Apothecary & Sweets, and I'm the sweets. Despite his appearance, he really is quite an extraordinary apothecary. People come to him from all over the kingdom, and sometimes even other kingdoms. Naturally, as a Protector you would use his services. You use to come quite frequently to see him for remedies, potions, for cuts, sprains, bruises, and worse. I only thought you were here to see him because you haven't come to this shop for my sweets since you were about four years old."

"Really?" Avery asked, finding that hard to believe.

Everyone she knew, knew she had a notorious sweet tooth. In fact, for lunches back on Earth, sometimes she would make due with a soda and candy bar, unhealthy to be sure, but always enjoyable.

"Oh, yes," Mrs. Bott told her, "you weren't like Jade or Skylar. They were in here all the time for breads and cookies, mostly after a battle or hard training session." Mrs. Bott laughed at the memories playing in her head, "I think Jade was in here more than she was at home…such a pistol of a girl"

That, Avery could believe, especially with Jade. That girl ate like a horse, any and everything she could get her hands on. It always amazed Avery how Jade managed to stay so thin, when it looked like she ate more than she actually weighed.

"You, on the other hand," Mrs. Bott said smiling, resting her hand on Avery's shoulder, "were always the little soldier. You made sure you stayed in perfect physical condition. You never put anything in your body that wasn't good for you. So, I suppose you never had any reason to come and see me." Mrs. Bott still smiled as she said this, but Avery could see a slight hurt behind her round bright eyes.

Avery squirmed a little in the tight belt strapped around her ribs, thinking about how her past Orcatian self would feel about all the pizza, soda, candy, and tacos her Earth self had consumed over the past sixteen years. For some reason she couldn't understand, especially considering they were technically the same person, but she took pleasure in the knowledge that it would probably piss her Orcatian self off.

"Well, Mrs. Beatrice Bott, you can guarantee that this Avery will be stopping by frequently for your delicious delights." Avery said this to Mrs. Bott, slightly to cheer her up, but mostly because it was the truth.

Mrs. Bott clapped and smiled fuller than Avery had seen yet.

"Would you like something now?" She asked and ran inside her shop, not bothering to wait for Avery's reply. It didn't really matter, since Avery's reply would have been a definite yes.

Wilbur smiled softly as he watched his wife bounce off into her shop, "I think you just made her day." He told Avery warmly.

"Trust me, the feeling's mutual." She told Wilbur.

Mrs. Bott came bounding back with a pink colored sack full of sweet smelling goodies. She slipped the thin handle of the sack between Avery's thumb and forefinger, the only place Avery had left to hold on to anything. Avery left the smiling Mr. and Mrs. Bott, promising to come back soon for more treats.

The sight of her own house, with its soft light pouring out of the windows, lighting up the space in front of it, and multiple flower beds, gave Avery a feeling of relief. She didn't necessarily consider it home, that space in her heart belonged to a little peach adobe house back in Redemption, but the thought of the soft bed waiting for her and her family somewhere inside, comforted her more than anything else could on this planet.

Just as she was about to step up to her front door, movement at the stables to her right caught her eye. She turned her head and saw a small, scraggily looking man lifting a saddle half the size of him off of the ground by the hitching posts and teetering with it into the barn. Avery watched him stagger from side to side then front to back, before getting a small semblance of balance.

It took Avery a second to decide what to do; after all, she had made it so close to peace and rest. Avery sighed long and hard and looked up to the black sky with its blanket of stars, "Typical." She said under her breath. She set all of her weapons down on the wooden bench to the side of the door. The bag of treats Mrs. Bott had given her and the long steel dagger that had given her the case of déjà vu both slid off of the bench as she let go of the pile of weapons. Avery made a grab for the sweets, letting the dagger fall to the ground and into the dirt.

"That was close." She said, delicately setting the bag down, then bending over, picking up the dagger, and tossing it back onto the weapon pile.

Avery walked over to the entrance of the stable where she had seen the man stagger into. The musky smell of hay and horses hit her. It caused her nose to tickle a little, but other than that was quite pleasant, even soothing. She entered the stable and looked around. The stalls and inside walls were made out of the same dark wood as the outside of the stables, and the entire ground was covered with straw-like yellow hay. To Avery's left, was an extremely large walkway with stalls of horses lining both sides. To Avery's right, there was a much shorter walkway with a few stalls of horses on one side and rows of saddles protruding out of the wall on the other side. The stalls themselves were good sized, with crescent moon shaped stall doors. In between each stall was a small, round, opaque glass lamp, casting everything in a dark firelight. In front of Avery were two bulky barn doors. Avery was about to grab onto one of the doors hefty metal handles, when the door swung open out towards her, and the little man she had followed in came scurrying out, carrying a bucket of oats.

Avery shrieked in an embarrassingly high pitch and jumped back. At the same time, the man hollered loudly and dropped his bucket, spilling the oats out all over the ground.

"Jumpin' June bugs!" the man shouted, bending down to pick up his bucket, "Sneakin' about like a troll in the night, what's wrong with ya?"

Before Avery answered, she tried to calm her breathing down. Even though she had caused him to drop a bucket of oats, he had startled her just as much as she had startled him.

"I wasn't sneaking," She gasped out, "I was coming to see if you needed any help."

The man huffed, "Do I look like I need any..." he looked up at Avery before he had finished what he was going to say and stopped mid-sentence.

Now that he was looking at her, Avery could see he was a man in his sixties, with tufts of graying hair encircling a small bald spot on top of his head. His skin was tight and leathery, like he had been working outside in the sun and elements his entire life. He had thin drawn lips that made his face look even tauter than it actually was. All in all, he looked quite unpleasant, except for the kind brown almond shaped eyes that stared up at her.

"Ms. Avery," he said, blinking, "I didn't know it was you. I'm sorry if I sounded a bit harsh." His voice was genuine, and as he talked to her, he hugged the bucket he had picked up against his chest, like a child clinging onto a stuffed animal for comfort. It gave Avery the impression she was making him nervous in some way.

"That's fine," Avery told him, faking a smile, "it really wasn't that harsh anyway." Not compared to some of the things Gumptin had shouted at her during training, "I'm Avery." Avery said, holding out her hand. She was aware that the man obviously knew that, but since she had no idea who she was talking to, she felt introductions were in order.

The man stared at her for a moment, then at her outstretched hand, then back at her, looking uncertain. Eventually, a slow smile began to form on his face.

"Oh, I forgot…ya don't remember a thing do ya?" He reached out his hand and grabbed onto Avery's, shaking it vigorously, "Well, I'm Thomas, Ms. Avery, Thomas Mullimany. I run these here stables, have for the past forty years." Thomas's chest puffed out slightly. It was an apparent source of pride for him, and Avery had to admit, they were the cleanest stables she had ever seen.

Avery remembered Pip telling her he worked for a man named Thomas in the stables.

"Well, it's nice to meet you." Avery said, this time with a genuine smile, "The stables look awesome. You and Pip do a really great job."

Behind Thomas's leathery tan skin, Avery could swear she could almost see him blushing, "That's might kind of ya."

Avery pointed outside, to the heavy saddles by the hitching post, "Did you need help with those?" She asked Thomas.

"Oh, no, I wouldn't want ya to strain yourself." Thomas joked, laughing heartily at his own humor. He knew Avery was strong enough to carry all of the saddles with hardly any effort if she wanted to.

"Are you sure?" Avery persisted, "I've supposedly got the strength of like ten men. It would be no trouble for me."

To Avery, Thomas looked like he barely had the strength of a child, let alone one grown man. How he managed to carry the first saddle in all by himself was a mystery to Avery.

Thomas shook his head, "No, no, Ms. Avery, it's me job. Plus, I've still got to clean and polish them."

Avery accepted Thomas's refusal without further argument. After all, she hadn't really wanted to help carry the cumbersome saddles in the first place; she just knew how guilty she would have felt if she hadn't asked.

"Well, if you ever need any help, you know where I live." Avery told him, "Of course, Gumptin keeps us so busy I probably won't be there, but you can always try." Avery turned to leave, but turned quickly back around, remembering something else she wanted to tell Thomas, "Oh, by the way, just call me Avery, no Ms. Avery…just Avery."

Thomas just stared at Avery for a few seconds, a small smile on his face, "Ya know, Ms. Avery....oh, sorry, just Avery. Anyway, ya know, I think this is the longest conversation we've ever had."

This shocked Avery, "But you said you've been here at these stables for forty years. That means you've been like fifteen feet away from me for my whole life."

"I watched ya grow up." He said.

Avery didn't understand, "So, why didn't I talk to you?"

Thomas looked at the ground and then back up to Avery, as if searching for an answer to her question, "Ya just had other stuff to do."

Avery didn't like that answer at all. She couldn't think of anything that she would have to do that would prevent her from having a short conversation with a perfectly nice man whom she had known for her entire life.

Then, a thought popped into her head, "Oh, my God, was I a bitch?!"

"What?! No, no," Thomas said quickly, dropping the bucket he had been holding and raising his palms in the air to stop her current train of thought, "ya were very polite. Ya'd say 'hello' and 'goodbye' and sometimes ya'd even ask me how I was doing. Ya just were so busy with everything. Ya didn't have time to think about anything but being a Protector, about doing your job and doing it well. Ya didn't have time for people like me."

Thomas's words hit Avery like a slap across the face. Avery hoped against hope that whoever she had been, hadn't given Thomas and the other villagers the impression she didn't have time for them. No matter what being a Protector had in store for them, she could never imagine isolating herself off from the people she saw every day. As disgusted as it made Avery to think that people could feel as if they weren't important enough for her to concern herself with, she also knew the person she was now would never give off that sort of perception. Avery walked over to Thomas and picked up the bucket he had dropped twice now.

Handing the bucket to him, she said, "Thomas, I promise, that's not me. This time around you'll get a lot more than just 'hello' and 'goodbye'. So much so, that you'll actually probably wish I would just shut up."

Thomas took the bucket from Avery's hands, keeping his eyes on the ground, and even though he wasn't looking at Avery, she could still see him blush slightly again, a small close lipped smile on his face.

Thomas cleared his throat and glanced up at Avery, "Thank ya," he said, "but like I said before, ya were never unkind, just preoccupied. Plus, anytime ya came in the stables before, it was usually for your boy."

Avery tried to decipher Thomas's sentence. She could assume that he wasn't actually talking about a real boy. To help Avery out, Thomas pointed to his left, and Avery's eyes followed to what he was pointing at. Straight down the short walkway to Avery's right, in the very last stall, facing outward, an enormous black horse stuck its head out as far as the stall door would allow him.

"He's yours," Thomas told Avery, "name's Phantom…good, good horse. Never a day went by that ya didn't see him, so he's missed ya quite a lot."

Avery had always loved horses. When she was younger, she and Skylar had taken horseback riding lessons at a ranch outside of town. From then on out, she had always wanted her own horse, but knew not to ask since her parents wouldn't have been able to afford it.

The big black horse whinnied softly, stomping his front foot upon the ground as Avery approached him. She walked past four other horses before she reached him, a medium sized dark brown horse, with a circular nameplate on his stall that said 'Ajax', a petite all white horse, whose star shaped nameplate read, 'Dancer', a good sized dusky gray horse that had the name, 'Belle' written on its nameplate, and an athletic looking buckskin with a square nameplate and the name, 'Steel' carved into it.

When Avery reached Phantom's stall, he dug his huge head into her torso and started to rub her with it. The initial force knocked Avery back slightly, but she recovered herself quickly, patting him on his large nose. He was the biggest horse Avery had ever seen, a good foot taller than the rest of the horses. He was completely midnight black, except for the shaggy white hair around his massive hooves. His breath was hot against Avery's stomach, and she giggled as he started to nibble on her dirty shirt.

"Did you miss me?" Avery asked, brushing Phantom's long, shaggy, silky mane out of his eyes.

Phantom reached his head up and lightly brushed Avery's cheek with his warm nose.

Avery laughed, "I'll take that as a yes."

Avery spent another twenty minutes with Phantom, brushing his soft coat, feeding him oats, and basically enjoying his company. Thomas told Avery that Phantom and the rest of the Protectors' horses had been rigorously trained, due to the fact they were with the Protectors for every battle and every mission and needed to behave accordingly. So, at Avery's request Thomas showed her all of Phantom's commands, and Avery haltered up Phantom and took him to the large fenced in pasture behind the stables to practice the commands on him. She practiced getting him to stay, coming to her when she whistled, kneeling down on his two front legs, rearing back on his hind legs, walking, trotting, and running on command. Phantom was so well trained, it didn't matter if Avery was giving the commands correctly, he still knew what to do, something Avery was thankful for.

Although Avery could have stayed out there for hours in the cool night air, working with Phantom, it was getting late, and she had promised Jade she would get a good night's sleep. Avery walked Phantom back into his stall and unhaltered him. She gave him one last handful of oats and a pat goodbye. She could see why the old Avery had spent so much time with Phantom. Unlike training with Gumptin, it was actually enjoyable, and she didn't feel the need to vomit after twenty minutes.

As Avery was about to leave the stables she saw Pip walk in from the back entrance.

Pip smiled widely when he saw her, "Thomas told me ya were here. I don't know what ya said to him, but he's in an awfully good mood."

The thought that something she had said put Thomas in a good mood made Avery feel warm all over, like she had made up for her past transgressions, "We just worked Phantom out for a little bit." Avery told him.

Pip might not have been convinced that was all Avery did to put Thomas in a good mood, but he didn't question Avery, "Well, whatever ya did, ya made him happy."

Avery smiled, "I'm glad."

Pip stared at Avery intently a small furrow forming between his brows. Then, after giving Avery a quick look up and down his face relaxed into a small sideways smirk, "Ya know, it's strange," Pip said to Avery, shaking his head, "I know you've had a whole other sixteen years on another planet, but to everyone here, you've only been gone a few days. It's just weird to see ya so different. It's almost like you're a whole new person."

"You know, I'm going to take that as a compliment." Avery wasn't sure Pip had meant it as one, or if it was just an observation, but after the very few details she had learned about her former self, she was going to take it as a compliment whether it was intended as one or not.

"Well, ya seem a lot more open now, more…warm." Pip said, "So, I suppose that's a compliment, but I always liked who ya were."

"Pip…" Avery was about to ask Pip exactly what that girl, who he had always liked, had precisely been like, but she stopped herself, not quite sure she was ready to hear the entire version of her old self. So, instead she finished with, "I'll see you tomorrow."

Pip pursed his lips together, looking slightly disappointed, as if he had known Avery was about to get more personal, but decided to stop herself.

"Night." he told Avery, walking away to help Thomas with the nighttime stable duties.

Avery meandered back to her house. The weapons and sweets were lying on the bench where Avery had left them. She bent down and piled them all back into her arms. They seemed even more difficult to hold onto this time than they had before she set them down.

As Avery struggled with the large doorknob on her front door, cursing Gumptin for making her carry home so much bulky junk, she heard her three dogs run up to the door, barking. Once she did finally manage to turn the knob and open the door, her two rambunctious German Shepherds charged her, leaping up on her and knocking everything except the bag of sweets, which she held onto with an iron grip, out of her arms. Avery pushed the fallen weapons to one side of the entryway and proceeded to give each of her slobbering dogs a giant bear hug. She intended to pick up the weapons later when she actually needed to use them. After giving each dog equal amounts of love, Avery looked up and saw her parents and Cinder sitting down at the dining room table.

"Avery!" Cinder shouted, jumping up from her seat at the table and running towards her big sister with her arms flailing wildly.

Cinder made her way through the wall of dogs and wrapped her arms around Avery's waist. Normally, Avery would have bent down to hug Cinder tightly and pick her up into her arms, but today, Avery's tired body just wouldn't allow that to happen. So, instead, she remained upright, hugging Cinder around her shoulders.

"You know what I did today?" Cinder asked, staring up at Avery, resting her chin against Avery's stomach, "Guess what I did today. You'll never guess what I did today. Guess what I did today." Cinder jumped up and down, unable to control her excitement, her blond curls bobbing up and down with her.

Avery was too exhausted for guessing games, but Cinder seemed so excited, she didn't want to burst her bubble, "I don't know, what did you do?" Avery asked, trying to sound eager to hear Cinder's answer.

"Well," Cinder said, grabbing hold of Avery's hand and walking her over to the dining table, "first, this morning, when I was still tired, mommy and I went out to the garden and planted purple flowers. Then, we picked some tomatoes and lettuce. Then, we picked some apples off a tree. Well, Mommy picked them and handed them to me and told me not to eat them till we got inside. Then, I helped Mommy bake some bread, which made the house smell really really yummy. Then, we walked down to the store and bought more stuff I wasn't allowed to eat, and I met a really nice girl named Ginger. She's a year younger than me, but that's ok, 'cause she's still nice and likes cats. Then, I came home and colored, and then I helped Mommy with dinner."

"Wow," Avery said, rubbing her little sister on top of her blond head, "it sounds like your day was a lot busier than mine."

The square dining room table had a purple and green plaid tablecloth strewn over it, and in the center, sat a green ceramic vase with bright bell shaped pink flowers sticking out of it. There was a basket full of warm sliced bread, still slightly steaming, a big pot of what looked like vegetable soup, a pitcher of water, and a leafy green salad sitting on the table.

Avery sat down across from Cinder where a place for her had already been set. Her mother ladled her a bowl of soup and as the smell of spices and broth hit her nose; Avery could feel her stomach lurch. Avery was too hungry to even bother with a spoon. She picked up her bowl with both hands and slurped down the warm salty broth and chopped vegetables. Cinder giggled as she watched Avery attack the basket full of bread, slamming a large piece into her mouth.

"Avery, honey, maybe you should slow down." Her mother told her, holding her own spoon above her untouched soup.

Avery held up her finger to her mother as she tried to swallow her large mouthful of bread, "Mom," she swallowed hard, "if you knew what Gumptin had put us through today, you'd be asking me why I only downed my little bowl of soup, instead of the whole pot. To which the answer is…I was trying to be polite."

"Speaking of today," her father said, slurping his own soup up, "how did everything go?"

There were a hundred different answers running through Avery's mind, like, 'horrible', 'I hated it', 'my life officially sucks', 'if the Emperor doesn't kill me, Gumptin's training will', but, "Fine." Was the answer she decided to go with.

Her mother looked at her with concern, "Did Gumptin say anything?"

This question puzzled Avery slightly. She wasn't quite sure what her mother was asking. After all, Gumptin had said a lot of stuff, most of it insulting, and definitely nothing her mother would be concerned with.

"About what?" Avery asked.

"About how your training was going. Does he think you're at the level you were before Earth? Is he going to make sure you get an adequate amount of training before you're actually expected to go into battle? Does he know anything about the Emperor's plans? Do those plans include the Protectors? How does he plan to get you better prepared this time?" Avery's mother rattled off her laundry list of questions without any pause, looking intently at her daughter, fully expecting an answer for each question.

Avery just stared at her mother, one dark eyebrow raised. She stuffed another piece of bread in her mouth, stalling for a little time. There was no way Avery wanted to discuss any of that with her family. She wanted to keep all the conversations involving her previous and possibly future death between herself, the other Protectors, and Gumptin. She wanted to keep her family, especially Cinder, removed from that worry, both for their sake and her own sanity.

"We just trained, Mom." Avery told her mother, knowing full well it wasn't the answer her mother wanted, "I don't think Gumptin feels there's really too much to worry about right now." Avery lied.

The look on her mother's face showed Avery she really didn't believe her lie.

Avery's father reached over and rested his hand on Avery's arm, "Are you alright, sweetheart?" He asked.

Again, Avery didn't know how she was supposed to answer. Of course, she wasn't alright; she had just spent the entire day going through Gumptin's boot camp from hell; she was going to spend tomorrow doing the same thing and all for the purpose of getting her and the other girls prepared to face the psycho who had already killed them once.

"Why wouldn't I be alright?" Avery asked, then chugged a giant gulp of water to stop herself from showing any emotion.

"Well, your mother and I were just worried that maybe this all might be a little overwhelming for you." Her father told her, "That, maybe you might not be able to handle it as well as you did before."

Her father's words caused Avery to prickle slightly. It annoyed her that her father would suggest that her old self, who had died, by the way, was more capable of handling anything better than she could now.

"I'm fine." Avery said in a clipped tone, not trying to hide her irritation.

Avery saw her mother glance at her father, then back at Avery, then back at her father, and then both of them glanced back at Avery, concern written all over their faces.

That was enough for Avery. It had been far too long of a day for her to sit there and deal with this.

After one more chug of water, Avery informed her parents, "I'm going to bed."

She stood up out of her seat, walked over and gave Cinder a kiss on the top of her head, "Night, Cin. Goodnight Mom and Dad." Avery told them.

As Avery clumped slowly up the stairs, she heard her sister chanting, "Goodnight…sleep tight…don't let the bedbugs bite!"

The moment Avery entered her room; she ambled over to her bed and collapsed on top of it, not even bothering to get undressed.

The last thoughts that passed through Avery's mind as she lay on her stomach, face buried in her puffy pillows, were of her parents questions and concerns. She thought they were reasonable fears and didn't totally blame her parents for bringing them up; she just couldn't share them. Avery was sure that deep down inside of herself somewhere she had to be scared; it just hadn't become a real thing for her yet. She wondered if she was foolish, or just really dumb for not being scared of the Emperor. Then, she thought that maybe it was a good thing she was either foolish or dumb, because if she allowed herself to fully comprehend what she was going to have to face, she would run screaming into the nearest hole.

Avery sighed heavily, turning her face towards the night sky, framed by her balcony doors, before mumbling to herself, "I can't believe it's only been one damn day."

Then, she quickly fell into a deep dreamless sleep.

Chapter 8

The next week was a blur of exhaustion and pain to Avery. Gumptin had them up at dawn training harder and harder each day. It horrified Avery and the other girls to discover Gumptin had actually taken it easy on them the first day.

Along with their normal training routine, Gumptin had somehow managed to incorporate two hours of study time in the library for the Protectors as well. Gumptin had them learning about different beasts and Demons. They studied maps and were lectured to about the history of Orcatia. Avery and Bunny took to the studying easily, just as they had at school back on Earth. Of course, for Avery it was more of a fear of failure than actual interest in the subject matter. Skylar, due to her flightiness, and Avery suspected, possible ADD, got about a third of what Gumptin taught them. Even though Sasha seemed to spend more time painting her nails and applying balm to her lips than paying attention, she still managed to impress Gumptin with her ability to retain almost everything he told her. Jade, however, was another story. She and Gumptin butted heads more sitting in a library discussing a book than they did when Gumptin was screaming at her to push her body beyond its breaking point. When Jade wasn't playing around with one of her sharp knives, she was either sleeping, eating, or trying unsuccessfully to get Avery, who was trying to pay attention, to talk to her.

Mid-week, Gumptin incorporated the Protectors' horses into their training. They had to learn to use their weapons while on horseback, an exercise that left more than a few injuries. The worst of the injuries having been inflicted on Avery, who was grazed on the arm by a wayward arrow shot from Sasha's bow. It happened while Sasha was on her horse, Belle, about to release her arrow aimed at a distant target. Belle was at a fast gallop when she jumped over a log, causing Sasha's body to jerk forward as she shot. Avery, who had been chatting with Jade and not paying attention at the time, heard the slight whistle of the arrow a split second before it reached her. She leaned to the right, the arrow grazing her arm and sailing into a nearby tree, as opposed to landing in Avery's upper chest. It was all Avery could do to put aside her own rattled nerves and stop Jade from tearing Sasha down off of her horse and throttling her.

Gumptin, however, found the bright side of the incident by praising Avery for her speed and defensive maneuver. It was the first time since Avery had been told she was a Protector that she was actually grateful for the abilities that came along with the position.

Even though Gumptin had been quick to praise Avery and call the whole situation a valuable training exercise, he was also quick to make sure that from now on the girls all stood behind anyone who was shooting sharp objects.

After the weapons training on horseback, Gumptin had them practicing different maneuvers in the saddle. They had to throw their bodies to the side, holding onto the girth of the horse with their legs while picking up items off of the ground. It didn't start well when Bunny completely slipped off of her horse, Ajax, and rolled hard onto the ground. Skylar ended up swinging around past the side of the horse, down to its underside. She hung there until Gumptin shouted at her to command her horse, Dancer, to stop, an idea that had completely escaped her. Steel, Jade's horse, whose personality matched her own, decided to stop mid-run when Jade pulled down on his reins a little too aggressively for his liking. This sent Jade flying over his head and landing hard on her butt, still clutching the reins in her hand. Jade cursed aloud, then immediately got up and gave the reins a quick hard tug to let Steel know he better not dare do that again. For Steel's part, he just snorted and turned his head away from Jade.

The rest of the day went on pretty much the same, filled with injury and humiliation, and no one performing up to Gumptin's standards.

The day after their first training session involving the horses, Avery was convinced that her legs hurt her more than if she had actually broken them falling off of Phantom. She could barely stand, let alone, run, flip, kick, and heaven forbid, squat. Of course, that didn't stop Gumptin from having them work just as hard as he had them work the previous days.

It was the morning of the seventh day since they had arrived on Orcatia, and Avery still wasn't accustomed to the ridiculously early morning schedule Gumptin had them on. Every morning her father would have to come into her room and make sure that she was up and getting ready. Avery hadn't once been able to get up in time on her own.

That was why, on the seventh day, when Avery groggily awoke, snuggled under her thick comforter, she was surprised she hadn't needed her father's voice to rise her. Avery stayed hidden under her warm comforter for a few minutes, relishing the coziness of her bed. When she finally did muster up the will power to peek her head out from under her comforter, the burst of blinding sunlight that hit Avery's eyes sent her scurrying back under the covers. Avery cursed the brightness that had left white bursts floating in front of her closed eyes, until a panicking realization popped into Avery's mind. She realized that it was the sunlight she had seen, and if she had seen the sunlight that meant that it was past dawn, which meant that she was late for training.

"Gumptin!" Avery shouted in horror, throwing off her comforter.

She jumped out of bed so fast that her legs hadn't had a chance to wake up yet, and she collapsed to the ground. She picked herself up quickly, pulled on a pair of lace-less boots over a pair of knee-high socks, snatched a hair tie off of her dresser, and dashed out of her room, still wearing the black boyshorts and 'Evil Dead' t-shirt she had slept in.

Avery was so panicked as she rushed down the stairs and ran towards the door, that she made it half way across her living room before, out of the corner of her eye, she spotted Jade sitting on her couch, munching on piece of toast, and playing a game of 'Go Fish' with Cinder.

Now, Avery was really confused. She stood completely still for a few seconds, staring at her front door, trying to figure out what was going on. She quickly abandoned trying to figure it out for herself and turned to Jade.

"Morning sunshine," Jade said, lounging back on the couch and trying to suppress a laugh as she looked Avery over, "nice outfit."

Avery dismissed Jade comment with a shake of her head, "Jade, what are you doing here?"

Jade sighed, "Getting my butt handed to me by a seven year old." Jade threw her cards down on the table, signifying she had had enough of their game, "I know you're cheating, kid."

Cinder shook her head, "I'm not cheating; you just suck."

Jade had known Cinder since Avery's parents had brought her home from the hospital. She considered Cinder family, which meant she could say things to Jade other people wouldn't dare.

"Get lost, tater tot." Jade told Cinder, giving her an affectionate little kick on the bottom as Cinder ran off to the kitchen to join her mother.

It had always amused Avery, watching Jade's softer more playful side come out around Cinder, but right now, she wished Jade would focus on her and her question.

"Jade," Avery asked again, "what are you doing here?"

Avery's father walked out from his study, holding a copy of the village paper, "Hey, sweetheart." He said to Avery, "Oh, by the way, Gumptin came by early this morning, a few minutes before I was going to wake you up. He said he had an errand to run and to meet him in the library at eleven. I thought I'd let you get some sleep."

Although grateful to her father for letting her catch up on some much needed sleep, another part of her wanted to yell at him for putting her through such anxiety, especially when she first woke up. Avery wasn't sure her heart rate would ever be back to normal.

"What time is it?" Avery asked.

"A whopping nine fifteen." Jade told Avery, sliding over on the couch as Avery walked over and sat down.

"So, what *are* you doing here?" Avery asked for a third time, realizing her question had never been answered.

Jade grabbed another piece of toast off of a platter sitting on the coffee table, "Well," she said, taking a bite, "unlike your parents, mine actually woke me up at five a.m. to tell me that Gumptin had stopped by. I couldn't get back to sleep after that, so what else was I going to do?"

Avery snatched a piece of toast up for herself. Satisfied with Jade's answer and happy with the fact that she had been able to sleep in past nine, and the possibility of training being called off, or at least delayed, Avery let herself relax.

Avery lifted her piece of toast in the air, "Cheers, to tardy Gumptin." Avery and Jade tapped their pieces of toast together, took a bite, then picked up the cards Jade had thrown down on the table to play a round of Jade's favorite card game, poker.

They made it through three hands, Jade winning two of them, before Avery headed upstairs to get dressed properly.

As they walked to the library together to meet Gumptin, Avery marveled at how lovely Havyn was in the early afternoon. The gigantic trees provided a cool shade, with rays of intermittent sunlight lighting up the village in a gentle glow. All of the shops were open, the blacksmith, the seamstress, the grocer's. A few children came running out of Mrs. Bott's shop; all carrying cinnamon rolls the size of their head.

The village was bustling with life. People were walking in and out of shops. Ladies were standing or strolling together, talking and laughing, some carrying baskets of laundry, some holding satchels of food. In the distance, behind the tree houses, Avery could see a number of men, and a few women working in the fields.

It struck Avery that, although, she had been on Orcatia for a week, she had never actually experienced much of it, including her own village. Her days had consisted of training, studying, eating, getting what little sleep she could, and the occasional shower if she had enough energy to force herself.

After walking a few shops and houses down, Avery began to notice how differently the villagers treated each other as opposed to how they treated Jade and Avery. With each other, they were warm and jovial, walking up to one another with sunny smiles, handshakes, and hugs. Whereas, with Jade and Avery, they were more reserved, giving the girls a polite smile, gentle wave, nod of the head, and a 'hello'. It seemed as if they were hesitant to be too friendly.

Avery understood that if their previous life on Orcatia had been anything like the past week, then she knew the Protectors would have almost never seen the villagers. Plus, from what Avery had heard from the few villagers she had talked to, the Protectors seemed to be more revered as saviors than accepted as friends.

Jade didn't even seem to notice, but it bothered Avery a little. Especially coming from a small town back on Earth where Avery was use to everyone knowing everyone else. She was use to being a part of the town and thought of as just another neighbor. She was use to receiving the hugs, or at least an amiable pat on the back.

To make up for the alienation that Avery considered her past self had put her in, Avery waved enthusiastically at every villager she passed and gave each of them a huge smile with a lively, "Hello."

Some of the villagers seemed pleasantly taken aback by Avery's exaggerated friendliness, others seem slightly confused, but all the reactions she received from the villagers were better than the one she received from Jade. Jade looked at Avery like she had just grown another head.

"What are you doing?" Jade asked her.

Avery kept smiling and waving, "I'm just being neighborly."

"Well, knock it off, Mr. Rogers," Jade told her, grabbing Avery's hand and placing it down by her side, "you're embarrassing me."

When Avery and Jade walked inside the library, they saw Bunny sitting at the large round table reading a book on ancient runes. She was the first and only one there. A couple minutes later Sasha and Skylar came walking through the door together.

"What's up ladies?" Skylar yelled, did a little turn, then fell into the seat next to where Avery was sitting.

Avery laughed as Skylar leaned her head onto her shoulder, "You seem in a good mood." Avery told her.

"Avery, darling, I got to sleep in till ten." Skylar said, stretching her arms high up in the air, "I am ecstatic! Nothing could ruin my mood."

The door swung open and Gumptin came trotting in, looking more haggard than the girls had ever seen him. He immediately walked up to the front of the room and turned to address the girls. Before he said anything, he rubbed his eyes, which looked blood shot and puffy.

"Protectors," He spoke in a professional manner, standing up straight, voice clear and deep, "today is the day you put your training into use."

Sasha, who had been standing, now sat down, bracing herself for what Gumptin was going to say next.

Gumptin continued, "Very early this morning, I received word from a friend of mine, that a small party of trolls was making their way to the village Lilydale. I have confirmed it, and it appears to be true. The village is approximately five miles from here. They are known for their production of Everlily, a flower used in many medicinal balms. It helps keep wounds from becoming infected. Mr. Bott uses it in many of the balms used to treat your wounds. The trolls are most likely being sent by the Emperor to try and destroy the village's flower crops." Gumptin sighed and ran his hand through his beard, a maneuver Avery knew he did when he was nervous or upset about something. After a small pause, he said, "The Emperor is becoming bold. This is a test to see how strong you are. It is said that he has sent some of his strongest trolls for this mission. I am afraid this will not be easy for you. I wish we could have had more time for training, but..." Gumptin trailed off.

The girls sat in silence, not one of them even moving. Avery hadn't moved since Gumptin had begun talking, her eyes fixed on a small dark imperfection in the wood on the table in front of her, but her mind was far off and lost in Gumptin's words. She pictured the images of tolls she had seen in the books Gumptin had made them read, big and nasty, with wide slobbering mouths, carrying mallets and axes, anxious to pound her into a pile of broken bones and bloody flesh. Avery knew it was their duty and that they didn't have a choice but to try and stop them. She knew that if they didn't do anything now, then the trolls' next stop would be Havyn and they would end up having to fight them then anyway.

Sasha was the first one to speak, her voice sounding shaky, "Gumptin, don't tell me you actually expect the five of us to go out there and face these things on our own."

Gumptin shook his head, "I am sorry, but that is your job as a Protector. Lilydale needs your protection."

Sasha ran her hand through her perfectly done hair, messing it up slightly, "Do you think we'll be alright?"

The look of controlled sadness in Gumptin's eyes gave the Protectors their answer.

As Sasha continued to question Gumptin, Avery's stayed lost in her own head. Gradually, the image of herself being pummeled into an unrecognizable pulp was replaced with an image of the

Lilydale. In her head, Avery turned Lilydale into Redemption; she turned all the villagers into the people she had grown up with for her entire life. Then, in a flash, the image of her being beaten turned into an image of Cinder lying under a troll's club. Avery shook the image free from her mind and stood up in a jolt. All the girls' eyes turned to her.

"What's the plan?" Avery asked Gumptin, "When do we leave?"

Bunny looked terrified, Skylar kept a blank face, Sasha looked shocked, and Jade stood in a corner, leaning against the wall, swirling her dagger between her fingers, a small smirk on her lips.

"You can't be serious?" Sasha said, looking even more shocked than before.

Avery turned to Sasha, the images of the village being destroyed still tugging at the back of her mind, "We're Protector's Sasha, what else are we suppose to do?"

Sasha opened her mouth to say something, but then shut it, which was rare for Sasha. Avery knew Sasha was well aware that the Protector's didn't have a choice. Gumptin had made it quite clear that the Elementals, who had given them a second chance at life, fully intended them to use that life to fight evil.

Avery looked around the room at the others. All of them, except for Jade, seemed hesitant about the idea of riding off to face a pack of killer trolls. The last think Avery wanted was for any of them to get hurt; she wanted them strong; she wanted them to believe in themselves.

"Look," Avery said, trying to give the girls a little perspective and maybe some fire to go into battle with, "I've come to the realization that this planet has Protectors because they need them. They need us. It's simple…if we don't go then those villagers die. I'm not telling you to do this because it's our duty, I'm asking you to do this because it's the right thing to do."

So far, what she was saying seemed to be working. The look of terror was off of Bunny's face and Skylar was nodding in agreement. Even Sasha had stopped arguing and was intently staring at Avery.

"Come on," Avery told them, "we can totally kick those trolls' asses. Let's send a message to every evil thing out there, that killing us was the worst thing that they could have done."

Avery wasn't sure that they could really kick any ass, but she knew they had to at least try. It was the one and only thing she was sure about since she had come to Orcatia.

"Alright," Jade said, sliding her dagger into her belt and pushing herself off the wall, "since we're all seeing things clearly now, what's the plan?"

Sasha shook her head, she still wasn't convinced that riding off to possibly get killed was something she wanted to do, but she was done arguing.

Gumptin nodded at Avery, a wisp of a smile behind his scraggily beard, "Go home, get dressed in your battle gear, and get your weapons ready. I shall draw you a map to Lilydale. Meet at the stable in thirty minutes. I will have Thomas get your horses ready."

Skylar stood up, "Well, after Avery's speech how could I say no." She laughed, trying to sound light, but failing as the laughter cracked in her dry throat.

As they were all walking out of the library, Bunny walked up to Avery, "Do you really think we can do this?" She asked Avery, her face a portrait of how nervous she was.

Avery did her best to make sure she looked confident and calm, the complete opposite of how she felt, as she stared Bunny in the eyes, "Bunny, I'm positive."

Bunny nodded, looking very slightly reassured.

After Bunny left towards her house, Jade, who had been hanging back in the distance, came up to Avery, "That was a good speech in there." She told Avery, "I knew there was a reason they chose you to be leader."

"I thought it was because they knew I was the only one who you'd listen to." Avery joked, wanting to lighten the unease she was feeling.

Jade laughed, "You wish!" She gave Avery a light punch on the shoulder.

Avery laughed with Jade, and for a second her attempt at trying to make herself feel better had worked, but after the laughter died down Avery was left with the same pit in her stomach.

Jade, who had always been better at reading Avery's moods and expressions than anyone else, said, "It was all true, you know, everything you said in there."

"I know." Avery said, and unlike what she had told Bunny, she believed what she had just told Jade.

When Avery reached her house, she was surprised to walk in and find the place empty. She walked into the kitchen and gazed out the back window over the sink. Through it, Avery saw her mother and sister out in the garden. Her mother was pulling up radishes and placing them in a basket, humming a light hearted tune. While three feet away from her, Cinder danced around a large leafy tree, surrounded by a circular patch of short mossy grass. She was playing chase with their two German Shepherds, Justice and King, as their old Great Dane, Bailey, lied down in the grass, sound asleep.

In the distance, Avery could see her father and another man working in the fields. Her father bent down, picked up a bit of dirt, showed it to the other man, said something to him, and then they both started laughing.

Avery watched as her family went about with their lives. Each one of them seemingly happy, enjoying their day and their work. They were completely unaware of what Avery was about to have to ride off and do, and Avery didn't want it any other way. She didn't want them worrying about her. More than anything, Avery wanted to be out there with them, but since she couldn't have that, she was going to keep the image of them just as they were at that moment. She was going to keep that image and take it with her to Lilydale. She was going to blame the trolls for taking her away from that image, and she was going to make sure she beat the trolls, so that they wouldn't be able to come to Havyn and try to kill and destroy that image.

Avery went upstairs and opened her closet. She grabbed a pair of dark brown leather pants, a tight fitting long sleeve white tunic that she tucked into her pants, a fitted dark brown leather vest, and thick black boots. She laced up her black leather arm gauntlets and stuck one of her daggers in on the inside of one. She buckled her oversized belt and stuck another petite dagger through it on one side and a larger sliver knife through it on the other side. She fastened up the leather bodice contraption Gumptin had given her to hold her sword and bow and arrows. When Avery had finished suiting up, she looked herself over in the mirror. Avery thought she looked ridiculous. She had spent her entire life striving for comfort and just trying to blend in, but here she was, staring at herself dressed in tight leather and loaded down with weapons.

"I'm sure I'd fit right in back home." She said aloud, mockingly, doing a slight turn in the mirror.

As quickly as she could, Avery made her way down the stairs and out of her house, making sure none of her family saw her.

Jade was already waiting for Avery at the stables. She was leaning up against one of the hitching posts, dressed entirely in black leather, which made the silver of her weapons stand out like lights in the night. Her long black hair was pulled back in a tight ponytail. To Avery, Jade looked the part of a warrior. She looked dangerous, and mysterious, and like she might behead you just for looking at her the wrong way. Of course, the fact that she was munching down on a chocolate chip cookie and whistling an Ozzy Osbourne song took away a little of her mystique.

"You clean up nice." Jade told Avery as she approached.

Avery smiled and told Jade, "Minus about ninety percent of the weapons, and you look like you do almost every day."

Thomas and Pip had all of their horses saddled and ready by the time the girls had arrived. Pip brought Phantom out front and Avery strolled up to him. Phantom pranced around and stomped on the ground. He was a war horse, after all, and Avery could tell he knew something was happening, and he was excited about it. Phantom had on a black saddle that was just one shade lighter than the color of his coat. It had a white vine-like stitching pattern around the edges of it and sliver lightning bolt decorations on the corners. The bridle was black with the same white stitching and sliver bolts. Both were a far cry from the simple brown leather saddle and bridle Avery had been using during training.

"Thanks for getting him ready, Pip." Avery told Pip, taking Phantom's reins from him.

Pip exhaled sharply and waved his hand at Avery, "Oh, please," Pip said, "ya know it's me job, but even if it weren't, I'd do it anyway. Ya do so much for everyone; ya don't need to thank me."

Avery had seen Pip almost every day since she had arrived on Orcatia. She had liked him right from the beginning, but after getting to know him more, she truly thought of him as a friend. He didn't treat her like she was off limits or special like the rest of the villagers did, and Avery appreciated that.

"Thanks anyway." She said, smiling at Pip.

Pip didn't smile back, instead he said to Avery, "You be careful."

Avery nodded and pip walked over to help Skylar who was having trouble tightening Dancer's girth.

"Here is the map to Lilydale." Gumptin spoke from behind Avery.

Avery turned around and took the map out of Gumptin's outstretched hand. The map told Avery to take the Main Road, ride a mile past the path that led to the Ora Gateway, and then take the third road to the right, called the Harvest Road. Then, they were to ride on that road till they reached the first path to the left, marked with a marker that reads Lilydale. Gumptin had drawn a very precise map and made sure that it was easy enough to follow, but still, Avery knew riding on horseback through a forest, looking for small roads and paths, while heading towards a place they've never been before was not going to be a piece of cake.

Avery stood, waiting for Gumptin to give her some more instructions on how she should fight, or how she should lead, or what to do once they got there, but he said nothing. He just stood in front of her, head down, staring at the ground.

Eventually, right before Avery was about to give up waiting for him to speak and say something herself, Gumptin said, "Remember what you learned. You are a Protector. You are stronger than those trolls. You are stronger than you could even imagine." He gave a little cough, "Remember I am proud of you all."

Avery thought that was one of the nicest things Gumptin had ever said to her. She took a hold of one of Gumptin's shoulders and said to him, "You've trained us like crazy. We'll be alright."

Gumptin reached up and patted her hand, and Avery could swear he looked like he was about to cry. Before he let any more emotion show, he hobbled over to stand next to Thomas near the stable and left Avery to finish getting Phantom ready.

There were three tie straps on Phantom's saddle. One was for Avery's whip, another was for extra arrows, and the third was for gear, such as bedding if they were on an extended ride. Since she didn't have to worry about being gone overnight, Avery just tied on her whip and a quiver full of twenty extra arrows. When she had finished making sure everything was tied on and in order, Avery grabbed onto Phantom's saddle and pulled herself up into it. Avery sat on top of Phantom and stroked his mane. She could sense his desire to run, but he stayed still, waiting for his master's command.

All of the others were up and mounted, except for Bunny, who was having trouble with an excited Ajax. This wasn't a surprise for any of them; Bunny always had trouble with Ajax not wanting to be ridden. Jade always joked that it was because Bunny was better with plants than she was with people and animals. Bunny pulled down on Ajax's reins, laid her hand on his head, and whispered in his ear. Whatever soothing things she whispered worked, because Ajax calmed down and let Bunny mount up.

When they were all ready with reins in hand, Avery glanced around at the girls she had grown up with and just hoped beyond hope that they were strong enough and lucky enough to make it through today, herself included. She let her eyes rest on Jade, and Jade gave her an 'it's now or never' nod.

With a light tap of her heel, a click of her tongue, and a turn of the reins, Avery had Phantom galloping down the Main Road, followed closely by the rest of the protectors.

As Avery had expected, Gumptin's map proved harder to follow than it looked. None of the girls had any idea how to judge distance while riding on top of a galloping horse. Once they had passed the path that led to the Ora Gateway, they had to slow their horses down to a trot just to make sure they didn't pass the Harvest Road they had to turn down. While traveling down the Harvest Road, they literally had to slow their horses down to a walk so they wouldn't miss the next tiny path they needed. Eventually, Avery spotted a small white wood sign, covered with clinging ivy, and the word 'Lilydale' carved into it.

The girls took the path, and since they didn't have any more turns to watch out for, were now free to run their horses out at a full gallop. Avery knew full well the five mile trip to Lilydale had taken them much longer than it should have. She just hoped they weren't too late.

Avery heard the screams before she was able to see the village. The path they were on curved slightly before opening up to the village. Avery pulled Phantom up to a stop before they reached the curve, making sure the trolls couldn't see them coming. The rest of the protectors followed Avery's lead and stopped their horses behind her.

Avery inched Phantom up slightly so that she could get a better view of the village. The end of the path was surrounded by large trees and tall forest growth, so Avery was only able to see straight into the village and not what was going on to the right or left. The village would have looked like a quaint farming village, spattered with straw houses and flower gardens, if it weren't for the utter chaos engulfing it. A few of the homes and shops were on fire, leaving long trails of puffy gray smoke climbing up into the air. Villagers were running around in every direction. Women were screaming and clutching their children, trying to escape the violence. Men were carrying swords, pitch forks, axes, garden hoes, anything they could use as a weapon.

The smell of the trolls reached the protectors before they actually saw one of them. It was the most appalling scent Avery had ever come across in her entire life. She had experience dealing with horrible smells, like sick dogs, backed up outhouses during the Rodeo Day Festival, and teenage boys, but nothing could prepare her for this. It smelled like rotten eggs and dog crap being boiled in a large pot of vinegar. Avery had to cover her mouth to stop herself from retching. Behind her, Avery heard Jade gag, and Skylar slap her own hand hard across her nose and mouth.

"This cannot get any worse." Sasha whispered in a nasal voice, her nose pinched between her two fingers.

Before Avery had a chance to tell Sasha that repulsive smells were the least of their problems, a monstrous troll at least ten feet tall and weighing a good thousand pounds, crossed their path three feet in front of them. It was the color of green swamp water with large brown warts dotted across his body. It had a large round bald head with pointy ears that stuck straight up and a large underbite displaying a row of misshapen teeth and two large bottom canines that reached up above his top lip. Its clothes were sweat stained and appeared about two sizes too small, leaving its flabby belly hanging out of its shirt and over its belt. As detestable as Avery had expected trolls to look, this one looked at least ten times worse. The most menacing thing about it was the five foot long blood stained club it was dragging around behind it.

As it passed in front of them, Phantom moved around on his front feet nervously. Avery pulled back on the reins and patted his neck to calm him. The last thing she wanted was for the troll to spot the five of them huddled together on horseback, three feet to the left of it.

The troll walked on without seeing them, and every one of the Protectors let out an audible sigh of relief.

The sight of the troll made Avery's body clench up with fear, but as the screams of the villagers continued to ring through the air, Avery knew they couldn't delay any longer. She turned around in her saddle to address the girls.

Avery tried to ignore the fear in the other's faces as she told them, "Remember, that thing is nothing compared to what we are. We go in strong and hard. We can do this." Avery pulled her sword out of the sheath strapped onto her back, "Are you ready?" She asked them.

The girls unsheathed their swords, and Avery took it as them saying yes.

Right before Avery turned back around in her saddle, Jade mouthed the words, 'be careful' to her. Avery nodded in response.

With a swift kick, Avery nudged Phantom into a run and straight into the heart of the village. Once there, she was able to get a complete picture of where exactly all the trolls were and what they were doing. Avery tried to close off her mind to the surreal shock and horror of the scenes she was witnessing. She told herself to focus solely on their purpose for being there, to stop the trolls from destroying the village.

The troll that had passed in front of the protectors was making its way over to the extensive fields of bright yellow Everlily flowers. Already in the fields were two more trolls. One was seven feet tall with muddy brown skin and white tufts of hair sticking out of his saucer sized ears. It was carrying a large torch and attempting to light the flower fields on fire. A group of villagers were unsuccessfully trying to attack the troll with pitch forks while another group of villagers stood behind them, carrying buckets of water, in case the troll managed to get the torch to the fields.

Another shorter troll, but twice as fat, stood in front of the troll with the torch, swinging a massive sword at any villager trying to assist the other villagers in stopping the troll with the torch. The troll swung his bulky sword at one man attempting to make a rush past the troll with a wood ax in his hand. The sword hit the man in his midsection, sending him flying backwards twenty feet, blood spurting out of him as he flew backwards, misting the ground in a red rain.

Two identical looking trolls, both six feet tall, a murky pea soup green color, with matching tattoos of dragon skulls on their shoulders, were walking from house to house, lighting the buildings on fire.

There was a sixth troll, bigger than all the rest, a good twelve feet tall and built like a truck, its hulking muscles looked like they were about ready to burst through its yellow-green skin. The troll was walking through the village, picking off any villager that got near its gigantic hands or oversized club. After smashing one villager under his horrible weapon, the troll threw his head back in the air and gave a deep throated howl that sent vibrations down the Protectors' bodies.

Just when Avery thought she had seen all that there was to see, a troll no bigger than Gumptin stepped out from behind a house a few feet in front of her. The troll was the same icky green color as the first troll. He had long pointy ears and a small upturned nose. He wore a tan colored tunic with brown cotton pants and a brown leather belt with a tiny sword sheath attached to it. One of his big toes stuck out from his worn out shoes. He was the only troll out of all of them that seemed to wear clothes that fit him, not to mention the only one that wore shoes. He held a sword the size of Avery's forearm in front of him and moved his little body into an attack stance.

"We meet again, Protectors." The little troll said in a high pitched voice that hardly sounded menacing.

"Who the hell are you?" Jade asked, from atop her horse, directly behind Avery.

"Shut your mouth ugly human!" The troll yelled at Jade, "You know exactly who I am. I am Beetlebat, your sworn enemy, leader of the troll armies, and the harbinger of your imminent death."

Jade scoffed, "The only way you're gonna kill me is with your stench, you horrible little maggot bait."

They didn't have time for this. Avery dismissed the diminutive troll in front of her, turning Phantom around to face the other girls, "Bunny, Sasha, Skylar, you three go take care of the trolls by the fields. Jade, you got the ugly twins over there, torching everything. I'll take Mr. Gigantic."

The Protectors nodded, but before they could ride off to follow Avery's orders, in a loud high pitch shout, Beetlebat screamed, "The Protectors are here!"

His voice carried farther than any of the protectors would have thought with him being so tiny. Every one of the trolls stopped what they were doing and looked over towards Beetlebat and the protectors.

"Kill them!" Beetlebat shouted again, "Grind their brains and bones into paste!"

The ground began to shake slightly as all six trolls began to make their way over to the protectors. Avery quickly shot down the panic aching to take over her entire body. The rest of the protectors froze as well, trying to fight their own panic.

"Now!" Avery shouted at the girls, "Plan still stands. Let's go!"

Smacked back into the reality of the situation by Avery's words, Sasha, Bunny, and Skylar, turned their horses and took off towards the three trolls making their way out of the flower fields.

Before Jade rode off to take on the twin trolls, she pointed her sword at Beetlebat, who stood on the ground grinning from ear to ear, "I'm gonna knock every one of those teeth out of your wormy little mouth, and then I'm gonna take my sword and chop off your annoying little head." She told him.

Beetlebat countered, "I'd like to see you try it, pathetic weakling!" Although, he talked tough the smile had completely left his face, and what ugly green color he had in his face seemed to drain away.

"That's a promise." Jade said as she rode past him.

Instead of riding to meet her troll, Avery let him come to her. She got down off of Phantom and slapped him on his hind quarters, making sure he got out of the way.

"You're going to die, leader." Beetlebat spat at her, "You're going to die…again."

Avery still had a few seconds before the enormous monster of a troll reached her. She walked up to Beetlebat, grabbed onto his little hand that held his sword before he could do anything with it, and punched him hard as she could in the nose. Beetlebat uttered a small plaintive cry, and then fell to the ground, unconscious.

The troll reached Avery and brought his club up high above his head. Avery somersaulted out of the way as he slammed the club into the ground where Avery had been standing. As Avery stared at the crater the club had left in the ground, she knew she had to get that club out of the troll's hands.

The troll swung its club towards Avery and she dropped to the ground, feeling the breeze from the swing swirling her hair. Avery rolled onto her back and handsprung onto her feet, flipping out of the way as the troll swung his club back around. Avery was getting tired of being on the defensive. She knew it was only a matter of time before the troll would actually land one of his hits.

Deciding to take the offensive, Avery sheathed her sword and grabbed her bow from where it was strapped onto her back. She knew from the books Gumptin had made them read that arrows weren't always effective against the armor-like skin of the trolls, but Avery wasn't going to aim for its skin. She pulled out an arrow, set up the shot, and took aim, all within a few seconds. Her arrow ripped through the air, past the troll's gigantic club, and straight into his right eye. The troll howled in pain, but didn't go down. He dropped his club to the ground, pulled the arrow out of his eye socket with one hand, and covered the wound, now gushing thick blue blood, with his other hand.

Avery took advantage of the troll dropping his weapon. She threw her bow to the ground, unsheathed her sword and ran towards the troll. Out of his good eye, the troll saw her coming. It angrily grabbed at Avery with its left arm, but Avery spun under it. Then, it made a grab for Avery with his right hand, the hand he had used to hold his club. A second before he would have been able to get a hold of Avery, she back flipped over his hand, swinging her sword as she flipped and chopping off his thumb. The troll let out a bellowing growl as a spray of blue blood stained Avery's white shirt.

The moment Avery's two feet landed on the ground, the toll kicked out with his right leg, kicking Avery square in the chest. Avery was sent flying backwards, landing hard on her back. It took a second for Avery to register what had just happened. She had never remembered being hit so hard in her life. It felt like a charging bull had slammed itself into her chest. Avery tried to catch her breath, her ribs screaming as she inhaled. Her senses still weren't fully intact when the troll appeared standing over her, blue blood streaming down his face and stomach. The troll looked down at her and roared. It lifted its left leg up and tried to bring it down on top of Avery. Avery rolled right, then left, then right again, trying to avoid his crushing feet. The troll slammed his right leg down and Avery was barely able to roll out of the way in time. She turned her head and saw the troll's mud and blood stained foot an inch away from her face. Avery quickly reached to her belt and grabbed the dagger she kept there. She took the dagger and stabbed the troll through his foot with it. The troll hollered and staggered back a few feet, allowing Avery to lift herself up off of the ground.

Avery had just managed to get to her feet when the troll roared a guttural cry and came charging towards her. She tried to cartwheel out of the way, but the troll managed to get a grip on her arm with the four remaining fingers on his right hand. The troll clenched tightly onto Avery's arm, pulling her in towards him. In the rushed momentum, Avery wasn't able to free herself from its grasp. Avery struggled to free herself as the troll picked her up with both hands, but his grip was like a vice. Even though the troll had Avery's arms pinned, she lifted her leg up slightly, so that she would be able to reach the knife she had stuck in her boot, but before she could get her fingers wrapped around the knife's hilt, the troll threw Avery across the village with both his arms.

The world went black for a moment then flashed into bright color as Avery tried to blink away the spinning going on inside her brain. The enormous troll had thrown Avery thirty feet through the air. When the world started to gain more focus, Avery realized she was lying on her stomach on the ground. She picked herself up onto her hands and looked around. Behind her, Sasha, Bunny, and Skylar had taken one troll down. It was lying on its back in a field, not moving. Bunny was still on horseback, firing arrows at the two remaining trolls. Sasha and Skylar were on the ground with their swords drawn. Avery saw one troll whack Sasha across her right side with his fist. Sasha went flying, and Skylar went running to her side, helping her up off of the ground before the troll could get to her. To Avery's left, Jade was still battling with the twin trolls. One was crawling across the ground, blue blood oozing out from its mouth. Avery saw Jade look at her and saw the terror in her eyes as she tried to make her way over to Avery, but was stopped by one of the trolls punching her in the stomach and sending her wobbling backwards.

Avery felt a humongous hand grab onto the back of her vest and flip her over. The troll clamped his hand down on Avery's throat and across her chest, successfully cementing her to the ground. As Avery tried to shove the troll's tree limb of an arm off of her, the troll took a knife out from his belt the size of Avery's arm. The troll lifted the knife up and for a split second the sickening thought that she was going to die flashed into Avery's mind. Just as the troll brought his knife down towards Avery's chest, Avery lifted her leg up and kicked the troll's arm as hard as she could. His arm lurched to the side and the knife sliced down the side of Avery's arm. The sharp pain snapped Avery back into action. No way was she going to let this ugly beast carve her up. Avery wrapped both of her legs around the arm the troll was holding onto her with. She jerked to her left as hard as she could, sending the troll rolling away from her. Avery stood up and retrieved her sword that she had lost when the troll had thrown her. She and the troll walked towards each other. The troll swung his left fist at her and Avery lifted up her sword, so that his fist slammed into her sword as opposed to her. He had been swinging his fist with such force that the sword went into his hand and arm all the way up to its hilt. Holding onto the grip of her sword, Avery swung it to the right while it was still stuck in the troll's hand. This caused the troll to drop to his knees, snarling in pain. In a move that took less than ten seconds, Avery pulled the sword out of the troll's hand, and then with a quick spin she slit the toll's throat with the sword. Blue blood sprayed out from the wound, covering Avery's face and shirt. The blue of the troll's blood and the red of her own mixed to create a strange purple stain.

The troll gurgled and tried to gasp for breath, causing blue bubbles to form at the wound on his neck. He made one final lurch towards Avery; then fell to the ground dead.

Avery stood still for a moment, trying to push down the reality of what she had just seen, what she had just done, and what had just happened to her. Avery realized she was shaking, and she tried to tell herself that it was just because of the cold breeze and her clothes that were wet from blood.

A scream from Bunny focused Avery's attention. Avery looked over in the direction of the scream and saw that Sasha, Bunny and Skylar were down to just one troll left. The troll had just knocked Bunny off of her horse with his bulky club.

Without hesitating for a second, Avery rushed over and picked up her bow she that had discarded at the beginning of her fight with the troll. Once she had the bow in hand, Avery whistled for Phantom, who came running out of the forest, stopping in front his master. Avery hopped up into the saddle and galloped Phantom over to where three girls were trying to take down their last troll.

Avery pulled up Phantom at the edge of the Everlily fields. She jumped down and grabbed an arrow out of her back quiver. The last arrow she shot into the other troll's eye seemed to work pretty well, so she decided to try it again with this troll. Whatever happened, she was not letting herself get tossed another thirty feet. Avery took aim and shot the arrow into the troll's eye. Before the toll had a chance to reach up and pull the arrow out, Avery shot another arrow. This arrow smashed into the back tip of the first arrow, pushing it deep into the troll's brain. The troll swayed to the left, then to the right, then fell with a loud thud onto the ground, dead.

The girls turned around and looked at Avery with shocked expressions on their faces.

"What?" Avery shrugged, "Apparently, I use to practice with this thing all the time." Avery fitted her bow back into its back strap.

"Well, thank God for small favors." Skylar said, limping over towards Avery. She was holding her side and Avery could see some bruising forming up and down her arm.

"You look horrible." Sasha told Avery, looking her over.

Avery thought this funny considering Avery had never seen Sasha look worse than she did now. The left sleeve of her shirt was ripped off. Her shoulder was bleeding. Her face was smeared with dirt, sweat, and blue blood. She had a gash on her forehead dripping blood down the side of her cheek, and for one of the first times in her life, Sasha's hair was sticking up in every direction, mangled and frizzy.

Bunny stood behind Sasha and Skylar. Her clothes were dirtied, and she had a long cut running across her collar bone, but other than that, she appeared to have escaped the combat without any serious injuries.

After Avery was sure they were all alright, she turned her sights to Jade, who was still fighting. One of the twin trolls Jade had been battling with was lying dead on the ground, Jade's sword sticking out of the middle of its skull.

Avery ran towards the village where Jade and the other twin troll were fighting in between two houses. Jade had the troll pinned to the ground with a pitch fork stuck through its shoulder. As Avery rounded the corner to where Jade and the troll were between the two houses, Avery saw Jade jump on top of the back of the troll and place her crossbow directly up to the back of the troll's head, firing two arrows into his brain. Jade jumped down off of the troll and gave him a hard kick in his side.

"Are you alright?" asked Avery.

Jade turned towards Avery, her eyes filled with relief at the sight of her.

"Thank God." She said in a whispered voice, more to herself than to Avery.

Jade walked towards Avery, and Avery opened up her arms to Jade, thinking she was going in for a hug, but instead, Jade placed both of her hands on Avery's shoulders and looked Avery over.

"Are you alright?" Jade asked, staring at Avery's blood stained shirt, "That looks bad."

Avery shook her head, "I'm fine." She told Jade, "It looks worse than it is."

Jade lightly touched Avery's side where the blood stains were the most prominent, and Avery couldn't help but flinch. Her ribs were still screaming at her from the kick she had received from the troll.

"Really, it's fine." Avery told Jade through gritted teeth.

Whether Jade believed her or not, it didn't matter. There was nothing Jade could do about it. They were in the middle of a destroyed village, miles away from home after doing battle with a group of nightmarish trolls.

For as worried as Jade was about Avery, Avery noticed that Jade didn't look to unscathed, herself. She had a large bruise forming on her lower jaw. Blood was dripping down her arm from a deep slice on her shoulder, and a small trickle of blood was coming out of her nose.

They walked together to join the other girls who were now standing back at the entrance to the village. Avery stopped a few feet before she reached the girls. She stood in the smoke filled sunlight, glancing around at the scene surrounding her. The air was thick with smoke from the burning houses, lending to the surrealism of the moment for Avery. It made everything around her appear as if it was clouded by a thin gray curtain, like in a dream.

A group of villagers were putting out the flames on a small section of the Everlily fields that the trolls had managed to light on fire. Some of the villagers were walking around in a daze. Some were working to put the fires out in their homes. Others were holding each other and crying. Avery couldn't help but stare at a woman kneeling on the ground, cradling the body of her dead husband and wailing at the top of her lungs. Avery looked down to the ground around her feet. She could barely see the green of the grass or brown of the dirt beneath the blanket of red and blue blood.

Avery slowly lifted her head up as Jade's voice languidly seeped into her brain, "Well, well, well," she heard Jade say, "look who's trying to crawl back to his sewer."

Beetlebat had regained consciousness and was on his hands and knees, trying to crawl away into the forest. Jade walked over and picked him up by the scruff of his shirt.

"Unhand me, pathetic mortal!" Beetlebat yelled at Jade, swiping his small arms at her, trying to land a punch.

"I made you a promise." Jade said, holding Beetlebat at arms distance, so he wasn't able to touch her.

Jade drew her arm back to stab the tiny troll straight through the chest, when Avery yelled, "Stop!"

Jade looked at Avery, wide eyed, "What?" She asked, glancing back and forth from Avery to Beetlebat.

"Don't kill him." Avery told Jade, walking up to her.

"You have to be kidding me?" Jade said, still holding tightly onto Beetlebat.

Avery shook her head, "Let him go."

Frustration crept over Jade's face. She looked like a child being asked to give up their favorite toy, "Avery," she said, refusing to let go of the tiny troll, "this little cockroach is not something you want to let live." She shook Beetlebat back and forth, the troll hollering at her the whole time.

"He seems harmless enough." Bunny said, earning her a scolding from Jade, telling her to, "Stuff it!"

"He has to live." Avery told the girls, "He has to go back and tell the Emperor what went down here today."

As much as Jade wanted to slaughter Beetlebat, Avery could see in her conflicted face that Jade understood Avery's reasoning.

Avery reached under Beetlebat's chin and turned his face towards her, "Listen to me," Avery said, pulling hard on his chin, making sure she had his full attention, "You're going to go back to your Emperor and tell him exactly what happened here. You tell him we're just as strong as we ever were. Tell him he's just going to lose more of his soldiers if he sends them our way again."

Avery made sure she sounded a lot more confident than she actually felt. She thought it a good thing to give that illusion to Beetlebat.

Beetlebat made a bite for Avery's fingers, and Jade pulled him back sharply, giving him a hard slap to his head.

Jade gave one last unsure look towards Avery, and then reluctantly let Beetlebat go.

"I'll tell him you are all just as stupid and pitiful as you always were!" Beetlebat spat out.

Avery hadn't wanted Jade to spare Beetlebat's life just because she thought it important that the Emperor see the Protector's as strong, but also because she hadn't wanted to witness any more killing. She felt she had already seen more than enough for a lifetime. Of course, that didn't mean she still didn't want to wring the little troll's neck.

With that thought in her mind, Avery told Jade, "Why don't you give him something to remember you by."

Without hesitation, Jade landed a hard punch directly into Beetlebat's face.

Beetlebat fell backwards; then sat up slowly, moaning. As he spit a small amount of blood out onto the ground, one of his front teeth came out with it.

"We'll work on the rest of your smile another time." Jade said to him before she, Avery, and the rest of the Protectors turned their backs on him and walked away.

"This isn't over!" Beetlebat screeched from behind them, "Next time we meet you will taste my blade! I will make a maggot feast of you!"

Completely ignoring Beetlebat's threats, Jade said to Avery, "I don't know if it was wise to let toad boy live. He's a vicious little thing."

Avery knew that Jade had a point, and that someday she may come to regret her decision, but at the moment, she couldn't have imagined making a different one.

"Thank you." A man's voice said from behind Avery and Jade.

The girls turned and saw a man in his late thirties. His clothes were tattered and his face was covered with a mixture of blood and soot. Avery and Jade just stared at him. At first Avery couldn't understand why some strange man would be thanking them.

"News of your return has been spreading." The man said, and as he talked more villagers began to walk over and stand with him, until a large group of about thirty had formed. "We weren't sure we should believe it, but thank goodness it was true."

A woman wearing a brown dress, her hair tangled, with a long scratch down her face, told the girls, "You saved us." Her eyes began to swell with tears as she said it.

Throughout the group of villagers that had formed, were words of gratitude and 'thank you's'. Avery wasn't sure what to say. A minute ago she had been thinking about the tragedy of the situation, about what a shame it was they couldn't have done more.

Now, here they were, being thanked by over thirty people for what they had done.

"You're welcome," was all Avery could think to say, "I'm just so sorry we couldn't have stopped them sooner."

The man who had first thanked them, said to Avery, "Without the five of you, we wouldn't have a village left to live in. Most likely, we would all be dead."

Hearing him say that gave Avery a new perspective on what had happened. There was no way she was ever going to get the image of the human bodies lying dead around her out of her mind, but now, she thought, maybe she could try and focus on the ones they had saved.

"You're very welcome." Avery said again.

"I'm Markin," the man said, sticking out his hand, "the mayor of Lilydale, and you have our undying gratitude."

Avery took Markin's hand and shook it, "Thank you." She said, "I'm Avery, and this is Jade." She nodded towards Jade who was standing next to her. Jade shook her head and smiled. She was terrible with thank you's and was never quite sure how to handle them. Probably, because she never received many back home, "That's Skylar, Sasha, and Bunny." Avery pointed behind her to where they were standing. They each waved and said their individual hellos.

After accepting Markin's and the rest of the village's thanks, Avery whistled for Phantom, and he came trotting up to her. She mounted, thankful to be able to go home. They had only been there for about an hour, but to Avery it felt like an eternity. She had Phantom walk the path home, unsure if her ribs would be able to handle a faster pace. The ride home was a silent one. Each of the girls was lost in their own thoughts, unsure of what to say to each other after living through an ordeal like that.

When they finally reached Havyn, the sun was just beginning to set in the sky, covering the village in hues of purple and orange. It made the village look like it was on fire, which Avery thought was ironic, considering the village they had just left had actually been on fire. As they entered the village, dirty, disheveled, and bloody, a few of the villagers stopped and stared, but then quickly got back to whatever they were in process of dong before the Protectors had entered the village. It occurred to Avery, that it must be no new thing for the villagers to see them returning, looking like hell.

Thomas and Pip came running out of the stables when the Protectors approached.

Avery jumped down off of Phantom. She gave him a hug, scratching his neck, and telling him what a good job he had done today.

Pip walked up to Avery, carrying Steel's reins in one hand. Avery handed him Phantom's reins in his other hand.

"Ya look terrible." Pip said, looking over Avery.

Avery laughed weakly, "Thanks."

Pip shrugged and looked towards the ground, as if he was ashamed for what he said, "What I meant was, are ya alright?"

"Oh, come on," Avery said, "don't tell me you haven't seen us looking worse than this, before." With everything Gumptin had told them, and after reading old Avery's notes and journal entries, Avery found it hard to believe that they had ever gone more than a few days without looking as they did now.

"I ain't sayin I ain't use to ya lookin like you've gone three rounds with a boulder." Pip told Avery, and Avery cringed at the analogy, "I'm just sayin, that was the old you. I was askin about the you…you."

As ineloquently as he put it, Pip had hit the nail on the head for Avery. For what was just a normal occurrence for almost everyone else, having the Protectors go off and do battle, had been, up to this point, one of the most significant for the girls. They could no longer pretend they were just five girls from Earth, playing the part of a warrior. Today had made everything real.

Avery smiled, appreciative of Pip's perceptiveness, "I'll be fine." She told him, reaching over and squeezing his arm.

She gave Phantom one last pat on his withers, before Pip walked the horses inside the stables. Avery turned around and gasped as she saw Gumptin standing almost directly in front of her.

"Well done, ladies." He said, smiling slightly beneath his bushy beard, "Well done, indeed."

The last thing Avery needed at this moment was another possible heart attack inducing bushwhack entrance by Gumptin, "Gumptin," Avery shouted, "you really need to start making some noise before just popping up around us. Especially after today, my heart can seriously not take your little surprise appearance act. Shuffle your feet, or something."

Ignoring Avery's mini rant, he asked her, "How did everything go?"

Avery had to think about how to answer that. On one hand, they had just lived through one of the most horrible experiences of their lives. On the other hand, they had saved a lot of lives and kicked the asses of the most monstrous creatures Avery had ever seen.

Avery decided it was probably best to keep her emotions out of her answer and just give Gumptin the facts, "Well, we saved most of the village and most of the villagers. Ninety eight percent of the flower fields were untouched. We killed the trolls, and we didn't die. So, all in all, I think it was a pretty successful day."

"Yes, yes, this is very good." Gumptin nodded energetically, "The Emperor will realize you are not as weak as he had thought. Did anything else happen?"

"Actually, yes," Avery said, "Jade met a tiny troll that infuriates her more than you do."

"Beetlebat," Gumptin replied, without having to be told, "you have had encounters with him before. He has worked for the Emperor for a long while. He is from a clan of ancient valley trolls. They are very old and very rare. They are also the only breed of troll that can actually speak other languages besides that of troll grunts. That is why they are usually used as commanders for troll armies."

"See," Jade said, walking up to Avery and Gumptin, "I told you we should have killed him."

Avery rolled her eyes. She knew Jade wasn't going to let her live that down anytime soon.

"You did not?" Gumptin asked, looking slightly surprised.

Jade looked at Avery, slight annoyance in her eyes, "Nope, our moral leader told us to spare him."

Gumptin looked towards Avery, waiting for an explanation.

"I thought it would be a good idea if he went back and told the Emperor how we had beaten the trolls and saved the village." Avery said loudly, feeling herself getting somewhat heated. She didn't want to have to explain her actions, especially considering she had the feeling Jade might actually be right.

"Actually, that is not a bad idea." Gumptin told her, "The sooner word of the Emperor's troll army failing reaches him, the better."

Jade threw her hands into the air out of frustration. "You know it wouldn't kill you to agree with me, just once." She said to Gumptin.

"What does it matter?" Sasha snapped, from behind Avery and Jade, "Who gives a crap that one little ugly troll was let go…not me. So, just shut up and get over it, Jade. I want to go home, already."

Avery realized Sasha wasn't exactly taking her side, and that she just wanted Jade to stop arguing so they could all go home, but having Sasha Seraphina actually help her out in an argument was something Avery thought she would never live to see. It was now official; this day could not get any weirder for Avery.

Jade, never one to be talked to in a way she didn't like grabbed onto the hilt of her sword and said to Sasha, "You know, Sasha, I was already stopped once today from killing something that I really wanted to. I'd watch that mouth of yours; 'cause I ain't gonna let it happen again."

Sasha just folded her arms, completely unaffected by Jade's threat, "You're all talk, Kai. After what we've seen today, do you really think you scare me one little bit?"

"Alright, I think it's time we all head home." Avery said, deciding to stop things before they got any more heated, "We've had a really hard day." She placed her hand on Jade's bicep, squeezing it slightly, making sure Jade stayed put next to her.

Avery didn't need to say it twice. Sasha took off; limping towards home the second Avery finished her sentence. Bunny waved goodbye, telling them she would see them tomorrow.

Before Skylar headed home, she strolled up to Avery. In a rare moment of seriousness from her, she told Avery, "You did a real good job today, you know. I'm glad you're our leader." She said goodbye to Jade and Gumptin and meandered towards her house.

Jade and Avery were about to walk off together, when Gumptin called out, "Avery, could you stay behind for a minute? I need to talk to you about something."

Jade looked unsure about leaving Avery and Gumptin alone to talk without her there to lend her opinion, but Avery motioned for her to keep walking.

"I'll see you tomorrow." Avery told Jade as a goodbye.

"Avery," Jade said, before Avery turned around towards Gumptin, "Skylar was right. I just want you to know, that no matter what I say, you're probably the only person I would ever actually follow."

"I know." Avery said, and she did know.

After a few seconds, Jade turned and strode towards her house, while Avery waited for Gumptin to tell her why he had her stay behind.

Gumptin cleared his throat, "I thought you should know that I talked to the Elementals. They told me that they could not give me any information about the spell that had been cast."

Avery stared at Gumptin blankly. She had no idea what he was talking about or why he felt it was important enough to bring up to her.

Gumptin, sensing Avery's confusion, cried out, "Oh, for Wizarding sake, you have forgotten, haven't you?!"

"No!" Avery yelled, bristling. Of course, she had no clue as to what he was referring to, but she wasn't about to let Gumptin think of her as an airhead. There would be too many instances where he could use that against her.

The look in Gumptin's eyes told Avery he didn't believe her for a second.

Gumptin pursed his lips before he spoke, "Well, then of course, I do not need to remind you of the spell that was cast at the Elysianth altar in the clearing…the one where you were so disgusted by the charred bird bone."

The scene burst into Avery's brain, "Oh, that spell!" She gasped, excited to remember, "Ewwww, that was disgusting."

"So nice to see you did not forget." Gumptin said condescendingly, "Anyway, the spell in the clearing had something to do with a spell that was cast before your deaths. Whatever it is, it is a very powerful spell, well beyond my knowledge, and that scares me. There are very few beings who would be able to cast a spell that I do not recognize."

The way Gumptin was talking about the spell was beginning to concern Avery. It seemed to be causing Gumptin anxiety, which meant there was probably more involved with the spell than just Gumptin's ignorance of its purpose.

"Why does this spell worry you so much?" Avery asked, "We've got a crazy Emperor with troll and Demon armies to worry about. What affect could this spell possibly have on us?"

Gumptin shifted around on his feet, as if he didn't want to have to tell Avery the next part, "When you died and the Elementals brought you back, there was a bigger price than just the loss of your memories." Gumptin told her.

Avery wasn't so sure the loss of her memory should be considered a price. With everything she knew about her old self and life, she believed it to be a blessing.

Gumptin went on, "Before you died, there was a very dark and very powerful spell that was cast. They told me it was a spell that could possibly shift the balance of good and evil. They could only right that balance one of two ways; either they reverse the spell, or they bring you back to life. I pleaded with them to choose the latter. I suppose you know which one they chose, but as a consequence, they cannot interfere with the spell that was cast. They cannot even give me clues or ideas as to what the nature of the spell was, or who may have cast it."

All the talk of spells and Elementals was starting to give Avery a headache. She understood the importance of Gumptin's concern, but also knew very well there was no way they were going to figure anything out anytime soon. Avery wanted to keep her focus on the Emperor. If there was one rule she was going to enact as leader of the Protectors, it was going to be to focus on just one bad guy at a time. Avery rubbed at her throbbing head, trying to think of a way to make it sound to Gumptin like she cared more than she actually did.

"Gumptin, I have faith you'll figure it out eventually." Avery decided that sounded like the best answer, "Like you said, a spell this powerful can't go completely unnoticed. I'm sure someone will know something."

Gumptin scoffed, "Unlikely, this is a bone from a Hellrise Raven."

Gumptin reached into one of the pouches attached to his belt and pulled out the charred bird bone Avery had found in the bowl on top of the altar. He shoved it as close to Avery's face as he could, waving it around in front of her. Avery scrunched her nose and turned away. The sight of it still repulsed her.

Gumptin continued waving the bone around as he said, "Hellrise Ravens are very, very rare. They are only found in one place in all the universe, the Hellrise Mountains to the far east, across the Wasted Desert. They are magical and evil creatures. The application of their bones in spells is for the perversion of memory. It could have been used to erase memories, implant memories, change memories, or anything else involving memories." Gumptin began to get worked up as he carried on, "I do not know who the spell affected or to what end, and that is extremely frustrating. I also do not know what other elements were used in the spell, everything was burnt too badly. Depending on how powerful the being was who cast the spell, it could have very far reaching affects."

Obviously, Avery's first tactic at ending the conversation hadn't worked. So, she decided to try a new one, "Listen," Avery said sternly, "I understand that this is a big deal, but I just can't deal with it right now. There is absolutely nothing I can do about it. Spells and Wizards are your department. I just want to focus on what you've been training us for…to kill the Emperor. So, can we just focus on that?"

While listening to what Avery had to say, Gumptin seemed to calm himself down. He took a deep breath and placed his raven bone back in his pouch.

"You are right." He said, "One thing at a time. We will fine tune our efforts on simply defeating the Emperor."

Thank goodness, Avery thought to herself. The conversation had only taken around five minutes, which was five minutes too long for Avery.

Before Avery and Gumptin walked their separate ways, Avery towards her home, and Gumptin towards the library, Avery said to him, trying to lighten the mood, "You know, Gumptin, none of the Protectors have any of our old memories anyway. They were taken away by the Elementals. So, if that spell was designed for any of us, then the spell caster is out of luck. They can't mess around with something we don't have."

Instead of agreeing or arguing with Avery, Gumptin simply told her, "I was very proud of the five of you today. Today, you were truly Protectors."

It was so unexpected and genuine that Avery was lost for words. So, instead, she simply nodded and smiled, before turning to leave.

In her head, Avery counted the steps to her house. With every step she took, she realized she was becoming more and more nervous. Avery wondered how her family would react to her battle worn appearance. She wondered if they would seem different to her after what she had been through today. The thought that she might have left a piece of herself back in Lilydale, among the corpses and destruction, teased at her insides. Avery had counted up to step forty-two from the stable to her house, when she reached her front door. Before she entered, Avery rubbed at her face with her sleeve, trying to wipe off as much of the blood, sweat, and dirt as possible. She tucked in as much of her blood stained shirt as possible. She didn't want Cinder to have to see her looking like a victim from some cheesy horror movie.

One deep breath, two deep breaths, and she turned the doorknob and entered into her home.

The crippling thoughts Avery had of being too damaged to think of her family as she had thought of them just hours before were dashed away in a fraction of a second as Cinder, along with their three dogs, came hurtling towards her, just as they did every other time she had come home.

Avery kneeled onto the ground and swooped Cinder up into a crushing hug when the little girl reached her. She let the three dogs jump all over them, covering Avery's already dirty clothes and face with saliva and fur.

Cinder wrapped her little arms around Avery's neck and held on tightly, "Why are you all dirty?" Cinder asked, speaking into Avery's ear, "Mommy and daddy were worried about you. They wouldn't tell me why, though. Why were they worried? Where did you go? Why are you so dirty?"

Avery let Cinder keep asking her questions, without answering a single one. Avery just held on to Cinder like she was the last life vest on a sinking ship. She buried her head in Cinder's shoulder and tried to fight back the tears that were begging to come.

When Avery spotted her mom and dad coming out from the kitchen and walking over to her, she let Cinder go and rushed over to her parents, falling into both of their arms. Her parents clung to her, holding her tighter than she had ever remembered them holding her.

"Oh, thank God." She heard her mother whisper into her hair.

Avery had never been so happy to be home and with her family in her whole life.

When she felt like everything was getting a bit much, like she would burst into tears at any minute if she stayed around her family any longer, Avery excused herself. She told her parents that she would be fine, that she wasn't hungry, and that she just needed to rest. She told Cinder to be good and that she would see her in the morning. Then, she rushed up the stairs to the second floor.

The first thing Avery did when she got upstairs was to go into the bathroom. As she closed the bathroom door she caught sight of herself in the mirror above the sink. She didn't think it possible, but she actually looked worse than she had expected. As she removed her vest, she saw that her entire shirt was covered in blood and dirt, so that she could barely see any of its original white color. Her wild curls stuck out in every direction and had bit of grass and debris tangled up in it. She shivered at the thought of having to try and brush it. Even after rubbing off her face before she had entered the house, her face was still a mess. There was a small cut above her eyebrow that had matted her eyebrow in dried blood. There was another scrape tracing her lower jaw line. Beneath the dirt, she could see a circular bruise forming on her right temple.

She took off her tunic extremely painstakingly. Any little movement caused her chest to ache, and the wound she had received on her arm, from the troll's knife, was still throbbing. She felt the skin on the wound separate slightly as she lifted her arms to take off her shirt. When she finished undressing she looked over her injuries in the mirror. Both sides of her chest were covered in deep purple bruises. The bruises on her right side ran all the way up to her collar bone, over to her shoulder, up her arm, and to her elbow. The slice on her arm had started bleeding again, leaving streaks of bright red trickling down her arm, over the dark red of already dried blood.

Avery just kept telling herself over and over that Gumptin had said Protectors healed quickly, healing about ten times faster than the average human being. Giving herself one last look in the mirror, Avery hoped he was right, because if he wasn't, the only thing she would be doing for the next week would be laying in bed, nursing the pain.

The shower felt like heaven to Avery. The warm water rushed over her body, soothing her tired muscles. Avery leaned her head against the blue tiled shower wall and looked down. The water running off of her and pooling around her feet had been turned a murky brown color from all the crud being washed off of her body. Avery stood in the shower, head leaning against the shower wall, eyes closed, until the water began to turn cold.

Finally clean and wrapped in a towel, Avery stood in front of the large silver dresser in her room. She had shut and locked the door, insuring her privacy. The wound on her arm was still continuing to bleed, and she knew it was too deep to be able to close and heal on its own. Gumptin had prepared them for injuries like this. He had devoted an entire day of library studies to the treatment and care of battle wounds. He taught them basic stitching, bandaging, and bracing of bones.

Avery sat down in her dresser chair and tied her hair back, so it wouldn't get in the way. She reached down and opened the one dresser drawer she had hoped she would never have to use. The bandages, needles, thread, and scissors looked just as they had on the first day Avery arrived on Orcatia and was exploring her room. She remembered thinking how unpleasantly crazy her life must have been to of had the need for a drawer like that.

The thread Avery chose was sturdy and black. She tied it around a thin medium length needle and brought the tip of the needle up to her wound. Avery hesitated and took a deep breath. She told herself that this would all be over soon, that after doing this one last thing, she could go to bed and forget about this entire day.

In one quick move, Avery pushed the needle through one side of her torn flesh. Avery slammed her fist onto her dresser. She wanted to scream out from the sharp pain, but clenched her jaw tightly, making sure she kept silent. It took Avery a moment before she could will herself to go on. She kept the stitches close and tight, to make sure there would be less scarring. The blood began to flow more heavily as Avery continued to close the wound, so Avery tied one of her white shirts around her elbow to catch the blood from falling onto the floor. It took Avery a good twenty minutes to effectively stitch up the wound, mostly because she kept stopping and starting when the pain got too intense.

When she had finished with the stitching, she wiped the remaining blood off of her arm with the white shirt she had tied around her elbow. Then, Avery took out a small vile of yellow liquid. She had had Mr. Bott come over to her house a few days before and explain to her exactly what every one of the salves and concoctions she had in her drawers were used for. So, she knew the yellow liquid, which smelled like a mixture of alcohol and Everlily flowers, was used to disinfect wounds. Avery rubbed some of the liquid over her stitches. There was a slight sting, but it went away quickly. Next, Avery bandaged up the wound, tying it tight

After Avery had finished with everything, she got into her nightshirt and delicately slipped into her bed. As she laid there, all the thoughts she had been trying to hold back the entire day started playing out in her mind. Images of the dead villagers and burning village were seared into her brain. Avery tried to fight back the tears as she thought about all the pain she had experienced. She began to remember the terror she had felt in the moment where she thought the troll was going to kill her. Avery had never come that close to dying before, at least, not that she could remember. She couldn't even begin to imagine never being able to see Jade, or her family and friends again. The harder she tried not to think about it, the more the idea of dying and losing everything was the only thought she could focus on. Avery felt one single hot tear roll out of her eye, and then another one, followed by another. She allowed herself to cry herself to sleep, making sure to keep her face buried in her pillow, so her family wouldn't be able to hear her sobs.

In the morning, Avery was awakened by knocking on her bedroom door. She heard the knocking, but didn't respond to it, hoping whoever it was would get tired and give up, leaving her to sleep.

"Avery." She heard her father call out.

"No!" Avery shouted from under the covers, refusing to get out of bed, "If Gumptin wants me for anything, he can go screw himself!"

There was no way Avery was going to be forced into any sort of training exercises after what her body had gone through yesterday.

Avery peeked her head out above her covers, keeping her eyes closed to the sunlight flooding in. She told her father, "There's no way I'm getting out of bed before ten. Gumptin's going to have to walk his old butt up here and drag me out of bed!"

"Avery." Her father said again.

"No!" Avery yelled and buried herself back under the covers.

Her father knocked twice more, then said, "Sweetie, it's already like nine forty-five, and Gumptin's waiting for you downstairs."

Crap, Avery thought. She wanted to kick herself for saying ten instead of noon.

"Dammit! Dammit! Dammit!" Avery shouted, kicking the covers off of her and hopping out of bed.

The first thing Avery realized when she stood up, besides the fact that her tears from crying the night before had glued her eyelashes shut, making it even harder for her to open her eyes, was that her body didn't feel nearly as sore as it had before she went to sleep. Avery stretched her arms high up into the air, a move that would have caused her to keel over last night, now just caused a slight ache.

Avery walked over to her dresser mirror and lifted her oversized Batman nightshirt up over her ribcage. The bruises covering her torso were already starting to dissipate. Now, instead of the dark purple they were last night, the bruises had turned into a yellowish brown color. Avery was tempted to undo her bandage and check to see how the slice on her arm was healing, but decided it was best to let it wait a few days.

After slipping on a pair of socks, Avery walked downstairs to see what Gumptin wanted with her. Halfway down the staircase, she heard her father and Gumptin talking. From the sound of it, she had come into the middle of a conversation.

"They are doing extremely well." Avery heard Gumptin say, "They still retain some of their cruder Earth habits, and they are lazier than a mountain ogre, but they are doing far better than I would have expected."

Avery's father's voice followed, "We just worry about them and not just about their safety. Of course, that's our first concern, but these past years, the girls have been happier than we've ever seen them. We just don't want them to lose their spirit."

"Well," Gumptin said, "it has been my experience training with them over this last week, that for better or worse, their spirit is not going anywhere. It makes training them severely agitating, but I must admit, I think I may miss their new zeal for life if they lost it. Although, I would ask you not to let Avery know that I feel that way."

"Gumptin," Avery said loudly, causing Gumptin to jump, "what are you doing here?"

Gumptin coughed and straightened his belt, hanging lopsided on his waist. He seemed befuddled and lost for words. So, instead of saying anything, he lifted his arm and pointed towards the study, motioning for Avery to go in.

The dark green walls and brown leather furniture were doing nothing to help Avery feel more awake. Gumptin shut the door behind them and Avery curled herself up into an overstuffed leather chair, covered with a hand sewn patchwork quilt.

"How are you feeling this morning?" Gumptin asked her.

Avery just shrugged. She didn't think Gumptin's question required an answer. Besides the fact that she thought it was a pointless question, Avery wasn't quite sure how she was feeling. A good cry and a long night's sleep had wiped away some of the more nightmarish elements of yesterday's events, for Avery. Looking back, she found her perception changing. She was beginning to focus on the people they had saved and their grateful 'thank you's'. Plus, she had to admit, that being able to kick major ass, felt really good. Of course, her new, more optimistic outlook was helped by the fact that she was in far less pain than she was yesterday. Even though, Avery was beginning to feel more positive about the endeavors involved with being a Protector, she wasn't about to let Gumptin know this. She could see a bright side, but that didn't mean she wanted to be sent out to do battle with more trolls anytime soon, at least, not until she was completely healed.

"So, why are you here?" Avery asked Gumptin, intrigued by the fact he had come to her house to talk to her in private. It was out of the usual for Gumptin, which meant it was probably for something big.

Gumptin sat down in a chair across from her, his little legs sticking out in front of him. If it weren't for his long gray beard and hair, Avery was sure he could have been mistaken for a child.

"Before you died," he told Avery, "you had a tentative plan on how to defeat the Emperor."

So far, Avery wasn't exactly thrilled with what Gumptin had to say. She figured if she had a plan, the fact that she died meant it probably sucked.

"You see," Gumptin said, "the problem with killing the Emperor, is actually getting to him. His fortress is surrounded by mountains, a large wall, and his armies, so even if you are able to reach him, his minions would surround you in a matter of minutes. I believe that is how you died in the first place."

"But you don't actually know how we died, right?" Avery interrupted Gumptin, "For all you know, the Emperor could have killed us himself."

Gumptin gave a cynical snort, "That is very unlikely." He leaned forward, continuing on with what he was saying before Avery interrupted him, "At first, your plan was to gather large armies and attack the wall surrounding the fortress from all sides. The Emperor's armies would be kept busy. Then, once you broke through the gates, you and the other Protectors could hopefully take on the Emperor without having to deal with his followers."

"Well, that obviously didn't happen." Avery said, sarcastically.

Gumptin shook his head, "No, no it did not. There were a few problems that ended up discouraging you. You felt that you were running out of time, so you abandoned that plan and tried to find another way. Weighing all of our options, I feel that your first plan is still our best course of action. So, firstly…"

"Wait, wait," Avery said, cutting Gumptin off again, "before you tell me what you want me to do, you better tell me why I ended up so discouraged."

Gumptin began wringing his hands. He stared at the ground for a few moments, trying to think about how to word his next sentences, "Well," he began, "the obvious and most powerful army, not to mention, the only army that could spare their resources and were in close enough proximity, would be King Draven's. However, you were more than hesitant to ask for his help."

Avery waited for Gumptin to explain, but if like Gumptin said, she had been more than hesitant to ask for King Draven's help then Gumptin was more than hesitant to explain why.

"Why?!" Avery exclaimed, demanding he continue.

Eventually, Gumptin reluctantly said, "Your opinion of him was not very high."

Avery just stared at Gumptin for a moment. She couldn't believe she wouldn't have asked for help, just because her opinion of him wasn't great. Avery knew there was something Gumptin was reluctant to share. She chose not to push him any further, thinking he might have been trying to be polite and spare her feelings by not calling her a judgmental bitch. After all, that's what Avery was thinking of her old self. For all she knew, maybe Gumptin was too.

"Whatever." Avery said, not forcing Gumptin to elaborate on his crappy little explanation.

Gumptin looked relieved to be off of that subject, "Plus, there was an incident with the Fairies, and they refused to aid the Protectors in any way, but you will not need to worry about that till later in the week when you go meet with them."

Avery couldn't stop herself from laughing. She wondered how her life had gotten to the point when the mention of meeting actual fairies was considered a normal topic of conversation.

"Are you quite alright?" Gumptin asked, as Avery placed her face in her hands and shook her head, continuing to laugh.

"I'm fine," Avery said, keeping her face in her hands, "keep going."

"Anyway," Gumptin went on, sounding slightly annoyed, "with the loss of those two armies and time running out, you decided the plan was not worth it."

Avery got that Gumptin wanted to go back to the original plan, she just wasn't sure what exactly he wanted her to do today, "So, you want me to…" Avery said, trying to prompt Gumptin.

"Today, I want you and the other Protectors to travel to Knighton Castle, to meet with King Draven. I have sent word to him that you will be coming." Gumptin stood up from his chair, "I will go and tell the other girls. You will meet them at the stables in an hour."

Traveling to Knighton Castle meant no training for the day and no bloody battles. To Avery, it was like Gumptin giving them a vacation.

Avery stood up out of the chair and stretched, "I'll go get ready." She told Gumptin, feeling giddy at the thought of getting to travel to an actual castle.

"Avery," Gumptin said, stopping Avery before she got to the study door, "just remember we need the use of Draven's army. So, however he may act towards you, just be the charming girl that I know you have buried somewhere deep, deep, very deep down inside of you."

Turning back around towards the door, Avery tried to ignore Gumptin's words, especially since she had the notion that he might not have been joking.

As she walked up the stairs to her room, Avery heard Gumptin shout from the study, "And for Wizarding sake, try and look like a Protector. This is a professional visit."

Avery took Gumptin's words to mean, add weapons to the outfit and loose the shirt with the giant yellow bat.

Chapter 9

The route to Knighton Castle was far easier to follow than the one to Lilydale. Gumptin had told them all they had to do to get there was to continue down the Main Road. He said it would eventually lead them to Knighton Castle, in the heart of the kingdom of Nightfell.

Since there wasn't the sense of urgency to reach their destination quickly, like there had been for Lilydale, they kept their horses at a slow trot, enjoying the cool breeze and sounds of the forest.

"Did Gumptin happen to mention to you why exactly we didn't try this whole multiple army plan before?" Jade asked, riding beside Avery.

It surprised Avery that Gumptin hadn't said anything to Jade about her past incarnation's disapproval of the King, and her subsequent discouragement in the plan. Then again, it was Gumptin talking to Jade, and he usually tried to say and spend as little time with her as possible. For a second, Avery considered telling Jade exactly what Gumptin had told her, but then she thought better of it. She didn't want to have to deal with the questions that she knew would follow. Jade would want to know why Avery hadn't approved of the King, and what exactly the incident with the Fairies was. Avery didn't have the answers to those questions, and she knew Jade would just chastise her for not pushing Gumptin harder to give her the answers. Avery was enjoying the scenery and ride too much for that.

So, instead, she just said, "No, he didn't mention anything to me."

If Avery had hoped that answer would satisfy and quiet Jade, she was mistaken, "It just seems messed up, you know." Jade continued, as Avery rolled her eyes. "If we had a somewhat good plan, and I'll admit, this is a *somewhat* good plan, then why would we all ride off to this incredibly guarded fortress alone, on what seems to be a whim, and try to kill the Emperor."

Avery knew that Jade was making sense. She would have loved to been able to have the answer to that question, but the truth was she didn't even have the slightest notion why they would do something so reckless. From what Gumptin had told her, she doubted even he knew why they had ridden out to the Emperor's fortress that night.

"I really don't know." Avery told Jade.

"It sounds like a suicide mission. No wonder we died." Jade sneered, "There's no way I would have done something so stupid, unless there was a damn good reason."

Avery was sure that was true. For Jade to have ridden out that night, she must have either been confident in the plan, or else have a spectacular reason.

Not wanting to dwell on the subject of their deaths, or what led up to them, Avery decided to switch the topic. She asked Jade about Mrs. Bott's sweet shop and what her favorite treats were there. As Avery had already known, Jade leapt on the topic. One of the perks of being best friends and spending an obscene amount of time together is you know exactly what subjects they can't help but talk about. For Jade, it was food, music, motorcycles, and although only Avery knew this, eighties movies, Jane Austen novels, and Star Trek memorabilia.

The rest of the ride to the castle was a pleasant one for the girls. They traveled down the Main Road for over an hour, with nothing but the forest and its haunting serenity surrounding them. They passed over a dozen small roads, all marked with small wooden signs.

On the road, the girls passed the occasional traveler, a young boy dragging a donkey, loaded down with misshapen sacks, a scruffy looking man on top of a brown work horse, galloping in the opposite direction. The Protectors had to ride around a family of six loaded into a wooden cart, being pulled by a giant slow moving draft horse. The mother and father sat up front, while the children were packed into the back, amongst several baskets of dark red apples. When the family recognized them as the Protectors, they gave each of the girls one of their delicious looking apples and thanked the Protectors for the work they did fighting the Emperor. Jade was the first to grab an apple, scarf it down, and then ask Avery if she was planning on eating hers.

A little while later, the girls came to an old looking wooden bridge. A small sign, stuck into the ground in front of the bridge, had the words, 'Cooper Bridge' carved into it. Below that, it had an arrow and the words 'Wildpoint Lookout' carved on it. The arrow pointed to a small path leading off into the forest, to the right of the bridge. The bridge crossed over a softly moving wide river below. From what Avery remembered of the maps Gumptin had them study, the river was called Moonfound River and it started in the Stormfell Mountain range, ran all the way through the Darksin and Wildwood Forests, and ended in a giant lake called Ravage Lake, bordering the Wasted Desert.

As they crossed the bridge, the sound of the flowing crystal clear water below sounded like bubbling bells as the water bounced off of the smooth stones and riverbed brush.

After about an hour and twenty minutes of slow riding, the girls reached a section where the road diverged off into three separate paths. There was a large wooden post sign in the center of the three paths, with multiple directional signs pointing to different villages, nailed onto it. At the very top of the sign there was a board that pointed straight ahead. On it was written the name, 'Knighton'. Below it was nailed a board pointing to the right road, which read, 'Blackmore'. Below that, pointing to the left road was a sign that read, 'Stormfell'. Then, below that, another sign pointing to the right that said, 'Vowhollow'. Followed by a sign nailed beneath, pointing left, that read, 'Divinwood'. Then, a final sign, that pointed right, with the word, 'Darksin' written on it and a small black, X carved into the wood after it, in what appeared to be a warning. The sign made it easy enough for the Protectors to understand that they wanted to continue traveling straight.

The farther they rode past the sign, the denser the forest became. With less light able to shine through the compact tree tops, a darkness fell over them, and a thickness hung in the air. It felt as if the very atmosphere itself were pushing in on them. The trees began to grow so close together, that as the Protectors trotted down the road; it looked as if they were surrounded on either side bay a dark brown wall. When Avery did manage to catch a glimpse of the forest between the trees, the only thing she was able to make out were dark shadows and the occasional ray of light, illuminating a patch of ankle high green grass. The only real color Avery could see were the spattering of multi colored wildflowers lining the edges where the forest met the road.

After riding for about twenty minutes down the more primitive road, the path began to gradually incline up a large hill. The top of the hill was also where the forest ended.

The moment they reached the top of the high hill, the trees opened up and a flood of sunlight smashed into the Protectors' eyes. Avery pulled Phantom up to a halt, allowing her eyes time to adjust to the new brightness. The rest of the Protectors followed her lead. As she reached her hand up above her eyes to shield them from the sun, Avery scanned the horizon in front of her. What she saw almost took her breath away.

The dirt road they were on led down a hill of Christmas green colored grass, and as the wind blew through it, creating waves, it made the Protectors feel like they were standing in the center of a vast green ocean. When the road reached the bottom of the grassy hill, it leveled out into an expansive valley below. On each side of the road were scatterings of small straw farm houses, each with their own little section of land. From high above the valley, most of the farms looked like they were growing wheat and different types of vegetables. There were animals, sheep, chickens, horses, pigs, bunnies, and the occasional cow fenced into pastures around the houses.

There were two roads that led off of the Main Road once it leveled out in the valley, one to the right and one to the left. The roads led off into separate sections of the forest. Over a dozen people were using the road, most of them the farmers who had homes in the valley. They were using their horse and carts to take their crops towards the castle. The entire valley and castle were surrounded by the dense Wildwood forest.

It was the castle that was really leaving Avery in a state of awe. It was the biggest castle she had ever seen. Of course, up until this point, the closest Avery had ever come to seeing a castle was the pink and purple fiberglass castle on course four of Bobcat Bob's Miniature Golf World, back on Redemption. So she was completely unprepared for the magnificent structure her eyes were now gazing at.

The castle sat on top of a high hill and was surrounded by a large octangular stone wall. The Main Road they were on led up the hill to the outer wall of the castle and right up to the drawbridge, which led to an arched gatehouse. The outer wall was massive, with high battlement walls built out of a light colored stone. It had a total of eight square towers built into each edge. The top of every tower had a low battlement and circular balcony with arrowslits wrapping around it. The castle, itself, was comprised of a mixture of light and dark gray stones. The tallest tower, cylindrical in shape, was in the dead center of the castle. It had a dark blue cone shaped roof with a long pole coming out of it and a black flag with a silver wolf emblem attached to the top of the pole. There were four smaller cylindrical towers on each edge of the castle. Each had the exact same cone shaped dark blue roof and pole with the flag attached. Built into the castle wall, on the north and south side, were two more towers. These had a flat roof with high parapets. Every tower had a wide circular balcony wrapped around it, near the top. All except for two square shaped towers, bordering the entrance to the actual castle. Arched windows and arrowslits lined the walls of the castle.

From behind her, Avery heard Sasha say, "That's it, forget Havyn, we're staying there."

Avery nudged Phantom into a walk, and the Protectors continued down the path towards the castle.

The closer they got to the valley below the forest; they noticed people beginning to come out of their houses. Men who were working in their fields stopped and stared as the Protectors approached. A group of young children playing in a wheat field began waving at the girls. Avery waved tentatively back. It was an odd feeling, having people she didn't know interested in her presence. Back in Redemption, even if people knew you, it didn't mean they were the least bit interested in your comings or goings.

As they passed a large potato field, a man, who had been tending his crop close to the road, took off his cap as they neared him and said to them, "You is them, ain't ya...the Protectors?"

The girls nodded and Jade replied, "Yeah, I suppose we are."

The man seemed to get excited, and clutched tightly at the cap in his hands, "Might good to see ya!" The man ginned, "All of us here were just so happy to hear ya weren't dead!"

Jade let out a saucy laugh, "Us too, buddy."

After they had ridden a few feet away from the man, they heard him yell out loudly, "It's them!"

Sasha leaned in closer towards the other girls and said, "Let's move it a little faster, ladies. I don't want any more hick farmers telling me how excited I make them."

Avery looked back and gave Sasha a disapproving look, as Skylar laughed and told her, "You need to get over yourself, girl."

To which Jade responded by snorting and saying, "When horses shit apple pie."

They walked their horses up the hill towards the castle. When they reached the end of the road, the drawbridge was down, allowing them to cross the steep ravine between the castle and the road. Phantom and the other horses' hooves clomped on the heavy wooden drawbridge as they crossed it.

There were two guards posted at each side of the entrance to the castle. They were dressed in chain mail and wore a black tunic with a silver wolf's head on it, belted over it. The silver helmets they wore made their eyes the only visible features on their face. Each of them held in their hand a tall lance and had a sword attached to a belt around their waist.

Avery slowed Phantom up slightly as they passed the guards. It was an instinct, like when she used to slow down her car back on Redemption when she would pass a police car, even if she was going the speed limit.

Once inside the outer walls, it was like a whole other village had just opened up to them. There were wide flagstone streets. On both sides of the street there were multiple wooden shops, houses, and stands built up against the large outer wall and the castle wall. A hundred different scents and sounds accosted the Protectors' senses. The smell of food, and smoke, flowers, hay, and horses all mingled together with the smell of human sweat. There were people talking, and shouting, and haggling over prices of merchandise.

Avery glanced up and saw a guard, in uniform, posted every ten feet along the top of the outer wall. Along the walls of the castle, including the tower walls, there were also uniformed guards positioned every ten feet.

"Apples, ten in a bunch!" A woman to the right of them, standing behind a fruit stand, shouted.

To the left, a man hollered, "Fresh fish!"

Dogs were barking and children were crying and laughing. People were carrying baskets full of goods, pushing carts, and strolling along on their way. They walked in front of, behind, and in-between the Protectors and their horses. It was by far the busiest place the Protectors had ever been to on Orcatia. The bustle threw them off guard.

Avery looked behind her to the other Protectors, looking for a little guidance, since she wasn't quite sure where she was suppose to go to now that they were inside the outer castle walls. Unfortunately, the others were no help. Sasha ignored her, Skylar was distracted by a lean muscled blacksmith working nearby, Bunny looked more lost than Avery, and Jade just shrugged her shoulders and shook her head.

While she was still turned to the other Protectors, Avery heard a man's voice shout above the other noises, "I take it you are the Protectors."

Avery turned and saw a blond clean shaven man in his mid thirties standing in front of her. He was wearing the same chain mail and black tunic uniform the other guards had on, except he wasn't wearing a helmet. Behind the man were two rows of five guards, each in full uniform, and carrying the same tall lances the guards at the entrance had.

"Hello." Avery said tentatively, looking down at the man and weapon carrying guards.

"We've been expecting you." The man said, "I'm General Stone, I command the guards, but you can call me Ferris if you like." General Stone smiled up at each of the girls, effectively softening his authoritative presence. It immediately made Avery feel more at ease with him.

"Nice to meet you." Avery told him, and then proceeded to introduce herself and the other Protectors.

General Stone said hello to each of them in turn, then said, "If you could please follow me." He turned and walked towards the castle. The rest of the guards turned and marched along behind him.

Avery noticed that their little interaction with General Stone and the guards had captured the attention of a number of the people around them. Feeling a bit on display, Avery was happy to follow the General and guards towards the castle entrance.

When they reached the entrance, just a short thirty second walk from where they had been, they saw a large arched opening, about twenty feet wide and thirty feet high, with a heavy iron gate coming half the way down in front of it. On either side of the gated entryway were two guards. One stood next to a hefty wooden lever that Avery assumed controlled the rise and fall of the iron gate.

Once inside the castle gate, the Protectors found themselves in the main courtyard. The flagstone walkway had continued inside the castle gate and outlined a lush green rectangular yard the size of a hockey rink. A packed dirt walkway led up the center of the yard and was bordered by rows of five foot tall trees, all dappled with dark red flowers. On the right and left side of the courtyard, the castle walls were straight, but as the courtyard ended, sections of the wall protruded and portions seemed to be built on to the walls as extensions. There was a large rectangular building attached to the middle tower section of the castle, on the opposite side of the courtyard. It was almost the width of the courtyard and appeared to be about five stories tall. It attached to the right section of the castle wall with a small two story building. The connecting section had a walled archway through the middle of the first floor, to allow people and horses to walk from the courtyard to the back right section of the castle.

The part of the castle in front of them had a wide ten step white marble staircase that decreased in width the closer it got to the enormous arched heavy metal double door entrance, which had two large wolf heads etched into the metal of the doors. Above the entrance was a massive window that Avery thought was probably equal to the size of her house back in Redemption. She squinted to see if she could see anything behind the ridiculously large window, but the sun was gleaming off of it, allowing Avery to see nothing but a bright shine.

Three boys, all in their late teens, came running out from behind the tower section of the castle, through the archway in the small attached building. They were all in lightweight cotton pants and dark colored tunics. They ran up to where the Protectors sat on their unmoving horses and formed a straight line. To Avery, they looked like professional versions of Pip.

"They'll take your horses." General Stone told the Protectors, which gave Avery a little understanding of why they looked like three order following Pip's

Avery and the others dismounted, handing over their reins to the stable boys. They watched as their horses were led away and out of sight.

"This way." General Stone said to them and walked down the dirt path in the center of the courtyard.

The Protectors followed him, but the ten guards they had walked in with made their way down the left side of the courtyard and down a small path that led into a different section of the castle.

When the Protectors followed General Stone up the white marble steps and through the thick metal entrance doors, they found themselves in the most spacious room they could imagine. It was even bigger than their high school auditorium. It shocked them to realize that they were only standing in the entryway.

The floor was entirely covered in black marble, and the dark stone walls were lined with black and burgundy tapestries, depicting forest landscapes and battle scenes. There were two closed wooden doors to the left of the girls and an open archway to the right that led to a sunlit sitting room with crimson red walls and black cushioned chairs and benches. Avery looked up and saw that the rest of the floors had no floor landings above the square entryway area. She was able to see straight up to the dark blue painted roof. She was also able to see the stone railings for every floor above her. Avery counted them, one, two…five. There were a total of five floors above her. At least, that she could see.

About a hundred feet in front of them was a long dimly lit hallway. From what the girls could see, it had stone walls lined with suits of armor and unlit torches. On either side of the hallway entrance were the beginnings of two massive staircases. The staircases and railings were polished and carved out of a hard dark stone. They wound around in a crescent moon shape and led up to the high second floor, which in any other building would have been more like the third or fourth floor.

The Protectors followed General Stone up the right hand staircase. When the Protectors reached the second floor, they became level with the large window that Avery had tried to peer through from out in the courtyard. As unsuccessful as she had been peering in, Avery was able to see out completely fine. She walked over to the stone railing that stood between her and a fifty foot drop and gazed out the multi-paned window. From the height the window was at, Avery was unable to see the bustling society outside of Knighton Castle or the valley below, but she was able to see a great expanse of Wildwood Forest, with its tall lush dark green trees. She could also see the bright blue sky and cotton ball clouds. The sun shone down through the trees, illuminating the rich dark brown of the tree trunks. It was one of the most beautiful sights she had seen all day, and she was including the castle in that assessment.

General Stone let out a small cough, letting Avery know that he was waiting for her before continuing on. Avery tore her eyes away from the window and walked over to where General Stone was waiting for her. Both staircases continued winding up to the floors above, but General Stone led the girls down a long, torch-lit center hallway. A dark red carpeting ran down the middle of the hard stone floor. Large square canvas paintings, over at least two dozen, in heavy mahogany frames lined the hallway.

They passed one painting with a small silver plaque attached to the bottom of the frame that had, 'Ivyville', engraved on it. It was a painting of a smaller village, with spread out chalet-like houses that had brightly painted red and green roofs. There were no trees to be seen in the village, just open fields of long yellow grasses and a narrow but long river running through the center of it. Throughout the fields there were dozens of horses and foals running, standing, and munching on the grasses. The painting across from the Ivyville painting had a small silver plaque that said, 'Klover', on it. The village in that painting was lush and over abundantly green. It was in the middle of the forest, just as Havyn was, but the homes, instead of being built into trees, were built directly next to the trees. They were short one story homes, covered in vines and moss, so much so, that one of the only visible things about the homes were the windows and doors. Next to that painting, was a painting entitled, 'Lilydale'. It looked just as the girls had remembered it, except without any buildings on fire or dead villagers lying around. The straw homes of the village were intact. The yellow Everlily fields were in full bloom and it almost looked like the houses were built next to a giant field of sunshine.

It occurred to Avery that all the paintings lining the hallway walls were of different villages in the Nightfell Kingdom.

"Through here." General Stone told them. He was standing outside of two heavy oak doors with thick black rails. The panels of the door had the thematic wolf heads carved into them.

They were walking over to join him when Avery saw, that directly opposite the wooden doors, was a painting of Havyn.

"Check it out." Avery told the other girls.

Sure enough, the little silver metal plaque on the bottom of the picture frame had the word, 'Havyn', etched into it.

The painting looked exactly like their village. It even had the stone well painted into the center of the town and the rows of long picnic tables placed off to the very far right, near the forest. The gigantic trees had little windows, and doors, and chimney stouts coming out of them. Each one of the girls found their house. It was easy for Avery; she knew hers was the first one next to the little painted stable. From what she could see in the painting, it looked vaguely the same, except the door seemed to be painted a different color. She could even see a tiny light brown and black brush stroke, meant to be the balcony outside her room. The only girl who couldn't find their home was Bunny, who didn't live inside the trees like the other girls. She lived in one of the farmhouses located in the fields behind the giant trees. In the painting, all that was visible were green and yellow patches of field and little wispy color spots, meant to be the farm houses.

Jade looked at the painting and snickered, "All it needs is a little sour looking Gumptin figure standing in the middle of the village and yelling, 'You are late! Lazy Earth tainted oafs!'."

The girls laughed, completely agreeing with Jade's assessment and remembering back to three days ago, when Gumptin had said those exact things to them.

General Stone gave them a minute to scan over the painting, and then said to them, "Right through here."

Before Avery let the others go anywhere, and while they were still in a tight circle around the painting, Avery said to girls, "Now, remember, we're dealing with a King. So, we've got to be on our best behavior. Be professional and confident…we're supposed to be Protectors."

Avery and the other girls all turned their heads towards Jade.

"What!?" Jade asked, taking a step back and acting shocked, "I'm always on my best behavior!"

Avery raised her eyebrows, letting Jade know she definitely wasn't buying that statement.

"I get along with people just fine." Jade told each of them.

The girls scoffed, and Sasha literally stepped out of their circle and walked towards the doors, not willing to listen to Jade's ridiculous comments anymore.

"Hey," Jade said, shrugging her shoulders, "as long as you're not an asshole, I like you just fine and it's all smooth sailing. That's why I have so many problems with Sasha…it definitely ain't smooth sailing."

Avery knew that's the best she was going to get from Jade, so she walked over to join Sasha and General Stone. The General grabbed onto one of the chunky black metal handles on the door and pushed it open. He motioned for the girls to enter into the room and after they all had, he shut the door behind them, staying outside the doors himself.

The Protectors' shoes thumped on the hard stone floors as they walked farther into the spacious room. The torches around the room were unlit, so the only light coming into the room was from the five tall arched windows along the right wall. The windows were lined with thick black curtains, which prevented as much sun as there could have been from flooding into the room. As a result, some parts or the room were brightly lit and easy to see, while other parts remained in dark shadows. The walls were covered with red and black gothic themed tapestries, effectively adding to the dark feel. In the dead center of the room was a twelve foot by twelve foot platform that had a step leading up to it on every side. On the platform, sat a grandiose throne. It looked to be made out of black marble, with a strip of silver running down the arms and curved legs. The seat and back cushions were plushy black and a black marble wolf's head with blue jeweled eyes rested at the very top of the back of the throne.

The room was sparsely furnished, with only a row of dark chairs with crimson cushions against the back wall, a broad round black table to the left hand side of the throne's base that had a number of papers strewn across it, a larger black chair with a crimson cushion pushed up against the left wall, and a large black writing desk with a simple dark wooden chair, also pushed up against the left wall.

A small movement out of the corner of Avery's right eye caught her attention. When she turned her head in that direction, she saw a tall man leaning with his shoulders up against the wall, next to one of the long windows, his arms crossed over his chest. The man was shrouded by the dark shadows of the room and partially hidden by the thick black curtains surrounding the window. So Avery was unable to see anything but his lean silhouette. When the man saw Avery take notice of him, he pushed himself off of the stone wall.

"Well, well, well," She heard a smooth deep voice say, "I never thought I'd see the day when Avery Kimball, leader of the *righteous* Protectors, would enter into my throne room."

There was a definite dripping of sarcasm wrapped around his words, but any inkling of offense Avery might have taken from his comment was wiped away when she heard her name said in his silky voice.

When he walked out of the shadows and sauntered over to his throne, Avery was shocked to see, not only a young man in his early twenties, but also one of the most hauntingly handsome men her eyes had ever beheld.

The man was tall, about six foot, and lean, without being thin. He had thick midnight black hair that came down to just below his ears. His dark eyebrows and lashes were the same color black as his hair, making his bright electric blue eyes even more prominent than they would have been. His skin was pale; more like someone's who doesn't go out into the sun, than Avery's naturally porcelain skin. He wore fitted black leather pants, tucked into black boots that went up to just below his knees, and a white tunic, with a black leather belt clasped around his waist. Attached to the belt was a black leather scabbard, which held a large silver-handled sword.

After the shock of the initial first sight of him, Avery collected herself and played back his comment in her mind. She really didn't know how to respond to it. So, instead, she decided to get straight down to the reason they had come.

"Gumptin sent us." Avery told him, trying to maintain a polished looking calm as she stared into his eyes. No one should have eyes that blue, she told herself, it's just not fair. Then, realizing her mind was drifting from the topic at hand, she gave herself a mental slap.

The man walked over to the black throne and leaned his arm up over the top of it, "Yes, I know." The man said to Avery, fixing her with a crooked side smile, "Your little magician sent me word early this morning, telling me to expect the honor of your presence."

Again, his words were twinged with sarcasm, and this time Avery couldn't find it quite so easy to ignore.

"Is that all he told you?" Avery asked, wondering if Gumptin had mentioned the reason for their visit.

"Should he have told me something else?" He asked quickly, staring at Avery intently and not answering her question.

Avery hated it when people answered a question with another question. It was one of her pet peeves. She reminded herself to stay professional, just as she had instructed Jade to do.

She opened her mouth to simply tell him, no, when, from behind her, Sasha blurted out, "I'm Sasha, by the way, Sasha Seraphina. It's a pleasure to meet you."

Avery slowly turned her head towards Sasha, giving her a 'what the hell are you doing' look. When Avery turn her head back towards the man, he was smiling broadly at her, flashing a row of straight white teeth. He clearly enjoyed Avery's displeasure with Sasha's comment. Avery found it amazing how quickly his good looks had gone from mesmerizing to irritating.

The man moved his eyes from Avery, over to Sasha, "And it is a *pleasure* to meet you." He told Sasha, smiling his side smile at her, "I'm King Draven Night, but you can call me Draven."

Avery could almost hear Sasha smiling from ear to ear behind her. It made Avery want to gag.

"Anyway," Avery said, putting an end to that little interlude, "we came here to ask you for the use of your army."

Draven stared fixedly at Avery for a moment, and then burst into a slow deep laughter.

"*You*," Draven said, through his dying laugher, "came here to ask me for the use of my army?"

Avery failed to grasp the humor in her last statement.

"Well, it's not like we'd need you to give us the army right now." Avery said, only making Draven laugh harder.

That was it; Avery was officially completely over his good looks.

"Look," Jade said, standing next to Avery, "we don't have a lot of time to waste. So, if you could just listen to her," Jade pointed towards Avery, "it would be really helpful." Jade must have listened to Avery; because that was the most polite she had ever been to anyone who had even slightly annoyed her.

Draven stopped laughing just as quickly as he had started, which led Avery to suspect that his laughter might have been just for show.

"Oh, I'm sorry," He said to Jade, "I wouldn't want to keep you from running off and getting yourself killed again."

Avery felt Jade's body stiffen next to her. Jade took a deep breath before telling Draven, "We were thinking about keeping that off of our 'to do' list."

A serious look came over Draven's face, darkening his blue eyes, "I'm not sure that would be a very safe bet."

"Who do you think…" Jade had started to take a step towards Draven, but Avery grabbed her by the arm and pulled her back, stopping Jade not only in her tracks, but also mid-sentence.

Draven smirked, watching Avery take control of Jade, "I believe Havyn's missing five little girls." Draven told them, wiggling his fingers, signaling them to leave, "You should run on home now."

Avery had had enough. She wasn't going to go back to Gumptin and tell him that they had failed miserably. She could already see the horrible look of disappointment in Gumptin's eyes. So far, in the matter of a few minutes, Draven had mocked her, laughed at her, and called her a little girl. Taking all of that into account, Avery was going to make damn sure he at least heard what she had to say before being dismissed.

"No." Avery said sternly.

She stepped up onto the platform and walked up to stand in front of the throne. When she approached, Draven flinched back slightly, not expecting her to get so close to him. He took his arm off of the back of the throne and crossed his arms, as if he was creating an invisible shield to block her with.

Avery could tell she wasn't going to get anywhere with Draven by being overly aggressive. She also knew that if she was too passive, he would just walk all over her. Avery came to the conclusion to take Gumptin's advice and just be herself.

"I know that I didn't…" Avery tried to think of the right way to say what she wanted to, "think to highly of you in the past, but I don't remember any of that. Who I am now doesn't think of you that way at all."

Draven broke eye contact with Avery for a brief second, looking down, but then immediately looked back up at Avery. Avery saw his throat move up and down as he swallowed hard. It was the first time Avery had seen his cocky façade crack, even just slightly, and she was thankful for it. It meant that she just might be able to get through to him.

"I'd really like for us to start out with a clean slate." Avery stuck out her hand in front of her, "I'm Avery Kimball."

It took Draven a moment to pull his eyes away from Avery's and glance down at her hand. He hesitated for a few seconds, then stuck out his hand and took hers in his own. They shook hands longer than necessary. Avery's delicate hand fit comfortably in Draven's bigger, slightly rough hand.

"I'm Draven." Draven told Avery, his face soft, although he wasn't smiling.

Standing there having her hand held in Draven's, Avery almost forgot why she come to the castle in the first place; she almost forgot about the other girls standing there watching them, and she had definitely almost forgotten that less than a minute ago she had thought of Draven as an arrogant jerk.

Of course, all of those things came rushing back to her when Draven, seeming to realize they were still holding hands after more than a few seconds, cleared his throat and dropped Avery's hand back down to her side. He stepped down off the platform and away from Avery

"Well…um," Draven was uncharacteristically searching for words, "just because you don't hate me anymore, doesn't mean I'm going to hand over my army for you to play with."

It hit Avery again why she had thought him an arrogant jerk.

Avery rolled her eyes, "It's not like we're gonna go play, storm the castle. We do actually have a plan, and you…"

"I'll have to think about it." Draven said shortly, cutting off Avery.

Avery bit her tongue, keeping all the insults she wanted to throw at him to herself.

"Fine," Avery said, knowing it was probably the closest thing to an answer she was going to get, "you think about it, but before we go we need to see the records you keep on your army." Avery didn't ask if she could see them, she demanded it. She didn't want to be turned down again, so she thought it best not to give Draven that option.

"Why?" Draven asked.

Avery shrugged, she really wasn't sure. It was just something Gumptin had told her to get. He wanted the army records. He wanted to know how many men and regiments the King had and where they were all positioned throughout Orcatia.

"Gumptin wants to see them." Avery told Draven, "When we return them, you can give us your answer." Avery added the last part to let Draven know that she fully intended on getting an answer from him.

By the way Draven was looking at her, Avery thought he may try to argue, but instead he strode over to the throne room doors and pulled them open. He stepped outside and Avery heard him saying something to General Stone, who was waiting outside the door. When Draven walked back inside, General Stone was following him.

Draven pointed to General Stone, "Ferris will take you to the records room and make sure you get what you need."

As the girls began to follow Ferris out of the room, Draven asked, "Avery, could you stay behind for a moment?"

Avery and the others stopped in their tracks. She stood completely still, just staring at Draven for a moment, wondering if she actually heard him say what she thought he had said.

After a moment, without Draven correcting or elaborating on his statement, Avery hesitantly said, "Alright."

The rest of the girls turned and followed Ferris, all except for Jade, who stayed by Avery's side, not moving.

"Alone." Draven said to Jade.

Jade still refused to move, "Whatever you want to discuss with Avery, you can talk about it with me here."

Draven smiled at Jade, a smile that didn't reach his eyes, "Run along little watchdog." He told her, motioning with his hand for her to leave, "I promise I won't hurt her."

"Watchdog?!" Jade hollered

Before Jade could say something that Avery would regret, Avery grabbed Jade around the waist and pulled her to the door, where Ferris was waiting.

Avery whispered into Jade's ear, "He's a king, he's a king, he's a king, let it go."

Without bothering to free herself from Avery's grasp, Jade turned to her and whispered back, "Well, the *King* just called me a dog."

"Remember what I said about being professional." Avery told Jade.

To which Jade responded, "Remember what I said about assholes."

Avery had to literally push Jade outside the throne room doors, "Just go." Avery said, pointing down the hall to where the other girls were waiting, "I need you to go to make sure we get the right records anyway. Bunny will forget the information Gumptin wanted, Sasha won't care, and Skylar will get distracted by the first hot guy or sparkly object she sees!"

That seemed to strike some sense into Jade, which Avery knew it would. Jade may at times try to appear apathetic and indifferent, but she hated not getting a job done properly.

"Dammit!" Jade said through clenched teeth, then pointed at Avery, "Fine, but don't take long."

After Jade and the others disappeared down the hall, Avery slowly turned back around towards Draven.

Avery smiled nervously, "She'll be fine." She told Draven, hoping Jade's almost outburst wouldn't affect his decision about letting them use his army.

"I'm surprised you get anything done with that one safeguarding you all the time." Draven told Avery, walking over and closing the throne room doors back up.

It was one thing for Draven to give Avery a hard time, which she really didn't appreciate, but it was a whole other thing for him to talk about Jade. It was something Avery wouldn't tolerate from people who didn't even know her.

"She's my family. We protect each other." Avery said to Draven. Making sure her voice was stern enough for him to get the point to leave that subject alone.

He got the point. Draven shook his head, looking at Avery from out of the side of his eyes, "I've offended you." He said.

Avery wasn't sure if he was asking a question or making a statement.

"It wouldn't be the first time today." Avery said, laughing slightly, so Draven wouldn't think she was too upset by it.

Draven smiled, "I'm sorry." He said, and sounded more sincere than Avery thought him capable of, "I don't have a lot of contact with people. So, I can sometimes come off a bit…abrupt."

He walked over to the window he had been standing next to when the Protectors had first walked in. He leaned back up against the wall and stared out the window. Avery walked over and joined him, curious as to what he saw outside that window.

It was the same view that she had seen from the large window on the second floor. Except, the position of the room allowed Avery to see over the castle wall and partially down into the valley below. She saw a few of the farm houses and where the Main Road disappeared into the forest.

As Avery gazed out of the window, trying to count how many people were walking along the Main Road, she gradually became aware that Draven was no longer looking out at the view, but was instead staring at her. When Avery looked up, he quickly glanced away, back to staring out the window. Avery turned away from him and as she did, her shoulder grazed his chest. He shifted away uncomfortably, and she took up position leaning on the other side of the window. It made Avery happy to be at least a few feet away from Draven. It made it easier for her to think. She tried to think of something to say, anything to break the awkward silence starting to form between them.

"Why don't you have a lot of contact with people?" Avery asked. She had been curious about Draven's statement when he made it and thought now was as good a time as any to question it.

Draven seemed a little thrown off guard by the question. He looked at her, shifted again, and then looked away. He seemed to be contemplating exactly what to say to her.

"I was raised with my mother, far away from this place." He told Avery, matter of factly, no inflection in his voice, "I never had any real...experience with people."

Avery wondered exactly where Draven's mother raised him that prevented him from interacting with other people.

"I mean, sure I have to talk to Ferris, the Generals of my army, and a few others." Draven elaborated when he saw the shocked look on Avery's face, "Not to mention, other kings, diplomats, and aristocracy, but they're usually so boring that I just completely block them out."

"But, you're a king. You rule an entire kingdom." Avery said to him, pointing her hand towards the window and everything outside of it, "There are literally thousands of people who, I'm sure, would be willing to talk to you."

Draven shook his head, completely dismissing that notion, "I don't interact with my subjects."

"What?!" Avery asked, thinking that was a preposterous thing to say, "Why not?"

Draven pushed himself off of the wall and went to stand by his chair. Avery could see his back tense underneath his shirt. For whatever reason, he clearly didn't want to continue with where this conversation was going.

"What did Gumptin tell you?" Draven crisply asked Avery, turning around abruptly.

"N...nothing." Avery stuttered, taken aback by Draven's unexpected turn of emotions.

"Nothing?" Draven looked at Avery suspiciously, "He didn't tell you anything about why you didn't approve of me before?" When Avery hesitated, Draven continued, "Your friends aren't here now. You can tell me the truth."

So, that was why he asked to speak to her alone, Avery realized. So he could interrogate her about information Gumptin hadn't given her. It had nothing to do with discussing his army. It was just a waste of Avery's time and that thought pissed her off.

"What exactly should he have told me?" Avery asked Draven, stepping up to him. She figured she might as well answer his question with a question, give him a little taste of his own medicine.

It worked, a little. Draven seemed confused for a moment, searching for the appropriate reply.

"So, he didn't tell you *anything*?" Draven asked, getting his face dangerously close to Avery's face.

Avery was going to continue with the run-around questions, but Draven's eyes, only inches away from her own, looked so pleading, so questioning.

Although she didn't completely want to, Avery relented and answered Draven's question, "Well, not really, he basically told me I was a super warrior machine bitch, who didn't have a life and had a major stick up her ass about everyone in general."

Draven searched Avery's eyes; a furrow began to form on his brow. The slight side smile of his began to form on the left side of his face and he stood up, taking a few steps back.

"It's very doubtful Gumptin would have said that to you." Draven told Avery, covering his mouth with his hand, trying to wipe the smile off his face.

Avery shrugged, "I read between the lines."

Draven's smile disappeared, and he became calmly serious again, "You had your reasons to think what you did and act the way you acted. You're a Protector. You have to be a certain way to keep yourself alive."

"'Cause that worked out so well." Avery told him sarcastically.

Draven grinned, realizing what he had just said, "Still," he said, "you should really try to harden yourself a bit."

That statement was like a slap across Avery's face. She couldn't believe he was actually telling her to be more like her old self. The old self that seemed to make herself miserable and turn away from the people she loved.

"You don't know anything about me." Avery told Draven, trying to keep her anger under control, "The old me…died! She died with nothing to show for herself, except hard work and alienation. I am *nothing* like her. I may be soft and trusting, and you may think of that as weakness, but I really don't care." As she continued, she realized she was more venting now, spilling her frustrations, than yelling at Draven, "I have friends, and family, and interests that don't include beheading things. So, whatever you think, I'm already better off than that other girl was."

After a moment, Draven said to her, "I take it back." He made a slight little bow gesture, "Stay just the way you are."

Avery scoffed, thinking he was teasing her.

"No, I'm serious." Draven said, less than a second after Avery let out her scoff, "You know yourself, and you're able to connect with people. That's a gift not too many have the luxury of." He looked down as he said the next part, "Although, I'm afraid it will make things harder for you as a Protector.

That, Avery believed. Pretty shortly after she had come to Orcatia, Avery had figured out that her way of thinking and the way people felt a Protector should think were completely different. She knew it would probably make things harder on her, but she also knew that there was no way on Earth or Orcatia, that she would ever be able to change it. In truth, she thought she would rather die than switch over to old Avery's way of thinking.

"I'm sure, if you tried, you could connect with people to." Avery told Draven. His words had been the softest thing he had said to her so far, and they had managed to make her feel good about herself. Avery felt that she should try and return the favor.

Draven let out a hard cold bark of a laugh, "Trust me," He told Avery, flashing her his teeth, "that'll never happen. I don't do…people. I became King to keep my father's kingdom safe and protected. When he was alive, I let my father down in ways that no son should ever do." He clenched down hard on his jaw, "After his death, I made a vow to myself, that I would protect his kingdom and his people, to my very last breath. He loved his people, so I take care of them for him, but I do not want anything to do with them outside of that. It's better for everyone involved, that way."

That was far more information than Avery had expected or wanted. So much so, that she had no idea what she should say next.

"Unlike you, Avery Kimball, I do not connect with people." Draven spat his sentence out, and Avery was unsure if the cold tone in his voice was directed at her or just his feelings on the topic in general.

Avery thought about what Draven had said for a minute, and then said the first thing that popped into her mind, "Well, you're getting along just fine talking to me. I mean, sure you're a little aggravating, and from what I've seen, also a little moody, maybe bipolar, but things could be going much worse."

Avery's statement appeared to startle Draven out of his anger. He opened his mouth to say something, but quickly closed it.

When he opened his mouth again, Draven told her, "I don't...I don't mind talking to you." He seemed surprised, "It's strange, I hadn't really thought about it, but this is the most I've talked to anyone in a very, very long time. It's just, you...you're..." All of a sudden, a look something close to fear came over his face, and Draven quickly turned his back to Avery, "You're leader of the Protectors." He said in a short tone, "I have no choice but to deal with you." He turned back around, an arrogant smile plastered back on his face, "Truth be told, you're ludicrously annoying."

Avery smiled, it wasn't the first time someone had said that to her. In fact, she thought Gumptin had said something close to that just a few days ago.

"Well, I'm sure you're wanting to join your friends." Draven walked over to escort Avery towards the door.

"Hold on," Avery said, pulling her elbow away from him as he took it in his hand, "what about the army?"

After everything she and Draven had discussed and said, she felt that, surely she deserved more than an, 'I'll think about it'. She wanted an answer, something concrete to take back to Gumptin. Draven, however, did not see it that way.

He gave her a quizzical look and reached for her elbow again, "I told you," he said, "I'll think about it."

Again, Avery pulled her elbow away from him, this time taking a few steps backwards, to ensure she was out of his reach. When he steadied his jaw and made a move towards her, Avery gave him a pleading look, as told him, "I need more than that."

Draven's face softened, he stepped over to her and once again took hold of her elbow, except this time, instead of pulling on it, he let it rest in his hand.

"Avery," he said, "I told you, I took an oath to protect this kingdom, and that's exactly what I plan to do."

With her free arm, Avery reached over and grabbed a hold of Draven's arm, as it rested on her elbow.

"But, that's exactly what the Protectors want, to." Avery said, emphatically. She didn't understand why there was such an issue if they were working towards a common goal.

Draven looked down at Avery's hand on top of his hand that was holding her elbow. He quickly let go of her and backed away, almost pushing off of Avery as he did, sending her gently back a step.

Draven sneered at her, "You didn't seem to do that great of job your first time around."

His words stung Avery, just as he had meant them to. He wanted her gone and out of his chamber, and Avery could feel it, but if Draven thought he could so easily wound and dismiss her, he had another thing coming. She wasn't going to let him take this conversation back to her old self and her old failures.

"You know what…" Avery snarled, striding over to Draven, sticking her finger into his chest, "screw you!"

Genuine shock exploded on Draven's face, "Excuse me?" He asked, smiling slightly, which only angered Avery more.

"I said screw you!" Avery threw her hands around in the air and paced back and forth in front of Draven, unable to stop the tirade that followed, "I've just spent the last week and a half working harder than I've ever had to work in my entire life! I've pushed my body past its breaking point! I've left the only home I've ever known to travel to an entirely different *planet*, just to get yelled at by a psychotically militant gnome, fight creatures from horror stories, and come to the realization that the future of the planet is basically resting on my shoulders, and my shoulders aren't that broad! Oh, and not to forget, finding out that I actually already died once! Which, can only be made worse, by finding out that I was killed by the dude we're suppose to go fight!"

After she finished, Avery took in and let out a long breath. It hit her how much better she felt after her little outburst. They were things that had been coiled up inside of her for a while, and it was inevitable she was going to explode at some point. She just hadn't expected to do it in front of a king. Avery turned her head and looked at Draven. He stood with his mouth half open, a small smile on his face.

"I'm sorry." Avery said, quickly. She really was sorry. Although Draven had peaked her anger, none of that was really meant for him.

Draven cocked one dark eyebrow up, "You told me to, 'screw you'.

Ok, maybe Avery had meant that, in the moment.

Avery winced, "Well, you pissed me off."

"Noted." Draven told her, and then he slowly broke into a slow loud laughter that resonated off the chamber walls.

Avery couldn't help but notice how different Draven looked with a genuine smile and laugh on his face. All the arrogance and mockery were gone. The sternness of his sharp angles softened, making him appear more like a warm human being, than a cold marble statue. Crinkles formed at the edges of his eyes, making him seem even more approachable. Avery might have found his big smile and deep laugh more endearing, if he hadn't been laughing at her outburst.

"I don't know how you intimidate your enemies." Draven said to her, trying to calm his laughter, "You looked like a little angry dove, chirping about."

Avery pursed her lips, trying to let his comment slide off of her back, "Well, I usually try to have a sword in hand when facing my enemies, hoping they see that and not the angry little dove charging at them."

Draven tried to make himself look serious, which was hard to as a tight closed lip smile perked at his lips, "I'm sure that's very effective."

His smile, mixed with the image of a rabid dove running towards a troll, with sword in wing, began to break Avery down. Avery bit her lower lip, trying to stop the smile she felt coming, but it was too late. In a second one of Avery's giant bright smiles peeled across her face and a choked back giggle escaped her lips. In just a few minutes they had gone from yelling, and Draven almost dragging Avery out of the room, to standing just a couple of inches apart, smiling, Draven's electric blue eyes staring deeply into Avery's emerald eyes.

The moment quickly died, when Draven's smile abruptly left his face and he strode past Avery towards the chamber doors. Avery stood for a moment, staring at the place where Draven had been standing only seconds before. Now, instead of him, she was looking out a long window, noticing the change of color in the sky from a bright blue to an opaque yellow and wondering why exactly Draven seemed so reluctant to just let himself enjoy the company of another human being.

When she turned around to look at Draven, he was standing with the door held open, eyes pointing towards the ground. She walked slowly towards the door, looking Draven up and down as she came closer. She wondered if he was so difficult to deal with on purpose, or if he had serious emotional issues. Whatever it was, she was done trying to interact with him today. Charming one minute and exasperating the next was becoming too much for her.

Avery stopped a foot in front of Draven. She stood and stared up at him, waiting for him to say something. She was hoping for a, 'goodbye', at the least. Draven didn't say anything; he didn't even look at her. His eyes went from the floor, to staring at the far back wall of the throne room. Still, Avery waited, but the only response from Draven was the hard rise and fall of his breathing, which got heavy the longer Avery stood by him. Finally, giving up, Avery sighed and turned to leave. She thought to herself how disappointing this trip had been.

Before Avery made it two steps away from Draven, he reached out and grabbed a hold of her upper arm.

Avery didn't turn her head towards him, instead he bent his head down towards her ear, and said to her, "Before I give you use of my army, I'm going to need to have a full briefing on your plans, and I'm going to need to oversee it every step of the way."

In her excitement, Avery turned her head quickly towards him. When she did, her lower cheek smacked into Draven's mouth. For a few seconds, longer than Avery would have thought necessary, Draven let his lips rest on her cheek. This time when he pulled away, he did so slowly, with no abrupt jerks or back steps.

"Th...Thank you." Avery told him in a rushed whisper.

As Avery moved to walk out the door, she felt that Draven was still gripping her arm. When she delicately tugged it free, Draven's grasp collapsed in on itself. He cleared his throat and placed his hand behind his back.

"You know," Avery said, turning around before she made it completely outside the door, "I don't think I've smiled like that since I've been on Orcatia. So, thank you."

Draven nodded and appeared as if he wanted to say something, then thought better of it, then rethought it and told Avery, "I don't think I've laughed like that...ever. So, thank *you*."

Before Avery could respond, not that she would have known how to respond, Draven swiftly closed the door, leaving Avery staring at a thick plank of wood, two inches in front of her nose.

It took Avery's brain a little while before it was able to tell her feet to move. Her mind was spinning, trying to take in everything that had just happened. She took a small step back from the door, her face scrunched up in a confused expression. Avery shook her head clear and let out a small giggle. Whatever had just transpired, Avery was pretty sure she was going to be given use of Draven's army.

Avery glanced left, then right, and realized she really didn't have any idea exactly where she was suppose to go. Draven had seemed to be in such a rush to get Avery out of his throne room that he hadn't given her instructions on where to go to meet up with the other girls. There was no one in the hallway besides her, so Avery couldn't even ask anyone to direct her to the records room. She raised her fist to the throne room door, to give it a quick knock, but couldn't seem to make herself bring her fist down on the hard wood. Her emotions were already frazzled from dealing with Draven. She didn't know if they could take any more interactions with him. After a quick debate, she decided to head back down to the front courtyard and try to find the stables.

The high sun hit Avery as she walked out of the castle doors, soothing over her entire body. The bright sun and warm colors of the outside were in strict contrast to the cool dark castle. It felt to Avery like stepping into another world, the real world, and leaving the dreamlike realm of the castle behind.

The courtyard was empty, but there were still plenty of sounds floating around the air. From the outside of the wall, the sounds of everyday life were loud and clear. From inside the castle, Avery could hear the shouts of guards, giving and receiving orders. Then, to her left, she heard what she had been listening for, the faint whinnies of horses.

Avery walked down the path she had seen the stable boys walk with the horses. Once she had passed through the archway in the attached building, she found herself in a completely different courtyard. This courtyard was simply a large square green field of shortly cut grass, surrounded by a dirt walkway. To Avery's right, was a low-rise part of the castle, which seemed to be made out of wider and rounder stones than the rest of the castle. There were three large arched wooden doors on the bottom floor. The middle door was left partially ajar and the smells of baking breads and cooking meats were filtering out through it. Outside of the door was a small wooden bench with some kind of churn sitting next to it. In front of her was a higher part of the castle, with one of the towers attached to it. To her left, were the stables she had been looking for. The stables were a single level building made out of round brown and black rocks, with a straw roof. The front of the stables had a row of twenty large square windows, with horses heads sticking out of a few of them, whinnying at each other and over to Avery. A large rounded open entranceway was built into the middle of it. There was a wooden fence surrounding the stable that went out about twenty feet. It was split in the center by a small dirt pathway that led up to the entrance of the stables. Inside the fenced area were three loose horses on the right side and a few pigs and chickens on the left side. One of the stable boys that had taken the Protectors' horses was in with the pigs and chickens, shoveling manure into a cart.

    The smell of animals began to mix with the scent of cooking foods already in Avery's nostrils, causing Avery to feel slightly queasy. She puffed air out of her nostrils and headed over to the stables. She walked up the small path, through the entryway, and into one of the largest stables she had ever seen in her life. Not only were there twenty stalls of horses to her right and left, but the stable went much farther back than was visible from the outside. Avery ambled down the hay strewn pathway, past two tack rooms on either side of her and stopped in the middle of another row of horse stalls.

    In back of the main stable area was small walled in courtyard where there were more horse stalls built. These stalls were larger than the inside ones, and had both inside and outside access for the horse. In the largest stall, was a tall completely ebony black stallion. He was just as tall as Phantom, but not as bulky. On the outside of his enclosed stall, a gold plaque read, 'Drako'. The large black horse was on the inside area of his stall, munching on a large pile of green hay. Avery clucked her tongue and the horse lifted his head, a few straggly pieces of hay hanging out of his mouth. He finished munching on the hay already in his mouth, and then slowly meandered up to Avery. He stuck his large head over his circular wooden stable door and straight into Avery's face. Avery moved her body slightly to the left, to avoid being knocked over by him, and took his giant head in her hands. She scratched under his chin as he nibbled on a wayward lock of her hair.

"You remind me of my boy." Avery whispered into the horse's ear.

"Um, excuse me, Miss," Avery turned and saw another one of the stable boys she had seen before, addressing her, "that's the King's horse."

Avery got the implication that meant, 'hands off'. She gave the horse one more pat on his neck, then stepped away from him.

"I'm guessing my friends haven't come back, yet?" Avery asked the boy.

"No, Miss Avery." The boy said back to her.

Avery sighed, she wondered if she was going to have to have this same conversation with everyone she met, "Just call me Avery. No, Miss, alright?"

The boy looked completely confounded. He just stood in front of her, staring at the ground, not sure what to say next, or how to address her.

"Fine," Avery said, taking pity on the boy, "call me whatever you want."

"Thank you, Miss Avery." The boy told her, already more at ease, "Did ya want me to bring out the Protectors' horses?"

Avery smiled, "That'd be great."

The boy whistled and two more stable boys, one whom Avery hadn't seen before, joined him. They ran back to the last few stalls in the walled in courtyard and fetched the Protectors' horses from them. The stable boys hitched the horses up to the outside fence, and then Avery, sensing they all intended to wait out there with her and the horses, told them it was fine for them to get back to their work.

Avery sat on the top rail of the fence, in between Steel and Phantom, and waited for the others. She had to continually push Steel's mouth away from her, as Jade's horse kept trying to nibble on her leather belt. After about ten minutes, the rest of the Protectors came walking through the same archway Avery had come through. They were being led by Ferris, who smiled and nodded his head slightly when he caught sight of Avery.

"I hope you haven't been waiting long." He told her.

"Not too long." Avery said, hopping off of the fence.

Jade walked past Avery quickly, without acknowledging her. Before Avery could turn and say something to Jade, she noticed Bunny had a large satchel slung over her shoulder that she hadn't had the last time Avery had seen her.

"Are those all of the records Gumptin asked for?" Avery asked Bunny.

Bunny nodded, "Yes, Jade made me carry them down." Bunny shifted the loaded down satchel strap on her shoulder, cringing a little under its wait.

Avery grabbed the heavy satchel off of Bunny's shoulder, slipping it over her own, "You know," Avery told Bunny, "just because Jade tells you to do it, doesn't mean you have to."

Bunny sighed, "Jade's still not over the whole, me hitting her with a rock, incident yet. I figured I'd just try and be nice to her and do what she tells me to do for a little while."

Avery smiled to herself; she wasn't sure if that was going to be such a good idea. She could only hope Bunny's mostly meek personality didn't get trampled over by Jade's strong one.

"Well," Avery said, "if Jade tells you to go jump off a cliff, which she probably will at some point, just try and control yourself, alright?"

"I promise." Bunny laughed sweetly, smiling at Avery.

Before mounting up on their horses, Avery thanked Ferris for showing the other girls the records.

"Of course," He told Avery, "just following orders." Ferris shut his mouth, then after a slight hesitant look, said to Avery, "Orders that the King doesn't usually give. I don't remember the last time he allowed visitors into the records room. In fact, I'm not sure that he ever has."

Avery wasn't quite sure what Ferris was trying to say, "Well…" she said, "we're Protectors, and Gumptin sent us. So…" That was it. That was all Avery could think to say.

Ferris stared hard at Avery for a few seconds, smiling slightly, "I'm sure that's it." He waved goodbye to girls, "Have a safe trip home."

Avery jumped as Skylar, who had, unnoticed by Avery, come up and stood beside her, wrapped her arm around Avery's shoulder.

"That, Draven," Skylar said, slyly smiling down at Avery, "was the *tastiest* thing I have laid my eyes on...maybe ever."

"Skylar," Avery groaned, shaking Skylar's shoulder off of her, "you think every guy you see who is even mildly attractive is *tasty*."

"Oh, come on," Skylar teased, following Avery to the where the horses were hitched up, "don't tell me you didn't think he was gorgeous?"

Avery shrugged, "He was alright." She turned her head away from Skylar, making sure she couldn't see the blush of a lie forming in her cheeks.

"Whatever," Skylar shouted, pushing Avery in the shoulder slightly, before walking over to mount her horse, "I don't believe you for a second. Now, tell me what went down in that throne room, woman!"

As Avery approached Phantom, she saw Jade leaning up against Steel, arms crossed, one eyebrow up, staring Avery down.

"What is your problem?" Avery asked, laughing. She was too shocked by Jade's look not to laugh. For a minute, it reminded Avery of the look her mother gave her a few years ago when she had been caught sneaking back into the house after going to a concert her mother had told her she wasn't old enough for.

"I don't have a problem." Jade said in a clipped tone, shrugging her shoulders, "I'm just waiting for you to answer Skylar."

"Nothing happened." Avery said slowly, mounting Phantom.

Jade didn't move; she just stared up at Avery, a look of suspicion on her face.

"Nothing." Avery said again to Jade.

Jade shook her head, then turned to mount Steel.

It suddenly occurred to Avery, that while she had been so busy protesting that nothing had happened up in Draven's throne room, she had completely forgot to mention to the girls the most important thing that had actually happened in his throne room.

"I almost forgot," Avery said loudly, "I did get him to give us permission to use his army."

Jade, who was halfway through mounting Steel, fell to the ground as her foot slipped out of the stirrup.

"What?!" Jade shouted, wrapping her arms around Steel's neck, and picking herself up, "And exactly what did you do to convince him to do that?!"

Skylar let out a little wolf whistle, "That's my girl!" She giggled.

Sasha was looking at Avery like she had just sprouted a second head.

"Whoa, whoa, whoa," Avery said defensively, "I didn't *do* anything."

"Oh," Said Jade, mounting up fully this time, "so he just, out of the blue, decided to give us his army, which he so adamantly had to think about."

It was time for Avery to calm everybody down and clear the air, "First off," she said, "it wasn't out of the blue. I kept pushing him about it. Second, it comes with conditions. He wants us to bring him a full plan, and he wants to be involved in everything we do with his army."

"So, nothing really happened?" Skylar asked, sounding disappointed.

"We just talked." Avery told her.

Jade squinted at her, as if trying to pry into Avery's brain, "That was it? Nothing else happened?"

Avery's mind immediately flashed back to the electric feel of Draven's warm lips resting on her cheek, "Nothing else happened." She said to Jade, trying to block out the image.

"Good," Jade said, kicking Steel into a slow walk, "because if you decided to fall for the one guy on this planet or Earth, who called me a dog, I'd be forced to pound some sense into you."

Bunny followed Jade out of the courtyard, followed by Sasha, then Skylar and Avery.

"So," Skylar leaned over and asked Avery, when she was sure Jade was out of earshot, "what was he really like? You know, besides being hot."

Avery thought back to their entire interaction. She was as confused about it now as she had been after Draven had slammed the door in her face. There were moments when he was soft and open, telling her about his father, and their last moments when he had given her his army. Then, there were moments when he was closed off and abrupt, insulting Avery and trying to get rid of her. It aggravated Avery just thinking about him and his arrogant and aloof mannerisms, but she also couldn't help the warm tingle that rushed over her body when she thought about his laugh and the softer side she was able to see just below his surface.

After giving it a little thought, and realizing she really wasn't sure what she felt about King Draven, she told Skylar, "He's complicated."

Skylar looked at her a bit puzzled, "Is that good or bad?"

That was the question Avery was asking herself, "I'm not sure yet."

From the other side of Avery, Sasha said, "If I were you, I'd go with bad, because that boy is way out of your league."

Avery was always so completely shocked by Sasha's insults that she could never come up with a comeback in time. So, as she was staring at Sasha open-mouthed, Skylar said, "Oh, back off Sash, Avery's smokin'. You're just jealous because King Cutie didn't ask you to stay behind and discuss 'interrelations'."

Sasha scoffed, "Please, if I decide to go after that man…he's mine."

Avery suddenly had enough talk about King Draven.

"Alright," she said to Skylar, "despite his good looks," she turned to Sasha, "and despite your ego mutilating statements directed at me, can we please talk about something else."

Skylar was silent for about fifteen seconds, and then asked, "Did you guys see how hot that blacksmith was?"

"You're worse than a dog in heat." Sasha told Skylar.

Skylar acted offended, she shouted up towards Jade, "Jade, now I can join your club! I was just called a dog too! Now we need someone to say it to Avery, so our dog club has a leader."

Despite herself, Avery burst out laughing; she only hoped Jade didn't see her giggling.

It didn't help when Jade turned around in her horse and shouted back, "I think our club might be a little Ruff for her!"

Hearing something so corny come out Jade's mouth, caused Avery to throw her head back and let out one of her crystal bellowing laughs. It was so loud and contagious, that despite

Jade's previously sour mood, she couldn't help but let out a chuckle either.

Just as they were about to ride their horses out of the castle gates, Avery turned around in her saddle and took one last look at the castle. She looked up to the large window on the second floor, and then scanned a few windows over to the right. She knew these were the windows that belonged to Draven's throne room. Despite not being able to see much behind the windows, she could have sworn she saw a shadow moving inside one of the tall windows. Before she allowed herself to dwell on the thought of whom that shadow belonged to, she turned back around and followed the girls out of the castle walls.

Chapter 10

When they got back to Havyn, they dropped their horses off at the stables, and then walked over to the library to meet Gumptin.

Gumptin was seated at the large round table, reading a big red leather bound book, waiting for them.

"How did it go?" He asked the girls as they walked into the room.

Avery slammed the satchel she had taken off of Bunny's shoulder onto the table in front of Gumptin, "Here are the records you wanted." Avery told Gumptin, smiling proudly.

Gumptin opened the satchel and scanned through the documents inside it, "Are you sure this is everything?" He asked, looking up at Avery, "You remembered everything I told you I needed?"

Avery hesitated for a second. She hadn't actually been there when the other girls had gotten the records, so she wasn't quite sure how to answer.

"Well, it should be." Avery said.

Gumptin blinked up at Avery, "Could you please define what you mean by *should*."

"I'm the one who got the records," Jade stepped in and told Gumptin, "and yes I got everything you told us to."

Without thanking or questioning Jade, Gumptin asked Avery, "Where were you?"

Avery placed her proud little smile back on her face, "Oh, just getting Draven to agree to give us his army."

Gumptin looked a little stupefied, "You...what?"

Avery furrowed her brow, not understanding why he looked so shocked. After all, he was the one who had sent them to try and get Draven's army. Why would he have sent them if he expected them to fail?

"Is that surprising for some reason?" Avery asked him.

"Well...well...yes." Gumptin stammered, "I thought he would either tell you 'no', or give you some vaguely ambivalent answer. Then, after he had time to think about it, he might say yes. Or, I would go see him and convince him of your pure intentions. I had no hope that he would willingly give you use of his army without any argument."

"Thanks for your confidence." Avery said sarcastically, taking a seat in one of the chairs next to Gumptin, "Anyway, there *were* a few arguments, and a few catches. He wants you," Avery pointed to Gumptin, "to write down and give him whatever past Avery's full plan was, and he wants to be involved once he gives us use of his army."

Gumptin still just stared at Avery in amazement, "I am utterly astonished...well done. I will get to work drawing up the plan immediately." Gumptin shook his head, "I cannot believe you were able to get through to him with reason."

Jade let out a snort, "I don't think *reason* had anything to do with it."

Avery was starting to get sick of all the little comments made about her and Draven.

She turned quickly towards Jade, who was sitting next to her, and told Jade sharply, "Just drop it. What is your problem with Draven anyway?" Before Jade could bring up the dog remark again, Avery stopped her, "Besides that."

Avery knew Jade well enough to know that one offhand remark wouldn't bother her so much.

"I...I," Jade ran her fingers through her long black hair, "I don't know. He just gives me a weird vibe." She softened, staring Avery in the eyes as she said the next part, "I don't trust him."

"Do not be ridiculous." Gumptin cut in quickly, "He is the King of Nightfell. If anything, you, Jade Kai, probably give him a weird vibe."

"Says the weirdest of them all." Jade scowled at Gumptin, leaning back in a chair and putting her feet up on the table.

Gumptin continued to scan through the records the girls had brought back, "His army has more men than I had thought, very good." He said more to himself, than any of the girls.

When Gumptin looked up, it was as if he just realized the girls were still there, waiting for him to tell them what they were suppose to do next.

"Oh," he said, staring at them, "why don't you girls go on home now. I have much work to do. Plus, you should all get a good night's rest. You have training first thing in the morning tomorrow, and then I'm sending you out on patrol."

The girls stood up to leave; grateful they had the rest of the night to themselves.

"I'm gonna go home and change, then I'll see you at your house for dinner later." Jade told Avery, before walking out with Sasha, Skylar, and Bunny.

Avery stayed seated, staring at Gumptin as he read through the records, "Gumptin." She said, getting his attention.

"Oh, my dear girl," Gumptin said, looking up at her, his little reading glasses hanging off the end of his nose, "you are still here?"

There were some things Avery had been curious about since she left the castle that she knew would be bugging her all night unless she asked Gumptin.

"What's Draven's story?" Avery asked.

"Pardon?" Gumptin said, trying to make himself look as if he didn't understand the question.

"Well," Avery began, "he told me that he was raised by his mother, away from other people, and that he disappointed his father in some way. I was just wondering what his story was."

Gumptin pulled off the glasses from his face, staring dumbfounded at Avery, "He told you that?" Gumptin asked, shocked.

Avery nodded.

"Well," Gumptin said, clearing his throat and collecting himself, "I suppose, since he opened the door, I shall tell you what is commonly known. For the past seven hundred years, give or take a few, when the King of Nightfell decides it is time to marry and have children, he travels far away, far away to distant kingdoms. He marries a distant princess or queen and has an heir. Then, when his son is of age, he travels back to Nightfell and takes over the kingdom. It is said that Draven's father traveled to a distant kingdom, married a princess, had a son, and then died shortly there afterward. Draven was raised with his mother, and then came back to Nightfell a little over ten years ago."

"Ten years ago?" Avery asked, doing the math in her head, "How old was he when he came here, because he doesn't look over twenty-five?"

Gumptin shook his head, "I...I don't know. He is rarely seen outside the castle, so no one really knows."

Gumptin's explanation still didn't really answer any of Avery's initial questions, "But why was he only raised with his mother away from people? And how did he disappoint his dad?" She couldn't help but be curious.

"Avery," Gumptin said, slightly agitated, "I do not know. Perhaps you should ask him, instead of showering me with such nonsensical questions."

"Meow," Avery told Gumptin, giving him an insulted expression, "retract the claws kitty, I'm leaving."

Gumptin looked at Avery like he might take off his pointy hat and beat her with it. Instead, he fixed his glasses back on his face and turned his attention back to the records.

That night, Avery was able to enjoy a satisfying meal of baked fish, roasted corn, and Jade's favorite, blueberry pie. She and Jade played one hand of Jade's favorite game, poker, and one round of Avery's favorite game, chess. She then hugged Jade goodbye, without one mention of King Draven escaping from Jade's lips. She kissed Cinder, her parents, and four legged family members goodnight. She slipped into her extra comfy Dawn of the Dead nightshirt and curled into her overstuffed bed and thick comforter. It would have been the perfect night for Avery, if she hadn't stayed up for hours, tossing and turning, the image of Draven and his husky blue eyes piercing into her. She couldn't help but replay every little moment they had together in her mind. It was well after midnight when she made a final toss under her covers. She fell asleep with the picture of his hand wrapped around her arm, playing across the inside of her eyelids.

Early the next morning, Avery held onto the railing with a firm grip as she stumbled down the stairs with her eyes half closed. Of course, this was an improvement from her eyes being completely closed, which they mostly had been since her father knocked on her door to wake her up fifteen minutes ago.

As she sat down at the kitchen table for breakfast, Avery cursed King Draven for allowing her only four hours of sleep. She didn't care that it wasn't his fault. If he hadn't been so damn enticingly mysterious, she wouldn't have been up half the night thinking about him.

Her mother set something down in front of her, but Avery was too absorbed with thinking about all the reasons King Draven agitated her, to pay attention to what it was. Avery grabbed a pitcher sitting in front of her and poured its contents into the bowl in front of her.

"Avery, sweetie" Her mother said, "are you alright?"

Her mother's question shook Avery out of her Draven thoughts.

"What?" Avery asked, blinking her head clear, "I'm fine, why?"

"Um…" Her mother raised her eyebrows, "because you're pouring orange juice into your oatmeal."

"What?!" Avery gasped and looked down at her soupy, orange, ruined oatmeal.

"That's gross!" Cinder giggled through a mouthful of untainted oatmeal.

"Oh, my God!" Avery shouted, setting down the pitcher of orange juice and standing up, "It's not enough he ruins my sleep, now he's even affecting my breakfast!"

"Who?" Her mother asked, a puzzled look on her face.

"Who?" Avery repeated, not sure how to answer, since she most definitely didn't want her family to know that a king was beginning to take over her thoughts, "Um…well, Gumptin, of course. He has us all so busy that we're just…we're unable to function properly."

Her family just stared at her blankly. Cinder picked up an apple from a bowl in the center of the table and handed it to Avery.

"Here," her little sister said, "you can't ruin this."

Avery snatched the apple out of her sister's tiny hand and hastily said, "I gotta go."

Once outside of the house, she made a promise to herself that as much as she might be tempted to, she wouldn't let herself think about Draven again. Even if she had an inkling of a thought about him, she would immediately turn her mind to something else. Avery figured that was the only way she would end up making it through the day.

Training was just as exhausting and tedious as it always was, almost more so since they had gone two whole days without it. The only saving grace was that Gumptin cut it a few hours short.

While the sun was still high in the sky, Gumptin stopped their training.

"Today," He told them, "you shall go on patrol. It is one of the duties involved with being a Protector, and I feel you are all finally ready. You shall each patrol a separate area of Wildwood forest. Therefore, you shall each be patrolling alone."

"Alone?" Bunny asked, wide-eyed, "You mean, we're going to be in the forest all by ourselves?"

"That is what alone means, Bunny." Gumptin said, "If you run into anything you feel is too much for you to handle, ride back to the village and wait for the rest of the Protectors."

"That's pretty much a guarantee." Sasha said snappily.

"Do not worry," Gumptin told them, "you have done this over a thousand times in the past. If you remember your training and trust your natural instincts, you shall be just fine." Gumptin stared directly at Bunny when he said, "So, whatever you do…remember your training."

Avery flashed back to the maps hanging on her bedroom wall and all the little incidents her old self had written down on them. She was sure that more than a few had happened while they were on patrol. It terrified Avery to think of herself alone in the forest and running into a troll like the one she had fought in Lilydale, but it terrified her even more to think of the other girls alone in the forest, running into one of those trolls, especially Jade. Avery didn't know what she would do if anything happened to Jade.

After going home, changing, and gathering up their weapons, the girls met up at the stables.

Glancing around at the other girls, Avery could tell they were all just as nervous as she was. It was one thing to travel into battle together, it was a completely different story to go off on your own, without any idea of what to expect. Avery held onto Phantom's reins and pulled his large head down to her level. She rested her forehead against his and took a deep breath, trying to calm herself slightly before addressing the others.

"Hey," Avery said loudly, lifting her head off of Phantom and getting the other girls attention, "I'll see you guys soon."

It was a way not to say, 'be careful', and saying 'goodbye', which sounded so ominous, and 'don't be afraid', which just sounded stupid.

Sasha nodded and mounted Belle, "Like Gumptin said, we'll meet back at the library at four."

"See you guys at four." Bunny said, kicking Ajax into a trot, towards her designated patrolling area.

Gumptin had given each of them an assigned route. There were four roads that led off into the forest from the village. On the far south side of the village, was the small Rumor Road. Gumptin had assigned Bunny to patrol that road. Then, on the far north side of the village, next to the stables, was the Thorn Road, given to Skylar. Behind the village, past the farm houses, fields, and orchards, was the wild Oran road, which Gumptin had given to Sasha. Avery and Jade were told to take the Main Road and all the subsequent roads leading off of it, with Jade patrolling the half closest to the village.

Before Jade mounted up on Steel, she walked over to Avery. By the look on her face, Avery could tell she was just as concerned about her, as she was about Jade, if not more so.

"Avery," Jade said, her voice a little unsure, something that was unusual for Jade, "I'll…I'll see you later."

Avery smiled, "You know it."

Jade's eyes showed no reassurance of her concern, but she smiled nonetheless.

What had started out as a nerve-wracking experience for Avery, after an hour of patrolling, seemed like a quite uneventful and even pleasant experience. She had been riding in the forest for over an hour, keeping her eyes open and body prepared for trouble, but so far, nothing even remotely dangerous had happened. She had passed a man and his dog walking towards Knighton to look for work. She met a family from Klover who were headed into Lilydale, to purchase Everlily flowers for their village.

Wildwood forest was enchanting, lulling Avery into a state of serenity with its clean floral scents, crisp air, lush green surroundings, lullabies of animal sounds, and dappled sunlight. Avery was back out onto the Main Road, trotting up to Cooper's Bridge, feeling more at peace than she had in a long time, when she spotted a dark figure scurry into the forest about a hundred feet in front of her.

Avery's heart just about jumped out of her chest. The thing she had seen looked to be the size of a person, but moved more like a four legged animal. She fought the part of her that had been raised on Earth for sixteen years, that was telling her to run away from the freaky shadow and kicked Phantom into a gallop. When she reached Cooper's Bridge, she pulled Phantom up to a stop. She knew whatever she saw didn't cross the bridge.

To the right of the bridge, was the small path that led to Wildpoint Lookout. On the wet soft dirt, Avery saw two distinct footprints that led off down the path and into the forest. She turned Phantom down the path and headed into the forest. The path to Wildpoint Lookout was narrow and dense. If Avery were to reach out her hands, she would have been able to grab onto the trees. Wild mushrooms and tall grasses grew along the edge of path. It would have been charming, if Avery hadn't of know that somewhere out in those wild woods was a creepy moving creature.

After fifteen minutes of walking Phantom down the path, Avery's heart began to slow down. She thought maybe the thing she had seen was long gone, or maybe what she had seen hadn't even meant her or anybody else any harm. As Avery was debating turning Phantom around and heading back to the Main Road, her right ear zoned in on a slight whistle. The whistling sound came closer, and closer, and closer, until finally Avery had to lean back in her saddle far enough that her head was touching Phantom's back. The instant she laid her body back, she saw a large bladed ax hurtling above her face. It flew past her face and struck into a tree to the left of her.

Avery didn't even have time to panic. A humanoid creature leapt out of the woods to her right and tackled her off of her horse. Avery landed hard on the ground, knocking the wind out of her lungs. The creature would have landed on top of her if Phantom hadn't kicked his hind legs back, knocking the creature to the left of Avery.

Before the creature had a chance to recover itself, Avery placed her hands behind her head and flipped up into the air, onto her feet. She slapped Phantom hard on the hind quarters, making sure he got himself out of harm's way. Then, she reached her arm back behind her and pulled her sword from her back sheath.

The creature couched on all fours, a few feet in front of Avery on the forest path. It wore a long black cape with a hood that completely covered its face and body. Very slowly, the creature unfolded himself, standing straight up. On his two feet, it stood a good six feet tall. It reached its arms far out in front of it, revealing a pair of long, slender, humanoid hands. Its skin was a scaly texture with a yellowish hue to it. The fingers were a few inches longer than an average man's, and at the top of them were long, black, pointed fingernails, that looked as hard as steel. It brought its long fingers up to his overhanging hood. Avery watched in horror as the creature pulled back its hood, uncovering a face that resembled that of a man, but with a few distinct differences. His face was covered in the same scaly yellowish skin as his hands, and his forehead protruded out in a reverse triangle pattern. His eyes were a dark red color, and he had no nose, just two small slits. Behind his thin lips were a row of small pointed teeth, which he now showed off as he smiled widely at her.

    He moved his head back side to side, like a snake, as he stared her down, "Protector," His voice came out in a high pitched hiss, "you should not have followed me."

    Avery swallowed hard, trying to control her fear so the humanoid creature couldn't see it, "You're right," Avery told him, "you don't look suspicious at all. I totally should have let you scurry back underneath your rock."

    The creature clucked his tongue in a scolding manner, "You hide your fear behind sarcasm, little one, but I can see the truth. I can see how scared you really are." He let out a whistling laugh, "Nothing has changed. You are as pathetic now as you were before. As pathetic as you were on the day you died."

    Avery was thrown off. The thought that this creature might have actually been there on the day she died was like a mini bomb going off inside her brain.

    The creature took advantage of Avery's rattled state. It released a loud high screech into the air and charged towards her at full speed.

    The image of the snake man charging towards her, his body moving more in a slither than a run, would have made Avery scream at the top of her lungs, except she didn't have time for that. He was almost on her in a manner of seconds. Avery jumped back and swiped her sword out in front of her, towards his head, but before her eyes could even adjust to his speed, he flipped up and spun through the air, landing behind her. Avery kicked back with her left foot, kicking him in his stomach. He doubled over, and Avery spun around to backhand him with her left hand. He stood up and grabbed Avery's left fist inside his own, before she could land a blow. He took Avery's arm and used it to turn Avery, twisting it behind her back. Avery brought her right shoulder down hard into the creature's soft side, once, twice. The creature hissed and tossed Avery away from him, throwing her face first down onto the ground. As the creature approached her, Avery rolled herself over, stood up, and scissor kicked in front of her, slamming her foot into the creatures elbow. The creature hollered and grabbed onto Avery by her upper arms. He pushed her backwards, slamming her up against a large tree. He pinned Avery down with the right side of his body and held onto Avery's wrist with his left hand. He pounded Avery's right wrist and hand up against the hard trunk of the tree, over and over again, until she dropped her sword out of her right hand. Once the sword was out of Avery's hand, the creature placed his right hand over Avery's chest, holding her against the tree. He spread his left hand into a wide claw, his long sharp nails made ready to swipe at her face. Avery knocked the creature's right hand away from her chest and ducked just as the creature's nails sliced into the bark of the tree, leaving four deep claw marks where her face would have been. Avery drew back her fist and punched the Demon with all the force she could muster in the middle of his stomach. The creature exhaled sharply and staggered backwards. Avery advanced on him, punching him right in the jaw, and then slamming the base of her hand into his collarbone. She felt a snap and heard a loud crack, followed by the creature's ear piercing scream. She had snapped his collarbone in two. The creature fell to the ground, near the edge of the forest. Avery pulled the long dagger out of her boot and walked towards him. She twirled the dagger around in her hand, to get ready for a killing blow. When she reached him, she grabbed onto a clump of long, scraggily, black hair, pulling his head back and exposing his throat. Before she could run her blade across his exposed throat, the creature had grabbed onto a heavy log of wood. He looked up at her, laughed once, and then hammered the large piece of wood into Avery's chest, shoulder, and upper arm. A white hot pain immediately shot through Avery's shoulder. She cried out and flung herself backwards, away from the creature. When she looked down at her shoulder she saw that it was hanging at a disgustingly unnatural angle. Avery steeled her throat to stop herself from vomiting. She knew the creature had dislocated it. The creature stood up and charged at Avery once again, his dangerous wooden club held high above his head. Avery stood her ground, face scrunched up in pain as her shoulder screamed at her. The second the creature reached her, Avery grabbed a hold of his club arm, with her good arm, and turned the good side of her body into him, flipping him up and over her back. The creature landed on the ground, on his back, with his arm still firmly held in Avery's grip. While still holding onto the creature's arm, Avery lifted up her right leg and brought her foot down in the creature's face over and over. He spit up a large gulp of blood and one of his pointy teeth. The last time she brought her foot down, the creature lifted up his free arm and grabbed onto Avery's ankle. With all his might, he pushed back on her leg, driving her knee up into her stomach and causing her to falter backwards. While the creature was still on the ground, spitting up blood, Avery staggered over to the closest tree. She knew what she had to do. She couldn't fight with a dislocated shoulder, not if she wanted to live. Avery rested her shoulder up against the tree, a flame of terror rose up inside of her, but she pushed it down as she saw the creature begin to slowly try and get to his feet. She leaned her shoulder back, and then slammed it into the sturdy tree as hard and fast as she could. A popping sound exploded throughout Avery's body, along with the worst pain she had ever felt in her life. The pain caused her to cry out at the top of her lungs, she couldn't help herself. A warm tear slid down her cheek as she collapsed her body into the tree. The pain began to dull slightly turning more into a dull throbbing. Avery didn't have long to rest her wounded body, the creature was up and facing her, claws spread out in front of him. Avery stared him down, all terror of the creature gone; now she was pissed. They charged each other. The instant before they would have collided, Avery pulled out her knife from the cuff on her wrist, spun under one of the creatures swiping claws, and plunged the knife into the creature's back the moment he ran past her. It would have been a killing blow, severing his spinal cord, if he hadn't moved a fraction of an inch at the last second. Instead of grasping for the knife, stuck to the hilt deep in his back, the creature immediately spun around, swiping

Avery across the right side of her neck with his sharp claws. There was a stinging pain and a large spray of blood spurt out in front of her, staining the creature's yellow hand, but Avery could immediately tell that it hadn't punctured her jugular. She reached up to her neck and felt a stream of wet sticky blood, pouring out from four long claw marks, running across her neck and down to her chest. While her hand was at her throat, the creature leapt on her, pinning her to the ground. He brought the arm at her neck, across her chest and over to her other wrist, so that he was able to pin both of her hands down with just one of his hands. The creature stared down at her, his eyes flickering over to the wound at her neck. He brought his face down close to her face. Unhurriedly, he moved his mouth over to her wound, which was still bleeding. He stuck out a long, forked, pink tongue and dragged it across one of the claw marks. Avery thought she may vomit from the grotesqueness of the situation and die choking on her own bile. It would be better than laying here, watching him feed on her.

Deciding dying in a pool of her own vomit, wasn't the most dignified way of going, Avery wrenched her top wrist slightly to one side, then yanked with her arm as hard as she could. Her still throbbing shoulder begged her to stop, but she ignored it, finally wrenching her wrist free. The creature jerked his head up. He let go of Avery's arm, not bothering to hold them down, and instead, wrapped his hands around Avery's throat. Avery grabbed at his hands, trying to wrench his crushing grip off of her windpipe.

"Who do you think you are?!" He screamed down at her, "I am Sevil, a Serpentine Demon of the Drake Clan. You are nothing compared to me!" He laughed down at her, "You are still so stupid. Just like you always were, stupid and weak. They died because of you, you know. You led them into slaughter with your stupidity. Your weakness killed you…it killed all of them."

"Get the hell off of me!" Avery shouted, tugging at his hands. More than anything she wanted him to stop talking. It was a horrible realizing his words were hurting her worse than anything he could do to her body.

He laughed down at her, picking her up slightly and pounding her back into the ground, "You're just the same." He hissed, "You haven't changed. They're stupid and weak, too. They would follow you right into their deaths, just like they did last time. I'm really doing you a favor by killing you. Saving you the trouble of killing yourself and everyone you love."

"Shut up!" Avery screamed agonizingly.

"Don't worry," He whispered into her ear, "they'll join you soon enough. I'll make sure of that. I'll taste their blood too."

She let go of his hands and tried pushing on his chest, anything to get him off of her. His hands tightened around her throat and Avery chocked. She couldn't breathe and her vision was beginning to get fuzzy.

Not like this, she thought to herself, I can't die like this. I'm not ready. She thought about never seeing her family again, or hearing Cinder ask her a hundred nonsensical questions. She thought of her friends having to fight on without her, and she thought of Jade. She thought about never talking, or laughing, fighting with, goofing around, and touching the people she loved again. Avery couldn't let that happen, she knew she just couldn't.

She placed her hands flat on the creature's chest and pushed with all the strength she had left. As the world in front of her began to fade, she felt a warm sensation growing throughout her body. It began in the middle of her chest, and then spread out to every other part of her. A surge of searing hot energy went off in her body, snapping her eyes back into focus. A split second later, a blinding white light burst from her hands, sending the creature sailing backwards through the air, landing a good twenty feet away into the forest. Avery lay on the ground for a moment, shocked by what had just happened. She sat up slowly and examined her hands. They looked just as they always did, only covered with spots of blood and a few scrapes. She had no idea how she had done what she did, or where the powerful energy had come from. What she did know, is that whatever it had been, it was gone now, and she could see the creature painfully picking itself up from the forest floor.

Avery stood up, taking in a deep breath of the cool air that she had been cut off from not too long ago. She turned and walked over to the tree where the ax the creature had thrown at her was still sticking out of. Avery heard the creature behind her, running towards her at a hasty pace. The ax was stuck deeply into the wood, but Avery's Protector strength allowed her to pull it out with ease. The creature was less than three feet away when she turned around. She gave him a hard thrust kick to his chest, close to his broken collar bone. The creature cried out as he fell backwards onto the ground.

Avery strolled up to the creature, lying on the ground, clutching at his collarbone. On his chest, where Avery's hands had been when the electric energy had exploded out of them, were two large burn marks where his cloak had been singed away, and his scaly yellow skin was charred and bleeding. She looked down at the creature who had almost killed her. The last thing he had said to her, thundered in her mind, 'I'll taste their blood too'.

Avery lifted the ax high above her head, and as he wailed, "Noooooooo!" she brought it down on his neck, severing his head from his body.

The ax slid from her hands, and Avery gently backed away from the body. The adrenaline that had been rushing through her began to subside, leaving her feeling dizzy. Avery felt a tear sliding down her cheek. She hadn't even realized she had been crying. If at that moment, Phantom hadn't strolled up to her, giving her a sweet little nuzzle on the side of her face with his fuzzy nose, Avery was sure she would have collapsed into a shaking weeping ball. She wrapped her arms around Phantom's neck and let herself release a few more tears. The tiniest of smiles touched her lips when she realized she was alive. She had done it.

As she was about to mount up on Phantom and head home, Avery noticed a glowing orange light coming from around a curve in the road up ahead. She grabbed a hold of Phantom's reins and walked him up the path. When she turned the corner, she had to catch her breath slightly.

She had reached the end of the road. She was standing at Wildpoint Lookout. In front of her was one of the most awe inspiring views she had ever seen. The large trees of the forest ended, giving way to a small circular clearing about fifteen feet in diameter. At the other end of the clearing was a drop-off. Avery tied Phantom's reins onto one of the branches of a large tree and walked over to the edge of the drop-off and looked down. It was a sharp fall, at least a good thousand feet.

Avery took a seat on the cool grass, curling her legs up underneath her, and gazing out at the view below and in front of her. She could see everything. Directly in front of her was forest, green and lush treetops blowing in the breeze. She could see random clearings throughout the forest area. In a few of the clearings, she was able to see dots of tiny houses. Little puffs of smoke streamed out from a few of the clearings with houses. In the far distance was a mountain range. The sun was just beginning to set, lighting up the high rounded peaks of the mountain in a rust colored glow. In the very far distance, slightly to the right, Avery could see, what looked to her, like the outline of a castle. It sat mainly in a heavy forested area, only slightly elevated. Draven's castle stood proud and clear to the left of her. She could see the entirety of Knighton Castle, resting on its hill, its black flags clear and waving. Avery could see the valley below, with its small farm houses. People that looked the size of ants could barely be seen walking around. To her far right, Avery saw, clear as day and unmistakable, the Emperor's fortress. It was too far in the distance for Avery to see much detail, but what she could see gave her chills. The fortress was dark as night, with one high pointed tower in the center of it. The top of the tower was surrounded by high sharp pillars. The enormous wall surrounding it was heavy stone, with pointed towers protruding out from it. The fortress sat on top of a hill made of black ragged rock. The same black rock seemed to comprise the high mountain range that lay behind and to the east and west of the fortress. The forest that lay in front of the fortress looked nothing like the dense green Wildwood forest, teeming with life, that Avery was use to. This forest, which Avery knew must be Darksin, was filled with twisted and misshapen barren trees.

 Avery pulled her eyes away from nightmarish sight and focused on the beauty around her. When Avery leaned her head all the way back, she was able to see the round full moon beginning to take over the sky, chasing the sun away. The moon on Orcatia was unbelievably big, at least twice as large as the full moon back on Earth. It lit up the entire land, like a giant night light. Behind the moon, Avery could see a planet glowing brightly, a delicate purple shade. It was about a third of the size of the moon, with wispy white cloud-like areas dotting it.

 Avery lost herself in the peaceful beauty of the moment. She let her mind wander to thoughts she would have normally preferred to keep at bay. She thought about what the creature said about everyone dying being her fault. She wondered how much truth there was to his statement. It had hurt her more than she was even willing to comprehend. The thought of her friends getting hurt just because they followed her was unacceptable, and the idea that Jade could get hurt was just something that Avery couldn't let happen.

A little while later, Avery wasn't sure how long, but it was long enough for the sun to have almost set, casting the whole landscape in a bath of orange and purple, the sound of galloping hooves caught Avery's attention. A moment after that, a worried looking Jade galloped around the curve in the road. She pulled up Steel, her worried expression turning to one of anger.

"Where the flaming hell have you been?!" She shouted, jumping off of steel, "You were supposed to be back at the library over two hours ago! Everyone is out looking for you!"

Avery had completely forgotten that part. Although, after the fight she had just went through, she felt she deserved a little leniency.

"I'm sorry," Avery said, straightening herself up off the ground, "I guess I just lost track of time."

"You lost…you…lost" Jade raised her fist in the air, and clenched it tightly, trying to get control of her anger, "You just can't do that Avery! People worry about you! You can't just…"

Jade's words were cut short the second she walked up to Avery and took in the state of her. Jade's eyes immediately went to the four gashes on Avery's neck and the stream of dried blood that led down from them and covered her chest. Then she scanned over to the bruises left on Avery's neck by the creature's throttling hands.

"Oh, my God, Avery," Jade's voice came out in a rushed high-pitched whisper, "what happened to you?! Are you alright?! Was it that headless thing back there on the road?"

Avery laughed and it caused the wounds on her neck to twinge slightly, "I'm fine," she said, "they just bled a lot, but they'll heal soon. That creature was some kind of snake Demon…mean bastard to."

Jade nodded and took one more wincing glance at Avery's wounds, "I knew something had happened." Jade told her, "There's no way you'd be cruel enough to leave me alone with Gumptin, Bunny, Skylar, and Sasha for over an hour."

"Whatever," Avery scolded, giving Jade's foot a little tap with her own, "you know you love them."

Jade smirked, "I never said I didn't care about them; I just said that they bore me to tears. Seriously," Jade continued when Avery rolled her eyes, "I mean, what do I have to talk about with those people? Their knowledge of movie quotes is pathetic. Sasha doesn't even know the difference between Star Trek and Star Wars, and just a few days before we came here, Skylar referred to my Suzuki as 'adorable'. She should have just hit me...that would have been less painful."

When Jade lifted up her hand to tuck a loose strand of dark hair behind her ear, Avery noticed that her wrist had a white bandage wrapped around it.

"What happened there?" Avery asked, pointing towards Jade's bandaged wrist.

"Oh," Jade said, looking down at her wrist like she had completely forgot it was injured, "it's nothing, just a sprain. I ran into a group of dwarves trying to rob this family on some crappy little back road."

"Dwarves?" Avery asked, thinking how weird their life had become to have actual dwarves come up in a sentence.

Jade nodded, "Yep, they basically looked like really ugly Gumptin's. Gumptin said they were most likely dwarves from the Western Mountain Range, 'cause they're the only ones that have joined the Emperor so far. You should have seen Gumptin's face when I compared him to the dwarves." Jade laughed out loud at the memory, "I thought he was going to put some magical hex on me."

Avery smiled and nodded, her mind still preoccupied with what the creature had told her. She thought it was as good a time as any to breach some of the thoughts she had been thinking with Jade.

"Jade," Avery asked tentatively, "if something had happened to me, if I didn't end up coming back...you'd be ok, right?"

Jade looked at Avery like she had just spoken a different language, her previous laughter completely gone from her face, "What are you talking about?" Jade asked her.

"I mean, you wouldn't do anything stupid, right?" Avery pleaded with her eyes.

"Avery, what the hell are you talking about?" Jade asked again, her voice growing higher and louder.

"Think about it," Avery told Jade, "we all died last time. I was the leader, and we all died…and that's when I was crazy single-minded warrior Avery. If you follow me now, there's no telling what could happen to you."

"Well, it can't be any worse than the last time." Jade tried to joke.

"That's what I'm talking about!" Avery said passionately, "Jade, you could do anything you wanted. You don't have to follow me." As Avery spoke, the creature's words continued to play in her mind, "I'll have Gumptin talk to the Elementals. I'm sure if I promise to stay…"

"Just stop!" Jade cut off Avery, "You know I'm not going to let you go fight without me. Somebody's got to look after you. You're more reckless than an adrenaline junkie."

"I don't want you here, following me, because you feel like you have to protect me. That's stupid, Jade. This whole thing is becoming way too dangerous." The idea that her old self had possibly gotten Jade killed had put Avery in panic mode, "You have to get away from me. You have to think about yourself. This is your life!"

"Don't you say that to me." Jade said quietly, "Don't you ever say that to me."

From the look in Jade's eyes, Avery knew her words had hurt her. It wasn't what she had intended to do. In fact, right now, she wasn't sure what she had intended to do. She knew Jade would never leave her, and she had a pretty good idea that the Elementals would never really let any of them leave. Avery was just scared, and wounded, and thrown by what the creature had said to her.

All strength seemed to drain out of her and she collapsed back into her seated position on the ground, staring out at the sunset, "I just don't want you to get hurt." Avery said softly, on the verge of tears, "I don't know what I would do if you got hurt."

Jade stared off into the distance at the sunset for a minute, the deep orange and purple rays lighting up the sharp angles of her face. She then took a seat on the ground, next to Avery.

"I'm going to say this to you one time, and then we're never going to talk about it again, alright, because I never want to hear you talking like this again." Jade looked at Avery seriously, but softly.

Avery nodded.

Jade looked back out to the sunset and landscape as she spoke, "I never told you this before, probably because I never wanted to freak you out, or give you a complex, but my parents, and Skylar, Sash, and Bunny's parents always use to tell us to, 'watch out for Avery', 'keep Avery away from trouble', 'Make sure Avery doesn't get hurt'. I mean, I use to think it was because you get into more trouble than anyone I know." Jade laughed softly and shook her head, "It makes sense now, with you being the leader of the Protectors and everything, but I could never figure it out back on Earth."

Avery followed Jade's gaze out towards the landscape, she couldn't believe none of them had told her that before. They must have thought she was a complete weakling while growing up.

"Anyway," Jade continued, "Remember that day, I think we were about six or seven, and my mom was babysitting you and I, and we were out in front of my trailer, building a fort out of old car parts." Jade smiled warmly at the memory, "You wanted to walk out into the desert behind the trailer park and look for the perfect stone to place upon our fort. I didn't want to go, because I didn't want to get yelled at by my mom, but I followed you out there, because…well, because that's just what I do. We kept walking and walking, until the trailer park became nothing but a speck in the distance. Then, out of nowhere we came up on that big feral Akita dog, standing over the pack rat he had just killed, and he started growling and snarling at us. I jumped in between you and the dog and pushed you out of the way."

"I remember that," Avery said, replaying the memory in her mind, "you pushed me on the ground and I skinned my hands."

Jade rolled her eyes, "You would remember that part. Anyway, the dog eventually picked up the rat and ran off with it, but that was the moment everything became clear to me. I didn't put myself between you and danger because I was told to, or because I thought it was the right thing to do. It was instinctual, and I realized, that even at that age, you were the most important thing to me. You weren't just my friend, you were my sister. When I think of my family, I think of you."

Jade turned her face towards Avery, a small tear forming at the edge of one of her eyes. Avery gave her a little pouty smile, and fought back the tears from forming in her eyes as well.

"I love you, too." Avery told her.

Jade laughed and wiped at the tear in her eye, "Of course," She said, looking back out to the sunset, "about a week after that, I come over to your house and that crazy Akita dog is laying on your living room floor. You felt so bad for it. You begged and begged your dad, till he went out with you and set a trap in desert and caught that stupid dog."

Avery laughed, "Yeah, Bear, he was my first dog. He was such a good boy."

"I was so *mad* at you." Jade said, "I had just put my life on the line, jumping in between you and this wild beast, and what do you do…you go out, trap the wild beast, and bring it home." Jade smirked, "That dog loved you so much. After I got over my anger, I realized something else. I realized that you were the best person I knew, or ever would know. Both those realizations have lasted till this day. You're still the best person I know, and you're still the most important person in my life, and both those things will always be true. So, those are the reasons I follow you. Those are the reasons I'd die for you. Those are the reasons I don't *ever* want to hear you tell me that your path is too dangerous for me. Your path *is* my path."

Avery couldn't help but understand. She felt the same way. There was nothing Jade could ever do or say that could cause Avery to abandon her, so how could she ask that of jade.

"Plus," Jade added, "I get to kick ass and save lives, which, let's face it, is a lot better than any prospects I had on Earth."

"Oh, I don't know," Avery said, trying to control the smile threatening to take over her face, "I think your path from juvenile delinquent to downright social menace seemed to be going well."

"Be careful, Kimball," Jade warned, standing up and grabbing onto Avery's hand, to help her up, "we're standing at the edge of a very high cliff, and you look like you just lost a fight with a tiger. Pushing you over would be more than easy."

It was past dark when Avery and Jade finally rode back into the village. Avery was thankful for the darkness. She felt it would allow her to make her way home, without people noticing the monster claw marks on her neck and the trail of blood leading down from them. All of her hopes for an inconspicuous entrance were dashed, however, when Gumptin, the other girls, Pip, and Thomas came rushing out of the stables to meet them.

"We were about to send another search party out for the *both* of you." Sasha told them, an expression of slight relief unfolding on her face. It was such a rarity for Sasha to show any sign of concern, Avery knew she must have been really worried.

"Avery," Skylar gasped, "you look horrible!"

"Are you alright?" Bunny asked.

Pip ran up and grabbed onto Phantom's reins and Avery hopped down.

"I'm fine, guys." Avery told them, uncomfortable with the fuss being made over her.

"Are ya sure?" Pip asked, looking concerned, "If ya want, I could…"

"I'm fine." Avery said, cutting off Pip. She felt slightly guilty when she saw the hurt in Pip's eyes, as he lead Phantom back into the stables, but she had just wanted the subject dropped. Thinking about her injuries made her think about the fight, which made her think about what the Demon had said to her. Her talk with Jade had made her feel better, and she didn't want to be brought back down with dark thoughts.

"So," Gumptin inquired, walking up and inspecting her, "what did happen to you?"

Avery sighed, resigning herself to the fact that she was going to have to relive the fight, no matter how hard she tried to avoid it.

"Sasha encountered an ogre." Gumptin told Avery.

From what Gumptin had taught them, all Avery really knew about ogres was that they were slightly bigger, more agile, and human looking version of a troll. There weren't near as many ogres as there were trolls, and they were known for their glutton appetites, which, at times, consisted of feeding on human beings. Avery's mouth fell open, and she looked towards Sasha. She couldn't believe Sasha had encountered one on her own and still managed to look so calm and unharmed.

"Do not look so awed Avery." Gumptin told her, giving Sasha a discouraging glance, "Sasha, although, claiming to have been thoroughly vigilant, failed to not only kill the beast, but also find out what it was up to."

"Enough." Sasha snapped at Gumptin, placing her hands firmly on her hips. She turned towards Avery and told her, "Alright, so the thing got away," Sasha breathed out heavily, shaking her head, "but what Gumptin failed to mention, is that I *did* wound it. It knocked me off of my horse, I shot it through the knee with an arrow, and then it ran off."

Gumptin let out a disgusted sigh, "And chasing after a limping ogre is such hard work!"

Before Sasha could retort, which she was more than getting ready to do, Gumptin said to Avery, "Anyway, Sasha encountered an ogre. Jade ran into a small party of dwarves." Gumptin ignored Jade's snicker when he said the word 'small' in reference to the dwarves, and continued, "What happened to you? What did that to your neck?"

Avery reached her hand up and let her four fingers slide down along the four claw marks, "A Demon with a really bad attitude." Avery told Gumptin, letting her mind drift back to the fight she had been trying to forget.

"A Demon?!" Gumptin questioned, getting a little excited, "Avery, defeating a Demon is marvelous news! What kind of Demon was it?"

Avery didn't really hear Gumptin's question. Her mind was still back on the fight with the Demon, "An insanely bad attitude," She continued, "and icky yellow skin, red eyes, sharp little teeth, and," Avery pointed to the gashes on her neck, "*claws*...knife-like claws!"

A mixture of recognition and shock flashed in Gumptin's eyes, "This is very important, Avery." Gumptin said, making sure he got her attention, "What kind of Demon was he?" Gumptin looked anxious, waiting for Avery's reply.

Since most of the information the Demon gave Avery was when he was choking her, Avery was a little fuzzy on the details, "I think he said he was a Serpent Demon or something like that." Avery shrugged.

"Serpentine Demon?!" Gumptin shouted in excitement.

"Yep, that was is." Avery replied, not near as excited.

"Oh, oh, that is so…" Gumptin couldn't have been happier if he was a kid at Christmas, "did he say what clan he was from?"

"I think so." Was all Avery could give him. She barely remembered the type of Demon; no way was she going to remember the clan.

Gumptin helped her out, "Was he from the Vipa, the Fanish, or the Drake Clan?"

"Oooh," Avery said, getting excited herself at a familiar sounding name, "the last one, definitely the last one."

"Great goodness!" Gumptin exclaimed, "You must have killed Sevil. The Emperor only has five Serpentine Demons in his service and only one of them is a member of the Drake Clan."

"That's him," Avery said, remembering him telling her his name as he choked her, "he told me his name was Sevil."

Gumptin shook his head in disbelief, "Avery, I do not think you fully grasp the enormity of what you have done."

Avery just shook her head, she thought doing things like killing Demons was all in a day's work for a Protector. Although it had been a big deal to her, she hadn't thought Gumptin would find it so huge.

"Serpentine Demons are incredibly dangerous." Gumptin beamed, "Avery, in your time as a Protector, you have never faced anything as remotely deadly as a Serpentine Demon…except the Emperor, of course. I cannot believe…I am utterly astonished that you defeated it."

"Thanks for vote of confidence." Avery said sarcastically.

"Ha, ha, ha," Gumptin laughed and did a little circular dance, that just about knocked Jade over with mocking laughter, "the Emperor is going to want to eat rocks when he hears you beheaded one of his precious Serpentine's!"

Avery thought back to the gruesome fight, replaying the entire thing in her mind. She got up to the point where the Demon had his vice-like fingers around her neck. In that moment, she had really thought she was going to die.

"You know," Avery told Gumptin, "if it hadn't been for this crazy white light that shot out of my hands, the Demon might have been the one rejoicing right now."

Gumptin stopped his little dance, his back turned towards Avery. When he did turn around to look at her a few seconds later, complete shock was written all over his entire face.

Avery raised her eyebrows, as if to say, 'what?'

"That is...that is your power, Avery." Gumptin stuttered, "Remember, each of you were given a power by the Elementals. Jade has water, Bunny earth, Skylar wind, and Sasha fire. You, the leader, were given energy. The power lends to your strength and fighting abilities, but I never thought in my wildest dreams, you could ever learn to harness it."

"I wouldn't exactly use the term 'harnessing it'." Avery said, "It flowed through me, zapped the Demon off of me, and then it was gone. I had no control over it. I don't even think I could do it again if I tried. It was like...sneezing."

Gumptin cringed at Avery's comparison of her power to that of sneezing.

"You used a *power*." Skylar exclaimed, "That is so cool."

Jade gave Skylar an exasperated look, "Despite it being *so cool*, it didn't do anything to you, did it? I mean, you still feel...normal, right?"

Avery just knew that Jade would jump right into Mother Hen mode, which is why she hadn't said anything to her before.

"I don't feel any different." She assured Jade, "It felt a little hot and tingly when it happened, but then it was gone."

Skylar snorted, "Feeling hot and tingly is never a bad thing."

Jade reached over and slapped Skylar across the shoulder, disapproving of her humorous tone on what Jade considered a serious matter.

"How much power did you produce?" Bunny asked, looking almost more curious than Gumptin, "What did it feel like?"

Avery looked questioningly at Bunny, wondering when she had become a female version of Gumptin, throwing rapid fire questions at her.

"I'm just curious." Bunny said, "We all have powers; I was just wondering what I should expect when I get to use mine."

"You may never get to use yours." Gumptin told Bunny plainly, not bothering to spare her hopes, "You, as human beings, are more like vessels for your powers than wielders of them. It would take great oneness with yourself to be able to brandish your powers at your will. I am astonished Avery was able to use her powers so effectively, and as she is being very vague as to how she was able to use those powers…"

"Vague?!" Avery cut in, offended by the use of that word, "I've told you everything! I can't tell you what I don't know, and I don't know how or why I was able to use my power."

"Well, was there a trigger that caused the power to come?" Gumptin prodded, not letting the subject drop.

Avery thought back to the moment right before she felt the warm energy course through her, "He was choking me to death; I almost died."

Gumptin waved his hands dismissively, "You almost died a hundred times before. You did actually die once! Why did it not work then?"

"You're supposed to be the expert, Gumptin, not me." Avery told him, getting sick of the conversation. She regretted even bringing the subject up, and she dreadfully feared Gumptin wanting to add on 'power practice' to their already grueling training schedule, Avery faked a yawn and told Gumptin, "I've got to go home and get some sleep, or else I'll never make it to training on time tomorrow."

"That statement would mean something if you had ever actually been on time to training." Gumptin told her disparagingly, "Anyway, you do not need to worry about training tomorrow."

The girls' faces lit up.

"Seriously?!" Skylar asked, a huge smile on her face.

"Do not get excited, Skylar." Gumptin said, "The four of you will still have training and patrol tomorrow. Avery, I need you to travel to Vowhollow tomorrow and speak with King Audwode and Queen Vaniana. They are the rulers of the Vowhollow Fairies, the highest rank of Woodland Fairies, and one of the only Fairy groups that we have any hope of receiving help from. Vowhollow lies on the southwestern border of Blackmore, which means sooner rather than later, the Emperor will try to conquer them. They know they have no other choice but to work with the humans. They just need a little reminding of that fact."

"Why would they need reminding?" Avery asked.

"Oh, there was a small incident." Gumptin said, glancing sideways towards Jade, "I shall tell you about it later."

Jade and Avery shared a look, wondering exactly what the Wizard wasn't telling them.

"Meet me at the stables tomorrow fifteen minutes before training starts." Gumptin told Avery, "Then, I will give you an update of the plan and a map to get you to Vowhollow. It is about a day and a half ride, so make sure to bring your bedding with you."

Avery groaned. She went from not needing to worry about training, to having to worry about getting up an extra fifteen minutes early, sleeping on a blanket in the forest, and dealing with mythical creatures that reminded her of children's stories. All in all, Avery would have much rather had to put up with training.

"So, are these winged bugs expecting us, or is it an unannounced visit?" Jade asked Gumptin, refusing to use the word 'fairies' in a sentence.

Gumptin blinked up at Jade, "No, they are not expecting *Avery*. So, when *Avery* goes, she will have to take extra care to make sure her point gets across."

Jade stared down at Gumptin, "Well, when *Avery* tries to get her point across, *I* will be standing next to her."

"Absolutely not!" Gumptin passionately spit out, shaking his head, "Not you! You are not going!"

Jade was taken aback for a moment by Gumptin's vehemence, but she recovered quickly, "You are not the leader, little man. You don't give the orders or make the decisions, Avery does!"

If that was the argument that Jade wanted to take, then, from a leader's perspective, Avery didn't see why she shouldn't go alone. After all, she was a Protector, and what could happen to her that would be more dangerous than what she encountered today.

"I'm fine going by myself." Avery said, leaving Gumptin with a look of relief, "Besides, Jade, you're going to be needed for patrol."

"Oh, shut up, Avery!" Jade hollered at her, then turned back to Gumptin and told him, "I'm going and that's final."

"You just said I was the leader!" Avery shouted, wondering at how quickly her authority had been taken away.

Without even looking at her, Jade waved her hand dismissively and said, "Only when you don't make dumb decisions."

"You are not going and *that* is final." Gumptin told Jade, sternly.

Jade laughed, "You just try and stop me. Skylar, Sasha, and Bunny can handle patrolling. Just give them each a bigger area to cover."

Sasha, who hadn't cared enough to say anything about the matter until now, spoke up, "Jade, maybe you should take your own advice and shut up. You want to give the three of us more work, not to mention, putting us at more risk, just because you and Avery are perversely co-dependent."

Jade just stared at Sasha, not knowing how to respond to her comment, or if she even wanted to.

"I think it's a good idea for Jade to go with Avery." Bunny said, receiving looks of shock from both Jade and Sasha, "This is a dangerous place. I mean, just look at Avery." Everyone turned their heads and stared at Avery's clawed neck and bloody mess of a shirt, "She should have Jade with her in case she runs into any more trouble."

Avery was getting sick and tired of listening to everyone argue about plans that involved her without even consulting her. She remembered Jade telling her about how she and the other girls had always been told to look out for her. That was something Avery wasn't alright with. They needed to look out for themselves, just like Avery needed to look out for herself.

"I'm not a child!" Avery protested, "I don't need a bodyguard." Even if she had wanted Jade to keep her company on the long trip, there was no way she was going to admit it now.

Jade scoffed, and pointed towards Avery's wounds, "Until you learn how to come back without being covered in your own blood…you're a child."

Avery knew Jade far too well to know that this was an argument she was going to win. So, instead of standing out in the darkness and shouting about it for another hour, Avery just rubbed at her head, which had just recently started throbbing, and told Jade, "Fine, I don't care, come with me."

"Of course, I'm coming with you." Jade said to both Avery and Gumptin, "I don't even understand why this was up for debate. I'll see you tomorrow."

After taking a few steps towards her home, Jade turned around and told Avery, "Make sure you take care of those gashes when you get home."

Skylar groaned, as she headed off with Sasha and Bunny towards their houses, "Tomorrow's gonna blow!" She complained, picturing the extra work Gumptin was going to give the three of them with Avery and Jade gone.

"Avery," Gumptin said, before Avery had a chance to make her own way home, "may I have a word with you."

With his finger, Gumptin motioned for Avery to follow him into the stables. Not wanting to argue anymore, Avery obeyed and followed Gumptin.

Inside the stables, Pip was brushing down the Protectors' horses, while Thomas threw fresh green hay into the stalls.

"It was not just because of Jade's more than offensive attitude that I wished for her to stay behind!" Gumptin told Avery in a whispered yell.

"What are you talking about?" Avery asked, her curiosity slightly peaked by Gumptin's statement.

Gumptin sighed, "The Fairies will not take Jade's appearance in their kingdom very well."

Now Avery's interest was really peaked.

Gumptin continued, keeping his voice down, "Jade and the Royal Fairy Prince Eryk had a secret love affair before she died."

"What?!" Avery laughed loudly, causing a few of the horses to jump and Pip to turn around and stare at her.

Avery couldn't help it; she could never have imagined she would ever hear Jade's name associated with the term 'love affair'. Sure, Jade was as much of a fan of a good looking guy as most girls, but back on Earth, she preferred them just passing through, in town for a few days to help her have some fun and scratch a few urges, then out of her life forever. They never came close to anything involving love. Avery couldn't wait to tell Jade about her past romance, with a Fairy Prince nonetheless.

Perhaps seeing the joyous look of anticipation on Avery's face, Gumptin told her, "Whatever you do, you cannot tell Jade. You must keep her far, far away from Prince Eryk."

Avery didn't like that idea at all. She was already keeping what the Serpentine Demon had told her from Jade. Now Gumptin wanted her to keep Jade's own love life a secret from her. Avery was used to telling Jade everything. They never had any secrets before Orcatia, and she didn't like the feeling it was giving her.

"Gumptin," Avery said, "I don't think that's something I can keep from Jade."

"You have to!" Gumptin told her sternly, "Their affair was the reason the Fairies withdrew their support. When the Emperor first started gaining power, the Fairies worked with the Protectors to fight the Emperor. Prince Eryk leads their army, so he and Jade spent a lot of time together. Somewhere along the way they developed a relationship, one that they tried to keep secret from everyone. Unfortunately, the King and Queen found out. They were so furious; they ordered Eryk to never see Jade again and swore to never aid the Protectors again."

Avery thought that was one of the biggest overreactions she had ever heard of, "Why did they have such a fit?" Avery asked.

"Jade is human," Gumptin explained, "and Eryk must marry a Fairy princess, or he can never ascend to the throne. He is their only son and heir. It is out of the question for him to fall in love with a human. To the King and Queen, the Protectors betrayed them."

Hearing the rest of the story caused Avery's heart to ache. The thought of Jade having to be ripped away from the man she loved hurt Avery more than any Demon attack ever could. The only comfort she had was the knowledge that Jade didn't remember any of it.

"If the Fairies think we betrayed them, why would they even consider helping us?" Avery asked.

Gumptin shook his head, looking worn down, "I am hoping that your death and subsequent memory loss have alleviated some of the King and Queen's anger. Avery," Gumptin said, in such a serious tone that it demanded Avery's complete attention, "we need the Fairies and their army. Without them, there is almost no hope. Do whatever you have to do; say whatever you have to say, to get them to help you. You have to make sure they understand the severity of the situation."

Avery nodded, swallowing hard. Gumptin's words scared her. The longer she stayed on Orcatia, the more people she met, and the more monsters she fought, she realized just how serious the situation with the Emperor was.

"And Avery," Gumptin said, turning to leave, "whatever you do, make sure Jade stays away from Eryk."

After Gumptin left, Avery just stood in the stables, contemplating how she was not only going to convince the Fairies to help them, but also keep such pivotal information secret from Jade.

"Avery." She heard someone call her name, slowly pulling her attention away from her thoughts.

When Avery turned towards the sound of her name, she saw Pip standing just a few inches away from her. His hand was on her shoulder and he was looking down at her with care in his eyes. Avery blinked a few times, clearing her mind, until she was fully back in the present.

"I thought ya might need this." Pip said, handing her a soft blue cotton scarf.

It took Avery a second before she realized the scarf was to wrap around her neck, so that she could hide her wounds from her family. The fact that Pip would have even thought about something like that overwhelmed Avery with gratitude. After everything she had been through, getting attacked and almost killed by a Demon, learning she might have had something to do with them getting killed, dealing with the implications of Jade's heartfelt speech on the lookout, the prospect of having to lie to Jade once again, and the weight of getting the Fairies help resting on her shoulders, it was almost overwhelming to have such a small but kind act done for her.

Without even thinking about it, Avery stood up on her tiptoes and hugged Pip around his neck. If she hadn't already been so emotionally drained, she would have cried into his horse scented tunic. He instantly reached around Avery's waist and held her tightly.

"You're a good friend." Avery told him, pulling away from the hug and wrapping the scarf around her neck.

"Avery," Pip said, a cautious look on his face and one of his hands still resting on her waist, "I…" Pip averted his eyes away from Avery and let his hand fall to his side, "I want ya to make sure ya get a good night's rest." He smiled widely at Avery, a smile so wide that it almost looked forced, but Avery didn't pick up on it. She took off towards her house, the cool breeze outside the stables blowing her auburn hair and blue scarf into a peaceful dance.

Avery rushed inside her house and pushed back her charging dogs, dashing up the steps to her room before Cinder and her parents could get a good look at her. The last thing Avery wanted was for her little sister to see her all clawed up.

With too many emotions swirling around inside of her, Avery couldn't bring herself to join her family for dinner, instead she lay on to top of her bed, not even bothering to take off her bloody clothes, and just staring up at the dark wood ceiling.

"Can I do this?" She said into the darkness, the memory of the Serpentine fight vivid and sharp in her mind, "Can I really do this?"

The reality of what it truly meant to be a Protector was becoming clear to Avery. It was a life of struggle, and fighting, and carrying the weight of being responsible for keeping the people you loved alive. Just a few hours ago she had almost been killed, but she had also been strong enough to fight back, to use her powers, and defeat a Demon powerful enough to impress even Gumptin.

All Avery knew for sure as closed her eyes was that it had been the longest few weeks of her life, that she had seen things she could never have imagined existed, done things she never thought herself capable of, and that her journey was only just starting.

The End...
To be continued in Dark Fate: Book 2 in the Protectors Saga

About the Author

Paige Dooling was born and raised in Arizona, where besides a healthy love for writing, she also developed an obsession with Chuck Taylors, Jim Henson, and classic rock. In what little free time she has she enjoys writing fantasy, visiting observatories, and spending far too much time reading travel narratives.

If you enjoyed this story and want to find out more about upcoming books, the world of the Protectors, or the author; you can do so by following her at:

http://paigedooling.blogspot.com/

Made in the USA
San Bernardino, CA
01 December 2013